A DREAM HOUSE . . . A HAPPY FAMILY.

That was what Meg Kendricks was going to find. That was what they were going to be—when she and Tighe and her mother were all living together in a pretty little house in the Florida sunshine. While her mother got the real help she needed.

Tighe agreed. He loved her. They had both defied their families to marry. And had married in such haste that Tighe had to stay behind as Meg rushed to her mother's side.

But Meg hadn't reckoned on The Home. Had never imagined a man like Dr. Sommers. Kindly one minute, terrifying the next, what made him think that Meg and her mother belonged with him . . . belonged to him? That there was no happiness, no future, no possibility of life for them beyond . . .

THE HOME

Other Books by
DAVID LIPPINCOTT

E·PLURIBUS BANG!
THE VOICE OF ARMAGEDDON
TREMOR VIOLET
BLOOD OF OCTOBER
SAVAGE RANSOM
SALT MINE
DARK PRISM
UNHOLY MOURNING
THE NURSERY

THE HOME

David Lippincott

A DELL BOOK

Published by
Dell Publishing Co., Inc.
1 Dag Hammarskjold Plaza
New York, New York 10017

Dell ® TM 681510, Dell Publishing Co., Inc.

ISBN: 0-440-13703-9

Printed in the United States of America

First printing—July 1984

For my son Christopher's best friend,
Lawrence Whittemore
whose passionate devotion to the Dark Arts of Psychology
and Psychiatry was the inspiration for this book

Avant-Propos

(1972)

The Furies tore at her from both inside and outside the house, making her whole body tremble. The little girl wasn't sure which had awakened her, but she didn't really care; when you're only seven, the presence of fear is more important than its source.

Outside, the rain was lashing her windows, making them rattle with sporadic bursts of anger; the trees groaned as their branches were wrenched and twisted by the wind gusts. Every now and then, one of the branches would be pushed so hard against the house that the little girl could hear the smaller branches scraping along the siding and across the glass of her windows.

She shivered, sinking down as far as she could into the bed so that maybe the storm wouldn't see her and burst inside the room to rip her from her bed. The thunder muttered like an angry giant, but the lightning was distant and diffused; midsummer storms like this ran into too much ground heat to develop the blinding flashes and thunderclaps you got in cooler weather. The rain and the wind and the groaning of the trees was enough, anyway; the little girl was paralyzed with fear.

She thought of crying out for her mother or her father downstairs—the bedroom door, as always, had been left open to make her feel safer—but they were having one of their fights, and the voices were screaming at each other loud enough to make the storm seem gentle by comparison.

Sighing, the little girl decided against calling out for them—these fights of theirs terrified her as much as the fiercest of storms. Instead, she sank even lower into her bed; the girl would have liked to pull the covers clear up over her head, but then she wouldn't be able to see the *Thing* when it crashed through the wall and came to rip her to pieces.

She knew her friends' families had fights, too; they talked about them, they shared their fears about them, they discussed how it was that grown-ups who could be so nice during the day could turn into such monsters when their children were upstairs, supposedly asleep. They could find no answer.

Besides, the fights between her mother and father sounded different from what the other girls described. Theirs were more in the nature of arguments—usually, it seemed, about money; with *her* family they screamed and yelled at each other as if on the thin edge of madness.

The wind had dropped and the rain became a steady downpour; the girl grew braver, pulling herself up a little to listen to what they were screaming so violently about. As usual, her mother's voice was the loudest and her words the meanest and bitterest. Her father, although having to yell to make himself heard, appeared to be trying to reason with her.

"If I've told you once, I've told you a thousand times, damn it," her mother yelled. "You don't give me air to breathe; you're suffocating me with your goddamned possessiveness. If I'm five minutes late getting back from the store, you halfway accuse me of running out on you. If your daughter doesn't get back from school right on the dot, you cross-examine her like you thought she'd been carried off by Gypsies. It's intolerable. You're a sick bastard, and what you're doing is terrible for me and impossible for your child. For Christ's sake, grow up."

Her father's voice broke in, having to yell to be heard, but still trying to be reasonable.

"That's not fair, and you know it. Of course I'm concerned when you don't come home when you say you will. Of course I'm upset when my own child doesn't get home from school on time. The sick people that are out there on the streets today, why they're capable of doing anything. The sick people on the streets today—"

"Aren't half as sick as you are. I don't know what happened to you when you were a child, but you can't pretend it's simple concern when it's obvious that in the back of your mind you think I'm going to run out on you any minute."

There was a brief pause; the little girl knew her mother must be lighting a cigarette, preparing herself for the next stage of the onslaught. A desperate urge to call out to one or the other of them, to yell at them to stop, please stop, began to possess the little girl. If they hated each other this much while pretending they loved each other, did it mean they were only pretending, too, when they told her they loved *her*?

"I can't take it anymore, I tell you," her mother shouted in a complaining whine. "That's why this morning I made the decision."

"Decision?"

"I'm not going to let you destroy me and my only child. And that's what you're doing, damn it, destroying us. So we're leaving. Going away as far as we can get. So I can breathe again. Then you won't have to worry anymore that I'm going to run out on you, because I'll have already gone. I feel sorry for you, I really do. You're crazy in the head. But I can't take being suffocated by you anymore. Neither can your child."

Daddy's voice suddenly rose to a pitch of fury the little girl had never heard before, and for an instant she wondered if her mother had stuck him with an ice pick or something, the way she'd seen it on TV. "You *can't* leave me," her father pleaded, his voice suddenly strange-sounding. "You wouldn't do that, you *can't* do that, for Christ's sake."

"I can and I will."

"It would kill me. Look, I'll try. I'll go see another doctor. I'll work at it. I'll—"

"Be just like always the moment you think I'm calmed down. No, we're leaving. Not tomorrow, not the next day, but tonight. Do you understand me? Tonight."

A roar came from her father. "You're a fucking bitch, damn it. 'Made the decision this morning', you say. Balls! You've been planning it for months. Planning to leave me and run off with the lover you've got tucked away somewhere. Planning to take the only thing in my whole life that's ever meant a damn to me—my child. Planning—"

The little girl couldn't stand it anymore. People always described her father as a "weird man"—her friends never misssed a chance to point that out to her—but she didn't see anything strange about him. To her, he was gentle—usually anyway—and he was kind and wonderful to her. Of course, she loved her mother, too. But the edges were too rough, the voice too loud, the deliberate meanness too easy to see. Blindly, she began screaming for her father. "Daddy, Daddy, Daddy!" Over and over and over again, as if saying it often enough would change the terrible things she'd heard. "Daddy, Daddy, Daddy!"

A moment or two later he filled the door and came

over to her bed, stroking her hair lovingly. "Sweetheart, sweetheart . . . What's the matter? Storm wake you up, darling? A big girl like you shouldn't let a little thing like some thunder scare you. It's all gone away, anyway. Just slip way down under the covers and go back to sleep. Nothing's going to hurt you, sweetheart, I promise it. You're your daddy's big girl, and—"

"Those things Mummy was saying," the little girl sniffled. "About taking me away. I don't want to go away, Daddy. Please don't let Mummy take me away. . . ."

The little girl heard her father make a curious noise, like a distant door somewhere creaking shut, and then take a deep breath. "Of course I won't, sweetheart. I won't let anyone *ever* take my little girl away." She heard him blow his nose, and then suddenly he was hugging her, squeezing her so hard she couldn't breathe. Abruptly, he stood up, as if getting out of her room was of immediate urgency.

"Now look. Don't worry about anything, sweetheart. Daddy loves you, you know that. It's just like the storm; one minute it's thundering and blowing and coming down in buckets; the next, it's all gone away. Why, I bet if we looked outside right now we'd see the stars are out. Okay?" He leaned down and kissed her and then seemed almost to run from the room, stopping only to switch on the little light and gently pull the door shut behind him. Wonderful Daddy.

The little girl felt much better. Daddy always did that. Quietly, she got out of bed and went to the window to see if what he'd said about the stars being out was true. It wasn't. The sky was still dark and heavy, small black clouds racing across the night sky. His lie made everything else he'd said suspect, and the girl went over to her door and softly pulled it open so she could hear what was happening downstairs now.

Their voices were softer, but no more pleasant than before. "Tonight, I tell you," her mother said in a soft, terrible hiss. "And that's that. We're going to Maine to live with my sister until I can make other arrangements. Everything's already set up with her. Later, there'll be lawyers and all that crap. But I'm not going to rob you blind, don't worry. We'll get by; I've got enough. It's a small price to get away from you. And I don't want a big custody fight and all that nonsense. It's terribly hard on everyone concerned. . . ."

Her father's voice rose to a roar, something unusual for him, even during one of their fights. "No," he said flatly. "You won't go anyplace, and you sure as hell won't take *her* if you do. She's my child. The only love she's ever gotten came from me; you've always been too busy complaining about things. So that's all there is to it. She stays here."

The little girl heard her mother laugh, which struck her as strange. Then she realized it was a cruel, bitter laugh, and it made more sense. "I'll take you for every penny you've got," her mother said, suddenly calm and businesslike. "Don't contest custody and you get away free as a bird. No alimony, no settlement, nothing."

"Good Christ," her father yelled at her. "That's blackmail. You're trying to buy your own child. Trading your daughter for a promise of no alimony. Shit, you're the damnedest bitch I ever ran into."

Her mother's voice rose again. "Don't be more of a jerk than you already are. The court will give her to me anyway. You're not here from early morning until nighttime. Who would take care of her all day? Hire a housekeeper like that awful Miss Cricket and have her raise the child? Very good for her. Healthy as hell. She'd turn out a zombie. The judge would laugh in your face. Take my offer before I change my mind. Like I said, the court will give me custody anyway."

"No," her father bellowed. "No—absolutely no. I'm not selling my daughter, understand?"

Upstairs, the little girl began to tremble. She didn't want to go away from Daddy, but it was an awful picture her mother had just sketched. Being raised by Miss Cricket. Miss Cricket was a terrible woman. She was stiff and strict and wouldn't let her watch television. And she was old—so old she had long white hairs growing from her chin, waving menacingly every time she moved her head. No, no, no—no one would be so cruel as to have Miss Cricket take care of her. The last thing in the world she wanted was to be taken away from Daddy, but Miss Cricket . . . The little girl felt torn, as if two giants each had hold of an arm and were trying to tear her in half. She didn't want to go with her mother; she was afraid now to stay with Daddy. Miss Cricket . . .

Twisting her body around miserably, she tried to look at things from all sides like a grown-up would. Her mother did everything for her, she knew that—picking out her clothes and seeing that she washed her face and feeding her. But it was Daddy who made her laugh, Daddy who tickled and hugged her and kissed her. Daddy who made her feel wanted and needed and loved.

Even through the now closed door she could hear them, yelling at each other, now louder than ever. They were still fighting, even if the closed door kept her from hearing anything of what they were saying. At one point the little girl heard a terrible crash, followed by a thump like something falling, and heard her mother scream—no words, just a scream. The voices suddenly stopped completely, and she heard a door closing somewhere. They'd gone into the library, she supposed, to continue their shouting and yelling without waking her. Or maybe Daddy had killed her mother, hitting

her with something heavy, and had dragged her into
the library so that she wouldn't be found too quickly.
She'd seen that once on TV, too.

Shivering, she crawled back into bed, wondering what
happened to the daughters of men who have killed
their wives. It was too terrible even to think about, and
the little girl began trying to count sheep, but they kept
turning into "those people out there on the street" who
were capable of anything, strange monsterlike people
with saliva running down teeth that had hair growing on them. Suddenly the door opened again. Abruptly,
the lights in her room went on, and the little girl
blinked at the sight of her mother standing inside the
door, a suitcase in one hand.

"Quick, darling. Get up, and we'll pack your things.
We have to leave here tonight. We're going to stay with
your Aunt Brett in Maine. You'll love Maine. Snow—
lots of snow—to play in all winter long. It's like Fairyland.
Come on, come on. Get out of bed. Just pack what you
need; I'll have the rest of the stuff sent up later."

The little girl began to tremble all over. She wanted
to say no, she wouldn't go. She wanted to run downstairs and throw herself into Daddy's arms and beg him
to get somebody other than Miss Cricket and then stay
here with him forever. But in the sudden, harsh light,
she saw an ugly bruise under her mother's right eye.
Could Daddy have done something like that? Was that
the terrible thump and scream she'd heard from downstairs earlier? She didn't think so; Daddy didn't do
things like that. But if Daddy got mad would he hit *her*,
too?

Her mother's voice, hard and efficient as always, was
talking loudly into her ear, telling her, for Christ's sake,
to get out of bed and start packing. Automatically, the
little girl began to follow her mother's orders, but as
she stood up beside the bed, she decided she'd just

have to take a chance on Daddy. She was about to bolt downstairs to throw herself at him, when a sudden image of Miss Cricket's hairs waving at her crossed her mind. She couldn't, she just couldn't. She loved Daddy, but she just couldn't stay here.

Meekly, she walked into the bathroom and began getting dressed, her body shaking, her tears coming in sporadic little sobs like the rain against her window.

By the time the little girl and her mother were tiptoeing across the wide foyer, the storm had returned with a vengeance. This time it arrived complete with brilliant flashes of lightning that threw sudden, weird patterns of dark and light across the hall, each flash quickly followed by a crack of thunder so loud the little girl grabbed her mother's hand in desperate terror. Her mother seemed not to notice and continued, undeterred, across the foyer. As they reached the door the little girl stopped and planted her feet, pulling her mother down closer to her. "Aren't we going to say good-bye to Daddy?" she whispered. Her mother straightened up, saying nothing, but shaking her head grimly as she silently began to unlock the front door.

Outside on the little porch, her mother swore in a soft hiss. The wind had dropped a little, but the rain was coming down in great grayish-white sheets. The girl could see the Datsun station wagon was parked some distance up the driveway, which was probably why her mother was so angry at the rain. "Run and go get in the car," she said. "I'll be there in a second." The girl was wearing her yellow rain slicker and rain hat; her mother had on a raincoat, and her head was wrapped in a silk scarf. A Christmas present last year from Daddy, the little girl thought.

"No, you better come with me," her mother corrected herself. "He could grab you and try to take you away."

Who, the little girl wondered, was her mother worried would grab her and take her away? The *Thing*? Miss Cricket with the sinister web of white hairs drooping from her chin? *Daddy*? She didn't have any more time to think about it; her mother was pulling her toward the empty garage. There, in the dim light, only able to see anything when the terrifying flashes of lightning bathed the garage in blinding light, the little girl saw her mother hunt for something on the workbench, find it, and stuff it in her raincoat pocket. The girl hadn't seen what it was—her mother had jammed it into her pocket too quickly—but she had an impression of something vaguely shiny, long, and heavy.

"Now, we'll have to run for the car. Run fast or we'll get soaked. Watch the puddles; I'll be right beside you." Numbly, the little girl nodded. Tonight was becoming worse than the worst nightmare. The bone-rattling thunder and lightning were the final hideous touch; the *Thing* always appeared surrounded by both, as well as usually being wrapped in dense clouds of swirling fog. The girl shuddered. Maybe grown-ups were right after all when they said children shouldn't watch too much television.

As they passed the house, running, on their way to the car, the front door suddenly opened. The little girl gasped in fright. But standing in the lit rectangle was not the *Thing*, but her Daddy, wearing a fierce expression and walking toward them in the rain without even a raincoat to protect him. "So," he grunted at the little girl's mother, "you *did* mean it. I sort of expected that. I've been watching out the library window just in case you tried it."

"I told you where we're going and we're going."

Her father suddenly seized his daughter's arm and

began pulling her toward the house. "Not with my child, you aren't. Of all the goddamned bitches I've ever known."

The little girl felt her mother's hand, the nails sharp and painful even through the yellow slicker, seize her other arm and begin yanking her toward the Datsun. The little girl looked from one to the other, pleading, not sure what she was supposed to do. She remembered thinking earlier that she felt as if she were being torn in two, but as both of them began tugging at her, one from one side, the other from the other, the thought changed from thought into reality. "Stop . . . please stop . . ." she sobbed, the tears beginning to join the rain running down her face.

"Let go of her, you bastard," her mother screamed, pulling at her daughter with all her strength.

"The hell I will," her father roared, his suit turning black from rain, one hand still pulling her by the arm, the other wrapped around her shoulder and yanking her toward the house.

They were screaming and swearing at each other, both of them hauling and pulling her as hard as they could. Shrieking in pain and fright, the little girl pleaded with them to stop, but they seemed to have forgotten she was there, except as something to fight over.

The girl saw her mother's other hand disappear into the raincoat pocket, pulling out whatever it was she'd gotten from the garage. In a second of blinding brilliance from the lightning, she saw it was a monkey wrench. "Let go of her, damn it!" her mother screamed and suddenly brought the wrench up between her father's legs as hard as she could.

There was a sort of crunch, and her father fell to the driveway, rolling on the ground in agony, howling in pain. The little girl wasn't old enough to know what it meant, but she *was* old enough to know whatever it was had hurt her Daddy horribly. He was still howling when her mother grabbed her and pushed her into the front seat of the Datsun, muttering to herself and still cursing the rain, the storm, and Daddy.

The car started with a lurch, splashing sheets of water as she drove back and forth through the puddles to turn the car around. "Here we go," her mother grunted as she jammed the car into Drive and roared down the driveway. The car sent a great sheet of water over her father as it plowed through a large hollow of water beside him.

Daddy didn't seem to react, the little girl noticed, but remained sitting on the hard, rough surface of the driveway in his dripping-wet suit, one hand holding his crotch, an expression of pain still etched across his face. She thought she heard him call out her name weakly as the car raced past but wasn't sure; twisting, she looked out the rear window and saw him staring after them, baleful and defeated. Out of all the night's nightmare confusion a sudden wave of sadness swelled inside the little girl, as she strained in her seat to be able to see him as long as she could. Suddenly, she began to cry.

"Are we ever going to see Daddy again?" the little girl asked her mother between sobs.

For a moment her mother didn't answer; she was having trouble maneuvering the car through the downpour. Then: "Not if I can help it." Her voice was hard and cold, and the little girl looked at the determined, stern set of her jaw in wonder. The tears began flowing faster, and her mother glanced at her with clear annoyance. "Stop that sniveling, damn it. Stop it right now. It's hard enough driving without all that sobbing and moaning in my ear. *Stop it!*"

The little girl tried, but the harder she struggled against tears, the easier they seemed to come. "Oh, shut

up," her mother said, swearing at how ineffectively the
Datsun's windshield wipers were working tonight.

The little girl shut up. All of a sudden Miss Cricket
and her chin of waving hairs didn't seem so bad after
all.

Far behind them her father got painfully to his feet
and sloshed his way toward the front door. Like his
daughter, he was crying.

From outside the door he heard a frantic scratching
and a whimper. Dandy, the family dog. He opened the
door but stood blocking the cairn's entrance into the
house. "I saw you, you goddamned mutt. I saw you out
there trying to get in the car and leave me, too." This
wasn't quite fair to Dandy, and he knew it. Open a car
door, and Dandy would try to get in. Always. But the
man's mood was neither forgiving nor even terribly
rational at the moment.

"Okay," he growled. "You can come in this time. But
I'll get even with you." Later, you bitch.

Later, when the weather was better, he'd take Dandy
out and shoot her. That was the only way to handle
faithless objects, faithless people, faithless dogs. The
cairn came in gratefully and tried to jump up at his
legs, but he sent her whimpering with a vicious shove
of his foot. He shrugged.

Limping, he walked inside, getting out of his ruined
shoes and letting his sopping clothes fall to the floor as
he stripped them off. He walked into the downstairs
bathroom, drying himself and his soaked hair—it hung
down across his face like a drowned sailor's—and put on
the terry-cloth bathrobe he used around the pool.

Out in the foyer again, he stared at the puddle of wet
clothes by the door and decided to leave them where
they were; Miss Cricket could cope with them in the
morning. Now that he was going to be living here by

himself, his first step would be to replace that damned, crazy woman as housekeeper; she took good care of his daughter, he supposed, but she depressed him too much to keep her around in these new, strange circumstances.

The full impact of everything that had happened caught up with him at the same moment. Living here by himself. Damn it, it kept happening to him. It always seemed to. Suddenly, with no good reason, people up and go away from you. Desert you. Leave you by yourself. It had happened before; it would happen again.

As he walked across the library toward the bar, he made a sudden, silent vow to himself: the hell it would happen again. He would see to that. Never.

Turning back from the bar, he saw his daughter's drawing of him—primitive, childlike, but colorful— hanging on the opposite wall, and began to cry again. The loss of so much had earned him the right to cry as much as he wanted to.

But it would not happen again. Never.

PART ONE

Chapter One

(1984)

I'm having trouble with Mrs. Kendricks again. She says she's all better now and keeps asking when she can go home. Well, damn it, she can't. Not ever. I need her too much.

She was a psychological mess when she got here, and, okay, now she's pretty much cured. Oh, she'll always be a little out of touch with things, but basically, she's all better.

I don't tell her that, of course. Then she'd leave me and go home. Leave me, for Christ's sake.

So I just keep telling her that she may feel like she's better, but that she still needs a lot of treatment. It's worked for years. Recently, though, she seems to have caught on. It makes me beat the wall in sheer fury. After all I've done for her psychological problems, I don't see how she can even think of leaving. Some appreciation.

One thing I've never been able to stand is a patient's leaving.

So I make sure they don't.

Psychiatric & Personal Observations,
The Home, Alan Sommers, M.D., Director.

Sometimes, in the middle of the unthawed days of winter, Meg Kendricks felt she was a prisoner of the wind. She had been raised in the small, unpresuming town of Little Goat Bay, Maine; her father, as ungiving as the wind from the sea, had built a high wall around her, saddling Meg with Down East parochialisms, monitoring every moment, and insisting she stay inside the bleak, frigid world that was all Little Goat had to offer.

"You can certainly afford college for me, Pops," Meg had argued.

"Yes, but maybe *you* can't, Meg. Those colleges fill young girls' heads with a lot of stuck-up notions. Steer you away from the things that count. Little Goat builds *character*."

Her father, Lawrence Kendricks, could well afford college. (Actually, he was her stepfather, but her mother had remarried while Meg was still so young they had rechristened her with her stepfather's last name.) He was operating manager of Lavery's Boatyards—and like most of that fiercely independent breed of Yankee who flourished in this part of the world, he rarely spent a penny more of his ample salary than was absolutely necessary. There, in Lavery's, some of the largest and finest sailing yachts in this country were designed and built. Lavery's also handled the care and maintenance of many of them; some summers, to pick up extra money, Meg would work in the sprawling yards for a month or so, but neither the relatively minor scheduling jobs she was assigned to nor the business itself appealed to her in the least.

"I don't know why you keep wanting to go away somewhere, anyway," her father had growled. "One or the other of our family's been working at Lavery's for over a hundred years, and somebody's got to keep that tradition going after me," her father had added sulkily.

He always sulked when he and his only child, Meg, got into these arguments.

"Keep the tradition going, the tradition going." Meg mimicked him in a singsong voice, laughing. "You should have had a son, Pops. I don't plan to spend my life messing around with other people's boats, damn it."

Meg was treading on tender territory and knew it. She didn't mean to be deliberately cruel to her father—that sort of petty meanness simply wasn't in her—yet she was aware that that was precisely what she was being.

"You shouldn't talk dirty like that," her father had said in an effort to defend himself. With a grunt he threw his copy of the *Bangor Times* on the floor and stood up.

The argument had become painful enough so that Lawrence Kendricks knew he'd better leave the living room; the whole conversation hurt too much. And it hurt Meg as well, as she had slowly resigned herself to the icy prison of Little Goat next winter, too.

With the winter the piercing winds would be back roaring across Mount Desert, making her whole world shiver. She had never felt really warm her entire life, Meg decided. The bay would freeze solid. Mittens would become useless against the cold. The summer people would go. The natives on the streets would disappear behind their balaclavas, their personalities as frigid as the winds roaring in from the sea—silent, withdrawn, hostile.

Oh, God, Meg sighed to herself, for once—just once—to be really warm.

Not all the Mount Desert area is like Little Goat Bay. Mount Desert includes once-fashionable Bar Harbor—Newport gone to seed—Seal Island, and highly active Northeast Harbor, not very far from Little Goat. There, in summer, the boating rich from Philadelphia, Boston, New York, and Washington huddled together for safety, their great sailing yachts bobbing impudently in the waters of Northeast Harbor. The people her own age from Northeast simultaneously fascinated and repelled Meg. They were so studiedly casual as to be maddening; even the boys seemed to have been weaned on gossip and raised on a diet of pure malice. They all knew each other—either from prep school or college; they all knew the same older people; they all shared a vacuousness of mind that left Meg cold.

Yet, they gave fabulous parties at the Northeast Harbor Yacht Club, and Meg—a startlingly attractive girl of nineteen with a lightning mind—occasionally got herself invited to them. Apparently, she had an appeal that transcended class. Inside herself, she loved the noise and the laughter and the crowding that was part of their social ritual.

"Maybe," she had once suggested tentatively to her father, "we could get a guest membership or something. You certainly know enough of the members."

"Don't think they go for the laboring type, Meg."

"Ernie Westfield belongs—and he's further down the ladder than you are—by a long shot."

"I don't see why you want to belong to that place, anyway," her father had said, growing visibly annoyed. "Bunch of little twerps."

"That bunch of little twerps is who buys your damned boats."

"No, the little twerps' fathers buy the boats; their sons just like to act big sailing around in them. Banging them up, running them on the rocks, if they can manage it. You don't want to be tearing around with those creeps, Meg. They all look half-fag to me."

"For God's sake, Pops," Meg had said. "They have parties and dances and things, and there's lots of people around all the time." Meg paused a moment, trying not to let the real reason out of herself. It came anyway. "People. I *need* people, Pops. For Christ's sake, joining it wouldn't kill you."

Mr. Kendricks had heard enough; his face turned stern. "I don't want you messing around with *that* particular kind of people. Bunch of stuck-up little asses. No one in the family's ever belonged to it, and I'm damned if we'll start now. That's all there is to it."

This time, it was Meg who fled the room, only, unlike her father, she was crying. His strongest reason for not joining something that would have opened up a whole new world to her was that no one in the family ever had, and he was damned if they'd start now. Only a true, bedrock Maine type like her father could summon up so shallow a reason. Or maybe he really did hate her because she wasn't a boy. It was unfair, so damned unfair. And he wasn't even her real father, damn it. Meg was still crying when she finally fell asleep that night.

Funny, she'd spent a lot of time crying lately.

On the thirtieth of July the summer suddenly became an enchanted season for Meg. It was the date of her parole from the prison of Little Goat, and every single little detail of that day was burned into her brain like an etching on steel. She could remember the raucous scream of the sea gulls as they plundered the waters outside Lavery's Boatyards searching for food. She could smell the familiar mixture of hot pitch and wet paint and sanded-down hulls floating to her from the scraping sheds. She could hear the groaning and clanking as other boats were hauled up the yard tracks to have their bottoms scraped. She could still feel the warm, rough planks on the long dock against her bare feet as she started walking out it to meet him, clipboard clutched in her hand.

The *Rittenhouse II* had just picked up an anchor buoy, and she could see someone climbing spryly into the dinghy the *Rittenhouse* was towing astern. The schooner belonged to the Devlins from Philadelphia, and Meg had expected Mr. Devlin himself to bring her around for her end-of-July scraping and painting, but from where she was standing, the someone looked more like a boy than a man. As the outboard drew closer to the dock, Meg saw her guess had been right, and something inside her wrenched violently, although at the time, the reason escaped her. He was slowing the dinghy's outboard now, and Meg had a good chance to study him. The boy seemed about her own age—maybe a little older, it was hard to tell—and was dressed in the mandatory boating costume of Northeast Harbor: clean, well-pressed chinos, broad-striped rugby shirt, white wool sweat socks, and Top-Siders. Below a gleaming mop of ash-blond hair was the face of someone who spent enough time on the water to develop a complexion like aged bronze. Apparently, *this* Devlin took his sailing seriously.

Blinking, Meg suddenly realized she was staring at the boy, her eyes devouring him. His clothes might be standard for Northeast; he was not. To cover her embarrassment, she went to the end of the dock and busied herself with one of the mooring rings. It was a feeble cover-up, and she could hear his laughter floating up from the dinghy. Only, it suddenly occurred to Meg, he was not laughing *at* her, but *with* her.

"Are you planning to throw me a line or the brass ring itself?" the boy asked, an infectious lopsided grin sliding across his face. "Around here, there's not a hell of a lot of brass rings to catch, I'm afraid."

A bit put off, Meg threw the boy a line; he grabbed it

and made it fast to the bow-post of the *Rittenhouse*'s dinghy. She glared at him. "Not in Little Goat, you mean, but lots in Northeast?" Meg was surprised at the bitter tone of her jibe.

"I don't know about Little Goat. But certainly not in Northeast."

Meg considered, looking at the scheduling sheets on her clipboard to see if she could discover anything about him there. Only that the *Rittenhouse II* was to be hauled, scraped, painted, and put back in the water as quickly as possible.

She stared at the scheduling sheet again. "Well, you're not Mr. Devlin, Sr., because you're not old enough, and besides I know what he looks like. So you must be . . ."

Dangerously, the boy stood up in the dinghy, executing a little boy's dancing school sort of bow. The dinghy rocked. "Tighe Dexter Devlin III," he finished for her.

"Tighe Dexter Devlin III!" repeated Meg, trying to look properly awed. "It's a hell of a name, but it'll never fit on a T-shirt."

The boy began to laugh, rocking the dinghy so violently he had to grab the side of the dock to prevent disaster. "You should have to live with it," the boy sighed, still-laughing. "But my father copped Tighe Dexter Devlin, Jr., and my grandfather is still alive, so there had to be some way to tell us apart. Like branding cattle, sort of."

"Top U.S., Choice," Meg heard herself mutter, her eyes glued to a subtle khaki bulge in the front of his chinos. Tighe Devlin looked at her curiously—the muttering to herself, Meg imagined—and she began to fidget.

The reason for the fidgeting dawned on her gradually. He was staring at her as intently as she'd been staring at him earlier. Flashes of electricity ran between their eyes, crackling and snapping, like the jolts of static electricity they'd always shown them in the high school physics lab. Hand over hand, Tighe Devlin came up the ladder and smiled at her, shook her hand, and helped her make the line secure to the mooring ring.

He was still staring at her, exploring her face, her hair, her body with his eyes when he spoke again. "Okay. You know *my* name, but I don't know yours. You're . . . you're . . ."

"Meg Kendricks."

"Kendricks." He repeated the name, searching his mind for something. "Oh, sure," he said suddenly. "Your old man's the foreman here. I've met him a couple of times."

Meg nodded uncomfortably. Maybe that she was part of a family that built boats for rich people like the Devlins would make him laugh at her, or turn and run away to avoid further contact with the laboring classes. Maybe he'd never met the kind of people who spent even their winters in a desolate place like Little Goat and would consider her so foreign to anything he'd ever known, he'd turn pale and flee. Maybe . . .

"Wow," Tighe said, gesturing with his hand toward the *Rittenhouse*. "Then you had a hand in designing and building her. And what a beaut she is. Sometimes, when there's a good breeze and she's really slicing through the water, I swear I can hear her singing. . . ."

Relieved, Meg giggled. "No, that's me. I'm tied on every morning, just under her bowsprit, and *I* do the singing. Mostly opera, because that's what people expect from a bowsprit. I could try folk-rock for you—if that's what you're into—but I suspect it would sound sort of crazy with my mouth full of seaweed."

He laughed again—Tighe had a wonderful laugh, unforced, full, and totally genuine—then shook his head in wonder. This creature was not only the most dazzlingly attractive-looking girl he could remember ever setting eyes on, but she had a superb mind, funny, with an offbeat way of looking at the world, that enraptured him. Meg Kendricks was a far cry from the shallow inanity of the girls in Philadelphia, or, for that matter, Northeast Harbor. His eyes went serious and returned to studying her solemnly.

The electricity between them no longer was static flashes; it was a surging and ebbing currrent that Meg could feel coursing through her whole being, making places and parts of herself she never would have imagined writhe in impossible ecstasy, a pulsing current that made her whole body react with inner spasms of a kind she couldn't entirely describe.

Tighe seemed to be feeling the same thing; his lips had moved slightly apart; he appeared to be having trouble breathing; the subtle khaki bulge was no longer so subtle. Abruptly, he blushed violently, tried to speak, but only produced what sounded more like sighs than words. Finally: "Do you . . . what I mean is . . . you see . . . that is . . . well, okay, we only just met, but . . . I was wondering . . . it's terribly short notice and everything. I know that . . . but there's a great movie over in Northeast tonight, and maybe we could go to that new little restaurant afterwards and grab a bite . . . hell, I'm sorry to be sounding so crazy; it's like a schoolboy asking for his first date, but—"

"I'd love to," Meg said quickly, afraid that Tighe would talk himself out of it in sheer embarrassment if she didn't say something immediately.

"You *would*?" Tighe looked amazed, turning his head a little as if he weren't sure he possibly could have heard her right. The look of wonder was abruptly replaced by one of his lopsided smiles, this one hyper-charged with delight. "You would? You *would*? Great! Wow! Awesome!" Tighe did a boyish little jump of extrava-

gant pleasure that almost dumped him over the edge of
the pier. The childish exuberance in him was completely out of keeping with the studied hauteur of the
other boys from Northeast and delighted Meg. The
details of time, et cetera, for the evening were discussed and set, and Tighe bounced down the ladder
into the dinghy. Beginning to laugh, Meg wondered
how long it would take him to realize what he'd forgotten.
The outboard was started and the painter thrown aboard;
then she saw realization hit him, and he turned the
motor off again. Sheepishly, he climbed back up the
ladder to face her; she was doubled over with impish
laughter. His face looked miserable.

"The *Rittenhouse*. What I came for. I forgot about
the *Rittenhouse*."

"She's a little big to forget very long."

He tried to look annoyed. "I was waiting for you to
hook yourself to the bowsprit and do *Aida*."

Slowly, the arrangements were made for hauling out
the *Rittenhouse II*. Tighe had a list—dictated by his
father, Tighe said—of special things he wanted done.
Trying to keep a straight face, Meg carefully wrote it all
down on her worksheet. Still kicking himself for almost
having left without doing what he had come to do,
Tighe once more climbed down the ladder. "I'll probably pull the wrong lever and drop the outboard into the
ocean," he said somberly, waving good-bye and reminding Meg of what time he'd pick her up that night.

Meg hardly needed reminding. For a long time she
stood on the end of the dock, watching the dinghy until
it grew small on the water, the sunlight gleaming on
Tighe's hair like a young god setting out on a benign
sea. New ideas and thoughts kept racing through Meg's
head and made it hard for her to focus her eyes very
well. How could it happen like this? One minute Tighe

and this mysterious and wonderful set of emotions didn't exist; half an hour later she was drowning in them.

And it wasn't just her. It would have taken an idiot not to realize that Tighe was as affected as she was. Her whole world, with its life sentence to Little Goat, was exploding around her in a radiant phantasmagoria of happiness.

As the summer raced past, the weeks began to pick up speed, an enchanted roller coaster moving ever more quickly, as if to plunge to its inevitable finish in the fall. By now Tighe and Meg were seeing each other just about every night, either alone, or at one of the endless succession of parties and dances at the Northeast Harbor Yacht Club. To the people in Northeast, Meg had become an accepted reality; her charm and radiant beauty quickly buried any of the usual questions that might otherwise have been asked about her origins. In Little Goat, it was as if Meg had fallen off the globe; no one saw her anymore.

The sudden closeness of Tighe and Meg was not lost on either the Devlins or the Kendrickses. Neither family—each for their own reasons—looked kindly upon the sudden liaison between their children. Mr. Devlin had even considered speaking to Kendricks but couldn't think of a polite way to put what was bothering him; besides, Lavery's head foreman was a crusty old bird and had always slightly terrified Tighe Dexter Devlin, Jr.

Meg was to feel that crustiness almost nightly. "Off to Northeast again with that Devlin boy, eh?" Mr. Kendricks would say grumpily if he ran into Meg getting ready to go out. "I guess old Little Goat just isn't good enough for you anymore." He would sit in his chair staring at her as if she were a stranger, the *Bangor Times* resting, unread, on his knees. "I told you they were a stuck-up bunch of little snobs, and they are. Don't let that Tighe kid get away with anything, you hear?"

Mr. Kendricks raised his newspaper and tried to pretend he didn't realize Meg still stood in front of him; the paper would remain raised until she'd left, when he would lower it and stare out the window angrily at the roar of Tighe's car being started. Damn kids. (Inside, some secret voice was telling him that eventually Tighe would knock his stepdaughter up and then vanish, laughing with his friends about what a great lay she was. Did Meg know about the pill? He supposed she did, he concluded sadly. These days, everything was so different.)

The Devlins tried a more subtle approach, but were, if anything, more obvious. Seeing Tighe getting ready to leave, his mother would say innocently, "How nice you look tonight, Tighe. Who are you taking to the dance?"

Tighe would try not to laugh. "Oh, well, I dunno. Maybe . . . I thought maybe I'd take Meg Kendricks." The air of innocence in his answer was a perfect match for the unsubtle innocence in his mother's question.

His father would get mad. "Very funny, young man. We're not dumb. All kids think their parents are dumb, but, usually, they almost never are."

"Dumb?" Tighe would answer, clinging to his child-like artlessness.

"Well, dear," his mother would suggest gently. "I mean, it's not that we don't know and understand these things. And of course, I've always thought Meg was a sweet child—and certainly a beautiful little thing. It's just that"—she would begin falling apart, groping for words that wouldn't make her sound too insufferably old-fashioned and snobbish, both of which she was—"How do I put this, dear? I mean, Meg's an absolutely wonderful girl, you know, but well, that is, the two of you were brought up so completely differently—you with Philadelphia, Exeter, now Williams, and Meg with, Meg with . . ." His mother ground to a halt, unable to define Meg's world of Little Goat with anything more specific than a helpless waving motion of her hand. Bracing herself, she would begin again. "Those kinds of worlds don't mix very well. Oh, maybe at first, but then . . . they don't last, if you follow me dear. And I don't want to see you get hurt. . . ."

"Balls." Tighe's muffled explosion, unusual for him, left both his mother and father shaken.

"Don't say things like that in front of your mother, damn it. It's childish and offensive," growled his father, trying to keep a lid on his temper.

"Then she shouldn't say things like that in front of *me*."

"But, dear," his mother would argue, trying to calm things down.

"Damn it, Tighe," his father would roar.

Tighe ignored them both, checking his watch. "I'm late already."

Walking quickly across the room, Tighe would kiss his mother dutifully on one cheek and promise not to be out *too* late. At least, he thought gratefully, they didn't wait up for him anymore. By then his father would have disappeared back behind *The New York Times*.

Precisely as with Mr. Kendricks in Little Goat, the paper would not come down until Tighe was well out of the house. Then, he would throw it angrily on the floor and stare at his wife. "Trouble with that boy is too damned *much* balls. Meg Kendricks, for Christ's sake!"

His wife would gasp; she always gasped when her husband used words she would have liked to use herself.

Hearing Tighe's car roar out of the driveway, Mr. Devlin would stare at the black square of the window, fuming. (Inside, he was picturing an artful Meg, egged on by her canny father, deliberately getting herself pregnant so that Tighe would *have* to marry her, slip gracefully into Philadelphia society, and go to work on running off with his own money. Over his dead body, damn it. There were good lawyers who knew how to handle such things discreetly. Abortions. Homes that disposed of unwanted babies. Lots of things. The sanctity of class could be preserved.)

Oddly, neither Tighe nor Meg ever mentioned the problems they were having with their families to each other directly. It was too obvious, Meg supposed, to need saying. Besides, instead of moving them apart, it seemed to drive them closer together—two lonely children fighting a common enemy, battling misunderstanding, struggling against parental tides to be grownups in their own right.

The wonder of love ignored parental pleas, soaring above what both considered simple, familial pettiness. As the summer dwindled down to a handful of days, Meg and Tighe came very close to making love in Tighe's Alfa Romeo. Breasts were fondled, the khaki bulge explored, their bodies pressed together so tightly Meg could hardly breathe. Suddenly, Tighe sat bolt upright, moving away from her, his face flushed, his breath coming in gasps. "We'd better stop," he said, leaning his head against the steering wheel for support and looking miserable. "I know this probably sounds ridiculous in this day and age, but I'm still a virgin. I'd be lousy. Please, Meg, please don't laugh at me."

"Why would I laugh, for Christ's sake? So am I."

"We must be the only two left in the whole goddamned world."

Meg laughed. "No, not with girls anyway. A lot of them are too afraid. Scared to death of getting pregnant. For a while, anyway. Men"—Meg giggled—"well, maybe you plain just don't *like* girls. My father says all the boys from Northeast Harbor are half-fag anyway."

Tighe pretended to be furious, beating Meg over the head with his hands, cursing and swearing at her. She loved it.

Another link had been forged, another tumbler had fallen into place, another door of common understanding between them had opened.

Chapter Two

Mrs. Tibald again. Scratched one of the practical nurses badly this morning. Thorazine treatment, NG. Tried electroshock two months ago, results negative. Insulin shock a possibility.

Roof of West Wing leaking badly. Damn.

Patients keep complaining about the water dripping into their rooms, but don't know where to get money to repair roof. The Home is an old house originally built by an eccentric Northerner who wanted to spend his winters alone. He lasted one winter, then decided it was too lonely here. Place sat empty for years until I bought it to make it The Home, but the years of neglect keep showing up.

If the eccentric Northerner came here now, he'd find lots of people to keep him from feeling so lonely. He might even enjoy the patients I have here. After all, any man would have to be just a little crazy to build a house in a place as isolated and forlorn as this.

Psychiatric & Personal Observations,
The Home, Alan Sommers, M.D., Director.

The day Tighe left for Williamstown was the worst day Meg could remember living through. Both of them tried to be so damned brave. Tighe joking, Meg laughing, neither of them quite pulling it off. "Well . . ." was a word that cropped up a lot when they talked, an unfinished sort of "well" that implied a great deal about things left unsaid, things left undone, and a future that suddenly seemed very far away.

It turned out to be not quite as distant as Meg had originally feared. "Look," Tighe said suddenly, grabbing her by both arms and squeezing them until her flesh hurt, "after I get myself set up and everything—this year's courses and stuff—I'll start trying to come up every other weekend. Except around exams. We can hole up in my family's house. No heat, no water, probably colder than hell. But we'll survive. And what counts is, we'll be together. Hell, it isn't much, I know. But it's the best I can do. I've got to get at least sophomore year at Williams under my belt before I bolt the place."

Staring at him with a mixture of incredulity and qualm, Meg had to ask something that immediately bothered her about his plan. "But someone must look in on your house all the time. Won't they tell your father . . . ?"

"Virgil Clark. Summers, he does gardening and stuff. Winters, he checks the house a couple of times a week. But Virgil always needs cash; he's a greedy old bastard. I'll slip him fifty or a hundred and tell him to keep his mouth shut. He'll play ball; he's known me since I was a kid."

It was left there. For the balance of the time, what had begun in summer survived in winter mostly by mail. Both of them were prolific letter writers, although Meg always felt that Tighe's had a certain polish she could never match. His letters always arrived in typed envelopes, but with the actual letter written by hand, which Tighe felt was more personal.

In his letters to her some odd little ideas rapidly became conventions, appearing in all of his letters that followed. For instance, for reasons unknown to Meg, he always addressed her as "Kitten," a term she couldn't remember his ever using to her face. Worse, in spite of repeated questions, he would never explain it either. During the summer she had frequently made fun of his weighty name; in his letters, as a running joke, he always gave her the full treatment, signing them all "Tighe Dexter Devlin III." Once, the signature was even festooned with a red sealing-wax impression of his signet ring, underneath which was a dazzling array of ribbons fastened to the paper.

Meg's were more serious, although she never lost her sense of humor. However, she wasn't good at the boyish little games Tighe clearly loved to play in his. Every day, Meg would wait for the mailman, her nose pressed against the frigid windowpane waiting for the blue and white truck to arrive; then, she would race out and pluck out his latest. Some days, of course, there would be no letter, sometimes because the mail system was jammed up, other times because, as Tighe would sheepishly confess in his next letter, he'd gone out and gotten bombed with his roommate or there'd been a party he had to go to, or sometimes even that he had been studying until three A.M. for a test the next day and was so tired when he finished he could no longer make sense. She forgave him, hating but understanding it; Williams was not Little Goat, and she had far more time for writing than he did, locked away in her cell with only the frozen cries of gulls and the icy pounding of angry seas to distract her.

Finally, Tighe arrived for his first visit from Williamstown. When he got out of the car, he was half frozen; Alfa Romeos are designed for the sunny, balmy weather of Italy, not the frigid blasts of Mount Desert Island. For herself, Meg was equally frozen; by agreement she waited for him at the gas station at the intersection of two roads, one leading to Northeast, one to Little Goat.

Holding her hands out toward the black, potbellied wood stove, Meg still felt violent shudders of cold sweeping through her body. Caleb Price, the station's owner, had known Meg since she was a little girl and looked at her with concern. "Get your whole body closer to the stove, child. You look near to shaking apart. Not enough heavy clothes. I don't know what's wrong with you kids. . . ."

Meg figured it was impossible to get any closer to the stove without climbing inside, but moved her feet forward a few inches to avoid a prolonged lecture from old Caleb. "It was the Jeep, Caleb. I drove over in the open Jeep, and the cold really got to me. I'll be all right; someone's picking me up here—it should be any minute now—and I can get *really* warm." Thinking, Meg realized that hadn't come out at all how she meant it and blushed furiously.

Caleb Price looked at her quizzically. In Maine privacy is a sacred thing, second only to solvency, and while visibly curious, he would sooner have died than ask her *who* was supposed to pick her up here.

Meg avoided his eyes. She'd known Caleb for so many years it embarrassed her to be waiting to launch a tryst under his stern gaze. Slowly, she could feel sensation returning to her fingers; the damned open Jeep was a stupid car to use, but she had no other choice that wouldn't have brought down a barrage of questions from her father.

About half an hour later, the Alfa Romeo's *vroom-vroom* shook the frosted-over windows of the station. Caleb started to put on his coat and hat to go out and gas up his customer, but Meg stopped him. "It's all right, Caleb. That's the person picking me up. Thank you for letting me stay here and get unthawed."

Blinking, Caleb looked first at Meg, then the car. He knew the Alfa; he knew who owned it. His expression was not disapproving, just a little surprised. "Anytime, Meg, anytime. . . ."

Pulling her stocking cap down over her ears as far as it would go, Meg opened the door and quickly shut it behind her so that Caleb's wouldn't get any colder than it already was. As she walked quickly over to Tighe's car, she turned back and waved one more time, calling out "Thanks again, Caleb." Dimly, through the frosted front window, she could feel Caleb's eyes following her. He *couldn't* know anything. Then why, she asked herself, did she feel so guilty about what she was doing? She could still feel Caleb's eyes until she opened the far door of the car and grabbed Tighe's hand. "Let's get out of here," Meg said urgently. "I feel like a thief."

The Devlin mansion seemed colder inside than the air outside it. Inside, both of them shaking with the cold—and maybe something else—Tighe took her in his arms and kissed her until she could barely breathe. Suddenly, he stepped back. "Christ, this dump's freezing. First thing to do is build a great big fire in the fireplace and sit on top of it until we feel human again."

The memory of Caleb's eyes still haunted Meg. "You're *sure* no one's going to know we're here?"

"Stopped off at Virgil Clark's house in Trenton on the way. Seemed to understand. Just asked me not to mess up the place. He won't bother us."

The wood was dry and the kindling already laid. In a few minutes the fire was roaring in the hearth, crackling and snapping, sending off waves of blessed warmth. Tighe raced back to his car and returned with a heavy paper bag. "Sandwiches. Cake. There's booze already here. And a primus stove so we can make coffee or soup or whatever. We'll have to melt snow for water. Sorry it's so damned primitive."

Meg giggled, although inside she was deadly serious. "I'm the primitive type, anyway. When I'm not lashed to a bowsprit, I wear animal skins and live in a cave. By comparison this place is very *luxe*."

"If you face the fire," Tighe said, ignoring her, "your ass freezes. If you turn with your back to the fire, your front freezes. Damn it, I don't know which is worse."

A few minutes later Tighe had solved the problem. Meg heard a thump-thump-thump on the stairs as Tighe dragged a huge double-mattress over in front of the fireplace. With him, he'd brought a pile of fluffy poufs which he spread across the mattress. "Climb in, Meg. If *they* don't keep us warm, we'd better give up."

It didn't take long; they began kissing, their hands exploring each other's bodies. This time Tighe wasn't so shy. Clothes were unbuttoned and kicked to the bottom of the makeshift bed. Lips joined, bodies meshed, and Meg had a sensation that the room was spinning. It was only a matter of minutes before they had lost their claim to being the only two left in the whole world. To Meg it was a moment of sheer, shuddering ecstasy, her whole body heaving and thrashing, as he entered her again and again. Finally, Tighe fell back, breathing heavily, apparently exhausted. "Was I all right? I mean, well, you know. . . ."

"Do I know! Fantastic." A moment later Meg turned her head toward him and fixed him with a lofty stare, still running one hand back and forth across his smooth, flat stomach. "Which isn't half bad," she added solemnly, "for a Northeast half-fag."

Tighe roared in fury, pounding the poufs, then her. She let her hand slide all the way down his stomach and knew he was ready for more. Some instinct—Meg never knew where it came from—made her head follow her hand, and she placed her lips around it. Tighe began thrashing and groaning. His stomach moved in and out, almost violently, his toes pointed and back arched, his breath coming in gasps and groans. "Oh, my God, my God, Meg . . ."

Meg looked up at him impishly. "Shhhh . . . I was always taught not to speak with my mouth full. *Shut up!*"

A second later Tighe's entire body seemed to rise off the mattress into the air; a sensation of labored spurting surprised her; Tighe's body fell back onto the mattress as if some secret inner spring had been released.

They fell asleep, holding each other, exhausted and spent, but filled with a glorious closeness neither of them had ever known before. It went on like this for the entire two days. They rarely left their warm cocoon in front of the fire except to get sandwiches or more wood.

When it was time for the leave-taking—actually past the time—so Tighe could get back to Williamstown, it was, if anything, considerably worse than when he'd left in the fall. They clung to each other for hours, until Tighe finally forced himself back into his clothes, swearing at the world for its unfairness.

But in the minds of both, settled over them like a gloriously happy cloud, was the certainty that in two weeks he would be back. This week she'd told her father she was spending the weekend with her friend Meg Ruley; she'd have to decide whether to use Meg or someone else for that weekend.

To Meg, the frigid winters of Little Goat had never seemed as cold or as lonely as when she watched Tighe's car disappear into the frozen darkness.

As the months moved on, every two weeks Tighe would arrive. They talked of life; they talked of love; they talked of early the next summer when Tighe would have finished his sophomore year and they could get married. Inevitably, they talked of their families. "Pops isn't really a mean man," Meg told him. "He's just a born Down Easter. If someone in the family hasn't already done something, well, he's damned if he's going to be the first of them to do it. Most people in Little Goat are like that—very set in their ways—and he's more set than most."

"Well, my family's like that, too, only in a completely different context," Tighe answered. "They don't set out to be mean; they just manage it by trying to make me think the same way they do. I don't, and I won't have to pretend to much longer. A month from now, I go twenty-one. My grandfather set up a trust fund years ago, and there's not a damned thing they can do about it—I start getting the income then. I'll be free. Free to quit Williams, free to live where I want, free, damn it, to marry you." Looking at Meg, Tighe suddenly blushed. He'd said more than he had planned to; the difference in their financial setups was too obvious to get on the subject. "I mean, it's not a hell of a lot, of course, but . . ."

Meg laughed. She'd never known anyone with a trust fund before, she told him, and she just hoped it *was* a lot. "I have terribly expensive tastes," she added.

On and on they talked, about everything and nothing. Lost in the exquisite pleasure of each other. But only every other weekend.

Two days out of fourteen Meg was delirious; the rest of the time was sheer hell, filled only by the endless writing of letters back and forth. It was no ideal arrangement, Meg knew that, yet she had never been happier in her whole life.

The idyll ended suddenly, as if the hand of God had reached down and struck it dead for giving them too much happiness. Tighe's letter tried to explain it, but written between the lines was his own anguish at the disaster that had claimed them.

> . . . and there's not a damned thing I can do about it. My father's call up here made that brutally plain. Maybe the $50 I gave Virgil Clark wasn't enough, or maybe he just got scared that someone else would tell my father before he did. Anyway, he finked on me. Wrote a letter to Dad— I suspect Virge doesn't write very often, maybe two letters a year—but the message was clear. Said exactly what I'd been up to and with whom, and that he knew it probably wasn't any of his business, but that he felt Dad should know. Didn't mention the fifty, the bastard.
>
> Anyway, they've changed the locks on the house up there, and Dad told him if I showed up and got in somehow anyway to call the State Police. Some father, that guy. Anyway, from now on it'll have to be just letters until spring vacation.
>
> What can I say to you, Meg? What can I say to *myself*? I'm heartbroken. It makes me want to chuck everything and just run away with you now.
>
> Oh, Meg, just when everything was so close to working out, that damned father of mine pulls this.
>
> Forgive me, can you ever forgive me? Please, Meg . . .
>
> > Every ounce of my love,
> > Tighe Dexter Devlin III

Meg read and reread Tighe's letter, as if maybe reading it enough would change what it said. She spent a lot of time in her room, crying. Her father never said anything, just looked at her as if he somehow knew what had happened and was secretly delighted. (He *did* know. In a small town like Little Goat everybody knew everything; he had been on the point of talking to Meg—growling would have been a better word—but then someone else ended the situation before he was forced into a showdown with his daughter. The word drifting around town from Virgil Clark was that it was Mr. Devlin who had lowered the boom.)

For days Meg sat in her room, restless, lonely, completely dispirited. She had to find something besides writing letters to keep her mind off the tragedy of Tighe and the bleakness of the winter. The year before, faced with only the deadly bleakness, she had taken courses in psychiatric casework in Bangor. Because of her mother, psychology had always fascinated her. It was not, however, a career she had any intention of following. Now she needed something to kill time this dreadful winter.

Wearily, she hauled out the University of Maine's listing of courses; maybe something in it would give her the inspiration to get out of the house and go back to studying. The syllabus was dull; the courses struck her as ridiculous. She left the booklet on her desk, planning to get back to it the following day.

Meg never did. That night she made her every-other-week call to her mother. Her mother's tone of voice, the strange new things she said, her crying, rattled Meg completely. Usually, her mother sounded quite content about being in The Home, something Meg had always had trouble understanding. It had been the cheapest sanitarium her stepfather could find, run-down and dilapidated. Inexpensive. Her stepfather, Meg knew, could be a total bastard, a conclusion that was reinforced the more she heard about The Home. Cheap, cheap, cheap. She also suspected that he had chosen a place as far away as the Florida Keys so that no one could expect him to go visit her. That her mother hadn't objected violently years ago said a lot about how removed from reality she had become by the time she was sent there. Meg's secret dream—she sometimes mentioned it to her mother when she was in a depressed state and needed a boost—was to someday buy a little house somewhere down in the Keys and take her mother out of The Home. They'd find some place near Key West, for instance, where the best kind of psychiatric help would be available. She trotted out the dream for her mother again over the phone tonight, but this time her mother was not so easily put off.

Suddenly, Meg's mother, crying as she spoke, dove into an area she'd never touched on before. "Oh, Meg, darling, I've *got* to get out of here, I just do. I know I'm better, and I keep telling Dr. Sommers that, but he just says I need more treatment and changes the subject. I'm very fond of the man, but I don't understand why he keeps saying things like that. I know I'm better, Meg, I'm absolutely sure I'm better, but the doctor won't even discuss it. It's like he didn't *want* me to be better. . . ."

Meg wasn't sure how to handle this new twist to things. Her mother had always seemed content enough at The Home. "But, Mom," Meg began, trying to buy time, "maybe you should hang on awhile until you're really *sure* about yourself. . . ."

"I *am* sure, Meg, very sure. And I look at the other patients—they've always been a little frightening—and, Meg, I swear to you I think most of them are getting worse instead of better. I don't want to have that happen to me. I'm all better. Cured. In great shape. I don't know why Dr. Sommers can't see it; he just doesn't seem to want to."

"Mom," Meg pleaded, trying again, "I'm sure the doctor isn't—"

Her mother's voice rose in a sudden wail, shaking Meg badly. "Meg, sweetheart, somehow you've got to get me out of here. Right away. Why should a perfectly sane person be locked up in a falling-apart, run-down nuthouse like this? I can't stand it anymore. . . ."

For a moment there was silence, then her mother again. "Somehow, Meg, you have to manage it. You just *have* to." The tears again, rising, then gradually lessening as her mother struggled to control herself. The sound was so desperate, so pitiful, Meg found her own eyes had to blink hard to hold back the tears. At the moment what her mother was asking was impossible. Where would she go? Her cheapskate stepfather wouldn't put up with someone as troublesome as her mother now was, she was sure of that, and wouldn't pay for her to go someplace nice to live. There was nothing Meg could think of doing but cursing; she held the receiver away from her as she did so it wouldn't upset her mother, a little girl's reaction from an almost forgotten childhood.

Abruptly, she tried a new tack: logic. "Have you talked to Dr. Sommers about it, Mom? I mean, directly about it. I know he likes you. I've spoken to him quite a few times, and he always says what a fine woman you are and how fond he was of you. . . ."

There was a long pause from her mother's end of the line, then: "Yes, I talked to him about it. I forced him to talk to me about it. But . . ."

The silence again. Meg could hear her mother breathing into the mouthpiece and thought she heard her beginning to cry again.

"But *what*, Mom? Tell me, Mom, please tell me."

There was a sigh. Haltingly, her mother began speaking. By the time she had finished, she was crying again, worse than before, her words interspersed with sobs. "Well, like you just suggested, I came out and talked to him about how well I was. And he went into his usual thing about how I needed more treatment.

That made me mad, Meg, and I got a little smart-alecky. So I told him—it wasn't really very nice of me, I'm afraid—that if I wasn't cured, then he damned well ought to give me more time in therapy. Why, sometimes I don't have a session with him for weeks at a time, you see. And he laughed—that wasn't very kind of him, was it?—and it *really* made me mad—you know how my temper can go wild sometimes, Meg—and I got nasty and said that since he didn't want to give me any more therapy time and found my asking about it funny, it just proved what I'd been telling him for months: that I *was* cured, so I'd be leaving as soon as I could make arrangements for someone to pick me up."

Cautiously, afraid of upsetting her mother further, Meg asked the key question. "What did he say, Mom?"

Her mother's voice suddenly became hard to understand; the new attack of crying and sobbing were jumbling all her words together. "He went crazy, sort of. Furious. Livid. I know you'll have a hard time imagining it, but he stormed around his office, snorting, sort of screaming at me, and breaking things on his desk and throwing things against the wall. I was frightened to death he was going to pick up something and hit *me* with it. Terrified. I don't know why one little thing like that should upset the man so. Usually, he's so wonderfully calm. But what I said I was going to do turned him into a wild man.

"And what's even more frightening in its own way: now he acts like nothing ever happened that day in his office. Why, he still always smiles at me when we pass in the hall, and sometimes, we stand and chat about nothing. But I can see it in his eyes—he remembers what happened as well as I do. He's just pretending. I guess that's why I haven't had a therapy session since. Because he *does* remember and is afraid I'll bring it up again. Oh my, it just doesn't make any sense at all."

More nose-blowing, more effort to bring herself under control. "Meg, dear, I know it won't be easy for you, but if you could just come right down and take me away." Another pause, a new burst of crying. "I'm frightened. My God, I'm scared to death."

Something in her mother's voice chilled Meg; she found herself shivering. Her mother sounded so helpless and lost, like a little child waking up in the middle of the night and suddenly finding the light beside her bed won't turn on.

"It's not safe down here anymore . . . I'm frightened . . . my God, I'm scared to death." Meg was baffled as to what to do. Her mother sounded completely rational, but hopelessly terrified.

Abruptly, her mother began pleading again, once more the frightened child. "Please, Meg, darling, *please*. For God's sake, come get me. . . ."

Reluctantly, Meg went back to an earlier idea of hers. "I suppose I could call up and speak to Dr. Sommers," she began.

"No, no, no," her mother said frantically. "He'd get terribly upset. No, Meg, please don't call him up. He might start screaming at me and throwing things again. Please don't call him, Meg, just come down and get me."

With a sigh Meg told her she'd try to find a way, but that it would take several days to work out, and it was just possible she wouldn't be able to manage it at all. A moment later her mother was back in tears; Meg told her not to worry and that she'd call her in a few days to see how things were going.

Sitting by the phone, Meg tried to figure out how to weigh her mother's panic. It was totally bewildering. After a few minutes she decided to break her promise and call Dr. Sommers anyway. She was surprised when he answered the phone himself. He was, as always, very charming and beatifically calm. When Meg mentioned the conversation with her mother, he laughed genially. "Well, your mother's right on one point. Things got terribly busy here, and I haven't had a chance to have a session with her for—let's see—ten days. It's something I plan to correct tomorrow or the next day." Dr. Sommers sighed, but his tone of geniality remained constant. "Missing sessions always upsets a patient, I'm afraid, however valid the doctor's reason may be. They're like siblings in a large family, you see, and always resent the time the doctor spends with other patients. It's very common, something we psychiatrists have to cope with and try to handle as best we can. . . ."

"I can understand that," Meg said. "It's just that . . . well . . . Mother said that when she said she felt she was cured and wanted to leave—"

Meg was surprised to hear Dr. Sommers's voice lose its genial, professional calm completely, taking on a defensive, angry sound. "She probably said I screamed at her and threw things. That's what she accused me of at our regular session yesterday. Ridiculous, of course. But many patients attack their psychiatrists with things like that." The doctor's voice became a near scream; he'd lost control. "You have to remember that your mother is a patient in a psychiatric clinic, damn it. And if you're going to take her word over mine . . ."

"No, but I . . ." The doctor's flash of temper had startled Meg; she wasn't at all sure how to handle it. Somehow, it seemed the wrong reaction for a psychiatrist. There was a sullen silence from the other end of the phone; she could hear the doctor breathing heavily, trying to bring himself under control. "Dr. Sommers," Meg began again, "I didn't, certainly, mean to upset you. I'm sorry if—"

Dr. Sommers suddenly sounded highly professional again, cutting off her apology with another genial laugh.

"Nothing to worry about, Miss Kendricks. You see—oh, excuse me for a moment."

Meg could hear Dr. Sommers's hand cover the mouthpiece, presumably while he talked to someone at the other end. A moment later his voice returned, crisply efficient. "Miss Kendricks, I would love to go into this at much greater length, but the head nurse just handed me a note. I'm needed elsewhere, I'm afraid. One of the hazards of running a place like The Home. I'm sure you understand. . . ."

"Yes, yes, of course. I just wanted to repeat that—"

But before Meg could even get to her apologetic statement, there was a click and Dr. Sommers was gone. The call left Meg troubled; she wasn't entirely sure why. That a psychiatrist in Dr. Sommers's position could suddenly descend into petulance was one thing, of course. But there was something else. The doctor had lied, first saying he hadn't had a therapy session with her mother for over ten days, then saying he'd had their regular session only yesterday. Why? It was possible she'd misheard him, but she didn't think so. It worried Meg. Her mother also worried Meg. There was something wrong, something she couldn't put her finger on. Meg shivered.

A little later she told her stepfather of the conversation with her mother. Mr. Kendricks looked at her over the top of his paper and said she must be crazy to listen to her mother. "Christ, one nut in the family is enough," he added.

When she told him she thought perhaps she should go down to The Home to see what was really happening, he lowered his paper and stared at her. "Meg, will you promise me one thing? That this sudden emergency's real name isn't Tighe Devlin?"

She stared at him unbelievingly. "Pops," she said

finally, "sometimes you're nothing but a big, fat shit."

For the first time Meg could remember, her stepfather didn't raise his paper to hide behind. He couldn't. He had dropped it on the floor.

Chapter Three

Mrs. Kramer's family came and took her out of The Home today. I tried to stop them, but they accused me of trying to make her stay here because I needed the money. Bastards. Mrs. Kramer was no favorite of mine, but I still didn't think she should go.

One problem any psychiatrist has is that transference is a two-way street. Patients frequently become too involved with their psychiatrist, but psychiatrists are equally vulnerable to becoming too involved with their patients. It's a pattern I've always been overly vulnerable to. Acton-Phillips claimed I became so involved with my patients I couldn't bear to discharge them, even when they were better. That's not true, of course, but the idea of a patient's leaving me did always upset me, and I will confess to a higher degree of involvement with my patients than was probably healthy for me.

Psychiatric & Personal Observations,
The Home, Alan Sommers, M.D., Director.

Getting Tighe on the phone at Williams was something Meg rarely tried. It was almost always impossible. A series of male voices—people living on the same corridor, she assumed—would follow one another onto the phone, finally reaching a consensus that Tighe must be out. This time, because she pleaded with them, they kept trying. Perhaps fifteen minutes later she finally reached him. As concisely as she could, she told Tighe about the talk with her mother, how frightened she had sounded, about the doctor's peculiar behavior, and that she thought maybe she'd better fly down to the Keys and find out for herself what was going on.

She sounded so upset that Tighe found himself saying things like "of course, you have to" and "there's probably absolutely nothing to worry about, but you won't feel right until you've seen it with your own eyes. . . ."

Listening to his warm, reassuring voice, Meg began to crumble; she could feel her body trembling and her chest heave. After her mother's panicky pleas, Dr. Sommers's self-contradictory unpleasantness, and her father's petty meanness, Tighe seemed so nice it was heartbreaking. Suddenly, as surprised by it as Tighe was, Meg began to cry. Over the phone she could hear him calling her name softly, trying to reach her, trying to get her attention without yelling at her. Struggling, Meg forced herself back under control. "I'm sorry—" she began.

"Don't be sorry. There's a lot on your mind; you've got every right to cry." There was a long pause; she could hear him breathing, pondering something, but the sound of his voice was distant, like thunder far out over the ocean. Abruptly, Tighe began speaking again, firmly and full of conviction.

"Look," he said in a tone that announced he wasn't going to be argued with. "Look, damn it, it's not something you should have to handle alone. I'm going with you. I mean it. I'm fed up with Williams. College sucks. The hell with finishing sophomore year. What good would two years of college be anyway? I was twenty-one two weeks ago—you know that—so the trust fund's mine now, and we'll be able to buy that little house for your mother you've been dreaming of for years. A nice, proper home for her. And we can live there with her until we find the right kind of housekeeper and get her the best damned psychiatric help in the country to boot."

Stunned, Meg had trouble believing her ears. Oh, Tighe had talked about this before, but she had always assumed it idle dreaming. One facet of his suggestion bothered her, the product, probably, of her Maine upbringing. "Why," she asked him bluntly, "why should you take on *my* problem with *my* mother? The money you'd be spending and everything; I'm not sure I could accept it. It's simply not your problem."

"The hell it isn't. Any problem of yours is a problem of mine. The money—hell, I lied to you a little. There's quite a bit."

Everything Meg had ever dreamt of was suddenly being handed her. Her mother, out of that damned looney bin, The Home. The right kind of treatment for her. The cottage for her Meg had dreamt of half her life. And most important of all, spending all her time with Tighe, something in the front of her mind ever since the first time she'd met him. Meg couldn't think of what to say, so she said something that made very little sense at all; it was a minor stumbling block. "But your family . . . my stepfather . . . I—"

"Fuck 'em," said Tighe, quickly putting the stumbling block into perspective. "We'll take off soon as I can get my room cleared out. Then, it's the Keys and your mother. You're in a very understandable hurry to get down there and find out what's up, so you fly. I have some things I have to clear up with the bank in Philly and the trust fund, so I'll drive down a few days later. You won't be missing anything, Meg; it's a lousy drive. One big speedtrap. I can probably wrap up here

in a couple of days, then I'll be set to start." Tighe gave
a long pause. "Only first . . . we get married."

Clutching the receiver so tightly it was a miracle the
plastic didn't shatter in her hands, Meg gasped. "Get
married. . . ." Meg's voice was weak and trailed off into
nothingness. In fact, she suddenly felt weak from her
head to her knees and had to sit down in the little chair
by the phone or she'd have crumpled to the floor. "Get
married. . . ." she repeated in a small voice, stunned
by the suddenness of things, the room reeling with
happiness over what Tighe had just said.

"Get married," Tighe said again firmly. "I mean, you
still *do* want to?"

Everything exploded inside Meg at once. The worry,
the withering frustration at Mr. Devlin's closing his
house to them, the pain of her and Tighe's forced
separation, the telephone call to her mother, the mourn-
ful comments of her bastard stepfather—everything.
Meg burst into tears, so happy she was sure something
terrible had to happen to their plans, God's cruel punishment for a wayward sinner's having been suddenly
given something she didn't in the least deserve. The
sobs and cries rolled out of her in waves, punctuated by
short little yelps of pure joy.

"Gee," Tighe said, laughing. "Most of the girls I
propose to at least *pretend* to sound happier about
it. . . ."

"Oh, shut up." Meg laughed along with him. "It was
just so sudden and everything. . . ."

They both were laughing now, then Tighe's whole
manner abruptly changed. Meg could hear him arguing
with someone in the dormitory hall. A moment later he
came back on the phone, sounding defeated. "Some
clown's jumping up and down and says he's got to have
the phone right now. Worse than that, he's bigger than
I am—biggest damned bastard I know—and says he'll

beat the shit out of me if I don't give it to him right now. He's given me thirty seconds, and he's checking it with his stopwatch. Look, Meg, get your stuff ready. I'll phone and tell you when I'm coming up to get you." A brief pause while Tighe apparently tried arguing with the giant who stood clocking him. "But, for Christ's sake, don't tell anybody, Meg. Not your friends, not your stepfather. Particularly not your stepfather. He'd only—"

A sudden new voice came over the phone, as deep and percussive as a tympani. "Look, Meg whatever-your-name-is, congrats on landing the guy and all that crap, but I got a girl to call, too, so if you'll forgive me for breaking into lover-boy's time here, good luck and good night."

"Tighe—" Meg began, but realized the phone had gone dead. The giant bastard had hung up the phone. Meg giggled. Boys were so crazy, like children, really. Even giant bastards.

The wedding was a small one. That the church, St. Bardolph's Episcopal, was a very big one only made the wedding's smallness seem smaller, its vaulted Gothic arches continually threatening to overwhelm them all. Never in a million years would St. Bardolph's have been the church Tighe Devlin would have chosen to marry Meg in, not his beloved Meg. But because the vestry of St. James, the smaller but elegant church the Devlins had used for generations, included friends of his family, Tighe had reluctantly decided that to use St. James was to invite disaster; even though his parents were in Hobe Sound at the moment, word was sure to get to them. It saddened Tighe a little; St. James was where he had been christened, where he had been confirmed, where he would presumably be buried, and, in normal circumstances, where he would have been married. It was a shimmering jewel of a church, fitting for someone as beautiful as Meg.

On the other hand no word would make its way to his family from St. Bardolph's. Once upon a time it had been a very select, elegant church, where some of Philadelphia's best families worshipped. But the city had changed complexion, and the church was now surrounded by once-fashionable town houses converted into low-cost tenements crammed to their roofs with Puerto Ricans, Haitians, and Blacks. On a good Sunday at St. Bardolph's, a congregation of ten or twelve was considered spectacular.

For the wedding itself only a handful had been invited. Two or three longtime cronies from Friends Academy, where Tighe had gone to grammar school. A small contingent of friends from Exeter. A fistful from Williams. Two cousins from New York, sworn to secrecy. The governess who had raised him—and who wept throughout the entire proceedings. His godfather, William Biddle, who thought Tighe's father was just as unreasonable as Tighe did. A gaggle of uncles and older friends who shared Biddle's opinion of Mr. Devlin. There were no bridesmaids, no ushers, no best man, no wedding dress, no cutaways. Instead of her father, sitting as unknowing in Goat Island as Mr. Devlin was sitting unknowing in Hobe Sound, William Biddle gave Meg away. It was like a hurried last-minute wartime wedding. Even though the service was held off to one side of St. Bardolph's to minimize its vastness, Meg still felt lost in its awesome interior.

"Dearly beloved," the minister began, "we are gathered here today in the sight of—" The minister stopped abruptly, looking anxiously over his head. Meg followed his eyes upwards, startled by a sudden flapping sound and small, shrill cries that seemed to come from nowhere.

The minister ducked. Meg and Tighe ducked. The small gathering behind them ducked.

It was a pigeon, a pigeon suffering an agony of panic. Somehow, it had made its way into St. Bardolph's—probably through one of the broken windows to the rear of the church—and now couldn't find its way back out. The crashing chords from the organ had terrified it, the hostile humans below threatened it, and that it was enclosed inside a building instead of being able to fly freely at will had stampeded it.

Circling crazily, flapping its wings wildly, the terrified pigeon kept swooping low over them in its panic. Meg could not explain it, but the trapped pigeon was a dark cloud passing across her happiness, an omen of something sinister that made as little sense as the pigeon did.

Buzz de StPhalle, an old friend of Tighe's from Exeter days, leapt high to grab the pigeon on one of its lower swoops and get it out of the church; his hands were able to catch hold of only one of the frantically flapping wings and a single leg; the pigeon screamed—something Meg had never thought a pigeon could do—and got away. The church deacon appeared and began trying to trap the poor creature in a large net fastened to the end of a long pole—apparently pigeons, sparrows, bats, and other birds quite frequently got inside St. Bardolph's. The deacon's assault only made the pigeon more frantic than ever, swooping down over the people seated in the front pews like an errant bat. The women were covering their heads with their hands; the analogy to a bat appeared to have occurred to them, too.

Meg felt the dread inside her growing senselessly; she gripped Tighe's hand so tightly he looked at her oddly. Up toward the altar, the deacon and his pole-net finally captured the bird. Pulling the pole back hand over hand, the deacon almost had hold of it when the

pigeon suddenly struggled free of the net and began
flying aimlessly around near the altar screen. To calm
it, the deacon signaled the organist to stop playing.
Almost immediately the pigeon calmed down—the boom-
ing organ apparently was one of the things about the
church that terrified it the most—and exhausted, settled itself on the top of the ornately gilded altar screen.

For a moment the minister studied it to see if the
pigeon was going to stay there long enough to get
through the wedding and decided it was. Once again he
faced Meg and Tighe and the gathering. Meg found it
difficult to concentrate on what he was saying; for her, the
whole thing was so filled with nameless warnings that
she felt cold shudders running through her. Stupid,
stupid, she kept telling herself, but the feeling would
not go away. She was getting as batty as her mother,
Meg decided. Pulling herself together, Meg clutched
Tighe's hand for reassurance and received an answering
squeeze; he appeared more amused than frightened by
the pigeon's performance.

"Dearly beloved," the minister began for a second
time.

It was a brief service, but everyone appeared relieved when it was finished. The only living creature
that really appeared to appreciate the modest little
wedding service was the pigeon. The exhausted bird
had tucked its head under its wing and fallen sound
asleep.

After the wedding itself a reception was held at the
Biddle home, where Tighe and Meg were going to
spend their wedding night. The reception was almost as
small as the wedding—perhaps there were fifteen more
people—and Tighe felt as badly about it as he had
about St. Bardolph's. Someone as precious and beautiful as Meg deserved a far grander reception. At the
Marion Cricket Club or someplace that didn't have the

last-minute informality of even the Biddle's opulent living room.

It was, in fact, a beautiful home, and Mrs. Biddle had covered every table and other flat surface with vases of flowers; in the dining room she had even provided a small wedding cake. But to Tighe there was something sad about the reception; it looked more like a cocktail party than the grand wedding celebration Meg so richly deserved.

When Tighe took Meg to one side during the party, her reaction baffled him. "I wish it were bigger," he said sadly. "Bigger and dressier."

"Oh, I think it's a very pretty setting, Tighe," Meg answered, trying not to show what was bothering her. "Only . . ."

"Only what?"

"You're just going to laugh at me, Tighe. But that pigeon. That damned pigeon at the church. It scared me. I couldn't tell you why in a million years, but that crazy bird got me all upset. It's like it was trying to tell me something. . . ."

Tighe laughed. "For God's sake, Meg, it was only a pigeon, not a vulture. And if it *was* talking to you, telling you something, hell, we ought to race right back to St. Bardolph's and catch it. A talking pigeon could make millions."

Meg's temper flared. Damn it, he was trying to kid her out of something she felt deeply. Just as she was about to try again, Mr. Biddle brought two older friends of Tighe's over to talk of old times and to introduce Meg. Her words froze in her mouth, and she was never able to really get back to the pigeon and its effect on her.

The drinks kept being poured, the buffet kept disappearing and being replaced, the laughter kept growing louder and more intense. It was, Meg thought, as if she were on some sort of insane carousel, driven by forces unknown to go constantly faster and faster.

The only telegram that came was from Peter Longtree, a Williams friend of Tighe's Meg had met last summer. He had also been Tighe's confidant in the arrangements made for the Devlin house in Northeast Harbor earlier that winter. It was a telegram Tighe *should* have read before reading aloud to the gathering. Addressed to Meg, it consisted of only two words: "Act surprised."

Everyone at the Biddle's laughed—the older guests a little uneasily—and Meg found herself blushing furiously. With effort she finally brought herself to join the laughter. Peter Longtree was a close friend of Tighe's and knew about everything, which, to her, made his "funny" telegram all the more unfair. "Act surprised," *indeed*.

Neither she nor the telegram's playful sender would have been laughing very hard had they known the series of ugly surprises that lay ahead of her.

The next day Meg listened to the whining roar of the jet as it climbed skyward and headed for Miami. Out her window she could see Philadelphia rapidly disappearing behind her. She was not sorry to be leaving it; the city's lone recommendation was that Tighe had been born and grown up there. A few minutes earlier at the departure gate, Tighe had kept reassuring her that it was only a matter of days before they would be together again.

"Some honeymoon," Meg said with an attempt at a smile. "The bride heads six states south; the groom heads for his bank."

"Just a matter of days," Tighe had repeated, taking her in his arms and squeezing her as hard as he could. Walking down the long ramp, Meg kept turning back and waving to him forlornly; Tighe kept smiling and waving back.

As soon as the outskirts of Philly had disappeared into a blur of smudgy dots below her, Meg fell fast asleep, worn out by all that had happened in the last few days. She was awakened by the stewardess, who smiled while gently shaking her.

"Are you all right, miss?" the stewardess asked in her professionally concerned voice. "You've been having a nightmare, and the lady in the seat beside you was getting quite worried."

Meg apologized, first to the old lady beside her, then to the stewardess. "Terrible things, nightmares," the old lady said, and looked as if she were about to attempt conversation. Meg turned away quickly; she bit her lip and squeezed her fingers together, forcing herself fully awake.

Meg didn't want to go back to sleep; of that she was sure. Some women have nightmares about seeing their children drowning and being powerless to save them; others have nightmares about being raped by foul-smelling, unshaven madmen.

But Meg's nightmare had been about a pigeon—a pigeon that flew wildly around inside her head, flapping its wings frantically, beating itself against the inside of her skull, and screaming a cryptic warning that Meg couldn't understand.

For the rest of the trip she stared moodily out the window.

Chapter Four

Damn it, that call from her daughter got Mrs. Kendricks all shook up. She's been talking about it lately, anyway—saying she's all cured and that it's time for her to go home—but Meg Kendricks's call really stirred her up. Just saying it to someone else convinced her she's right. Okay, so she is—she doesn't need her daughter's help to realize it.

That woman is too important to me. She's filled the pale void in my life that my wife and daughter's running-out on me left. Daughter or no daughter sticking her nose in things, I don't plan to have Mrs. Kendricks running out on me, too.

I'll tell that little broad her mother's a total flake, that all my patients always think they're cured and want to leave, and not to be conned by her mother's apparent sanity. I can be very persuasive on things like that. By the time I get through, Little Meg will want her mother to stay here—lock her up and throw the key away. Just watch me.

I knew something was going to go wrong—the ear was high in its jar this morning. That always means trouble. This time for Meg, if she doesn't do what I want her to and keeps stirring up her mother.

Psychiatric & Personal Observations,
The Home, Alan Sommers, M.D., Director.

The bus taking Meg from Miami to Matecumbe Gut had looked, when she had first boarded it, respectable enough, but as it bounced along U.S. 1, it became increasingly uncomfortable. Perhaps, Meg told herself, it was the highway rather than the bus, and patted the leather armrest protectively.

The ride grew increasingly unpleasant. As they got farther away from Miami—across the causeway and onto the Keys themselves—the towns on either side of them became progressively smaller and more dilapidated. Along some stretches of the road she could see no sign of any houses at all—nothing but stretches of flat, wind-blown sand dunes and a handful of withered, twisted trees.

Meg's nerves began to crumble. Finally, she walked up beside the bus driver and asked when they would reach Matecumbe Gut. "Oh, thirty minutes, maybe," he answered, looking at her oddly. "Don't get many people want to go to the gut," he explained. "Nothing there no more."

"I'm visiting a place there. A sanitarium. They call it The Home." The driver looked at her strangely again, shifted in his seat uncomfortably, and, when he spoke, there was an uneasy tone to his words. For a moment more he appeared to hesitate, then: "Well, I know where it is, lady, sure." Another long hesitation. "See," he added, without really explaining anything, "The Home's kind of a creepy place. Always has been. I'll tell you that straight out. See, it's—well, lemme put it this way—*I* wouldn't want to spend any time there. No, sir."

Meg felt a small shudder run through her and tried to find out what the man was talking about. "I'm afraid I don't follow. . . ."

"Not my position to talk about things like that, lady,"

the driver said apologetically, shrugging and turning away from her.

The Home, clearly, was not a place he wanted to talk about. His reaction was not a reassuring one; the trapped pigeon in Meg's head began beating its wings again.

About half an hour later Meg felt the bus slow down. Looking out her window, she could see a small, sandy road that crossed U.S. 1 and headed toward the ocean. When the bus had finally hissed to a full stop, the driver twisted around in his seat and looked at her. "Matecumbe Gut is down that road, lady." He looked away quickly, as if to be sure not to get involved in another conversation.

"Thank you," she said as he handed her and her two suitcases out of the bus and onto the road.

The driver shrugged and climbed back behind the wheel. Only seconds later the bus took off down U.S. 1 with a roar.

Standing beside the road, Meg suddenly felt small and helpless. She was out in the middle of nowhere, with the salt wind moaning forlornly across empty stretches of flat, sandy dune. There was no town in sight ahead of her; there were no houses visible along the road. A battered sign in peeling white paint with black lettering reading Matecumbe Gut and an arrow pointing ahead was the only indication that humans had ever been there. With a sigh Meg picked up her two suitcases and started down the road. After the first hundred yards, the bags had become unbearably heavy, and she wondered if she'd be able to make it; the bags couldn't be abandoned in this wilderness, yet, to be able to carry them, she would have to stop and put them down every hundred feet or so.

From behind her Meg heard a sudden clatter and the sound of an ancient car horn. Turning around, she saw a battered pickup truck slowing down to stop beside her. Its driver appeared to be a farmer, his face covered with benign cancers from working too long in the sun; besides an overlarge straw hat, he was dressed only in faded denim overalls.

"Need a lift, miss?" he asked in his rich drawl.

"Boy, do I!" answered Meg, watching the man come out of the cab and easily hoist her two bags into the rear of his pickup. "Thank God you came along."

"Those bags looked too heavy for a pretty young thing like you to be struggling with, miss," the man noted, smiling a thin, crooked smile. "Glad to help out," he added. "No one much comes to the gut anymore. Town just upped and moved away. It's nice to see a new face now and then."

The springs on the pickup had long ago suffered defeat at the hands of small back roads like the one they were on, and Meg found it almost impossible to carry on much of a conversation with the farmer; accustomed to the jouncing of the pickup, the farmer talked on about the weather, the effects of salt air on tomato crops, and a new kind of fertilizer that seemed to be working particularly well.

Suddenly, the road became smooth again, and Meg could ask the man a few questions. Yes, he had lived here all his life. No, he didn't mind the isolation of Matecumbe Gut; maybe, well, maybe yes, it would be nice to have more neighbors, but a farmer didn't have a lot of time to talk with people anyway.

"Do you know a place called The Home?" Meg asked. "Is it down this road or what?"

The farmer, like the bus driver before him shifted uncomfortably in his seat, and Meg could see his jaws suddenly clamp shut. The Home was not anything *he* wanted to talk about either. She asked a few more questions, but his answers were cryptic. Pushed by

Meg, he finally answered her angrily. "Not right to have a nuthouse in a God-fearing place like the gut, not right at all. Specially one like The Home. Nossir." This pronouncement frightened Meg. She grabbed his near arm with her hand and pleaded. "Please," she said, "please tell me. Is something wrong with The Home?"

The farmer shrugged. Finally he gave a long sigh. "With The Home," he said, "it's more a matter of nothing is *right*." Meg desperately wanted to ask him more about The Home, but the set of his jaw told her he had said his piece and nothing more would be forthcoming.

About a mile farther down the road they reached the town of Matecumbe Gut, and the farmer stopped his truck. To Meg it looked more like a western ghost town than a seaside village on the Florida Keys; only a handful of the houses showed any sign of being lived in; tall dune grass and weeds poked up through the slatted sidewalks; peeling signs from a better day swung back and forth in the wind.

"Only 'bout a hundred yards to the left, miss," the farmer grunted. "Down by the water." He got out, plucked her bags from the pickup's back, and put them down on the street. As he turned to climb back behind the wheel, he stared at Meg for a moment and sighed. "The gut's seen better days, miss, but, hell, it's our hometown and we're partial to it." With a small sigh he climbed back into his truck. His wave was perfunctory. With a great rattling and coughing, the truck started up and drove away in the opposite direction.

Back lugging her suitcases, Meg had gone perhaps a hundred yards along the water's edge when she came to a small raised pier. On it sat a weather-beaten little bench and a sign reading The Home—Ring Bell for Car. In front of Meg was an old-fashioned ship's bell supported on either side by heavy beams. When she grabbed the rope, the bell swung back and forth, its hollow boom ringing across the water.

A few minutes later there was a tremendous clanking and grinding sound, and a small, beat-up gondola car—hanging from the twin cables of an aerial tramway—began moving toward her from an island she could barely make out through a gray wreath of swirling fog. Meg shook her head in confusion. Until now she had not realized The Home even was on an island.

More clanking and grinding and groaning and the car arrived, finally scraping to a halt not far from the great bell. Viewing the car with mistrust—Meg hated machines like this that raised you up and moved you along without your being able to control them—she opened the car's small sliding door. It creaked and squeaked as she moved it back and forth, put her bags in, and climbed in herself. Below the front window was a button and a small metal sign, Push to Start. With a deep breath she closed her eyes and pushed it.

Meg was taken aback when nothing happened. For a moment she wondered if she should leave the tramway car and find a phone to call the island. But just as she reached for the door handle, the tramcar started with a sudden violent lurch, knocking her off her feet onto a small wooden seat in the rear of the car. As the wind caught it, the tiny tramcar began swaying wildly, suspended from the two heavy cables that stretched between mainland and island. Meg squirmed and shuddered; it was turning out to be a frightening, if not dangerous, journey.

Catching her breath, Meg studied the interior of the car. What she saw was not encouraging. It was old and badly in need of refurbishing; here and there, thick patches of rust showed through the peeling paint. Beneath her feet the floor was fashioned of aging wooden slats, much of it apparently rotten and crumbling. Several broken slats rose jaggedly straight up from the floor. The windows were gray with dirt, spattered by a long accumulation of salt spray and apparently never washed. Meg hoped the two heavy cables that the tramcar hung from were in better shape than the car they supported far above the water.

As she looked out through one of the windows, trying to clean a patch on the inside of it with a piece of Kleenex from her handbag to see better, she was struck by the speed of the current running through the gut below. As it reached the calmer water at the end of the narrow opening, it churned up a patchwork of white-caps, angry and ominous-looking. For Florida the water had an unusually grayish look, and although the sun had been out when she left the nonexistent town of Matecumbe Gut, racing wisps of fog made it appear from the car that she was entering a world of perma-nent overcast and threatening weather.

By now Meg had accustomed herself to how the little car swung back and forth in the wind; she could not adjust herself to the frightening, creaking lurches the car made while moving along its cables. Holding on to either side, Meg gingerly made her way up to the front of the car to find out if she could yet get a decent view of the island. Slowly, the car lurching and swaying, she was able to get a better look, not only at the island, but at the house that served as The Home.

Meg gasped softly. The building appeared endless, with wings and attached outbuildings stretching in every direction. It looked, however, in about the same state of repair as the car she was riding in. Once, apparently, the house had been white, but the paint had been stripped off by years of high winds that followed the racing waters of the gut. From the air no effort to repaint it seemed to have been made. Shingles were missing from the walls and the roof; chimneys had been allowed to crumble, their bricks, in some places, still lying on the roofing where they had landed and stuck. Some shutters were totally missing from their windows; others still swung back and forth, unfastened, banging against the windows as they were seized by the wind. It had the foreboding look of an abandoned house somewhere along a deserted stretch of the New England coast.

Even from her location—the island itself was quite narrow—Meg could see the great waves that crashed constantly against the rocky offshore side of the island. Meg discovered she was trembling. The Home was a throughly depressing place, and Meg cursed her stepfather for putting her mother in a sanitarium so run-down just to save money. If someone was only slightly unbalanced when they arrived here, it wouldn't take them long to go completely crazy in surroundings like these.

The car shuddered, passed a tower on the outer edge of the island, and began its descent toward another small platform, much like the one she'd left from. The platform appeared empty, but she had sent a telegram telling her mother approximately when she'd arrive and expected her and possibly Dr. Sommers to appear any moment. As she neared the platform, Meg could feel a wave of dread reaching out from the shore. Ridiculous, Meg told herself; The Home was old and run-down and grim, but she had known that before she arrived. In spite of trying, Meg could not shake her sense of the ominous; the pigeon was back battering its head against the inside of her skull, screaming a warning of things too foreign to understand.

On the platform Meg discovered there was still no one around. A flight of steep, crumbling stairs led up the bluff ahead of her; somewhere at the top of the stairs was presumably The Home. Awkwardly, Meg picked up her bags and started down the path; a mo-

ment later she put them down again. She would never
be able to climb those stairs carrying anything so heavy.
Meg picked up the lighter of the two and started up the
path toward the steps. A sudden sound of rustling
shrubbery and some indistinct talking made her heart
jump. "Hello?" she said tentatively. "*Hello?* Is anyone
there?"

A youngish man—almost a boy—stepped out from a
side path she hadn't seen, studied her for a second, and
then smiled. "You Miss Kendricks? I'm Kenny."

Meg was relieved. Kenny must be one of the staff
sent down to help her with her baggage. Meg was just
about to say something to him when the same rustling
sound she'd heard before came again from the side
path, and a short, stout lady of perhaps sixty joined
him. "And I'm Mrs. Belagio," the lady said warmly,
smiling broadly at Meg. "Welcome to The Home."

"We heard the bell and knew someone was coming
over," Kenny said, looking suddenly wistful.

"The bags, Kenny," Mrs. Belagio said, pointing to
where Meg had put them down. Obediently—Mrs.
Belagio must be Kenny's staff supervisor or something—
Kenny picked up Meg's bags and started forward. Mrs.
Belagio put her arm through Meg's and led her forward,
too.

"Have you worked here long?" Meg asked Mrs.
Belagio, but stopped when she saw Kenny had halted
and turned back toward them, still holding her suitcases.

"When I heard the bell, Miss Kendricks, I thought it
was my mother. She's coming to take me home, you
know. This week, maybe, or next at the latest. I always
come down when I hear the bell ring, because—"

"Oh, Kenny." Mrs. Belagio laughed. "You know just
as well as I do that your mother's been dead for five
years." She turned toward Meg, who was squirming
with discomfort. "I hate to be so blunt to the boy, but

Dr. Sommers said we all have to help make him face the truth. And the truth is that his mother's dead. And has been for over five years, I think it is. Not being able to accept that is one of the reasons Kenny is here."

There was a thud as Kenny dropped Meg's bags on the pavement. His face filled with anger. Slowly, one finger rose and pointed at Mrs. Belagio. "That's not true. Take it back, you bloated old bag, take it back! You're always saying awful things just to hurt me. She's not dead"—his eyes turned toward Meg, pleading to be believed, his voice beginning to sound like an angry child's—"she's not, she's not, she's not!"

For an instant he stood in front of Meg, staring at her with eyes half filled with tears. Then, he turned toward Mrs. Belagio, who stood beside Meg, her head slightly cocked to one side, smiling at him sympathetically.

"She'll be back for me, you lying old bitch, you'll see. . . ." Kenny hissed at her. Abruptly, he began running down the path until he suddenly plunged into the bushes at one side and disappeared. Through the undergrowth, Meg could hear him screaming to himself. "She'll be back, she'll be back, she will, she will, she will. . . ." Gradually his voice faded into nothingness, although for a few seconds more Meg could hear distant crashes and the sound of snapping branches as Kenny ran to hide.

Meg stood motionless, unsure of what to make of it. Kenny was obviously not one of the staff but one of the patients. The line between sanity and insanity was frighteningly thin, Meg reflected.

Still following the distant sounds of Kenny's flight, Mrs. Belagio sighed and shook her head. "Dr. Sommers works very hard with that boy, but he doesn't seem to get anywhere. Sad." Mrs. Belagio was puffing so hard from climbing up the steps she gave up further conversation.

Meg wasn't sure that Kenny's state was as sad as it was frightening. He had seemed perfectly normal until challenged on his mother's being alive. Before her eyes Meg had seen him turn into something completely different.

From the courses she had taken as a parapsychiatric trainee in Bangor the winter before, Meg knew that *any* of the patients here could, at any time, turn violent. It was a hard thing to accept and made Meg squirm uncomfortably: there was something frightening about the thought.

"Here we are, dear," Mrs. Belagio said, still puffing, and threw open the front door. The change from the brightness outside to the dimness of the interior left Meg's eyes blind. So her first impression of The Home came through her nose—the place had a strange sweet-sour smell to it that Meg couldn't identify. A smell that was mixed with the odor of permanent dampness. Slowly, her eyes began to adjust to the dimness, but she had just begun to examine the front room when she felt Mrs. Belagio touch her arm. "The first thing you'll probably want to do is find your mother, dear. I'll ask at the desk."

She had only advanced about two steps when Meg seized her arm. From somewhere came a terrible screaming, uncontrolled, unshaped, unending. It sounded like a woman in agony. The question on Meg's face made Mrs. Belagio smile and pat her hand.

"Don't worry, dear. That's only Mrs. Tibald. She's always doing that. Poor old thing, she's one of the two people they have to keep locked up in the cells downstairs. I've never seen her, but I understand she keeps trying to scratch out the eyes of anyone who goes near her cell."

From downstairs the scream suddenly took on additional dimension; the woman was swearing and cursing as well as shrieking. Mrs. Belagio was apparently unfazed by the racket. "She's in good voice today, I must say that." Abruptly, a stricken look crossed Mrs. Belagio's face. "My goodness," she clucked at Meg, "what a strange first impression you must be getting of The Home."

Mrs. Belagio smiled sweetly and then suddenly walked away, disappearing without explanation.

Chapter Five

That girl's due to show up today. I'm terribly fond of Mrs. Kendricks and most of the time have no trouble with her at all.

But her damned daughter will probably ask a lot of questions, get her mother all stirred up again, and for all I know, even start reinforcing that crazy idea of hers of going home and leaving me.

Well, Mrs. Kendricks is one patient I'm not going to have leave me, and that's all there is to it.

Psychiatric & Personal Observations,
The Home, Alan Sommers, M.D., Director.

For some time Meg stood in the dimness of the lobby, blinking at the strangeness of the room and its bustle, still unsettled by the sudden departure of Mrs. Belagio. One minute the woman was there, the next she was gone—without explanation, without apology, without apparent reason.

Her first step, she decided, would be to talk to the nurse behind the reception desk and ask where to find her mother, but the woman seemed deeply involved in talking to someone on the phone, her lips pinched tightly together, her expression one of high irritation. The entranceway appeared a busy place; people—most of them patients, Meg supposed—shuffled past her. All of them stared at her inquiringly as they passed, some wearing expressions of distinct hostility.

Meg felt increasingly uncomfortable; there wasn't even a chair to sit in while waiting for the nurse to finish her conversation. It was an awkward feeling, standing in the middle of the room being stared at like the unknown, unwanted guest at a cocktail party. Finally Meg marched over to the desk and planted herself in front of the nurse. The woman studied her a couple of times and finally hung up the phone with a sigh. "Yes?" she asked, making little effort to sound pleasant.

"I'm Meg Dev . . . ah, Kendricks."

"I'm Midge Cummins, the head nurse. You're Mrs. Kendricks's daughter, then. Don't look much like her, I have to say, but that doesn't mean anything, does it?" Midge Cummins studied her again, then: "Is there anything I can do for you, Miss Kendricks?" The head nurse's question was more a challenge than an inquiry.

"I was wondering if you knew where my mother might be. I want to see her and . . ."

Midge Cummins stared at her for a couple of moments, then apparently decided as requests went this was a reasonable one. She pointed across the room with one long, gnarled finger. "I think if you go through those double doors over there on the other side of the living room, you'll find her out on the terrace. I'd go with you, but I'm terribly busy."

The nurse was obviously abrupt, rude, and—uncaring. She was a tall woman, with sullen, pinched cheeks, a permanent expression of distaste, and a sour, turned-down mouth that when opened revealed uneven rows of teeth. Like the building, the condition of the grounds and the house—like the rust patches inside the tramcar—

Meg decided that Midge Cummins was a sorry excuse for a head nurse.

Meg looked at the woman with disbelief, resenting that the head nurse, however busy, wasn't going to make the effort to take her to her mother herself. Midge Cummins, Meg decided, was one cold fish.

There was no point going any further; the nurse was already back on the phone.

Feeling uncomfortable, Meg walked across the long Main Room, studying the other patients there as she went. The patients stared at her with varying degrees of hostility; any stranger apparently made them feel threatened. Some of them were playing cards, a handful were reading, some watched television, many of them simply sat where they were, staring emptily into space. Very quickly Meg stopped looking at them.

The din from the television sets was overwhelming, beating against her eardrums in a babble of voices, music, and canned laughter. In this one room alone, Meg counted four sets, each tuned to a different channel, some with a small gathering in front of them, others unwatched but nevertheless playing with the sound turned up as far as it would go. It was an electronic Babel.

As she neared the room's end, she saw, half hidden behind heavy faded drapes, the French windows that presumably led out to the terrace. Slowly, she made her way farther down the room. She felt herself growing increasingly apprehensive; the vacant eyes of the patients followed her progress, watching her every movement, studying her, measuring her. The effect was profoundly disturbing.

On the terrace she suddenly saw her mother lying on a chaise, far to one side, eyes closed, head thrown back, face aimed toward the sun. A thousand childhood memories rushed into Meg's mind, brought back by the familiar pose. She could feel tears crowding into her eyes.

"Mother," she said, "Mother—it's me. Meg."

Her mother's eyes flew open, unbelieving, a film of confusion beginning to grow across them, as if Meg were an alien newly landed on the planet. She blinked at her in surprise.

"Meg . . ." she said in disbelief, "Meg . . . Meg . . . Meg . . ."

Suddenly, she leapt to her feet and wrapped her arms around Meg, laughing, crying, screaming, all at the same time. "Oh, darling, darling Meg. You came, you came. My darling little Meg!"

Listening, Meg suddenly felt almost embarrassed. It was so long since she'd set eyes on her mother that it was as if a stranger were hugging and kissing her, someone she might have known long ago, resurrected before her eyes and only pretending she was her mother.

Her mother abruptly sat on the edge of the chaise, indicating Meg should pull over one of the smaller chairs for herself. "You look thin, Meg. Are you sure you're eating enough? You never were very much for food. And your hair. I don't think it's right for you. You should do something about your hair, dear. And you look pale, Meg, so terribly pale. Well, this good Florida sun will put some color back into your cheeks in no time. . . ."

The stranger vanished. Meg could remember almost a lifetime of the same questions and comments, thrown at her day after day, the incessant clucking of a mother hen. It was no stranger; it was her mother. She had run through every element of her bygone litany except to ask Meg whether she'd been to the bathroom, and Meg didn't know whether that omission came in recognition of her age now or because she'd simply forgotten to get around to it.

They chatted for almost an hour, covering everything and everybody from Little Goat to Matecumbe Gut. One thing became quickly clear to Meg; her mother was completely lucid now; the old days when she was continually out of touch with reality had gone. Regardless of what Dr. Sommers might say, her mother was cured. Adroitly, Meg began maneuvering the conversation toward some of the areas her mother had brought up with her over the phone to Little Goat.

"Mother, some of the things you said on the phone when I called were very upsetting. Are you really sure you're ready to come home? You said some very upsetting things about that and Dr. Sommers."

Her mother abruptly became evasive. To Meg it almost seemed as if she was afraid she would be overheard if she said what she meant. Her eyes shifted around the terrace, seemingly groping for something to talk about that couldn't get her into trouble.

"Well, dear, you can see how run-down this place is. Shocking. Inedible food. Glop. Rats running around. Building about to fall down. Hopelessly incompetent staff. . . ."

Setting her jaw, Meg realized she was becoming quite angry. Bad food and a few mice were not why she'd left Tighe and flown all the way down here. "Damn it, Mother, either you're better or you aren't. And if you *are*, there's no point in staying locked up in this place."

Patting her hair nervously, Meg's mother was clearly upset. She began to make excuses, but it was a half-hearted effort. "Dr. Sommers has been talking to me a lot. That man. He can talk me in or out of anything. . . ." Her eyes searched Meg's face, looking for understanding.

Swallowing her irritation, Meg was nonetheless determined to remain firm. "It all boils down to one thing, Mom. Are you or aren't you well enough to go?"

"Oh, Meg, I'm all better, I really am. You can tell that. But Dr. Sommers . . . I'm so fond of the man. . . . But he keeps saying I should stay longer. . . . And after I talk to him, I begin to wonder if he may not be right. . . . I just don't know. . . . The doctor—"

Meg exploded. "For God's sake, Mother. The doctor's not the point. If you think you're better, you can't let him brainwash you. Stand up for what you believe. Otherwise you'll be here forever. Doctors aren't gods."

For a second her mother sat on her chaise, nervously toying with her hankie. The notion that she might be here for a long time—forever—finally shook her real feelings loose. "Oh, Meg. You're so terribly right." She reached over and seized Meg's hand, gripping it so hard Meg winced. "Meg, please. Please take me away from here. I'm all better. Please take me away. Quickly, darling. *Now.* It's not just frightening here, it's actually dangerous. I don't know why I let Dr. Sommers bend me around his finger so easily. Please take me away before something happens. Dr. Sommers will be so mad there's no telling what he might do. Take me away *please.* Today, if you can. . . ."

Meg could feel her mother's hand trembling. She didn't know what Sommers's hold on his patients was, but it was obviously powerful. She didn't know about the others, but her mother was frightened to death.

"Then you want to leave?" Meg asked. Considering her mother's phone conversation of the other day, it seemed a strange question to be asking. This Dr. Sommers must be a very persuasive man to switch her mother around so easily.

Meg's mother stood up and clutched at Meg, shaking, trembling, holding on to her desperately. "Oh, my God, Meg, yes. It's not safe here . . . please . . . today . . . please. . . ."

From inside came a sudden commotion. Looking in,

Meg could see a man making his way among the patients. The card game stopped; the readers put down their paperbacks; even an old lady watching children's cartoons abandoned her TV set. It had to be Dr. Sommers. He stopped and chatted with each person in the huge Main Room; they seemed enraptured.

Meg's mother rose from the end of the chaise and pulled Meg inside the French doors. "You'll like Dr. Sommers," her mother assured her. "Everybody does." When Sommers looked in their direction, she called out his name and gleefully pointed to Meg. The doctor smiled and waved, indicating with a gesture he would be over to see them in a moment or two.

"I know you'll like him, I just know you will, Meg," her mother said excitedly. Her abhorrence of The Home but fondness for Dr. Sommers was a duality that Meg couldn't fathom. She studied the doctor as he moved on among the patients; he certainly didn't appear the kind of doctor who would talk a patient into staying on at The Home after they were cured, or who threw things and yelled. She considered her mother's ambivalence— could it be confusion? Was her mother really still insane?

Considering the number of years it had been, Sommers looked remarkably unchanged from the stormy night he had wound up sprawled on his driveway, crying as he forlornly watched the car taking his wife and daughter away from him forever.

Chapter Six

This morning Mrs. Tibald managed to get close enough to Midge Cummins to rip a real gash down the side of her face. Sometimes I think I should send that woman to a full security institution, but I'm damned if I want to give up the fees her family pays.

Meg Kendricks is a delightful little thing. With her here, my make-believe family is complete again. The tricky part will be talking her into staying here. Christ, do all daughters run out on you like my real one did?

Psychiatric & Personal Observations, The Home, Alan Sommers, M.D., Director.

The Home, as the building began to unfold for Meg— her mother was showing her around the inside before luncheon—was a rabbit warren of small sitting rooms and game rooms surrounding the Main Room, which, until now, was all that Meg had seen. All of the rooms were as shabby and dirty as the Main Room: the couches sagged; the upholstery was stained and worn. There were rugs, but thread showed through in many places.

The walls had once been white, Meg decided, but had turned a mottled gray from not being painted; here and there what paint there was was peeling from the walls in graceful curlicues. All of it was cracked and flaking.

At lunchtime Dr. Sommers sought her and her mother out, personally guiding them to his special table. The dining room was an incredibly noisy place, something Dr. Sommers and her mother appeared quite used to. For Meg the ruckus was hard to believe.

The first time it happened, Meg had spun in her chair to see what could possibly have happened to cause such a soul-shattering sound.

Apparently nothing. A middle-aged woman was sitting at her table, her head thrown back, screaming as if the Furies had descended upon her. The people on either side of her paid no attention. A moment later the woman stopped screaming and abruptly resumed eating her lunch. Several times during the meal the same thing happened with other patients—they would stop eating, start screaming or yelling, then stop, and start eating again.

From what Meg could see, the patients got their own food from a dilapidated serving bar, finally sitting down at one of the tables seating eight. The meal appeared to be one long fight. For some reason Meg couldn't fathom, some of the tables were more preferred than others. The result was that those who wound up at a less desirable table were constantly at war with those at the more preferred; shouted arguments erupted at one table after the other, food was occasionally thrown, water spilled, and there were undulating waves of angry shouting and screaming. To Meg the meal was a shattering experience; neither Dr. Sommers nor her mother appeared affected.

At Dr. Sommers's private table food was served by the hulking giant Ernie, who doubled as grounds keeper. He also, Dr. Sommers noted, handled any patient who suddenly became violent. By craning her neck a little,

Meg could see that the food they were served at Dr. Sommers's table was far superior to what the main body of patients was eating. None of this was lost on the others. Hard as she tried, Meg found it impossible to ignore the hostile, resentful stares she was getting from the patients. She was startled when Dr. Sommers suddenly reached over and patted her hand—startled that the doctor should have noticed her discomfort, surprised that the doctor should treat her as you might a little child.

"Don't mind the strange looks, Meg; patients in a place like this always stare at anyone unfamiliar to them." Dr. Sommers paused while he cut himself another slice of filet mignon, put it in his mouth, and chewed it. Then: "You also have to remember that I have never been known to have a patient and her daughter sit at my table before. They take that very personally."

On this score Dr. Sommers was completely right. Each course they were served brought with it a cascading chorus of hoots and catcalls. Meg squirmed in her chair.

"As I told you on the phone, Meg, running a place like this is like trying to keep peace within a large family of siblings. They're fighting for my attention all the time. Anyway, you know how the patients work a little now; don't let them disturb you."

Meg was upset to notice a small look of faint pleasure on Dr. Sommers's face. More upsetting, when she looked at her mother, she seemed to be smiling, too.

Her mother, obviously, was firmly in Sommers's control, a thought that for some reason sent small shudders of concern through Meg. After a little additional chatter between her mother and Sommers, Dr. Sommers and her mother were smiling openly at each other. Studying them, it became obvious that the doctor was as fond of her mother as she was of him. Why then was she so frightened and desperate to get out of The Home? None of it made sense.

As the conversation returned to normal, Meg became suddenly aware that Sommers was also paying a good deal of attention to her, listening to everything she said with a look of absorbed interest, smiling warmly at her continually, telling her funny little stories, frequently patting her hand. What upset Meg the most was the doctor's treating her as if she were a little girl. "Oh, it's so wonderful to have a young person around here who isn't off the wall, Meg. I can't tell you how much I've missed it. You're obviously very bright. A great credit to your dear mother here." Simultaneously, Sommers managed to pat both of their hands. Her mother beamed. Meg forced a smile and shifted un- comfortably in her chair.

On the whole, though, Dr. Sommers was totally charming. His stories were both interesting and funny; his recounting of his difficulties as the director of a sanitarium was thoroughly entertaining; he was a highly intelligent man with a sense of humor that was rare in his profession. Still, Meg wished Tighe were here to give her his own reading of the man; he was always very good at that kind of interpretation. Oh, hell, she just wished Tighe were here. Days now, only days.

"Oh, but you must, Meg, you really must." Meg had been so lost in her thoughts that she hadn't heard the first part of what Sommers was saying at all; she knew it had followed some talk between the doctor and her mother, but that was all. She must *what*? she wondered, searching Sommers's face for some clue to what he had been talking about.

Unwittingly, her mother supplied her with it. "The doctor says there's only one motel anywhere near here, Meg. And that it's a horrible, falling-down wreck."

"It would be a favor—both to your mother and to me," Sommers said smoothly. "We certainly have enough room here. You and your mother will be my guests at all meals, so the food I can vouch for. There's a beautiful room on the second floor, and I think you'd be very comfortable in it. I, certainly, would be absolutely delighted to have you."

Meg hesitated. Some inexplicable voice was whispering inside her head, telling her not to accept Sommers's invitation, warning her not to, but Meg found herself caught between forces.

"Oh, please say you will, Meg, darling," her mother pled. "It would mean so much to me, having you right here with me . . . like it used to be. . . ." Her mother's chin began to tremble again; Meg's resistance began to crumble.

Meg vacillated. "Well, I don't know. . . ."

Meg desperately wanted to tell him that The Home frightened her as much as it did her mother, that she and her mother had agreed it was time she went home, and that her husband would be arriving soon to take them both away from here, but she stopped before she even began. She hadn't yet told either Sommers or her mother that she was married. To prevent upsetting her, she had to pick just the right moment to tell her mother about it; if she told Sommers in private, he might let it slip to her mother. Her marriage to Tighe was going to come as a terrible shock to her mother, who had doubtless built a little dream by now in which the two of them were living together somewhere. It was, after all, the dream with which she had been feeding her mother for years.

"Oh, *please*, Meg," her mother repeated, her eyes beginning to fill with tears. "Please say you will. . . ."

Meg gave in, some part of her still crying out that she was making a mistake. "Great," Dr. Sommers announced.

Her mother struggled with a yawn, saying the day had been too exciting for an old lady like herself. She hoped they'd excuse her if she went to lie down a little while.

"Let me walk you around a little, Meg," Sommers said shortly after her mother had left the table. "This old house is really quite fascinating. Someday soon I'll give you a real tour of the place, but you'll want time to unpack."

The last thing Meg was interested in at the moment was walking around The Home, but it would be a good chance to talk to Sommers about her mother, so she gave in.

Following Sommers, it became obvious he knew every inch of the house, its history, and that he was as aware of its state of decrepitude as Meg was. "Place never recovered, really, from being left empty and uncared-for so long before I bought it."

In the first room they went into, Dr. Sommers paused to show Meg a startlingly lifelike stuffed animal grouping. "My hobby, taxidermy," Sommers explained. Unlike anything else in The Home, the specimen, a stuffed lynx with a rabbit in its jaws, lacked the usual covering of dust; someone kept it immaculately clean. As they moved to other rooms, Meg was surprised to see how alive each of his stuffed animals looked: they appeared as if they might spring to life any second and attack you. The doctor was a consummate artist in the way he posed them. Lifelike, yes, but increasingly unsettling.

"Someday I'll show you my workroom downstairs. That is, of course, if you're interested. Other people's hobbies can often be a terrible bore."

"I certainly *am* interested," Meg lied. "You really have a feeling for it."

Sommers beamed, and they moved on, moving slowly from room to room; in each, another animal grouping, each grouping more savage and violent than the one before. To Meg the worst was a giant hawk, wings spread wide, talons outstretched to seize a helpless chipmunk, which was making a futile, desperate effort to escape the winged death descending to devour it.

In another room they came to the only truly restfully posed animal in the house, a small dog, its head cocked to one side, sitting up as if to beg for a morsel of food from the doctor's table. "My first pet here on the island," the doctor said wistfully. "I loved that dog. But he kept chasing off with other dogs—wild strays—on the island," Sommers added with a sigh. "Trying to leave me, I guess." Sommers shrugged his shoulders sadly. Stuffing your own pet dog struck Meg as curious, and she was about to ask something about it, but decided not to.

As the afternoon wore on, Sommers showed Meg the kitchens (antique and filthy), the exercise room, his own office (beautifully paneled and in magnificent shape), the nurses' station and their small sitting room behind it. With each of these places—with the exception of the doctor's office—Meg felt the same run-down aura she'd noticed in the huge living room and dining room.

The staff, as Sommers introduced them, gave Meg a similar feeling. Midge Cummins, the head nurse, she already knew. But as Meg studied her, sitting in the staff living room, her shoes off, a wilted cigarette dangling from one corner of her mouth, she not only seemed as unpleasant as ever, but appeared as dissolute as she was acerbic.

She only rose halfway to her feet to shake Meg's hand when Sommers formally introduced her, barely looking up long enough to say, "We met."

Sitting on a small couch together were the two young practical nurses who rounded out the nursing staff. At least they stood up when Sommers introduced them, but once she'd met them, Meg found them highly unimpressive. Their uniforms were messy, and one devoted herself almost entirely to the gum she was chewing. Neither spoke, but merely giggled. Earlier, Sommers had formally presented Ernie, the giant who doubled as waiter and controller of the violent. The staff, Meg decided, were a seedy lot.

Dr. Sommers suddenly looked at his watch. "Oh, my," he said in chagrin, noting the time. "I was due in my office for an appointment half an hour ago. Patients get very upset if I'm late for their appointments. Forgive me. I'll see you at my table tonight."

Sommers smiled—it was not a very convincing smile; obviously he was mad at himself for being late for his appointment—and hurried off.

Good God, what a place, Meg thought, and went upstairs to take a bath. Looking in, she found her mother sound asleep on her bed and withdrew quietly, without waking her. She was glad somebody in this insane place could sleep so soundly.

Sitting in the living room that night, Meg and her mother were chatting with each other after Meg's second meal at Dr. Sommers's table. He had been in one of his more charming moods.

Meg was exhausted. The plane trip, the bus ride, the nightmare crossing on the careening tramcar, and the effort of trying to remain pleasant to Dr. Sommers had combined to take their toll; she had difficulty keeping her eyes open as her mother droned on happily. Meg cursed herself; she had yet to have a real talk with Sommers about her mother.

Wearily, Meg watched a young man—he appeared younger than even Kenny, the boy who had met her tramcar and then run off in a fury—standing in front of a couchful of other patients, who were sitting finishing their after-dinner coffee. She saw him nod at what they were saying several times, although Meg didn't see him say anything himself. Suddenly, the boy unzipped his trousers and calmly began to masturbate in front of them. Meg had trouble believing what she was seeing. She looked around. The people on the couch in front of him were ignoring him completely, as if the boy didn't exist. Stunned, Meg grabbed her mother's arm.

Her mother shrugged, then smiled at her. "Don't mind Roger," she said indifferently. "He's always doing that. Two or three times a day. Can't help himself, Dr. Sommers says. That's why the poor boy's here, I suppose. Just ignore him."

Perhaps half an hour later both Meg and her mother went upstairs to go to their rooms. On their way down the long hall, one of the doors suddenly opened, and a haggard, gaunt, elderly lady reached out and seized Meg's arm.

"Thank God, Doctor. Thank God you've finally gotten here." Her fingers bit into Meg's arm; the woman's eyes burned into Meg with an intensity that frightened her. "They made a mistake somewhere, Doctor, and sent me here instead of back home."

The crazed eyes studied Meg, and the fingers bit deeper into her; she suddenly spun and grabbed Meg's other arm as well, facing her and beginning to shake her in fury. "You're not going to be like the rest, are you, Doctor? That other doctor—Sommers—keeps telling me it wasn't a mistake and that I *do* belong here, but I think he just wants the money."

The woman began shaking Meg harder. "I don't belong here, Doctor, you can see that, can't you? Shit," she hissed at Meg suddenly, "you doctors stick together. You probably want the money, too."

The old lady heard someone coming down the hall, dropped Meg's arms after one final shake, and moved back into her room, pulling the door almost shut, her eyes suddenly wide with hatred. "You'd better not be like the others, Doctor, or I'll take a knife and slit you down the middle, from collarbone to cunt. I demand an appointment for the morning, Doctor. Oh, hell, what's the fucking use. . . ." The door was pulled violently shut. Inside, Meg could hear her cursing and swearing.

"It's Mrs. Crane," said her mother. "She thinks you're the new doctor. She thinks *everybody* new she sees is the new doctor. Completely bats, poor old thing."

At her mother's door Meg leaned forward and kissed her mother good night. Her mother smiled happily. "I'm so glad you're here, dear. I've missed you terribly. Try and get some sleep now; you look tired."

Tired? Meg asked herself as she got undressed. She was about to drop. Yet, when she climbed into her bed she found she couldn't get to sleep. There were too many things crowding in on her, too many ideas, too many half-formed fears rattling around in her head.

Lying there in the dark, Meg tried to put the day together for herself. Added together, the pieces were frightening. The patients, with hidden violence simmering under frequently benign appearances. The people in the dining room, screaming and fighting with one another about nothing. The ceaseless staring at her with ugly resentment. The peeling paint and the cracking walls. Mrs. Tibald, the lady locked up downstairs, waiting to tear any passerby's eyes out, alternating screaming with cursing.

Dr. Sommers's collection of viciously posed animal groupings. His attitude when telling about the dog he loved and how he had stuffed him. *Stuffed* him, for Christ's sake.

Finally, the otherwise perfectly pleasant young man, Roger, suddenly masturbating in front of the whole living room while everyone pretended not to notice.

"Just ignore it," her mother had said. How in the

world could any sane person possibly just ignore it? As sleep finally began to close in on her, Meg smiled grimly. For a moment she had forgotten: there weren't any sane people at The Home. What the hell was *she* doing here?

Chapter Seven

This whole thing is getting complicated. Mrs. Kendricks clings to the notion that she's all right now, which, of course, is correct. That could give me a big problem, except she's easy to manipulate. That's been true, sick or well, every since she was put here.

She'll tell herself that she's all well—and she'll begin to believe it passionately. I'll tell her she's still sick—and she'll believe that just as passionately.

I'm winning, I think. And if she starts to believe herself more than she does me, there's a few tricks I can think of to make her decide she's a very sick lady.

If only Meg doesn't louse things up. She's not easy to manipulate. Too damned bright.

At the moment, keeping them both here is the most important thing in my life. Mrs. Kendricks has always been a replacement for my own wife. Meg is my child returned.

She even looks a little like what I suspect my real daughter has grown up to look like. There's something about the way she laughs that's so familiar it's frightening. About the right age, too. The coincidence is eerie.

Psychiatric & Personal Observations,
The Home, Alan Sommers, M.D., Director.

Meg wouldn't have been smiling, grimly or otherwise, as she lay tossing in her bed that night, if she could have seen what was going on down in Dr. Sommers's office at that moment.

Sommers walked in, carefully locking the door behind him. In the dark he walked carefully across the room until he reached his desk. There was a dull click as he turned on a single, very dim light. His eyes were open, but the doctor appeared almost in a trance. Muttering, he walked out from behind the desk and moved slowly over to the wall on the far side of the room. Like the other three, it was lined with bookshelves running from floor to ceiling. For a moment the doctor stood in front of the shelves, his eyes drinking in the rich walnut paneling. Slowly, his hand stretched forward and pressed a button, simultaneously pulling slightly on the bookcase's center. From behind the shelving somewhere came a faint whirring sound and the bookcase opened, both halves of the shelving swinging slowly into the office.

Sommers gave a satisfied sigh. Behind the open shelves was a deep shadow box, starting perhaps three feet off the floor and running almost to the ceiling. When the doctor pressed a switch, a light came on in the shadowbox, one even dimmer than the light on the doctor's desk.

Lining the rear wall and both sides of the shadow box was a collection of curious objects that made no sense to anyone but Sommers himself. To him each of these objects represented a moment of pain—or in some cases, a moment of happiness.

In front of them all, for instance, stood Dandy, the cairn who had tried to scramble into his wife's car the night she left him. Like the dog downstairs that had also tried to run off, Dandy was stuffed, the small round hole where Sommers's rifle bullet had entered its head easily visible. For a moment Sommers ran his hand around the dog's shoulders as if he thought it might still be alive. "Man's best friend, eh?" he asked the motionless figure. "Sure, you are. That's why you wanted to run off with *her* that night. Faithless mutt. Well, you won't be running off with *anyone* anymore, will you?"

Behind the stuffed cairn hung a picture of his former wife. She stared at him angrily; even the best photographer had been unable to erase the expression of unpleasantness. Arranged around and below the frame were some of the small personal items that, to Sommers, were the essence of the night she had grabbed his daughter and run.

The glass she had been drinking from when they first started arguing in the living room. The doctor had tried to preserve the actual drink she'd been sipping, but of course it had evaporated years ago, leaving behind only a dirty brown ring around the glass. The comb, still with stray wisps of her hair sticking out from its teeth, that she had used getting ready to go.

The monkey wrench she'd damned near castrated him with. A pair of driving gloves she'd forgotten, leaving them on the hall table. In spite of the humidifier he had finally built into the shadow box, the leather of the gloves was cracked and dried-out, so mummified it looked as if it might crumble into dust if you touched it.

A half-empty pack of Pall Malls. What, Sommers often wondered, had she smoked in the car? If the bitch didn't have a cigarette every fifteen minutes or so, she would begin to tremble from withdrawal symptoms. That woman had been laden down with a host of unpleasant habits, the least pleasant of which was deserting a husband.

A collection of painful reminiscences, sad mementoes

of someone who had left him, someone he could never forgive for it.

On the right rear wall of the shadow box, in a frame identical to the one holding his wife's picture, was a picture of Meg's mother. In contrast to his wife, Mrs. Kendricks had been smiling broadly when Sommers took the picture. The doctor had posed Mrs. Kendricks in such a way that, with the exception of the warm smile versus the angry frown, the photographs were remarkably similar; both she and his wife were looking at the camera from exactly the same angle, and even the backgrounds appeared identical. Fond as he was of her, Sommers decided he would kill Evelyn Kendricks before he'd let her leave him; fond as he was of Meg, he would kill *her* before he'd let her talk her mother into abandoning him.

Cocking his head, the doctor studied the photograph, feeling a glow of warmth surge through him. Below her mother's picture was an empty frame, waiting for Sommers to get the right picture of Meg—his surrogate daughter .

This real daughter was below her own mother on the other side of the shadow box. In a frame like the empty one reserved for Meg, she was squinting in the sun and smiling shyly at the camera. In her arms she held Dandy, the faithless cairn. Attached to the same surface was her favorite china doll. Alongside was the nightie she'd been wearing when she screamed in terror at the storm beating on her window—the nightie she'd had almost ripped off her body when her mother forced her into her clothes.

To the other side were several stuffed fish: two angels, four tetras, a small catfish, and a huge snail—the entire contents of her fish tank. Sommers felt a wave of resentment sweep over him, thinking of how she'd left him.

She was only a child, he told himself, and perhaps

she hadn't really wanted to leave him at all. But if his little girl had really wanted to stay with him, weren't there things she could have done? Couldn't she have hidden from her mother somehow that night? Couldn't she have run away from her mother when they reached Maine and gotten back to him somehow?

Suddenly, shaking his head angrily, it didn't matter to Sommers anymore. His daughter, damn it, was just as guilty as her mother.

Above all of these items, stretching from one side of the shadow box to the other, were mementoes of a much earlier tragedy in his life.

The sepia-tinted pictures of his mother and father stared out tragically from their ornate oval frames. Dr. Sommers reached forward and touched them.

They had left him, too. Deserted him. Abandoned him. When he was only twelve. One minute they had been there, the next, they were gone. That damned automobile accident. He had been sitting in the back of the car, chattering, when there was a terrible, shattering crash. A little later the police and ambulances and doctors had come: they pronounced *him* unscathed; they pronounced his mother and father dead.

He could remember crying and crying and crying, later, when he'd been taken back home. At first Sommers was thoroughly convinced that somehow it was all his fault. He was talking, wasn't he, even after his father had told him to pipe down?

The conversion had been made. In Sommers's mind— as is so often true with children—his mother and father had left him because they *wanted* to leave him, because he had been disobedient and bad and evil, and their punishment was to get themselves killed and leave him alone in the world.

Their bodies had been duly laid out in caskets in the dining room, where once the whole little family had celebrated Thanksgiving and Christmas and Easter and other special festive occasions. That their caskets remained closed was simple good sense; their heads and faces had been mangled and smashed. But, looking at the sepia prints in their frames again, Sommers could remember as if it were today how he had sneaked down to the dining room the first night they were back in the house awaiting the next day's funeral. Searching, the boy had found the screws that fastened the tops to the caskets and softly opened them.

The sight of their shattered faces shook him terribly; they didn't look like his mother and father at all, anymore. Their heads were wrapped in bandages, like Indian Sikhs, foreign strangers with mangled faces and the white turbaned heads.

Reaching up underneath the bandages around his mother's head, he had, with a pair of scissors, been able to cut off a longish swatch of her hair. Sommers had held it up and looked at it fondly. This was some part of the mother he could remember, not something belonging to the two torn-apart strangers lying stiffly in their wooden boxes. The patch of his mother's hair was placed inside a bottle and fastened to the black velvet rear wall of the shadow box. Sommers looked at it now, staring at it intently, almost as if he half expected it to begin talking to him.

His father was not as simple. When Sommers had reached up underneath *his* bandage, he discovered the head had been shaved. There was no lock of hair to cut off; the hospital, he remembered someone's saying, had tried brain surgery. For a moment the boy had stared at his father's mutilated face. Then, tiptoeing so as to make no noise, he had gone to the kitchen and returned with a carving knife. With the sharp knife he sawed off his father's left ear. For a second the boy had worried; did dead people bleed?

Later, the caskets screwed shut again, he had put the ear into a jar of formaldehyde. It floated there even today in the slightly cloudy liquid, some days appearing to float higher in the jar, some days lower, but there for him to see anytime he wanted to look at the jar—it had been a peanut butter jar, he remembered—fastened beside the lock of his mother's hair against the black velvet rear wall.

Tonight he swore gently at the entire display and then, suddenly, laughed. The objects in the case could no longer torture him. With the arrival of Meg Kendricks and the long-established close relationship with her mother, the pain the contents of the shadow box were once able to produce had vanished. The many conversations he'd shared with the objects over the years seemed likely to remain in the past.

His release had started four years earlier with the arrival of Evelyn Kendricks as a patient. He had loved her ever since. There was something about her that reminded him both of his mother's continual sweetness and of occasional flashes of kindness his former wife had been capable of letting him see. Evelyn Kendricks had something that kept reminding him of the blurred sepia print in its oval frame. She was here at The Home, she was his, he was fully convinced he could control her so that she would be here forever.

And now—he had difficulty believing his own good fortune—her daughter, Meg Kendricks, was here, too. She was his own disappeared little girl grown up. Startlingly alike in so many little ways. The way she laughed—an adult carbon copy. The way she smiled at him—a grown-up version of that half-shy, half-devilish little grin. The way she could make him melt just by being near him—all of these things were his daughter all over again.

Gently, he turned out the light in the shadow box,

closed the bookshelf again, turned off the light on his desk, and stood in his door looking at the closed shelves which concealed the shadow box. The box suddenly seemed superfluous—a sad remnant of bygone days when his life had been empty.

With Meg and her mother here at The Home, his family was back, whole again. And unlike so many of the people represented in his shadow box, they would never leave him. This time, he would make very, very sure of that.

When Dr. Sommers stepped out into the hall, he heard it almost at once. Mrs. Tibald, in her cell downstairs, was raising an unholy racket. The shrieking and cursing for her were normal, but it sounded like she had somehow gotten hold of something, some object of wood or metal, and was banging whatever it was back and forth between the bars of her cell. This noise—new for her—combined with her screaming made it sound as if the devil himself were calling for help. Damn.

Quickly, the doctor walked down the hall to see where the nurse on night duty was and why she hadn't gone downstairs to halt the riot of sound. The nurse's station itself was empty. Growing progressively angrier, Dr. Sommers walked behind the desk of the station and into the nurses' sitting room behind it.

Sommers could smell it the moment he entered the nurses' sitting room. Vodka. That meant Midge Cummins must be the night duty nurse; her constant drinking, although it rarely interfered badly with her actual duties, always infuriated Sommers. Several times he had thought of firing her, but one of the reasons he had been able to hire her in the first place was a job history heavily dotted with reports from various sanitariums noting her drinking problems with pained disapproval. He didn't dare dismiss her. Very few other qualified psychiatric nurses would have accepted a position in a tattered place like The Home, and Sommers knew it.

To his surprise Midge Cummins was not stretched out on the beat-up and torn vinyl couch where he usually found her when she was bombed. Dr. Sommers swore again. She could be anyplace. He started to stalk out of the room, but a moan from somewhere stopped him. Slowly and unsteadily, from behind the couch, Midge Cummins's head and face appeared; she gripped the top of the couch and studied him with loathing. "Bastard," she hissed at Sommers.

"Get out from behind there, damn it," Sommers growled angrily. "Mrs. Tibald needs attention; she's raising an unholy racket."

Keeping hold of the couch, Midge Cummins maneuvered around to the front of it and sat down heavily. "Mrs. Tibald *always* needs attention, the bitch. I'm tired of her. Go take care of her yourself."

Dr. Sommers drew himself erect. "Miss Cummins, we've talked about your drinking before. But being drunk when you're alone on duty is something else. Frankly, you surprise me."

Midge Cummins threw her head back and laughed raucously. "And I'm surprised, Doctor, you're not with your little sweetheart, Meg Kendricks. You talk to her all day long, you have her at your table every day, and God knows what you do with her at night." The raucous laugh again. "Why don't you . . ."

Sommers was livid. "Go upstairs to your room. Right now. I'll get someone else to cover for the night. We'll discuss this tomorrow."

"Shit," Midge Cummins said feelingly, and made her way out of the nurses' sitting room, looking at the doctor and sneering.

Sommers sighed. He had felt so good coming out of

his office. Now he was boiling. He'd have to go wake one of the practical nurses and make her come downstairs to take over.

Midge Cummins's crack about Meg and himself lay beneath a lot of his anger. Shit.

In vino veritas, God damn it.

Chapter Eight

I've realized for a long time I should get rid of Midge Cummins. But she has me by the balls and knows it. No one worth their salt would work here. So tomorrow she'll promise to lay off the booze, and I'll promise to give her a lighter load, and each of us will know the other is lying. Damn.

The only good thing that's happened around The Home in a couple of months is Meg's turning up. God damn, but she's great. Last night I even had a dream about her, but in the middle of it Meg suddenly turned into my real daughter, only grown up.

One thing still bothers me about it. In the dream, my daughter was in some kind of danger. Does that mean Meg is? I wonder what the dream was trying to get at, and what lay underneath the symbolism.

That's a stupid question. I'm the shrink; understanding people's dreams is supposed to be my business.

Psychiatric & Personal Observations,
The Home, Alan Sommers, M.D., Director.

Tired and irritable, Meg came downstairs in the morning feeling mad at the world. That crazy screaming in the night; it took her forever to get back to sleep. The

Home was getting to her, and she knew it. The patients were creepy. The place was spooky— frequently frightening. Their special food was pretty good, except that there was a sameness to it. And it involved having meals with Dr. Sommers. There was as much a sameness to him as there was to the food. That got to Meg, too.

Everything was getting to Meg—except Tighe. Where the hell was he? Several times Meg had thought of phoning him in Philly but each time had decided against it; he would think she was crazy.

When everything was finished and done, he would call her and tell her he was on his way. In the meantime she would just have to try to ignore his absence. Fat chance.

Walking toward the dining room—Meg hoped that Dr. Sommers wouldn't show up for breakfast—she heard a lot of yelling and commotion coming from the Main Room. She looked inside. A number of patients were clustered together near one wall. In front of them Meg could see Dr. Sommers and Ernie. Sommers appeared to be talking directly into a shut door.

"Now, look, Van, it's silly to lock yourself up in there. No one is going to hurt you. Come on out, Van; I'll let you use one of the little sitting rooms and you can close the door and be by yourself. It's much nicer than standing in a dark closet, Van. I'll make sure no one bothers you in the sitting room. Come on, Van." He walked around the room for a moment, muttering, "The stupid son of a bitch. Doesn't he know I've got a lot of things to do today? Fuck him."

From one of the practical nurses, Meg finally found out what was behind this curious tableau: Mr. Hodgkins had ochlophobia.

"Do you know what ochlophobia is?" the nurse asked. From her parapsychiatric courses in Bangor, Meg was familiar with the disease. Someone with ochlophobia went crazy anyplace where there were other people. Usually, Mr. Hodgkins stayed in his room, but this morning *had* to come out when his bathtub overflowed and the floor was covered with water.

"See," the nurse said, "Mr. Hodgkins came downstairs with me, took one look at all the people sitting in here, and panicked. Headed right for that closet. Now they can't get him out. Mr. Hodgkins got the doorknob and the lock off the door from the inside."

Meg could see Sommers growing livid as he continued to yell through the locked door. His face had gone red, and he suddenly started pounding on the door as hard as he could. "God damn it," Sommers yelled over his pounding, "put the handle back on and come out, you stupid bastard. Fucking creep! Come out this minute, goddamn it!" He began pounding again, as hard as he could.

For a moment Sommers stopped pounding and walked away. After thinking for a second the fury in him rose to a new level. Spinning, Sommers began kicking the door with all his strength, yelling through the wood panels of the door as if he'd let his anger unhinge him completely. "I hope you suffocate in there, you stupid fucking bastard," he yelled through the door. "Who the shit do you think you are? Causing all this crap. Choke, you turd-head. Smother. Run out of air. Turn blue. If I could get through this door, I'd strangle you myself. . . ." With a final kick at the door Sommers spun and stalked toward the door of the room, muttering and cursing.

When Sommers got as far as the entranceway, his entire manner changed. He'd just realized that Meg was standing there. "Why, Meg, I didn't know you were watching all this." Dr. Sommers laughed, but the laugh had a forced sound to it. "Lot of fuss over nothing, really. They'll talk him out of there, given time." Sommers reached over and patted her arm and, still smiling broadly, left the Main Room.

Afraid he might be going to their table, she stayed around to watch. Breakfast with the doctor was too much to contemplate. Both Ernie and Midge Cummins tried talking through the closet door, but Van Hodgkins, presumably huddled in the corner in panic, didn't even answer. Finally, Ernie reluctantly produced a crowbar and slipping it under the edge of the door pried at it until the door came off its hinges, hitting the floor with a thundering crash.

Meg gasped. Mr. Hodgkins was not huddled in the corner in panic. While Dr. Sommers was yelling and pounding, while Ernie tried to soothe him and talk him into coming out, Mr. Hodgkins had taken the string off his pajama bottoms and hung himself from an old pipe running across the ceiling of the closet.

Meg felt her stomach shrivel. Hodgkins's body swayed gently back and forth, the air around him disturbed by the sudden tearing-off of the door; his pajamas hung down loosely around his ankles looking, somehow, lewd; his eyes bulged; his tongue was swollen and protruding. Crowds would no longer frighten him; in his last act on earth, he was frightening *them*. The din in the room was earsplitting, although some of the patients virtually ignored what had happened and simply withdrew further into themselves. Dr. Sommers was sent for. To Meg his reaction, in its own way, was as frightening as the sight of Hodgkins. "This is the first time anyone's been so desperate to leave me they went this far. What the hell's it take to keep the patients here, damn it?" A small, grim smile flickered on Sommers's face. "Faithless, disloyal pricks, the whole bunch of them." Sommers's reaction stunned Meg. Was the man trying to be funny, or was he a little crazy? Meg shuddered.

She fled.

Meg thought she had left the pigeon behind in Philly. It was back. She shivered.

By lunchtime, without having had any breakfast, Meg was ravenous. Hopefully, Dr. Sommers would be too busy with the follow-through on Van Hodgkins's death to appear at their table. But a few minutes after her mother and she sat down, Dr. Sommers joined them. Apparently, the details hadn't taken long to clear up; the State Police had come and gone (Meg saw them from her window), and the rest of the work was apparently being done by Midge Cummins.

The meal today was particularly painful. Sommers was on edge—Van Hodgkins, Meg assumed—although he tried very hard not to show it. The doctor was a good storyteller and made little things that had happened at The Home over the years engaging and funny. Nothing was said about Hodgkins by anyone during most of the meal, but his presence was almost palpable, hanging over the napery and gleaming silver of Sommers's table like an uninvited ghost.

"Oh, dear," her mother said toward dessert, without realizing the dangerous waters she was sailing into, "so much has happened today I feel completely exhausted. Poor Mr. Hodgkins. I didn't know him—in fact, I didn't even know what he looked like until I saw him hanging in that closet—but I *feel* as if I knew him. Such a waste."

Sommers gave her a sour look, almost a sneer, and ground his teeth in frustration. "It was a waste, all right," growled Sommers, grinding his teeth again. "Left his waste all over the closet floor. Thoughtless bastard."

The thought was too much for her mother. "Well, if you wouldn't mind, Doctor, I think I'd like to go lie down a minute. It's been very unsettling."

"Of course, of course," said Sommers, reaching over and patting Meg's hand, a gesture that always made her uncomfortable.

"I hope this hasn't upset you too much," Sommers said.

Meg *was* upset. Not just by the horrible picture of Van Hodgkins swaying lifelessly back and forth in the closet, but by a lot of things. Her mother's behavior confounded her. When she was with Meg, she thought it was time to leave The Home, complaining that the place terrified her. When she was with Sommers, she said that she had to stay here with him.

After lunch Sommers suggested he and Meg finish the tour of The Home they had started the day before. Meg thought it would give her time to discuss her mother's condition, so with a silent shudder she agreed. But somehow, the chance never came; he was too busy showing her things.

Bathed in a satisfied smile—smirk, really—he showed her the room with the electroshock apparatus in it. Meg recoiled at the bare metal table with restraining straps running from it. "A very effective device," Sommers said, "if the patient doesn't break something straining against the straps when we turn on the juice. . . . Maybe if we'd used it on Van Hodgkins . . ."

From Meg's expression the doctor could tell that Meg was thinking of a patient breaking his bones straining against the current. Quickly, he walked her down the hall into the large anteroom where the cells were.

"That's Mrs. Tibald," Sommers noted, indicating a wild-eyed woman with a tangle of hair over her face, who stared back at them from her cell. Mrs. Tibald, Sommers explained, had been married when she was very young and very innocent to a man who was middle-aged and very experienced, given to brutal violence in intercourse. Her wedding night hurt so much, poor

Mrs. Tibald became convinced it was not a normal wedding consummation, but rape. Ever since then, she believed every man who even looked at her had rape in mind and reacted accordingly. "She's the one you hear screaming all the time," Sommers explained. "Crazy as a bedbug, vicious as a shark. Watch."

Dr. Sommers walked over to the cell, standing directly in front of it, and stuck his hand in through the bars of the cell. In his hand he held a small piece of chocolate, whistling at her softly, the way one would call a dog. For some minutes Mrs. Tibald remained motionless, staring first at the doctor, then at the hand with the candy.

"Come on, Ruthie. Come show the nice lady how nicely you can take the chocolate when you want to." The dog analogy must have struck Sommers as well as Meg; he was cajoling and teasing her as you might your cocker spaniel. Suddenly—and moving with such lightninglike speed Meg didn't even realize the woman was on her feet until she had crashed into the bars—Mrs. Tibald lunged across the cell and tore at the doctor's hand, screaming wildly.

Dr. Sommers had already yanked his hand back and stepped away, but Mrs. Tibald's hands were still stretched through the bars to where the doctor had been standing. Snarling and drooling, she screamed again.

"Too bad, Ruthie." Sommers laughed. "Missed again."

"Down, girl, *down*," he laughed, keeping the dog analogy going. Meg's blood ran cold. You didn't expect a psychiatrist to make fun of his patients and taunt them the way he did. The man was not just strange, he trembled on the edge of madness.

The other occupied cell had as its tenant Mr. Levin, a man in a deep, catatonic trance. "This is shown in a classic symptom which psychiatrists call a state of waxy immobility," Sommers explained. Meg stared at poor Mr. Levin, simultaneously repelled and fascinated.

"A person in the state of waxy immobility," Sommers went on, "can be put in any conceivable position, however painful, and they will remain in that position until someone moves them into a new one. Like the one you see here."

At the moment, Mr. Levin was standing on one foot, the other sticking out behind him, his right arm stretched out in front of him and raised slightly, in a pose like the Roman statue of the winged messenger, Mercury. In place of the caduceus staff that Mercury usually holds aloft, Mr. Levin held up a urinal.

Meg looked at Mr. Levin again and squirmed. She turned to Dr. Sommers, a pleading tone in her voice. "Couldn't we put him in some more comfortable position? That one looks like it really hurts."

"Oh, one of the nurses will get around to it later," Sommers said offhandedly. "Hell, he doesn't know the difference anyway."

"Please?"

Damn it, Sommers told himself. She could make him do things he didn't particularly want to with that one little word "please." His daughter had been just like that, too, wrapping him around her finger whenever she wanted to. The similarity was eerie. With a shrug Sommers unlocked the cell, and still muttering, straightened Mr. Levin out, then pushed him down hard so that he was stretched stiffly out on his bed instead of standing on one leg like an unwinged Mercury.

"Feel better now?" Sommers asked unpleasantly, still too annoyed at himself even to smile.

"Thank you," Meg answered. Sommers's indifference to Mr. Levin was upsetting, as was the smile of unpleasantness he was wearing now.

Again, Meg had a glimpse of Sommers's unpleasant

streak of madness; it upset her terribly. A moment later the doctor's whole manner changed; the unpleasantness disappeared, immediately followed by the return of his charm. His Polaroid hanging around his neck, bouncing up and down on his chest as he walked, the doctor took Meg from one spot to another, talking excitedly the whole time. It was strange, Meg thought, how clearly Sommers could see the dilapidated state of The Home on one hand, yet, on the other, remain as enthusiastic and excited about the place as he did.

"In this little shed—if it doesn't fall down while I talk about it," the doctor said, laughing, "is the motor, the generator, and the other stuff that moves the tramcar back and forth. Someday soon, it's going to cave in." Sommers patted the motor, once gray, but now virtually without paint at all and rusting badly.

Dr. Sommers remained ebullient. With his Polaroid he took several pictures of Meg standing on the end of the dock, where, he said, supplies came in by boat. Fighting to hold the camera steady, he found his hands were shaking badly from concentrating on Meg so intently. Sommers's fascination in taking her picture was something Meg found embarrassing; she tried to smile on command, but had a hard time pulling it off.

Back at The Home itself the doctor again took her downstairs, this time to see the outer workroom of several he used for his taxidermy.

The shelves running around the room, raw and unpainted as most of the workroom was, were filled with various kinds of stuffed animals, row after row of them, the eyes of one fixed on the tail of the one in front.

"This is the room where I add the finishing touches. Like this grouping here," Sommers said, leading Meg to a plain wooden table in the center of the room. "There's something still wrong with the chipmunk's expression; can you see where I mean?"

Meg could. This grouping—a cat with its front feet outstretched in the process of seizing a chipmunk—was another of Dr. Sommers's more violent ones. The terrified little chipmunk was trying to wriggle free of the cat's claws, but it was obvious that the cat was about to bite its head off to end its struggles. She looked straight at Dr. Sommers, upset: "I don't know why you're picking on a sweet little chipmunk. They're my favorites."

"Nature knows no favorites," Sommers pontificated.

Meg shivered. She knew the doctor was right. Still . . .

To change the subject and get away from the unpleasant tableau on the table, Meg continued to look around the room. On the far side was another door that presumably opened into one of the inner taxidermy workrooms. Sommers seemed to be doing a lot of clearing of his throat—Meg knew he'd sensed her distress at the chipmunk tableau—so she began talking, less out of curiosity than politeness. "That far door," she asked. "Is there another room beyond this one?"

Dr. Sommers's face developed an agitated, nervous look. "Yes," he answered; a bit snappishly, Meg thought. "A sort of unpleasant one. It's where I do my initial preparation of the specimens. Where they are eviscerated. Where their bodies are kept in the curing vats. I also do some experimental work in there." Meg could see that talking about this particular room disturbed him, but he kept on, his voice rising slightly. "It smells terrible. All that flesh and the curing solution itself. Besides, there's nothing in there you'd want to see." He thought for a second, one finger running back and forth across a shaggy eyebrow. His eyes stared at Meg intently. "Don't ever, Meg, go in there. For any reason. The sights and the smells would repel you, believe me. Will you promise me that, Meg?"

Meg believed him; promising came easily. Why in

God's name did he think she ever *would* go in? What was really in the room that he didn't want her to see?

The doctor suddenly seemed in a hurry to end the tour. "There's a lot more I want to show you, Meg, but I notice it's getting on toward dinner, and I expect you'll want to get washed up and everything."

Chattering nervously, he almost shoved her out of the taxidermy workroom and walked to the bottom of the stairs with her. She was about to thank him for taking so much time to show her things when something made her turn away for a second. When she turned back, Sommers had disappeared. Meg shrugged.

Dr. Alan Sommers was a strange man.

If Meg had been downstairs in the workroom just now, she would have quickly discovered that "strange" was a massive understatement in describing Sommers. He was more than strange, more than "maybe a little crazy," a phrase Meg had used once or twice to characterize him for herself. Put brutally, he was a dangerous psychopath with homicidal tendencies. But such a possibility would never have crossed Meg's mind.

Earlier, the objects in the shadow box had been whispering to Sommers, as they had the day they made him do it. "Mary Lou, Mary Lou," his daughter's china doll had taunted him. "She was just like Meg. You had to do something about Mary Lou; one day you're going to have to do something about Meg."

His father's ear, which rarely said anything, suddenly joined the whispering and the laughter. "Once you start a job, boy, finish it," the ear hissed through its private sea of formaldehyde. "Damn it, get going."

Sommers had winced. He hadn't really wanted to do what he'd done to Mary Lou; they'd made him. Now, they wanted more. Meg. Uncomfortably, Sommers went downstairs to his outer workroom, through the inner door forbidden to Meg and her mother, and into the preparation room itself. The description he'd given Meg of it earlier was accurate on one point: it stank to heaven.

Wrinkling his nose in disgust, Sommers walked over to the curing vat, a large zinc tub sitting on square wooden legs. Around the edges of the vat was a series of wires that disappeared down inside, ran under small pulleys at the bottom, and then were anchored by the shiplike cleats that ran around the whole top edge of the tank.

This elaborate system of wires and pulleys was necessary because the animals, once submerged in the curing solution, quickly built up gas inside their bodies and would soon have floated to the surface unless weighted and held down. Uncleating the wire allowed a specimen to rise to the surface for Sommers's examination.

Whistling softly, the doctor undid a green wire from its cleat; there was a rush of bubbles to the top of the tank and a woodchuck, huge teeth grinning horribly at Sommers, rose to the surface in a burst of foul-smelling gas. The doctor looked at the woodchuck for a moment, checking that the curing was progressing evenly, shrugged, and pulled the wire tight again, once more submerging the woodchuck and its arrogant grin at the bottom of the tank.

The oily surface of the solution, disturbed by the woodchuck's movement, was still rippling, sending wide, shiny circles of reflection off its surface. Sommers felt hypnotized. As if from a great distance the memory of what the shadow box voices had said came back to him.

"Meg makes fun of you, you dirty old man, just the way Mary Lou did," the china doll had shrieked, following her pronouncement with a peal of raucous, sneering laughter.

"She led you on, and then she ran out on you," the

cuddly, stuffed frog noted in his Stepin-Fetchit voice. "So will Meg one day soon. You know how we feel about people who run out on us."

"You can't trust a woman, even if she's only a little girl," his father's ear had rumbled. "Or a young woman *pretending* to be a little girl—like Meg. *Do* something, boy."

A bubble from somewhere in the murky depths broke the surface; in the strange pattern of smaller bubbles it left on top of the solution, Sommers could see Mary Lou's face. He shifted uncomfortably as the details swam back into his head. Islamorada. About a year ago he'd run into Mary Lou for the first time sitting on a dock in Islamorada. She was a radiant child, perhaps eight or nine, and Sommers had been stunned to see the resemblance between her and his own daughter. The same smile, the same laugh, the same moody high spirits.

Over the next couple of weeks Sommers had returned frequently to Islamorada and walked down to the dock where he knew he could usually find her sitting on one of the heavy pilings as if waiting for him, inevitably alone. First, Sommers brought her candy. Then Sommers brought her crazy little-girl toys; soon he was bringing her other small gifts—like a china music box—he knew she would like. Mary Lou accepted them graciously, like an empress accepting crude gifts from the natives of her colonies. The similarity between Mary Lou and his daughter continued to stagger him.

On the day the trouble began, though, Mary Lou, oddly, was not alone. Gathered around the foot of a huge piling were some of the little girls who were her friends. They watched, silent, as Sommers gave her today's present—a stuffed frog cuddly toy much like one he'd once given his daughter.

One of the little girls suddenly broke into laughter. "He's crazy, Mary Lou. Silly old man."

"You know what school says about talking with strangers, Mary Lou," said one of the other little girls. "He looks dangerous to me. Silly old man, crazy old man, funny-looking old man," she screamed, while all the other little girls picked up the chant, formed a ring, and began dancing around Sommers, hooting and shrieking with laughter.

For a moment Mary Lou stayed on her piling, watching her friends disapprovingly. Suddenly, she leapt to the dock and joined the other girls. "Silly old man, crazy old man, funny-looking old man," she shrieked, loosing a taunting laugh that was louder than any of the others. Sommers had watched, bewildered, as they abruptly stopped dancing around him, screamed in mock terror, and raced off down the pier. On her way Mary Lou threw the stuffed, cuddly doll into the air and then batted it into the water beside the pier.

Sommers was furious. One way or another, Mary Lou had to be punished for making fun of him, and more significantly, she had to be punished for running out on him. The way it always seemed to happen in his life. He would have to wait awhile before acting; it wouldn't do to have any of the other little girls remember him. He decided a year would be about right.

The year he had given himself was abruptly cut to a week with the arrival of Meg. The objects in the shadow box not only reminded him of Mary Lou, but of the similarity between Mary Lou and Meg, and the voices began clamoring for Mary Lou's immediate punishment every time Sommers opened the door to the shadow box. The doctor would really have liked to let the matter be forgotten; the voices would not let them be. Finally, three days ago he had gone back to Islamorada. Surprisingly, Mary Lou was in her regular place—sitting

on the piling and staring blankly out to sea, her head
cupped on her hands as if the weight of the world were
on her shoulders. She was still stewing over a morning
tiff with her mother.

Sommers cheered her up quickly. When he asked if
she'd like a ride in his speedboat, Mary Lou's eyes
glistened with delight. It was, Sommers explained, tied
up at the dock in Matecumbe Gut, but he'd drive her
there, they'd go for a spin in the boat, and then he'd
bring her back here.

Mary Lou had hesitated, noting she should probably
tell her family where she was going and with whom.
Carefully, Sommers talked her out of this, claiming he
didn't have that much time. The lure of the speedboat
was too much for Mary Lou; she'd never once in her
whole life had a ride in one.

Without anyone's seeing them leave, the two climbed
into Sommers's car and drove to Matecumbe Gut. Now
that Meg was at The Home, Mary Lou had lost a great
deal of her appeal to Sommers, but she still reminded
Sommers enough of his daughter so that doing what the
shadow box voices demanded was easy. When they got
to Matecumbe, Sommers explained that the boat was
tied up out on the island; first they'd have to cross over
in the tramcar. Mary Lou jumped up and down with
delight; the tramway was going to be even more fun
than the ride in the speedboat.

It wasn't. Once the car had taken off, Sommers suddenly dropped a green plastic leaf bag over her head—
although making a game of it—and then pulled the giant
bag all the way down to her ankles. The game was over.
With a piece of rope he tied the bag under her shoes,
completely shutting off her air supply. He could hear
her thrashing and writhing and shrieking inside, trying
to get out, but he'd found extra thick lawn bags and
used a double thickness of them; Mary Lou was helpless.

To speed up the process, Sommers held the bag tightly around Mary Lou's neck so that she only had the air around her head to use up before she would suffocate. By the time they had reached the island, it was all over. Only a few spasmodic twitches still came from the leaf bag—product of her automatic nervous system. Mary Lou was dead. Sommers had thrown the bag over his shoulder and gone directly inside.

The memory sent a shudder through Sommers as he stood, still seeing in his imagination each scene of the incident reflected in the dank fluid in the vat. Sommers shook himself, moving his head quickly from side to side to chase the chain of terrible pictures from his mind. With a shrug he reached over, uncleated a pink-colored wire, and released it.

There was an explosion of bubbles and a small cloud of spray where the specimen body broke the surface, the naked stomach arched high, the face just below the surface of the fluid. It was Mary Lou.

Her eyes were open, although dimmed by the murky solution; her mouth sagged down, the lips several inches apart, her white young teeth glistening even through the fluid; from her head the long blond hair floated beneath the surface, spread out like a model's in a hair-conditioner ad. Even halfway to being cured for stuffing, Mary Lou managed to look terribly vibrant and seductive, something about her that had always attracted Sommers.

Sommers leaned over and patted her, the way you might a faithful dog. "I think," he said, studying her face, "that you're going to be a credit to me, Mary Lou. I haven't decided yet, but I think I'll mount just your head; all of you would be too cumbersome. I hope you don't mind." Turning around, Sommers stared at two wooden plaques hanging from the far wall, one a deer head, the other a ferocious-looking wolf. "Yes, just the head, Mary Lou. You'll look very much at home with the deer and the wolf on either side of you; you combine the sweetness of one with the viciousness of the other. And, if it makes you feel any better, yours will be the very first human head I've ever stuffed. I only wish I could show it to a lot of people, but that, I'm afraid, is out of the question." Sommers studied the body for a moment, then: "I wonder if Meg is as vain as you were. Probably."

Sommers reached into the fluid, turned Mary Lou over, and pinched her buttocks. No mark was left where he pinched her, so he knew her flesh was being properly cured. Turning her over again on her back, he repeated the same test on her cheeks with the same result. No marks. Pure perfection. Mary Lou would make a superb specimen.

Sommers dried his hand on a towel, still studying Mary Lou. It was somehow fitting that Mary Lou was the first of his experiments in the stuffing of humans. She had led him on, she had accepted his presents, then she had made fun of him and tried to leave him. Well, she wouldn't be going anywhere now. Fixed on the wall forever; a trophy to the futility of trying to run out on Alan Sommers, M.D.

To punctuate this thought, Sommers once again tightened the pink wire, pulling Mary Lou to the bottom of the tank to finish being cured. As she disappeared, Sommers waved the tips of his fingers at her in farewell.

Walking across the room, Sommers felt suddenly sad. Eventually, he suspected, Meg would try to leave him, too. If the pressure he could bring on her was not enough, Meg would have to be anchored to the floor of this vat, just like Mary Lou.

Oddly, he found himself wondering if Meg's hair would float in a fan shape the way Mary Lou's did; it struck him as quite exceptional.

The sadness in him grew deeper. He didn't want to kill Meg. He just might *have* to. Women usually brought this kind of thing on themselves. He wasn't sure, though, this was true in Meg's case.

Poor Meg. He would miss her.

Chapter Nine

Killing himself was the last thing in the world I would have ever expected from Van Hodgkins. He was such a weak person. Hanging yourself takes a certain amount of guts.

The fuss he caused wrecked my whole day. The police were polite enough, I guess, and, thank God, perfunctory. But I still feel badly about Hodgkins. I can't stand to have any patient leave me like that. Sheer meanness on his part.

I tried to cheer myself up by taking Meg on an exhaustive tour of The Home. It didn't help; she was uncomfortable with me today.

Maybe it was the Van Hodgkins thing. Some people get upset by stuff like that. Me? I wasn't upset—just damned annoyed. I should have guessed that that bastard didn't care about anyone but himself.

Psychiatric & Personal Observations, The Home, Alan Sommers, M.D., Director.

Meg was so startled she almost dropped the phone. She had been leaning against the wall of the long hall outside her room, the dime in her hand, about to pick up the phone and dial when it suddenly rang. Automatically, she had picked it up and answered.

A loud, enchanted laugh over the phone made chills of delight run down her back. It had to be, it had to be. "They have you answering the phone now?" the voice teased. "You're awfully informal for an operator."

"Tighe!" Meg screamed. "You have to be psychic. I was standing beside the pay phone with the dime in my hand, just about to call you. I know you asked me not to, but I just *had* to. I was beginning to think you'd run off with some other girl."

Tighe laughed again. "I had several offers, of course, and I thought a little about one or two, but I just let them pine away."

"You're a bastard." Meg laughed.

"Total. How are things going down there?"

"Oh, fine, fine," Meg lied.

"Things here are fine, too," Tighe said. "I finished up with the bank much faster than I thought I could, so tonight I start driving down to the Keys."

"Hey, great," Meg said, shaking from head to foot with happiness; she didn't realize how ecstatic she really was until she saw the receiver vibrating in her hand. A new and frightening thought suddenly crossed her mind. "*Tonight?*" she asked. "That means you'll be driving all night. That isn't—I mean, well—that isn't exactly safe, is it, Tighe?"

"Well, okay, it's a lousy time to set off. But damn it, I want to see you as soon as I can."

Meg was beside herself with happiness. In the chatter that followed, she could hear Tighe's own gleefulness that their separation would soon be over. "Then," he pointed out to her, "we find that dream house for your mother and get her out of that awful place. And you're mine, all mine—forever." Abruptly, his voice turned serious.

"How bad is it? I mean, how really bad? I mean, if you were just about to call me, I can guess it's no picnic."

Meg sighed. In spite of her effort to pass it off with her "fine, fine," she hadn't fooled him for a moment. Still, she underplayed it with him; the driving at night thing continued to worry her, and she didn't want anything making him drive faster than he should.

"Well, it's pretty run-down, just like mother said. I'd hate to be in the place during a high wind. I haven't seen any of the rats mother talked about, though. . . ."

"The ship sounds like it's sinking; maybe they got the message and already left." Tighe, Meg knew, was doing his damnedest to be cheerful for her benefit.

"The place is vintage Charles Adams. As for the patients, Christ, they give me the creeps. You begin looking behind yourself all the time. Yesterday, one of them hung himself. Right in the living room. Some of them seem okay; some of them are really weird."

"Well, I'll be down there in a bit and we'll tackle it together. What you could be doing in the meantime is start looking for a house. Make it a nice one. Remember, we'll have to live in it ourselves with your mother for a while—at least until we can set up a doctor from Key West and organize some kind of housekeeper for her." That, Tighe thought to himself, should keep Meg busy for a while.

"Tough to do without a car," Meg said.

"Real estate agents will usually ride you around," Tighe pointed out. "And the sooner we can find the right place, the sooner we can take your mother out of there. The important thing is to get started."

Meg sighed to herself. For some reason the prospect of looking for a house—their first home, in a way— without Tighe at her side depressed her. She didn't let the feeling show. "I'll start first thing tomorrow," Meg said. "There must be an agent somewhere around here, but I'm not sure." She laughed. "Wait till you see the bright lights and mad bustle of Matecumbe Gut, Tighe. Blink—and you've driven clear through it."

Tighe laughed delightedly. "Christ, I miss you, Meg. If you only knew how much. . . ."

"Just don't miss me so much you get yourself killed driving down here too fast. You told me yourself the roads are lousy. And please, please, Tighe, don't start driving at night. That's asking for it. Drive during the day and stay at motels at night. Besides keeping you alive, it'll deliver you down here feeling rested. I have my own plans for tiring you out." She giggled. "Promise me, Tighe, promise me?"

"Oh, all right, I promise," Tighe grumbled. "You're worse than my mother."

They talked on a little longer, each reluctant to hang up. Finally, they managed it. For a long time Meg stared at the phone; from this innocuous, beat-up black instrument, screwed to a crumbling wall as dilapidated as everything else in The Home, had come the glorious word that Tighe was on his way. Incredible thought.

On the other end Tighe Devlin was also looking at the phone having his own incredible thought. Okay, he'd made a promise, and he wouldn't start tonight. But he couldn't see himself stopping *every* night at some fleabag motel and sleeping. He was too anxious to be back in Meg's arms.

Chapter Ten

Mrs. Tibald getting more vicious each day that goes by. This morning Miss Parmalee went into her cell to give her a shot, and Ernie didn't stick around like he's supposed to. Old Mrs. Tibald took the opportunity to grab the hypodermic and rip open Parmalee's face—up one side and down the other.

She looked like someone had been using her face to play tic-tac-toe on and had to get countless stitches from the G.P. in Marathon. He did his best, but knew that for her face to look right again, the nurse would have to go to a plastic surgeon in Key West.

That's what you get for having to use improperly trained personnel; a practical nurse, for Christ's sake.

Psychiatric & Personal Observations,
The Home, Alan Sommers, M.D., Director.

"I don't know where anyone is," Mrs. Kendricks told Meg the next morning. "The doctor hasn't showed up; the waiter hasn't either. It's very strange."

They waited for a few minutes, but neither the doctor nor the waiter appeared. With a shrug Meg suggested they get their own food. It was no great hardship, although the patients jostled one another standing in front of the battered serving bar.

The food the patients got, Meg discovered, *was* a hardship. Gelatinous scrambled eggs (probably powdered, as someone had told her earlier), cold greasy toast, and coffee so oily it tasted like it had been drained from someone's crankcase.

"I don't understand it at all," Meg's mother said. "Usually, the doctor's so prompt. And no waiter—I don't understand that either. As for the regular food, I'd forgotten how dreadful it was. I don't understand any of it."

Meg was afraid she understood it all too well. When she'd finished her talk with Tighe yesterday and hung up, she had been surprised to hear a strange noise from just down the hall. Someone was right around the corner. Listening? The damned creepy patients here were always doing things like that.

A moment later she had heard Midge Cummins's voice. "Good evening, Doctor." Meg was stunned. The eavesdropper was not a patient; it was Sommers. There had been no answer, but Cummins's appearance had forced Sommers's hand. Staring angrily at the head nurse, he had come out of hiding and walked around the corner with her; he had had no choice. He neither looked at Meg, nor returned her weak "hello." His face was black with anger as he walked past her without a word.

Furiously, Meg tried to remember if she'd said anything about being married that might have been overheard by Sommers. She thought not. Apparently, since he didn't know she was married, he had come to the conclusion, from what he'd heard Meg say, that she had a lover. That was enough. Sulking, for Christ's sake. It didn't make sense, but then, to Meg, Sommers was making progressively less sense every day.

When she'd first gotten here, she'd considered him a warm and highly rational man. Seeing the stuffed animals, the preserved family pet, and his reaction to Van Hodgkin's suicide, she'd moved him into the "strange" category.

Now, as she got to know him even better, she was rapidly deciding the doctor might be completely crazy. Meg struggled to conceal the small shudder that ran through her.

As Meg and her mother were sitting out in the Main Room, another facet of Sommers's imbalance surfaced. Midge Cummins, lips pressed tightly together, came over to where they were sitting to give Meg's mother a message. "Dr. Sommers asked me to tell you, Mrs. Kendricks. He had to leave the island on business early this morning, so he won't be able to have your usual therapy session today, I'm afraid."

"Oh, my," her mother said, fanning herself with a magazine. "Everything's topsy-turvy today, isn't it?"

But Midge Cummins had not stayed long enough to hear Mrs. Kendricks's observations. Meg could see her across the room, moving slowly among the patients, not talking to any of them, merely studying them as if they were particularly interesting specimens in a zoo. A few minutes later, though, as Meg walked toward the door of the Main Room, she heard one of the patients, Miss Dalton, shouting at Cummins (Miss Dalton always shouted; no one knew why).

"I suppose," Miss Dalton hollered at Cummins, "I suppose that means—I couldn't help overhearing what you told Mrs. Kendricks—I guess that means my session for today is canceled, too. Christ, old Sommers gives us precious little time as it is."

Midge Cummins consulted the small leather notebook she always carried in one hand. "No, Miss Dalton. You're set for eleven. Just like always."

"But you said the doctor had left the island," Miss Dalton thundered. "How can he—"

"Eleven o'clock, Miss Dalton," Midge Cummins said, spun on her heel, and walked away.

Her mother, walking beside her, was oblivious of the contradictions between what Midge Cummins had told her and what she had told Miss Dalton. Meg couldn't be. Damn it, she told herself, the doctor was taking out his displeasure on her mother to get back at *her*.

"Sometimes," her mother said out of the blue, "I think Dr. Sommers is upset that I'm all better. I'm really very fond of him, but there's something all wrong about The Home. And those damned rats. . . ."

"I haven't even spotted a mouse," Meg said.

"They're there, they're there," Mrs. Kendricks said ominously. "Dr. Sommers thinks I make them up, too. But I know they're there. I saw one this morning."

Her mother suddenly turned to her. "Meg, darling, I know it would be very difficult for you, but can't you please, *please*, somehow take me out of here? It's not safe. The other patients . . . the staff . . . the rats . . . Oh, please, Meg . . . I'm scared to death all the time."

"I'm working on it, Mother." It was the only answer Meg could think of.

Meg hadn't told her mother that she was going house-hunting later this morning. She had called the one real estate agent listed in the Yellow Pages last night and reached a severe, gravel-throated woman named Miss Groundly. "I'll drive up from Marathon and pick you up at eleven, dear," Miss Groundly had rasped. "But where?"

Meg did not give her the landing dock for The Home; it would raise too many questions. Neither had Meg yet told her mother that she was married and launching herself on a mission to find her the "dream house" they'd been talking about for so many years.

Meg sat down in the Main Room until it was close enough to eleven so she could go to the mainland—the idea of riding again on the rickety tramway swept across her like an ugly tide—and meet Miss Groundly.

She hoped the woman was less abrasive than her voice.

As Meg had very much suspected, Dr. Sommers had not left the island this morning at all. Instead, he had been working on a plan to keep Evelyn Kendricks here at The Home for the foreseeable future.

He was ready. Picking up a box off his desk, Sommers slipped quickly upstairs, pausing only to use one of his many peepholes to make sure Meg's mother was still in the Main Room. She was. Chatting with Meg.

On the second floor he stopped outside the door to Meg's mother's bedroom, listened, and went in. The box was carefully opened. Out tumbled ten or twelve rats, scurrying to hide in corners and under the bed in their panic. With a faint smile Sommers noticed they staggered a little when they ran, product of the drugged food and water he'd been feeding them for the last twenty-four hours. It didn't sedate them so much, however, that it stopped the pack's leader from sticking his head out from under the bed, whiskers twitching, red-rimmed eyes staring balefully at the doctor. Sommers waved his hands, and the lead rat disappeared back under the bed with a venomous little squeal, a sound picked up and echoed by the other rats from their own hiding places.

Sommers smiled and left, carefully closing the door behind him. He had reason to smile: Evelyn Kendricks might be all right—cured would be a better way of putting it—but she was still highly open to suggestion, which was not unusual for someone just recovering. The fear of rats was something he'd used on Evelyn Kendricks before. Now he would await the results of the actual physical presence of one of her deepest fears: being attacked by rats.

In the Main Room Meg waved as her mother finally left for her room. She had lied to her, Meg knew, and suddenly felt guilty. She'd had to. If she'd told her mother she was going into town to do some shopping, her mother would have immediately suggested she go with her. Instead, Meg had said that it was such a glorious day she wanted to explore the island from one side to the other. "But, Meg," her mother argued, "just relaxing in the sun would be so good for you." Meg shook her head.

"No, there's too much on the island I want to see. The terrain, the wildlife, you know. Tough on the feet, but otherwise great. I'll get plenty of sun tomorrow."

The lie, the evasion, the elaborate description of where she would be going when instead she would be going someplace quite different, brought back her childhood years. If she didn't lie to her mother in those days, whatever it was she really planned to do was almost always automatically forbidden. The recollection made Meg suddenly uncomfortable.

"Why don't you come exploring with me, Mother?" she asked, knowing in advance what the answer would be. Her mother shook her head firmly. Meg heaved a secret sigh of relief and went back inside.

Most of the patients appeared to share Mrs. Kendricks's assessment of the day. The Main Room was virtually empty—except for the immovables. The old lady still sat glued to her television screen, watching children's cartoons, and the other woman, who spent her days rocking in a chair clutching a rag doll, was in her usual spot, rocking, staring into space, as if the word of God were written there.

At one of the windows stood Kenny, sweeping the mainland with his binoculars, waiting for the first sight of his mother. "Today, today," he said softly several times. "I bet she comes to get me today. . . ."

Roger had walked in and stood in front of the old lady. That either Kenny or Roger, so young and vibrant, should be indoors instead of outside, for some reason surprised Meg. "Hello, Mrs. McComber," Roger said politely, unzipping his fly and pulling out his thing. A second later he was masturbating, his head thrown back, an expression of ecstasy on his face. The old lady continued to rock and stare, as if Roger weren't there.

An angry shout came from the window where Kenny was. "Stop that, damn it, stop it. What will my mother think if she comes in and sees you doing that? Stop it, right now."

Roger didn't stop, only smiled meanly at Kenny. "They gonna dig her up special so she can see me, Kenny?"

With a roar of anger, Kenny hurtled across the room and threw himself on Roger, his face livid. They wrestled back and forth, Kenny's binoculars, slung around his neck on a strap, making a hollow banging sound every time they hit the floor. It was a furious battle, and Meg wasn't sure what she should do.

Out of nowhere Ernie appeared and pulled the two apart, simultaneously yanking them to their feet. Roger looked ridiculous, his erect prick still sticking out of his fly.

"He insulted my mother," Kenny shouted. "He said she was dead."

"As a doornail," answered Roger with an ugly laugh,

turning to Ernie. "Old Kenny here always gets excited when he sees me doing that; everybody else pretends not to notice, but Kenny always *stares*. Likes to look at other guys' pricks, I guess. Sick, sick, sick . . ."

For a moment it looked as if the whole fight was going to start all over again, but Ernie, besides being very large, was also very firm. "You go in that direction, Kenny, you go in that one, Roger," he said sternly, pointing out opposite directions to each of them. "C'mon now, march! March, or I'll start knocking heads—and you guys know I can do it."

Neither of them seemed willing to challenge Ernie. Shrugging, each went out of the Main Room via an opposite door. Meg relaxed again. This fight between Roger and Kenny had been coming for a long time, she supposed. But it served once again to underscore how all of the patients, however affable they might appear, were in reality unexploded bombs waiting for their timing mechanisms, ticking away quietly inside them, to trigger the explosion that could destroy anything near them. It was not a comforting thought.

Meg glanced at her watch and saw it was getting close to when she should be leaving to meet Miss Groundly. She picked up her purse and went into the ground floor ladies' room, a dank, gloomy place, with one sheet of wallpaper coming loose from the dampness and hanging out into the room over the washbasin. Meg pulled a comb through her hair, pushing the hanging wallpaper back with one hand while she combed with the other; left to its own devices, the wallpaper almost entirely hid the mirror from sight. It was not easy.

Looking carefully to see that no one saw her, Meg slipped down the hill and stepped into the rusty tramcar. The outer door had been locked for some reason, and

Meg had had considerable trouble getting the door to open. When she pressed the button under the filthy front window—the day she left for good, Meg vowed, she'd make Sommers a gift of a spray can of Windex—she felt the car lurch forward and up.

Meg didn't know whether the trip was worse with her eyes open or her eyes closed; she tried both, but either way made her stomach shrivel. The car began swaying back and forth wildly the moment it was up far enough for the full force of the wind to catch it, apparently determined to turn upside down and hurl her into the raging waters of Matecumbe Gut far below. Outside, the wind moaned and whistled derisively, a dirty old man staked out on a street corner. The gondola of the tramway groaned and shuddered from the wind and the movement; above her Meg heard the cables that supported the car creaking and thumping as the gondola shifted its weight from one side to the other. Occasionally, there would be a loud clanking sound, and the car would suddenly drop a few inches as it passed over one of the upright support cables.

She tried looking down for a moment, but the sight of the raging water pouring through Matecumbe Gut made her insides shrink; she was a tiny, insignificant object separated from the angry waters only by a pair of cables so old and in such bad condition she could see flumes of rust fly across the window every time the car's traverse wheels passed over one of the junction points.

Meg wished she were anywhere in the world but in this damned, terrifying tramcar, but finding her mother a place away from The Home had so long been a dream of hers that she gritted her teeth, squeezed her eyes shut, and held onto a small railing until the gondola car finally slammed to a noisy halt at its wobbly wooden dock on the mainland.

When Meg climbed out of the little car and put her feet on the ground, her whole body was trembling; it was a tremendous relief to be back on the ground again.

At the foot of the street—the stores had long ago been shuttered, sand from the dunes blew forlornly across the street, and there was no sound except the constant moaning of the wind—Meg saw a lady parked at the curb wearing a dour expression. Since there were no other cars in sight, she assumed the driver must be Miss Groundly. The woman in the car made the same assumption about Meg, climbing out of her car and coming toward her.

"Miss Kendricks? I'm Esther Groundly," the woman said. Meg looked at her. Miss Groundly was built like a linebacker, her voice a full octave below Meg's. "Climb into my car," commanded Miss Groundly after amenities had been exchanged. "I have several different places to show you, but I'm still not sure, even after our conversation last night, exactly what your requirements are."

"Well," Meg said, pulling at her lip, "someplace farther down the Keys toward Key West, but not in it. It has to be big enough for my mother, a practical nurse or housekeeper we'll be hiring to take care of her, and for my husband and myself. And he likes a good deal of space."

Miss Groundly was a lady who went straight to the heart of things. "If you're really married why are you called 'Miss' Kendricks?" she demanded as the car barreled down U.S. 1. She held up her hand. "Never mind answering; I know how kids today are."

Meg forced a laugh and let it go at that. It saved a lot of explaining.

Miss Groundly snorted. "You mentioned your mother. . . ."

"Yes. She is why we're so desperate to find a house in a hurry. She needs a nice place to live right now. My husband and I will be living there for a while, too, which is why the house has to be so big."

Once each in Pigeon Key and Ramrod Key, Miss Groundly showed Meg a house; one was sterile-modern, surrounded by no trees and sitting in the middle of what appeared to be scrub growth; the other was almost as dilapidated as The Home, with boards falling off the siding and a damp, musty smell inside from having been too long without tenants.

"Well," Meg said, not quite sure how to explain that she considered both of them awful, "I think my husband has something directly on the water in mind. He loves to snorkle, you see, so a place with a stretch of ocean would be just about perfect."

"They're very expensive. All direct waterfront property down here is." Miss Groundly turned to look at Meg, as if challenging her to say she could afford so expensive a house.

"Tighe wants a nice place," Meg countered.

"Well," Miss Groundly noted, "it's always a difficult question to put delicately, but how much is your 'husband' prepared to spend? Knowing that will make finding a place easier."

Meg was thunderstruck. She'd never been in a position to buy a house before, yet Miss Groundly's question was a completely reasonable one. She had no idea how much Tighe was prepared to spend; she had no idea what a house should cost, or what was a high price or what was a low price. She waffled. "Well, my husband didn't exactly say how much. I mean, he doesn't want a mansion, yet he told me he wanted something on the water and something nice. I'm afraid—that is—

well, I never thought about price very much. That's up to Tighe."

She was so vague about it, Miss Groundly looked at her strangely. "That makes it very difficult," she said firmly. "However, I suppose I can show you a range of houses and then, when your husband arrives, you can ask him whether we're too high."

She showed Meg a couple more houses, but it was clear her heart was no longer in it. That someone would go looking for a house with no notion of what she could pay for it struck her as crazy. The looks grew stranger.

But it was when she asked where Meg was staying for the moment, and Meg had to tell her she was staying at The Home, that Miss Groundly began to look alarmed. She began driving faster and no longer spoke.

Meg wanted to laugh. Because of her own vagueness, Miss Groundly had obviously decided she was dealing with a patient from The Home, not only wasting her time, but perhaps risking her life.

Fighting off a giggle that desperately wanted to surface, Meg tried to be reassuring. "I'm only visiting my mother there, Miss Groundly. Really. She's all better now and that's why we want to find a house and take her out of there as soon as possible."

Miss Groundly snorted again; she obviously didn't believe a word of what Meg had said. They drove on in silence; Meg was damned if she was going to defend her own sanity any further. As they reached the outskirts of Marathon, however, she turned to Miss Groundly.

"Would it be out of your way to drop me off at Dr. Kirsten's? It's only going to take about fifteen minutes, but I don't want to make you wait. I'll call a taxi and get back on my own."

"Nonsense," said Miss Groundly in a very positive voice. "By the time you get a taxi in Marathon, it'll be tomorrow. It's no trouble at all to wait for you. I want to be sure you get back okay."

"That's awfully kind of you," Meg said, suspecting that what Miss Groundly was really thinking was that it was her duty to society to get this obvious lunatic back inside the sanitarium before she butchered someone with an axe.

Dr. Kirsten confirmed what Meg had already suspected for some time. "I would certainly think so," he told Meg. "You have all the symptoms, certainly. Enlarged breasts, cervical engorgement, the missed periods. Just to make absolutely sure, though, we will want to make a test. The results should come in pretty quickly—two or three days at the most. I'll call you at The Home. Let's see—Friday."

For a moment Meg sat transfixed, her mouth slightly open. She couldn't believe it. A baby—a son. She was sure it would be a boy. My God, Tighe will be in ecstasy. *She* already was.

Coming out of the building to get back in Miss Groundly's car, Meg was grinning like an idiot. Riding up U.S. 1, Meg could not erase the thought of the baby from her mind; with Tighe's arrival she would have everything in the world she could possibly want. She couldn't wait to tell Tighe; he would be so damned excited and happy. Meg began to fidget in her seat. She had to tell *somebody*. Twisting around in her seat, she stared at Miss Groundly.

"The doctor—the doctor—I can't quite believe it myself—said I'm pregnant. Oh, Tighe—that's my husband—Tighe will just be beside himself. I am." Meg suddenly laughed. "I guess that house of ours is going to need one more room." She giggled.

For the first time since she had met her, Miss Groundly suddenly appeared to warm to her. The snort was gone, replaced by a warm glow. "Yes, dear, it certainly is wonderful. The one thing I've always missed about being single is not having children. I've wanted a baby all my life. It's the one thing I've always desperately wanted. . . ."

Chapter Eleven

Tonight, we're having a cookout—a barbecue. The patients love anything that breaks their routine, so they're all excited. And of course, I'm all for it—it saves me money.

If I gave them hot dogs and rolls in the dining room, the patients would try to lynch me—probably with Midge Cummins and Ernie leading the charge. I don't really trust those two. In fact, I'm beginning to think I can't trust anybody. Even Meg lies to me.

On that subject, I suppose I'd be smarter to stop letting what I feel about Meg's young man show. From what I overheard her say to him on the phone, they're very close. He could even be her husband, for Christ's sake. Oh, God, I can't believe that's true.

*Psychiatric & Personal Observations,
The Home, Alan Sommers, M.D., Director.*

By the time Meg stepped out of the tramway car— still delirious from the doctor's news—it was almost dusk. Dark was settling around her, and she had to watch where she stepped as she slowly began climbing the long flight of stone steps up toward The Home. Each time she put her foot down on the next step, she would say "a baby!" still unable to quite believe what the doctor had said.

She was about halfway up the stairs when she noticed sparks flying up into the black sky, only then remembering the barbecue scheduled for tonight. To Meg it sounded dreadful, but she supposed her mother would enjoy it. A baby, a baby, a baby!—the wonderful words kept whirling around in Meg's head, all mixed up with the picture of Tighe's dumbfounded expression when she finally told him and the incredible look of happiness that would follow it. By now she was almost floating up the steep stone steps, largely oblivious to the world around her. Somewhere ahead, she could hear the patients trying to sing "In the Evening by the Moonlight, You Can Hear Those Darkies Singing"—their voices as out of key as their minds.

Abruptly, a new sound intruded into her consciousness. Someone crashing through the shrubbery. The sharp crack of twigs and small branches as a body moved at full speed toward her. Terrified, Meg returned to reality with a *thud*, her heart pounding, her insides twisting in fear.

Which one of the patients was coming after her? Would he be violent? Would he beat her up? Rape her? *Kill* her? My God, the baby. . . . Meg didn't know which way to run, up the stairs or down. Sheer, blind terror seized her, a cold steel hand grabbed her guts and began squeezing them.

Stunned, she watched, helpless, unable to move, paralyzed with fright, as Dr. Sommers suddenly appeared out of the shadows, his face twisted and livid. "You left the island without my permission!" he roared at her, grabbing her by both shoulders and shaking her as hard as he could. "You left the island without my permission!" he repeated, his voice rising to a thin scream.

Meg could feel his fingers pressing through the flesh into the bones beneath as Sommers began shaking her again, this time so hard she bit her tongue trying to clamp her jaws shut. Sommers yelled, Sommers screamed, Sommers bellowed, repeating over and over again, "You left the island without my permission!"—as if it were some magic litany written to be performed by a chorus of yelling demons.

Pushing one hand hard into his face, Meg tried to squirm out from under his hands but discovered Sommers was surprisingly strong, with a grip like a vise. She put the other hand in his face, too, and pushed back as hard as she could, screaming at him for Christ's sake to get his hands off her or she'd start screaming until someone came to see why someone was making such a racket.

Abruptly, the doctor released her. Panting, he stared at her in the near-darkness. "For God's sake, Dr. Sommers, that was terrible. And all wrong. I'm not one of your goddamned patients, and I can come and go as I like. And right now I think maybe I should go—off this island and stay someplace else." It was an empty threat— she couldn't leave her mother alone here in the insane place, and Sommers probably knew it.

Oddly, after her threat to go, Sommers's whole manner changed. He looked stricken, as if it were he who had been seized by the shoulders and shaken until he bit his tongue. "That's a dreadful thing to say, Meg," he whined. "You see—" Sommers had been trying to sound reasonable, but suddenly his anger returned in full force. "Everybody on the island," he yelled at her, "patient or guest, has to tell me when they're going off the island, where they're going, and why. Otherwise, it's impossible to—" Sommers halted in midsentence, muttering and cursing. "Oh shit," he groaned, studying the ground. On his face was an expression of weary defeat, of a battle lost, of a familiar failure. "You're just like all of them," he hissed. "Trying to trick me. Lying to me. Not telling me things until it's too late to stop them. Threatening to run away. God, God, God . . ."

Sommers suddenly turned and climbed slowly up the steps toward The Home, slumped over, muttering to himself. Meg stood where she was, waiting for her heart to stop pounding and her breathing to return to normal. Above her she heard the singing around the barbecue begin again, and once he had disappeared, started up the steps herself. Sommers's sudden appearance from the bushes had terrified her; his shaking her and screaming at her like that was even more frightening. For the first time Meg seriously began to think that maybe they shouldn't wait until Tighe arrived; perhaps she and her mother ought to get away from this place right now and stay at a motel or something until he showed up. Instinctively, she put her hand on her stomach, thinking of her baby; she didn't know why.

Leaving now was a silly idea, she decided. Tighe would expect to find her here. So here is where she would be.

The scene around the giant barbecue was pure Dante. Through with their campfire singing, the patients had formed a circle around the fire and were dancing around it as if possessed. From them came little groans and shrieks and shouted phrases—incantations, Meg supposed, against the devils inside them. The flickering light from the fire cast weird shadows across their faces, making them look like Stonehenge primitives, an undulating ring of demons worshipping unknown gods. Some had shed all their clothing; Roger, naked, was inside the ring, moving in the opposite direction from the rest of the dancers, his head thrown back, his face wreathed in an evil, grinning ecstasy as he practiced his usual, peculiar sickness. To Meg the shoutings and the moanings and the muttered incantations were a chilling sound, the cries of the damned writhing in a private torment from which they knew they would never escape.

Dr. Sommers was nowhere in evidence—sulking somewhere, Meg supposed—but across the ring and standing outside it, she could see her mother and Mrs. Belagio standing together. They were engaged in what appeared to be a very serious, agitated conversation about something, waving their arms and paying scant attention to the tribal dancers.

Wearily—Meg wanted no part of this weird barbecue, but knew her mother would be hurt if she begged off—Meg walked around the outside of the circle until she reached her.

"Meg," her mother said, her face suddenly lighting up, "I didn't know what to do. I knew you couldn't be exploring the island this late, and I was getting worried. I couldn't find Dr. Sommers, and Midge Cummins was no help at all."

Meg forced a laugh. "Oh, I got bored with the exploring and went across to the mainland to do a little shopping," she lied. "I tried to find you to see if you wanted to come along, but I couldn't."

Just then, Ernie gave a shout as he brought out a huge tray of hot dogs, followed by one of the practical nurses carrying a tray with the rolls. Fighting a losing battle, Ernie tried to put the hot dogs on the grill, at the same time ordering the undressed patients back into their clothes.

"I'm going upstairs to get into some slacks or something, Meg, I'm too dressed up for this," her mother said.

Mrs. Belagio laughed. "How about your simple, basic black straitjacket?"

Meg liked Mrs. Belagio, and had since the day she

arrived on the island. She seemed completely sane, and Meg sometimes wondered why she was a patient here. Sommers had once explained to Meg that Mrs. Belagio had lost her husband and son in a boating accident, and that ever since she had believed God had stolen them from her.

To explain the unfairness of life, poor Mrs. Belagio had made up a story about imaginary stolen jewelry, replacing her lost husband and child with it. Since then, Sommers explained, no one had been able to shake the fixation.

It made a rough kind of sense, Meg supposed, but she herself had never heard Mrs. Belagio mention the stolen jewelry, and the illness remained an abstraction to her.

Maybe it was Sommers who had the fixation, Meg thought; he didn't seem nearly as sane as Mrs. Belagio did.

Already looking forward to the thought of coming back out, Evelyn Kendricks walked slowly into The Home. It appeared empty; just about everyone was outside, but as Meg's mother passed through the front hall, she saw Midge Cummins behind the reception desk. The woman looked as sour as ever, didn't acknowledge Mrs. Kendricks's nod, and stared silently at her with a dull, vacant expression.

Mrs. Kendricks shrugged and went upstairs. She hadn't realized how dark it had become until she opened her bedroom door and saw that it was plunged into almost total blackness; as with many old houses, there was no switch near the door, and she would have to walk to the other side of the room, blind, until she could find the switch on her bed-table lamp.

Her hands stretched out in front of her, she stumbled across the room, running into several pieces of furniture which, with the usual perverseness of inanimate objects, weren't where she expected them to be. For a second she stopped; she heard a strange squeaking sound. Some animal outside her window, she decided. She thought she felt her foot brush something that felt strangely soft, but ignored it.

Groping, she finally found the lamp and pressed the switch. The squeaks took on added urgency, and Meg's mother spun around; they were not coming from outside. She gasped, seized by the dreadful realization; in her room, staring at her with their malignant red eyes, were what appeared to be dozens of rats. One sat impudently on her bed, twitching its whiskers and showing its teeth. The more timid had fled when she turned on the light, but she could hear them squeaking and scurrying around under bureaus, chairs, and other low pieces of furniture, occasionally sticking a vicious head into the light to study her. The pack rat, largest and meanest-appearing of the lot, firmly stood its ground in the center of the room, back toward the door, its sneering narrow head pushed forward as if daring Mrs. Kendricks to try to leave the room.

Mrs. Kendricks froze. Rats. Could they *smell* fear?

Rats. Hairy, vicious night-stalking rats, who only showed themselves after dark. Evil, foul-smelling razor-toothed rats, who glared at all humans with hatred. Mrs. Kendricks's most basic fear since she was a little girl and found one in her clothes closet. Looking quickly around the room, she searched for some effective weapon to use against them—something like a heavy broom or a fire poker. Nothing.

She knew that she had to get out of this room; so far, she had managed not to scream, but her deadly fear of the creatures was quickly overcoming the weak grip she had on self-control. Waving her arms, shouting and cursing at them, she took a tentative step forward. The pack rat chattered and more of the rats came out of hiding and tightened the circle around her. "No, no," she pled hopelessly. The pack rat seemed to be laughing at her, then turned deadly serious and began moving toward her.

The scream she had been holding in tore loose from Mrs. Kendricks's throat. Waves of it, screams for help, yellings for someone, *anyone*, to come help her.

The rats seemed suddenly to be moving around her, like the patients around the fire, squealing their own ritual incantations as they raced in an ever-tightening ring around Mrs. Kendricks. She grabbed the pillow off the bed and, still screaming, swung it around her at the rats as she raced toward the door. The pack rat raised one lip and showed his teeth, apparently determined to stop her, but a violent swing of the pillow sent him flying across the room. She shot out the door and slammed it shut behind her, leaning against the wall to steady herself.

Pulling herself together, Mrs. Kendricks rushed downstairs and ran up to Midge Cummins, still staring vacantly out from behind her desk. "Rats," she gasped. "My room's full of rats. Crazy rats. Someone has to go up there and take care of them. . . ."

Cummins looked at her as if, until now, she hadn't known she was in the building. "Rats? Nonsense. You're always saying that. There are no rats here—the exterminator comes twice a year. You're seeing things, Mrs. Kendricks."

Evelyn Kendricks grew suddenly angry. "There *are*, I tell you. I'm not seeing things, either. The whole room is crawling with them."

Midge Cummins yawned, and Meg's mother was enveloped by a sweet-sour cloud of half-digested vodka. "Somebody will look around up there tomorrow when they clean your room," Cummins said, looking bored, and suddenly lapsed back into her vacant look and paralyzed stance, as if Evelyn Kendricks wasn't even there in front of her.

Furious, Meg's mother went outside to look for Dr. Sommers. She couldn't find him. From a few feet away, her mother called out to Meg, frenzy in her voice. Mrs. Kendricks didn't really want to tell Meg about the rats, but had to let her daughter know she wasn't crazy. Finally, taking a deep breath, she sighed and told Meg about them, something which made Mrs. Belagio, standing next to Meg, gasp and begin fanning herself with her magazine.

"I told you, Meg," her mother said in a tone somewhere between triumph and terror. "No one would believe me. Not Dr. Sommers, not even you, Meg. Now you will. The building is full of rats. I knew it, I knew it!"

She and Meg talked a few minutes more, until her mother suddenly saw Dr. Sommers standing to one side watching the patients stuff themselves on hot dogs. He reacted with condescension toward Mrs. Kendricks. "There are no rats here, Mrs. Kendricks. Perhaps you're tired. Or perhaps it proves what I've been saying all along: that you're not as well as you think you are. Believe me, there are no rats in The Home. Nuts, yes. Rats, no." He laughed cuttingly at his own clever phraseology.

Bridling, Meg's mother became furious. "Damn it, Doctor, my room is full of them. Not imaginary ones, not products of a psychosis. If you won't . . ."

Appraising her with an expression of consummate pity, Sommers sighed and finally relented. "All right, Mrs. Kendricks, if it will make you feel better, I'll go up there with you and *prove* there are no rats in your room. . . ."

Twisting uncomfortably, Mrs. Kendricks avoided looking him in the eye. "Do you need *me* to go, too?

Couldn't you just go up there yourself and see what I mean without my having to—"

"Standard practice when someone hallucinates."

With a sigh Meg's mother followed him up the stairs and down the hall, stopping outside her room. "There's one great big one. And one was sitting on my bed, too. They're all over, Doctor."

The doctor threw the door open and walked inside, half-dragging Mrs. Kendricks behind him. There wasn't a rat in sight. The pillow lay on the floor where she had dropped it, the light was still on from when she first went into the room, but not a rat in sight. They had disappeared. "But they *were* here," Mrs. Kendricks whined, not understanding it at all. "I *saw* them, damn it."

"Not in this room, you didn't. There isn't a rat anywhere. Or so much as a cockroach."

Sommers had good reason to know there weren't. After Meg's mother had come screaming out of her room, Sommers had gone in. Knowing the semidrugged state the rats were in, he knew exactly how to catch them: he held a small flashlight in front of each rat's eyes while rotating it slowly. The creatures immediately became paralyzed. Sommers then picked up the hypnotized rat by the tail and dropped it into a large cardboard box. By the time he left to go downstairs, all of the rats had been accounted for and disposed of. He wore a faint smile while he was accomplishing this; Evelyn Kendricks walked too thin a line for this kind of mental abuse. She would be unsettled after a few more events like this one, and then it would be only a matter of time before she became a permanent resident of The Home.

Later, in bed, Meg's mother tossed and turned, waiting impatiently for sleep to settle over her. It did not come easily. Every time she heard the slightest noise, she imagined it was the rats coming back. Twice she turned on her light, just to make sure.

Earlier that day, when Meg had asked how she felt about fleeing and moving into a motel, Mrs. Kendricks had steeled herself and said the idea was silly. It made her sound too screwy. But as the minutes crawled by, lying in her bed and listening to the groanings and creakings of the old house and the occasional sound of someone scuttling down the hall outside her room, the idea kept coming back to her. Perhaps she was putting bravery ahead of rationality.

Chapter Twelve

Last night's barbecue was a big success. They always are. That great blazing fire seems to stir something primitive in the patients, as if they'd retrogressed into an earlier stage of human development. Stone Age savages.

One thing I've never understood—it always happens—is the way a lot of them tear off their clothes and dance around the fire naked. I can understand it easily enough in Roger—it's a weenie roast, after all.

Mrs. Kendricks, I guess, still listens when Meg suggests she's ready to leave. Damn bitch. I don't know if I can trust her anymore.

The rats should undo that in a hurry. By now, I'm sure Mrs. Kendricks doubts her sanity. Once you get someone questioning their own reason, you can do anything you want to them.

Bad for Mrs. Kendricks, good for me.

> *Psychiatric & Personal Observations,*
> *The Home, Alan Sommers, M.D., Director.*

The next morning Meg was surprised when Dr. Sommers showed up at their table. Along with him came the waiter and the specially prepared meals—no more powdered eggs.

Her mother said little but stared sulkily into space a lot. The rats couldn't be blamed on Sommers. That they were there one minute and gone the next were hardly his fault. His reaction to them was.

"The mean way you acted about those rats wasn't very nice," Mrs. Kendricks pointed out, fussing angrily. "You made me think I was bats." The thought of it made Meg's mother seethe.

Dr. Sommers shrugged, a small smile flickering on his face. Making Mrs. Kendricks think she was bats, after all, was his objective.

"It was unpardonable," Mrs. Kendricks continued.

"Rats—no rats—should make you wonder about being—as you put it—bats," Sommers snorted. "I'm sorry to be so blunt, but I don't know how else to put it."

Meg exploded. "That's not blunt, damn it, it's cruel. I don't think . . ."

Sommers wiped his lips on his napkin, staring accusingly at Meg. "You're quite right: you didn't think, Meg. Sorry, more necessary bluntness. When you left the island without my permission, you broke one of the key rules of The Home. What do you think would happen if all my patients did that . . . ?"

"I'm not one of your patients, damn it. I can come and go as I please."

Sommers sighed and smiled apologetically. He hadn't meant this argument to begin. Convincing Evelyn Kendricks she was still crazy was all he'd meant to do. "Now, damn it, Meg . . ." He swallowed hard; apologies never came easily to him. "I didn't mean to upset you," he told Meg. "I'm sorry."

She managed a halfhearted smile. A few minutes later the disagreement disappeared, and the doctor, after a couple more halfhearted stabs at apology, left.

Later that morning, while her mother was in Sommers's office for one of her infrequent sessions, Meg sat on the terrace with Mrs. Belagio.

As they talked, Mrs. Belagio began to unravel in front of Meg's eyes. "There's one thing about Dr. Sommers, though, I guess I'll never be able to forgive. Maybe it wasn't even his fault, but I still have never been able to get over it." She looked around and whispered the rest to Meg. "He stole all my jewelry," she confided. "Just like that. One day it was there, the next it was gone. Maybe the poor man's a kleptomaniac, I don't know. But the jewelry—well, it was worth hundreds of thousands of dollars."

"But you must have talked to him about it," Meg protested, beginning to feel uneasy.

"Oh, I talked to him all right," Mrs. Belagio whispered. "I talk to him about my jewelry every time I see him, whether it's in his office or just passing him in the hall. He denies taking it, of course." Mrs. Belagio looked around the terrace furtively and lowered her voice to an even softer whisper, leaning toward Meg to be sure she could hear.

"He tells me he has it locked up in the vaults for safekeeping, but I know he's lying to me." The old woman was considerably worked up by now; she had high blood pressure—like her mother, Meg thought—and the tiny veins on the woman's face were glowing a deep, dangerous red. "It isn't in the vaults like he says at all. Not for a minute, it isn't," Mrs. Belagio hissed. "He's sold it."

Mrs. Belagio began to cry softly, bringing out a small, lace-edged handkerchief to dab her eyes. It had become suddenly clear to Meg why Mrs. Belagio was at The Home. Dr. Sommers had many strange facets to his character; Meg doubted if jewel theft was one of them.

Mrs. Belagio suddenly brightened, but continued to speak only in a whisper. "I managed to save a few pieces, Meg; he didn't find them because they were the most valuable ones and I always kept them hidden. Would you like to see them? One look, and you'll understand why it upsets me so. The worth of the collection was staggering."

Meg didn't want to go; Mrs. Belagio was making her uncomfortable. But the old lady was pleading with her, and a part of Meg wanted to see the jewelry. If it even existed outside Mrs. Belagio's mind. In spite of herself, Meg caved in.

Upstairs in her room Mrs. Belagio asked Meg's help in moving her easy chair over against the door. None of the patients' rooms had locks, so this was the only way, Mrs. Belagio explained, she could be sure that Sommers wouldn't walk in while she was showing Meg her remaining jewelry and take it, too.

Gently, she opened the second drawer of her bureau. She lifted out the underwear and then pointed to a spot at the bottom of the drawer. Pressing it hard to one side, a sliding panel moved softly. "Some other patient must have carved this for himself," Mrs. Belagio said wistfully.

She pulled a chamois bag out of the compartment and spilled the jewelry on the top of the bureau. For a second Meg was dazzled by its brightness, but as she examined each article—Mrs. Belagio kept up a running commentary on each gem—she realized everything was inexpensive costume jewelry.

"Aren't they magnificent?" Mrs. Belagio asked, her face radiant with pride. "They're worth hundreds of thousands, you know, and he sold every last piece. Except these."

Meg nodded, unable to think what to say. There was

something so pathetic about it. Cheap costume jewelry Mrs. Belagio believed was worth a fortune. "They're certainly beautiful," Meg said weakly. She didn't have the heart to even challenge the sweet old lady's delusion.

Mrs. Belagio smiled at first, then looked at the remaining pile sadly, on the edge of tears. "There was so much more," she said in a strangled little voice. "All my beautiful things sold by that damned doctor and probably being worn right this minute by some chippie in Miami."

Patting her shoulder, Meg struggled to sympathize with her but had a hard time pulling it off. There was something infinitely sad about Mrs. Belagio, a poignant sense of loss that made Meg want to cry.

As they started toward the bedroom door, the old lady suddenly grabbed Meg by the arm and began whispering. "There's something else I want to tell you," she said, her eyes pleading. "But you have to promise you won't tell anyone. Except your mother; I've already told her myself. But no one else. Promise?"

"Promise," Meg said warily.

"It was his theft of my jewels that convinced me. But my sister in Tampa is coming to get me in a few days. She's an awfully nice woman. She's going to take me home with her. She agrees it's time I left The Home; she thinks it's doing me more harm than good."

It was a point on which Meg was inclined to agree; the old lady's eyes had taken on a strange glitter, and the more she talked, the more intense she grew. Mrs. Belagio began whispering again, even softer now than before. "Remember your promise, Meg. Not a word to anyone. Particularly to Dr. Sommers. He'll be terribly upset when he hears. In fact, I don't intend to let him know I'm leaving until after I've already gone—because he knows once I'm out of here I'll go to the police and have him arrested for grand larceny."

Once again, at the door, old Mrs. Belagio seized Meg's arm. "I want you to promise something else," she hissed. "It's not at all safe here for me now, and if Dr. Sommers somehow *does* find out I'm leaving, he'll panic. The police, you see. So if anything strange happens to me, dear—for instance, if I just disappear one day without telling you I'm going—I want you to promise me you'll do something about finding me." The old lady stared at Meg, her face suddenly a mask of fear. "Why, he could put me in one of those cells downstairs and tell everybody I'd become violent. Oh my, and nobody would believe me; they'd believe *him*. Or—and I hate to say this—he could even kill me. The police, the police, he knows I'll go to the police. . . ."

Meg tried to sound reassuring. "I promise, Mrs. Belagio. I won't tell anyone, and if you *do* disappear or something—I really don't think Dr. Sommers would do anything like that, so I wouldn't worry—I promise I'll tear the place apart looking for you. Okay?"

Numbly, Mrs. Belagio released her arm. "You're a nice girl, Meg. A very nice girl. No wonder your mother's so proud of you."

Meg smiled, leaned over, and kissed her. A second later she fled, glad to escape. Ever since she had gotten to The Home, one of the things that had made the patients so frightening was the way they could seem so rational one moment and so dangerously unbalanced the next. What made it more frightening was that frequently, as with Mrs. Belagio, you were never sure which side of sanity's thin edge they stood on at that moment.

Until today old Mrs. Belagio had shown absolutely no sign of instability. So little Meg had wondered why the old lady was even a patient here. Now, she knew. The old lady's story of Dr. Sommers stealing her jewels and her panic that the doctor might kill her to avoid being exposed to the police were all in her mind. Which meant Mrs. Belagio was just as nuts as any of the rest of the patients. I mean, Meg told herself with a grim little laugh, I *hope* it's all in her mind; after all, it was only a matter of time before she had to tell Sommers she was leaving herself—along with her mother and Tighe, a husband he didn't even know existed.

Going down the stairs a frown crossed Meg's face. Where *was* Tighe? Here any moment, she told herself. She wished he would call, but knew he wouldn't. His thing about phones. Just now, his little phobia rankled. My God, for all she knew there could have been some terrible accident. Tighe on a slab. Tighe buried in unfamiliar ground. Or would they send him back to Philly for burial? Everyone would know except her. She winced and continued down into the Main Room to wait for dinner.

Kenny was screaming at someone that his mother, damn it, was too alive. Meg could see it was a wasted effort. The old lady he was yelling at sat silent, rocking back and forth in her chair, clutching her rag doll, staring at him without understanding.

Other patients were also staring into space or starting small, pointless arguments with one another. Over it all came the sounds of children's television cartoons; someone had turned up the set to full volume to make sure the old lady who watched the cartoons from morning until night could hear what Pluto was telling Roadrunner. From Kenny came a sudden, explosive cry; someone else had just challenged that his mother was alive and on her way to pick him up. The similarity of recent stories suddenly made Meg wonder if Mrs. Belagio even *had* a sister in Tampa; maybe, like Kenny's mother, she had died years ago. Listened to, Kenny's ranting and screaming was like a nail being drawn down the blackboard of insanity. Hollowly, from her cell downstairs, came the shrieking and cursing of Mrs. Tibald again. Meg shivered.

She found it hard to breathe. The madness collected in this one room was almost palpable.

Chapter Thirteen

I don't understand how everything could go as wrong all of a sudden. Christ, for no known reason, without any explanation I can think of, everyone is suddenly trying to skip out on me.

My deadliest, most terrible agonizing dread—being left alone. It isn't fair, damn it.

First, Meg's mother, Evelyn. I love and need that woman. Can't she see that, for Christ's sake? And if Evelyn leaves, Meg will go with her. I need her, too. The two of them are my little family—surrogate wife and child to replace my real wife and daughter. It'll kill me if they bail out on me.

And there's others, too. Mrs. Belagio—she probably doesn't know I know it, but rumors fly around The Home like jet fighters, and I pick them up as fast as they're airborne.

I don't really give a damn about Bea Belagio as a person; it's that horror I have of anyone leaving me.

Well, not this time, none of them. They're all here to stay. For good. And if they're ungrateful enough to decide to leave me anyway, I'll have to take steps— unpleasant ones—to stop them.

Sometimes I think I'd get a positive charge out of twisting Meg and her mother's arms behind them as punishment. Or if I had to, killing them. They'd scream like crazy either way.

What was the song? Oh, yeah. "You Always Hurt the One You Love" . . . I may not be the greatest when it comes to loving, but I'm sure a whiz when it comes to hurting people.

Sort of like my stuffed animals, I guess. They never look better than when they're dead.

> *Psychiatric & Personal Observations,*
> *The Home, Alan Sommers, M.D., Director.*

At breakfast that morning Dr. Sommers again did not show up. The waiter, however, and the special food did. The waiter explained that the doctor sent his apologies, but that he was all tied up with something, so please go ahead without waiting for him. To Meg, Sommers's absence was a relief; her mother appeared halfway disappointed. The strange on-again, off-again bond between her and the doctor was still very strong.

About midmorning Meg knew she faced a job that was going to be unpleasant. With Tighe due here any day, she had to enlist Sommers's help in telling her mother she was married. Her mother, having just found Meg again, as it were, might consider the fact of Meg's marriage as a rejection. She really had no idea how her mother might react; Sommers might. The only problem was that neither did Meg have any real idea of how Sommers himself was going to take the news.

Twice during the morning Meg had walked listlessly down the long hall to his office, only to discover the blue light over the door was on—a sign that a patient was inside. The third time the pale blue eye was out, looking more sinister in its grayness than it did when lit—like the eye of a sleeping demon temporarily shut but capable of springing wide open any second and fixing her with its withering stare.

She picked up the small blue phone outside the doctor's door and pushed the button that rang inside. "Yes?" Sommers's voice said over the receiver, a cold, unfriendly ring to it.

"It's Meg," she said. "Could I see you for a minute?"

The cold unfriendliness disappeared. "Of course you can, Meg, of course." The buzzer on the door sounded, and Meg turned the handle and walked into Dr. Sommers's beautifully paneled office. The doctor was already on his feet, a wide smile on his face, coming around from behind his desk and advancing to meet her. "It's wonderful to have you here, Meg. I love this room. You should have come before."

A ripple of irritation surged through Meg. "I tried twice this morning," she said. "But your blue light was on, so I stayed away."

Sommers laughed. "Oh, that," Sommers said, laughing again. "You know, Meg, sometimes it's on simply because I forget to turn it off. Anyway, *you're* special. Anytime you want to see me, light or no light, just pick up the phone in the hall and buzz me. I'll always make time for you; I thought you realized that."

"Thank you." Meg's answer had a flat, empty sound to it; she wondered if Sommers noticed it.

"Make yourself comfortable, Meg." He waved his arm toward an easy chair covered in a bright, colorful print matching one on the chair opposite it, which he settled into, lighting his pipe as soon as Meg sat down in hers.

Meg twisted uncomfortably on the soft cushion.

"There was something I wanted to ask you," Meg said lamely. For no reason she could think of, she suddenly felt guilty; it was like being caught cheating on a test back in grammar school in Little Goat.

Dr. Sommers seemed not to have heard her, but rose and walked over to his desk, rummaging through the papers on top to find something. He found it and turned back to look at her, holding a new book of matches in his hand. "Trouble with smoking a pipe," he explained, "is that you wind up smoking more matches than tobacco. Damned thing never stays lit." Once the pipe was going, throwing out great clouds of whitish smoke, he let his eyes settle on hers. "You said you had something to ask me," the doctor reminded her, still standing in front of his desk.

"Oh, yes. It's about mother. I need your advice on how to tell her something. I haven't up to now, but I can't avoid it any longer." Sommers looked confused, puffing hard on his pipe. "You see," Meg said, "she doesn't know it, but I'm married. My husband's due down here any moment, so I really have to tell her. I don't know how she'll react to the idea; I don't know how she'll react to Tighe. That's my husband's name— Tighe."

The pipe was out of Sommers's mouth, about halfway between his mouth and his waist. He looked at Meg with astonishment. "Your *husband*?"

"I thought I'd told you," Meg lied. "Tighe Devlin." She forced a laugh. "We've only been married a short time, and I still forget sometimes and call myself Meg Kendricks, which isn't my name anymore at all. I just can't seem to get used to 'Meg Devlin'; it takes time. . . ."

Meg found she was talking to Dr. Sommers's back.

He had grunted and turned away from her so that she wouldn't see the stricken, furious expression on his face. Meg's talk faded into nothingness. Sommers appeared to be staring straight ahead of him at the bookcase behind his desk; she could see that he was clutching his pipe with all his strength, and she finally heard the stem break from the pressure. Dr. Sommers swore under his breath, although whether it was at her or because he had just broken his pipe, Meg didn't know.

"I guess I should have made it clearer before," Meg said lamely.

Sommers remained motionless. Suddenly he swore again and hurled the two pieces of his pipe against the paneling around the bookcase in front of him, his back still toward Meg. Pieces of broken pipe and lumps of dottle fell to the floor, making strange noises on their way down the wall.

Meg was baffled. Sommers seemed to realize his reaction was all out of proportion, too. He tried to be pleasant, although the hollowness of his words was transparent. "I'll be delighted to have him here, Meg. This place could use some young people. I'll have someone make up the other bed in your room right away."

A convulsive shudder seized Sommers's body. For the first time, he turned around and looked at her; his face was a mask of steaming fury. "Shit, what a bitch you are. . . ."

He spun around with his back to her again. "I'm sorry," Sommers mumbled, staring at the wall. "That wasn't a very nice thing to say." His arms flailed the air helplessly. "I'm tired. The work. I've been terribly busy. I hope you'll forgive me if"—he brandished a sheaf of papers he'd grabbed off his desk—"but . . ."

Gratefully, Meg seized the hint and began to leave.

"See you at dinner, Dr. Sommers," she said cheerfully. There was no answer, although his head may or may not have nodded up and down slightly.

The moment she was out of the room, Sommers stalked across his office and locked the door. Coming back to his desk, he stormed around it and threw open the bookcase to reveal his shadow box.

The things inside were whispering to him today. That was relatively new, but once they had started using their voices, they didn't seem to want to stop. His daughter's china doll looked at him beadily. "Married!" she screamed, laughing so hard she had to hold her sides. "That means Little Meg will probably be leaving you, you old fart." Sommers ignored her.

For a moment he stared at the rest of the contents and began muttering to himself. It was happening to him again, damn it. Meg's husband—what was his name? Oh, yes, Tighe—stupid name—Meg's husband would take her away with him, and maybe her mother as well. His carefully constructed little surrogate family would walk out on him.

Like hell it would.

That boy Tighe had to be disposed of; that much was obvious. He was at the root of the whole new set of circumstances shoved in his face.

Muttering and cursing, Sommers stared again at the contents of the shadow box, thinking hard. Suddenly, he reached forward and yanked out Dandy, the stuffed cairn, running one finger around the bullet hole in his head, talking to it as if the dog were still alive.

"I took care of you, Dandy," he muttered reflectively, "and I can take care of that creep husband of hers just as easily." He tilted the cairn to one side a little. "But I was pretty easy with you; being shot doesn't really hurt. For that idiot-boy prick-ass husband of Meg's, I'll have to think of something that'll really make him suffer, the son of a bitch."

The cairn threw back its head, laughing and barking at the same time.

Sommers put the cairn back in the shadow box. From it he pulled the Polaroid he'd taken of Meg earlier on their tour of The Home. It was not, he knew, a very good picture; his hand had shaken too much every time he aimed the camera at her. He'd have to replace it later. If there *was* a later. With a pair of scissors, he carefully cut the Polaroid so it would fit into the oval frame and hung it up opposite his real daughter's.

"Damn it," he groaned, staring at Meg's picture. "You're turning out like the rest of them. Trying to leave me, trying to desert me, trying to run away." Sommers waved his arms, shouting at the picture in the shadow box while pacing back and forth in front of it. He suddenly stopped and took her picture out of the shadow box, studying it, torturing himself with it, an expression of hurt and anger etched into his face.

"But if you do, Little Meg," he whispered, "if you *do* try to leave, well"—the color in his face deepened to a deep red; his hands shook; his voice climbed from its whisper back to a roar of rage—"If you do, I can take care of *you* just like I did Dandy, just like I will take care of your damned husband when he shows his face down here. Do you hear me, Meg? Do you understand me, Meg?"

"Oh, Christ Christ Christ . . ." Sommers moaned, slamming the doors of the shadow box shut with a violent crash.

Sommers looked around himself, lost in the dimness of his office and blinking—as if he were returning from a long voyage in space. The light on his desk was turned off with trembling fingers, and the doctor slouched out of the room, muttering to himself softly.

The slow shift that was always part of Sommers's relationships with people—from love to suspicion to hate—was tearing deeply at the edges of his soul.

At luncheon Sommers had already pulled one of his chameleon acts and was acting normal and charming. Meg found it difficult to understand: only yesterday he had been shaking her so hard her teeth had almost come flying out of her mouth; only an hour and a half ago he had been throwing things around his office and calling her a bitch.

Now—only a little later—the doctor was telling her how happy he was for her, and how he looked forward to meeting Tighe.

During the morning he had taken Meg's mother to one side and gently told her about Meg's being married. Secretly, Sommers hoped the woman would fall to the floor screaming, shrieking, cursing her daughter for doing such a hideous thing.

Instead, Mrs. Kendricks looked more confused than anything else. "Meg *married*?" she repeated several times. "It's wonderful, of course, but why didn't she tell *me*? Why wasn't I invited to the wedding? Meg must have been such a pretty bride. . . ."

Getting to his feet, Sommers seemed ready to declare luncheon over, but something suddenly struck him and he sat back down. "In fact," Sommers announced, "I'm so happy for you, Meg, I'm going to take you and your mother out for dinner. There's a wonderful restaurant—it's called The Purple Key—down below Marathon a bit, about opposite Pigeon Key. I hear the food is superb. It'll be my own little party to celebrate the upcoming arrival of your new husband, Meg. And to drink a few toasts and a little good wine. Oh, I'm sure you'll enjoy it. I'd consider it a privilege, Meg."

Meg's mind frantically searched for an excuse, some reasonably polite way to say no, but before she could find one, her mother had already accepted for both of them. Inside, Meg groaned. But she supposed her mother got off the island so seldom Sommers's offer was a big treat for her.

"Dinner tonight, then," Sommers said happily. "Seven all right?" Seven was all right.

At least with her mother and Sommers, it was.

That afternoon, standing in the middle of her room, Meg grew increasingly annoyed. It had been there this morning, she was pretty sure of that. But nowhere could she find the framed five by seven of her and Tighe, taken last summer in Northeast Harbor. It was one of her favorite pictures of Tighe, damn it. It had been sitting on her bureau; now it was gone.

Painstakingly, she searched the room again. Maybe she'd put the picture down someplace while she was dusting this morning. She did that with things sometimes and then couldn't find them for days.

She swore and kept on hunting for the frame and picture. It was nowhere.

It was nothing of importance, she guessed. The Biddles had had dozens of pictures of her and Tighe taken during the party at their house after the wedding. But none, Meg decided, as good as the one taken in Northeast Harbor last summer. Damn, damn, damn.

Thinking about the Biddles' reception made her think about the church—St. Bardolph's—and thinking of St. Bardolph's made her think about the ominous pigeon beating its head against the church windows and screaming its unintelligible warning. And for no reason she could think of at all, Meg began to connect some of her dread about the pigeon's ominous screaming to her misgivings about the disappearance of the picture.

Crazy, she told herself.

Not so crazy. Sommers's effusiveness, warmth and charm at lunch were pure hypocrisy. The only honest moments came when he wistfully held forth on the wonders of a family and of a child. Later, this thought made him angrier than sad. His wife had deserted him, hadn't she? His daughter had abandoned him, too, hadn't she? Some family.

He was in his office, door locked behind him, the bookcase open to reveal the shadow box. On his desk lay the framed five by seven of Tighe and Meg. Carefully, he slipped the picture out of its frame. With his scissors he cut Tighe—that little bastard Tighe Devlin—out of the picture. Trimming further with the scissors, he cut the portion with Meg in it so that it fitted inside the frame identical to his daughter's and slipped it in. Far better than the out-of-focus Polaroid he'd taken. He gazed at Meg's picture with love as he hung it back up on the black velvet interior of the shadow box. Beautiful girl, bright girl, wonderful girl.

The remaining section of the picture—the part with Tighe on it—he stared at with hatred. Bastard, son of a bitch, prick Tighe, stupid-name fucking creep.

The more he stared at Tighe, the angrier he got. Taking a match from his pocket, he set the picture on fire, holding it between his fingers and turning it so it would burn completely. The searing flames reached the thumb and forefinger that held it. The charred remains he dumped into his giant, pipe smoker's ashtray.

Once again Sommers looked inside the shadow box, admiring Meg's picture anew. The Polaroid he slipped inside the drawer beneath the shadow box. The picture wasn't at all good, but *any* picture of Meg was worth saving.

Looking at Meg's picture once more, Sommers's eye fell on something he'd almost forgotten was there. On one of the doors hung a collection of keys. Sommers began yelling at them angrily; they were the keys to the different offices in different sanitariums he had worked in during his career. At the top of the arrangement, hanging above and a little separated from the rest, was the key to his office at Acton-Phillips Clinic. Acton-Phillips was synonymous with prestige; there, he had practiced the most sophisticated sort of psychiatry in the country. He had been their protégé, their fair-haired boy, their darling. Other psychiatrists across the country envied him his position. Sommers had gloried in it.

Acton-Phillips was where he was working at the time his wife and daughter suddenly deserted him. Acton-Phillips was where Sommers was working when he began falling apart.

He muttered at the key, touching it with his fingers as if to be sure it was real. The key began muttering back at him, sketching in his mind for perhaps the thousandth time his final moments at Acton-Phillips.

"Sit down, sit down, Alan," Dr. Whittemore, the director, had said, waving Sommers toward a chair near his desk. Whittemore himself came around his desk and took a seat in the chair that faced Sommers's. Sommers had never been able to explain why—some sort of inner prescience, he supposed—but a feeling of fear was flooding through him. There was no reason for it, he had told himself; Whittemore was the man who had pushed him the hardest, promoted him the most, and was largely responsible for the high position Sommers now held at Acton-Phillips. Why, all of a sudden, should he be afraid of him?

Dr. Whittemore seemed to be having trouble getting to his subject. Randomly, he talked about weather, about patients in other clinics, about new treatments he had read about. Suddenly, he had drawn himself up and faced Sommers directly.

"Alan, I really don't know how to put this. We've been friends and associates for so long it's very difficult. A great deal of the work you have done here has been utterly brilliant. But . . . but—Christ, Alan, I just don't know how to say this—but I'm afraid we're going to have to part company. There have been too many complaints. . . ."

Sommers had heard the words but was unable to react to them. What Whittemore was saying was some sort of nightmare. He would wake up from it any moment. It was impossible. "I don't understand, Lawrence," Sommers had said truthfully. "I'm not certain I heard what you said correctly. . . ." Sommers's eyes raised and stared into Whittemore's in confusion.

"I said," Whittemore explained slowly and meticulously, shifting uncomfortably in his chair as he spoke, "I said I was afraid the time had come when it would be better for everyone concerned if we—if Acton-Phillips and you—parted company. I can't put it any plainer than that, Alan."

"But why?" Sommers had asked, trying to keep his voice from caving in on him. *"Why?"*

Dr. Whittemore touched his fingers together and first studied the tips, then the ceiling of his office. Again, he shifted uncomfortably in his chair. "Alan," he said after a few moments of not saying anything. "I realize the severe trauma you suffered when your wife left you and took your daughter with her. It had to have been a terrible shock to you, and I think, Alan, you may need a little time in some sort of position that is less demanding than your work here. Someplace where you have time to sort things out in your own mind. I would, ordinarily, suggest a leisurely vacation for you, but I know that you live for your work, so a vacation would only add to your troubles. A position at some place where the requirements aren't as stiff as ours would seem to me the answer but . . ."

Sommers had gotten to his feet, clenching and un-clenching his hands, feeling the sweat running down his body. "I still don't understand, Lawrence," Sommers said, his brain beginning to whirl. "I don't think I'm doing anything different than I ever did, and that was always good enough for Acton-Phillips before. My wife and daughter leaving me, hell, it shook me up for a few weeks, but I barely think of it anymore," he lied.

Dr. Whittemore made a face. Anything like this was always unpleasant; it was doubly eviscerating when the man you were doing it to was your protégé and friend. He knew now that fairness demanded that he explain the rest. "Look, Alan, I mentioned complaints. Well, there have been a lot from your patients' families in the last couple of months. I ignored them at first, because I know how brilliant you are. But they have kept on complaining. The families say you refuse to release your patients even when by your own statements, you have told them the patients are pretty well cured. They say you seem to feel the patients *belong* to you personally, that, for some reason, you want your patients to stay here with you forever. At first, I thought it was absurd, but the same kind of complaint kept coming to me. Informally, I set up a panel of other doctors to check out your personal roster of patients; I was stunned to discover how many of them *had* been well enough to go home months ago. Alan, I have tremendous respect and affection for you. . . . I'm heartbroken to have to take this step. . . . But with the kind of patients we treat here . . . the grants we depend on . . . to have our prestige questioned . . . the complaints . . . the threat of the bad publicity that it raises . . . well . . ." Dr. Whittemore threw up his hands, suddenly unable to continue.

Sommers's face flushed a deep red; anger coursed through his body. "You bastard!" he screamed. "You had spies put on me, other doctors who don't hold a candle to me—and you know it. You don't have to say another word, Lawrence. I know when I've been zapped." He had spun on his heel and started toward the door. As he reached it, he turned back for a moment. "Fuck you and fuck Acton-Phillips!" Livid, he slammed Dr. Whittemore's office door behind him, walked down the hall, and never again set foot in the building.

The memory of the sound Whittemore's door made still echoed through Sommers's ears. Looking at the other keys hanging on the door, Sommers roared in fury. Each one represented another downward step from the prestige of Acton-Phillips to some of the third-rate sanitariums he had ended up working in. Each of them had finally let him go for the same reason: Sommers felt his patients were his personal property and would never release them, even when cured.

To Sommers the desertion of him by these clinics and sanitariums, second- and third-rate as they were, was as punishing a blow as his mother and father leaving him or his wife and daughter leaving him or Acton-Phillips abandoning him or now the threat of Meg's deserting him. He ripped all the keys off the door and hurled them violently across his office, where they clattered against the paneling and fell to the floor. Briefly, he looked around his office. He had bought and set up The Home himself; he owned it. The Home was the one thing in his life he was certain *couldn't* desert him.

Tighe would be taken care of—and Meg, too, if she tried to leave—he promised the collection of objects in the shadow box. Most of the things inside snickered at him. His father's ear, though, floating in its peanut butter jar of formaldehyde, seemed to rise and sink in the liquid, as if in agreement. Slowly, Sommers sank into his office chair, holding his head in his hands, looking as if he might burst into tears.

By the time he took Meg and her mother out to dinner, though, Dr. Sommers was back in good form, charming and thoughtful. He scanned the wine list of The Purple Key and picked out an excellent champagne. The food was delicious, the atmosphere convivial. Even Meg felt herself relaxing and letting herself fall under Sommers's spell. Her mother was on the upswing cycle of her on-again, off-again relationship with the doctor.

Raising his glass, Dr. Sommers abruptly turned toward Meg. "I want to make a little toast to Meg and her new husband."

Meg gasped. How could Sommers be crazy enough to mention something like that casually in the conversation? Sommers looked at her and laughed. "It's all right, Meg. These things are best handled by professionals."

"And I'm delighted, Meg darling, of course. How wonderful! I can't wait to meet him when he gets here," Mrs. Kendricks said.

Meg was stunned; it was as if Sommers had left her in a hypnotic trance of some sort.

"May their lives be long, and their happiness endless.

And that, of course, goes for Meg's charming mother as well. *Santé.*"

Mrs. Kendricks rewarded him with an unconvincing smile.

Meg felt a small shudder pass through her.

The pigeon trapped inside her head had begun screaming again.

Chapter Fourteen

The animals in my zoo are getting restless. I could sense it last night before I took Meg and her mother out to dinner. Today, it will build up and get worse. I've never quite understood why this happens from time to time with patients. I do know we'll have to keep the staff on full duty all day to make sure the explosion doesn't get out of hand. I've told the kitchen crew to pile on the food; a full stomach's a damned good soporific.

Dinner at The Purple Key last night made me feel even closer to Meg and her mother than ever. My whole little family enjoying superb food, superior wine, and me. It makes the thought of that bastard Tighe's eventual arrival all the more painful for me. Tighe—well, Tighe is going to have to be disposed of relatively quickly. On the other hand, doing it too quickly could make Meg suspicious. If she somehow begins to connect me with the thing, Meg herself might try to leave. Over my dead body. Or rather— over hers.

Psychiatric & Personal Observations, The Home, Alan Sommers, M.D., Director.

The next morning, her head throbbing slightly from last night's champagne, Meg was seated at the table with Sommers and her mother, when she sensed something wrong. At first her instinct was to suspect her hangover was worse than she'd thought, but looking around the room, she slowly realized there was an almost electric tension running among the patients at the other tables.

"I don't understand it, Doctor. Maybe it's my imagination, but I've got this crazy idea that your patients are up-tight about something."

Sommers shrugged. "You're not crazy, Meg. Any institution gets that way sometimes. I've never been able to pin down what causes it; all I know is that it happens every now and then."

"There's nothing you can do, Doctor?"

"Nothing. It's like a disease; one patient or another becomes disturbed by something—usually some small thing that ordinarily wouldn't bother anybody, even these kooks—and pretty soon all of the patients come down with the same infection. There's nothing anyone *can* do to head it off. I don't understand it; it just happens that way." For a moment he looked around the room, then turned his eyes on Meg. "Maybe it's the moon." Sommers laughed.

Meg wasn't laughing at all. The thought of being captive on a small island, badly outnumbered by patients all suddenly suffering from a simultaneous attack of nerves, was a frightening one. "God," Meg said feelingly, "it's a little scary."

"Nothing to worry about. Happens all the time, Meg."

To Meg, Sommers's offhanded indifference was not reassuring. She knew the patients resented her because Dr. Sommers gave her so much attention. If, as the doctor predicted, the whole mob of them suddenly turned violent, she and her mother were likely targets.

Meg studied her mother to find out why she'd suddenly become so quiet. She was all better—Meg was convinced of that— but the agitation of the other patients was getting to her. She hadn't said more than a dozen words since they sat down. It was as if she were on another planet, staring at a point somewhere over Dr. Sommers's head, utterly soundless.

"Mrs. Kendricks . . . Mrs. Kendricks . . ." Sommers tried gently, taking her hand and moving it back and forth. She seemed unaware of his voice or that he was holding her hand.

By now Sommers had lifted her wrist quite high off the table; from it the fingers drooped limply downward, like a rag doll's. The doctor stared at her mother for a moment, then suddenly let go of her wrist. The hand crashed to the table, upsetting her water glass, but she still didn't react at all. Sommers sighed, shrugged his shoulders, and looked at Meg. "No response. Nothing to worry about though. It's one way some patients— even those in the most stable mental state—react. Like no one else were here with them. She'll be fine by tomorrow."

Meg was startled when her mother suddenly rose to her feet and looked at the doctor with contempt. "Stop pretending I'm not even here, Alan," she yelled at him, leaning over and slapping his face. "I'm just as much here as you are, damn it." Meg was again startled. In her entire life, she couldn't remember ever hearing her mother say anything stronger than "heck" or "gosh-darn."

She spun on Meg. "Your mother—the woman no one seems to think is here—is going upstairs to her room to lie down." With a sniff of irritation, Mrs. Kendricks marched out of the dining room.

"Should I go with her?" Meg asked Dr. Sommers.

"Just leave her alone. When the electricity goes out of the rest of the patients, she'll be back to her normal, wonderful self again. In the meantime, I shall miss her."

Meg studied Dr. Sommers with curiosity. The bond between him and her mother was something Sommers only ever mentioned obliquely, and it surprised Meg that he was willing to be this open about it. An expression of concern must have crossed her face; she received the inevitable Sommers hand-pat.

They were just having their second cup of coffee when violence exploded across the room. The electric tension had affected Roger in about the way you might expect. Only now he had stepped up onto a chair and from it onto the center of the table at which eight people were eating their unusually ample breakfast. The zipper was unzipped, and Roger went to work.

"Stop that, stop that!" screamed Kenny. "It's vile. Disgusting. Sick. If my mother walked in now . . ."

"It would be a genuine miracle," Roger finished for him. "For Christ's sake, Kenny, she's been pushing up daisies for almost five years and *you* know it." An idea suddenly made Roger laugh, causing him to lose his concentration. "Hey, if she *does* show up, Kenny, maybe she'll give each of us one of the daisies. Nothing like flowers to brighten up a place."

It was too much for Kenny. He hurled his tray at Roger, who ducked it, and began laughing even harder at him. Roger watched the tray sail by his head and hooted.

The more Roger laughed, the more livid Kenny

became. Suddenly on his feet, he dove across the table and threw Roger to the floor. The other patients at the table calmly picked up their plates and went back to the serving counter; one old man, Keith Lichter, saw that his own plate of scrambled eggs had landed on the floor right side up. Instead of picking it up, Mr. Lichter lowered himself to the floor and continued to eat off his plate. On the floor beyond the table, Kenny and Roger were wrestling violently; in Kenny's hand was his fork, with which he repeatedly tried to stab Roger. The din was earsplitting. At other tables plates and glasses were being thrown, some at other patients, some simply into the air. A small cheering section of patients had gathered in a circle around the wrestling match between Kenny and Roger—some cheering one, some cheering the other.

Dr. Sommers kept on talking to Meg about the psychological implications of a day like today, ignoring the wrestlers and the hurled tableware as if nothing at all unusual was happening. Meg saw him nod imperceptibly to someone across the room. Ernie, who had been acting as their waiter, strode across the room and pulled Kenny off Roger, shaking him like an errant puppy. Holding onto Kenny's jacket so that his feet were off the floor, he turned to Roger. "Get up off the floor," he yelled at him. "Zip up your fly. Stop causing trouble and shut up." Meekly, Roger did as he was told; no one wanted to take on a giant like Ernie.

Picking Kenny up by the neck, the huge Ernie carried him over to the dining room door, where a dyspeptic Midge Cummins was standing with her arms folded, waiting, her mouth set in an even grimmer expression than usual. "The doc says give him a shot," Ernie told her. As she led Kenny away, Meg could hear Midge

Cummins telling him with relish: "Come on, Kenny. A nice little shot of Thorazine in the ass and then you go bye-bye."

Leaving the dining room, Meg walked into the Main Room. The noise was unbelievable. There was a running series of pointless arguments between patients; people muttered, screamed, and cursed each other; even the lady who watched children's cartoons all day had abandoned her TV set and was standing in the center of the room, her head thrown back, screaming at the ceiling. Ernie stood inside the door, braced for whatever might happen next; a few minutes later Midge Cummins took up a position at the other end of the room, her pinched eyes on the hunt for more trouble.

Meg knew she couldn't take it in this room for long. Looking around, she was surprised not to see Mrs. Belagio. She didn't know how the electric tension might have affected her—as with some patients, possibly not at all—and Meg was wondering if it wouldn't be a good idea to find her and ask her to go try to cheer up her mother.

Meg decided she had to get away from this suddenly frightening group of patients. She'd go upstairs, put on her bathing suit, and then go lie in the sun on the terrace. It would relax her, she decided. While changing, she'd check on her mother as well as see if Mrs. Belagio was well enough to go talk with her.

Silently, Meg opened her mother's door and peeked in. "Everything all right?" Meg asked.

There was no answer. With a sigh Meg walked down the hall and knocked on Mrs. Belagio's door. There was no answer. Surprisingly, though, the door was a crack ajar. Meg knocked again and then pushed the door open and went in.

What she saw stunned her. The bed had been stripped and its mattress rolled up at the foot of the bed. When Meg opened the closet door, she found no clothes hanging there. Mrs. Belagio was gone. An idea suddenly hit Meg, and she raced to the bureau. It was empty, too. Carefully, Meg slid open the secret panel to the compartment where Mrs. Belagio kept her few remaining precious "jewels." The costume jewelry pieces were still inside their secret compartment. A sense of dread swept over Meg. The old lady, confused as she was, would never have left the jewels behind if she'd left under her own steam; to Mrs. Belagio they were the most precious things in her life.

The worry kept gnawing away at Meg. Downstairs on her way to the terrace, in her bathing suit and with a bath towel slung over her shoulder, she went up to Midge Cummins, who was standing behind the reception desk at the nurse's station. "I'm a little baffled, Miss Cummins," Meg began.

"Everybody's baffled here today," Midge Cummins snapped at her.

Meg ignored her unpleasantness and went on talking. "I was looking for Mrs. Belagio, but I see her bed's been stripped and all of her clothes are gone. Do you know what—"

Midge Cummins looked even more unpleasant than before. "Mrs. Belagio? Doctor said her sister came by very early this morning and took her with her to Tampa to live. He might have told us she was leaving. The night nurse doesn't think the doctor told her anything about Mrs. Belagio leaving either; no one tells us anything. How can the staff run things if no one tells them what's going on? I've told the doctor a million times he has to—"

Midge Cummins found she was talking to herself; she watched as Meg walked through the Main Room and out into the sun. Cummins snorted. Rude. Today's young people were so damned rude it made you sick. . . .

As Meg walked on she became sure Dr. Sommers must be lying. In no circumstances would Mrs. Belagio leave her damned "jewelry" behind. As if from a great distance, Mrs. Belagio's words came back to haunt her. "If something funny should happen to me, dear—if I should just disappear or something like that—get the police, dear. Come looking for me. That damned jewel thief Sommers could lock me up downstairs in one of his cells to keep me from telling anyone, or—and I probably shouldn't even say this—he could even kill me. Do you promise to look for me, Meg?"

And Meg could remember solemnly promising, thinking it was one of those promises she would never have to keep. Now, precisely as the old lady had predicted, Mrs. Belagio had disappeared. Meg struggled with herself. Should she check out the room with the cells? It was tough to know. She knew Mrs. Belgaio, in her delusions, had lied terribly—as in the case of the jewelry—and for all she knew, there might *be* no sister in Tampa—or anyplace else. But the fact that the jewelry was still in its compartment and Mrs. Belagio was gone was not a lie, it was a fact. Damn, damn, damn.

Out on the terrace, lying in the glowing warmth of a beneficent sun of a glorious day, Meg was annoyed that the sun and balmy warmth couldn't give her the escape from tension she had hoped for. Mrs. Belagio's words kept spinning around in her head, pleading with Meg to come look for her, and if she didn't find her, to go to the police. Should she herself simply go to the police?

The question had tightened Meg up completely again. She was frightened, she was worried, she was confused, and she kept shifting her position on the chaise trying to find some way to get more comfortable. The idea of taking her mother and leaving The Home to wait for Tighe in a motel somewhere came back and hit her with new force. Her mother should be back to normal by tomorrow, Sommers had said, and maybe then she should—

Meg felt her heart shrivel. There was no longer any reason to accept anything Sommers said as rational. The man, who had once struck her as charming, then, as a little strange, she now considered clearly crazy.

There was no other explanation for his performance earlier in the day. Crazy. As crazy as his patients. Jesus, Meg shuddered. A madman in charge of an island full of lunatics. Terrifying.

And all the more reason to get herself and her mother to a motel and wait for Tighe there. Tomorrow. Tomorrow she would pack them up and take her mother to—

Suddenly, from behind her, a pair of strong hands grabbed her head and clamped it in their powerful grip like a vise. Meg felt her heart shrink in panic, her whole system seized by shock. Meg gave a shriek of pure, undiluted terror—the shock would have been terrifying in any circumstances, but her nerves were so taut both the shriek and her reactions were magnified— tore herself loose from the hands, and shot out of the chaise, screaming.

Ahead of her, Meg saw the entranceway to the flight of stone steps down from the terrace. Meg raced straight for them, stumbling and gasping. At the top of the steps she had to stop. A board had been placed across the steps as a barrier, and too late, Meg remembered that Ernie had torn up the steps to reset them.

From behind her she heard her attacker moving around and cursing to himself. Spinning, she turned to face him; the steps were impassable.

There he was: Tighe Dexter Devlin III, standing behind the chaise, laughing while he fanned one hand to try and ease the painful scratches she could see her fingernails had made in it. "Don't you love me anymore, Meg?" he asked sadly while wearing a wide grin. "Christ, I've gotten more hospitable receptions from girls who hated my guts. Jesus . . . those fingernails—"

Tighe never got to finish his sentence. He suddenly found his mouth was too filled with Meg's. She had raced back across the flagstones and literally thrown herself at him, almost knocking him over, smothering him with kisses, holding him, crying with relief and happiness. She kept running her hands over him, feeling him, touching him, as if to make sure he was real. When she saw the deep scratch marks on his hand— already oozing blood—she looked up at him, half-laughing, half-crying, and whispered, "Oh, Tighe . . . my damned nails . . ."

"It'll stop bleeding in three or four hours," he moaned. "What I get for playing games with a nervous lady."

"Oh, God, Tighe. Oh, Tighe, Tighe, Tighe . . . I'm so happy you're here. . . . I've missed you so much. . . . My God, I'm so glad. . . ." For a delirious moment they held each other tightly, trembling with ecstasy, reveling in their happiness.

There was one onlooker who wasn't feeling in the

least bit happy. Out through his office window, drawn there by Meg's first shriek, Dr. Sommers stood staring at Tighe, resenting him, hating him, loathing him.

The enemy had landed.

PART TWO

Chapter Fifteen

Patients gradually coming off their electric high. Still muttering and wailing and an occasional shriek, but the worst is over. They'll sulk all through dinner and go to bed early; by morning, they'll have forgotten it ever happened. Thank God. It's days like today that make running The Home sheer hell.

That bastard husband of Meg's showed up. Everything about him is ridiculous. Take his first name: who the hell ever heard of anyone named Tighe? Taken all together, the whole damned name is as pretentious as he is himself: Tighe Dexter Devlin III. Stuck-up little snot.

I can't fathom what Meg sees in him. Oh, he's good-looking enough—almost pretty, I'd say—and he has a certain charm that took me by surprise. He even made me laugh, damn it. Bastard.

Well, he won't be laughing for long. I hate to upset Meg by how I plan to get rid of the boy, but I can't have him around poisoning Meg's mind against me. A few days, so it doesn't look too contrived, and then Tighe goes to join the Tighe Dexter Devlins numbers one and two.

Thank God I'll get him out of the way before Meg has a chance to start working on a Tighe Dexter Devlin IV.

Psychiatric & Personal Observations, The Home, Alan Sommers, M.D., Director.

The knock on the door was a soft one, almost tentative. Meg and Tighe looked at each other; Meg's nerves were so taut she had jumped at the sound, pulling herself abruptly out of Tighe's arms.

Shaking her head Meg went to the door and opened it. Outside stood Ernie, his hand still raised to knock again. "Excuse me, ma'am," Ernie began uncertainly, blushing. "Dr. Sommers asked me to give you a message." The huge Ernie's eyes glazed a little as he struggled to repeat the message exactly as given. "Dr. Sommers would as how he'd like to have you and your husband—Mr. Devlin, that is—join him for dinner." Meg stared at him; they'd only gotten to their room five minutes earlier and already their lives were being interfered with. Blinking, Ernie went on with the rest of his message. "It's not in the dining room, ma'am; it's going to be in his office. We're setting it up now. A real special dinner to welcome Mr. Devlin like."

Meg turned toward Tighe helplessly. They had planned to go down to Marathon so they could be alone and catch up on things, but Meg could guess that refusing Dr. Sommers would be taken in the highly personal way he took everything. Tighe raised his eyebrows as if he were asking if they really had to, and Meg nodded her head up and down imperceptibly. She saw Tighe sigh unhappily and shrug his shoulders in defeat. "Tell Dr. Sommers we'd love to," Meg told Ernie, hoping

God wouldn't send a thunderbolt crashing through their ceiling for the blatancy of her lie.

"I'm sorry, Tighe, but there really wasn't much I could do but accept," Meg whispered the moment Ernie had gone.

"Christ, I've only been here ten minutes and already the man's interfering with my life." Tighe studied Meg's stricken expression for a moment, then: "Oh, cheer up." He laughed. "You look like you'd just been backed over by a diesel."

Tighe wouldn't have been quite so cheerful if he had had any idea of just how permanently Dr. Sommers planned to interfere with his life a few days later.

Surprisingly, the evening was an enchanted one. Tighe's arrival alone added a glow to Meg's world; the long, leisurely cocktails made Meg feel even better.

Dr. Sommers's office itself was part of the enchantment. Meg had barely seen it before but knew it had been the owner's library, back in the days the house was still a private home. The man had obviously spared no expense; ceiling to floor, the room was handsomely paneled in some warm, rich wood that gleamed with a deep satin patina. Because sometimes the evenings became chilly this time of year, Dr. Sommers had had Ernie light a blazing fire; underneath the beautifully curved mantelpiece, the flames crackled warmly, adding a soft golden glow to everything in the room, otherwise lit only by blazing candles.

"The man who had this place built certainly knew how to live," Dr. Sommers said with a small smile. "This, as you might expect, is my favorite room. Sometimes, I like to sit in here thinking how much the man who built this house must have enjoyed living here

by himself. Blissfully **alone. It's a luxury** I can't afford.
Morning till night I'm surrounded by people—some of
whom, I have to admit, I absolutely despise." Dr.
Sommers allowed himself a sad, philosophical smile.
"It's one of the penalties of my profession, I suppose—
along with a certain degree of poverty."

To her surprise, Tighe took to Sommers immediately.
("It's the man's frankness, I guess," he was to tell her
later.) She knew the doctor was making an effort to be
charming—and it bothered her a little that he'd won
over Tighe so easily. Tighe managed to be pretty damned
charming himself, kidding Meg and even kidding the
doctor a little. On the other hand, Sommers even found
himself becoming a victim of Tighe's easy charm. It
only made the doctor despise him all the more. It
wasn't fair, damn it, it wasn't fair.

The dinner was lavish, served by Ernie—immaculately
turned out in a black alpaca coat—and by a maid pressed
into service from the kitchen staff, and seemed to go on
forever. Smoked salmon, a curious-sounding but delicious mixture of lobster and steak served with a venera-
ble red; dessert (Key Lime ice) called for champagne, a
highly respectable bottle of Moët.

As Tighe and Sommers sipped their cognac, Meg
realized that for the first time in ten days she felt
completely relaxed, completely happy, completely safe.
She knew Tighe was exhausted by his days and nights
of driving, but the wine and the food and the cognac,
while making his eyelids droop a little, seemed to have
left him feeling completely at home.

Upstairs in their room Meg was afraid that Tighe
would be too exhausted to talk about the things she was
dying to tell him or to make love. She was right about
his being too tired to talk, but wrong about his reservoir
of passion. It was a wild, flailing sort of lovemaking,

their bodies thrashing and twisting after their long separation.

"Jesus," sighed Tighe and stared at Meg in contentment. Ten seconds later his eyes fell shut, and she heard a soft, gentle snore of fulfillment rising from him. Well, the things she wanted to talk about would just have to wait until morning. Gently, she slipped Tighe's naked body under the covers, running her hands over him, fulfilled, holding him, blissfully happy now that he was with her at last.

Outside, in the hall, the reaction was neither one of happiness nor fulfillment. Sommers stood there with one angry eye pressed hard against a concealed peephole into their room, positioned to one side of a watercolor of the sea crashing into the shore of Matecumbe Gut. His face grew livid as he watched their lovemaking—the furious coupling of Meg and Tighe, the accelerating up and down of Tighe's buttocks, the twisting and heaving of Meg beneath him. Meg's love for Tighe troubled, upset, and infuriated him. What business did she have loving him? Through the thin wall he had heard Meg's moans of ecstasy rise to a crescendo, the groans that came from Tighe, and at the end, Meg's sudden cry as she lost herself in shuddering waves of delirium.

Sommers remained standing there, not wanting to watch, but unable not to. Only when he saw Tighe's eyes fall shut and saw Meg pulling the covers up over him, running her hands across his body (Was that really necessary, for Christ's sake?), was he finally sure that they were finished for the night. Some lover, he sneered to himself, cursing softly. How could she possibly be in love with a creep like Tighe?

Walking down the hall Sommers grew angry that the

sight could send him into such a frenzy. It wasn't fair either, damn it, it wasn't fair. Why should that bastard Tighe be allowed to use and corrupt and make Meg love him like that? With a soft groan Dr. Sommers headed down the steep stairs. Any slight reservations he might have had about how he planned to eliminate Tighe vanished as he replayed what he had just seen over and over in his head, trembling with rage in an orgy of self-flagellation.

The next morning, over coffee and croissants delivered by Ernie, Meg finally got her chance to tell Tighe a little of what she felt about The Home and Dr. Sommers. Some parts she edited out; she grew increasingly aware of how paranoid she was beginning to sound.

"There was this nice lady . . . Mom's only real friend here, I guess . . . a Mrs. Belagio. And, oh, Tighe, yesterday she just disappeared. She'd said she might, but I never thought . . ."

Slowly, with difficulty, Meg led Tighe through the story from the costume jewelry to the mysterious sister from Tampa.

"Well, maybe she *does* have a sister in Tampa, Meg; maybe the sister likes to get up early in the morning, and that's why no one but Sommers saw her. Myself, I hate getting up at all—especially with you around to keep me in bed all day—but they're a curious lot up in Tampa, and who knows? Maybe it's just like Dr. Sommers says."

Tighe had laughed, but Meg had only shaken her head. There was too much wrong about the whole story to accept it that readily.

Picking up Meg's mood, Tighe turned serious. "How do you think your mother is?"

Meg pursed her lips, trying to pin down an assessment. "Well, she says she's all better. That she's cured. And damn it, I have to say that I think she's right. . . . Oh, there's a kind of vagueness sometimes, but beyond that, she's as sane as we are. . . .

"And hardly an hour goes by that she doesn't start pleading with me to take her away from here. She's afraid, she says. And a lot of the time, so am I. Hell, this place frightens *me* more every day. There's something wrong here, something I can't put my finger on. I dunno, maybe it's Sommers. Jesus, you should have seen him the day I told him I was married."

Meg shuddered, remembering the episode in Dr. Sommers's office, his breaking his pipe between his fingers.

On the bed Tighe rolled over on his back, taking her hand in his and squeezing it gently, a small quizzical smile slipping across his face. "I don't know what *you* could be frightened of, Meg. Your mother . . . well, that's something different. But there's nothing you—"

Meg stood up from the bed quite suddenly, looking at him and beginning to grow angry. "No, damn it, you *don't* know, Tighe, and yet you're making judgments as if you did."

Sitting up, Tighe looked at her in confusion. Her sudden anger baffled him. "Jesus, Meg. I don't understand you. . . ."

"Maybe it's because for two weeks, while you were galavanting around Philly, I was stuck here with a bunch of loonies. Some of them are just sort of vague, or disconnected; others of them are pretty damned nuts, going after one another with forks or fists, whatever's handy. And I know, even if you don't, that every damned one of them could turn violent any moment. Poor

Mom—no wonder she's scared. After five years of living with this bunch, you'd have to be crazy *not* to be scared. And she's not crazy. What about me? *Me* scared? Damn right I'm scared. Rats in Mom's bedroom one minute, gone the next. Men hanging themselves in the closet while everybody stands around outside the door waiting to see the gore. A shrink who maybe's crazier than any of his patients. A head nurse that's half in the bag most of the time. Alone, on a stupid little island, with the only way to get ashore a tramway so old it takes your breath away. Let me change what I said before. We've not only got to get Mother out of here before she's scared into a heart attack, but we've got to get the former little Meg Kendricks out of here before she winds up babbling as badly as the rest of the inmates. Yes, Tighe, I'm scared. And I don't give a damn who knows it."

Turning over on one elbow, still baffled by her reaction, Tighe tried to reassure her. "There's nothing to worry about, damn it. Okay, the place is spooky. But as soon as we find a house, we can move ourselves bag and baggage to—"

Meg spun on him, her eyes bright with urgency. "It's not soon enough, Tighe. I'm too frightened. What I was wondering was if we couldn't find a motel someplace around here, and move ourselves and Mother there. Just until we find the right house, Tighe."

Tighe suddenly hooted. "I saw the only motel around when I was driving in," he explained, as Meg's eyes studied him. "As dilapidated as this place—maybe worse. Scare you even more than this wreck. The night manager, I understand, is Tony Perkins. Look—"

"Damn you, Tighe," Meg whispered. When he saw his attempt at humor was less than appreciated, Tighe deftly took the blame on himself, smiling his crooked little smile and suddenly sitting up on the bed alongside her, holding her hand in his.

"Besides," he said, "it's *me* who wants to stay here. Blame your crazy husband. You know how I love to snorkle and, hell, the waters around here must be great for it. I was planning to buy a rubber boat and a small outboard and take a peek. The undersea life on the far side must be spectacular. Just stick it out for a few days more until we find a house or I get waterlogged. You can take it just that long, can't you?"

Meg sighed. Tighe was trying, but it didn't help very much. From what he'd said, it was obvious he didn't really understand what she found so frightening about The Home. In a way she had to accept this; she didn't completely understand it herself.

"Well," Meg said, changing the subject entirely, "you ought to call Miss Groundly—she's the real estate lady—and we can start looking right away. There's a pay phone just down the hall. We can pick up your snorkling gear after we've looked at whatever houses she can come up with. This afternoon. Okay?"

"Okay." Tighe reached over and pushed Meg backwards onto the bed. "And remember, darling. You're not alone anymore."

Downstairs, perhaps half an hour later, Dr. Sommers stood staring blankly out his office window, fists clenching and unclenching, unable to rid himself of a searing resentment. How the hell could she love him like that? The sex was proof of it. The picture of Tighe and Meg kept flashing through his brain in an agony of jealousy. He had spied, he had watched, he had absorbed; now he was paying dearly. Rhythmically his fist kept pounding the wall beside the window as Sommers tried to eradicate the picture; a fever of jealousy had enveloped him all morning, torturing him, infuriating him, washing across him in thundering waves of sadness and fury. No matter how hard he tried, the memory kept forcing itself violently back into his thoughts—Meg's cries of ecstasy, the plunging of Tighe's lithe young body, the groans and the thrashings and twistings. The minutiae of profound love. In a searing flash of jealousy, Sommers remembered the sudden scream from Meg at the end, the spasms that ran through Tighe's legs, the animal movements as Meg finally surrendered to orgasm. Then, spent silence.

As if from a great distance Sommers heard the phone on his desk ring—a strident, insistent jangling that demanded to be answered. Angrily, he picked up the receiver.

The voice on the other end was unfamiliar, the message infuriating. Sommers spoke for several minutes, barely keeping his anger under control. He was livid when he finally slammed the phone back on its hook.

Swearing and cursing, Sommers stalked across his office, slammed the door, and locked it. Still swearing at a treacherous world, he tore open the bookcase to get at the shadow box behind it.

When he looked inside, they were all there, looking unusually surly. He was about to say something when he heard it. At first, there was only the usual faint whispering. A moment later he realized it had turned into giggles. Pretty soon it became hoots and catcalls.

"Stop that, damn it. . . ." Sommers roared. This only made them all laugh harder than before.

His daughter's favorite doll blinked her big eyes at him and sneered sarcastically. "Oh, wow," the doll said, laughing. "You saw them screwing and so you know they love each other and that he's going to take her away. Her mother, too. It made you want to cry. Some man *you* are. No wonder everybody leaves you, you old fart."

"There was nothing I could do," Sommers whined, trying to defend himself. The whole damned world was against him today.

The stuffed, cuddly lamb shot to its feet, kicking its heels behind it, waving its forefeet to make itself noticed in the shadow box. "There was lots you could have done, Doc. Like stopping them before they started. Your wife, your daughter, Evelyn Kendricks, Meg. A stitch in time and all that shit," the lamb screamed, shaking with laughter.

It quickly was taken up by the other objects, becoming a sort of chant. "A stitch in time . . . a stitch in time!" they all hooted at him.

Sommers didn't know whether to cry or to scream; he sank into the chair behind his desk, his fists again clenching and unclenching, his body shivering from the sudden rivulets of sweat coursing down.

Fuming, he gave the groan of an animal in pain and yanked open the small drawer beneath the shadow box. From it he withdrew the fuzzy Polaroid he'd taken of Meg during their tour a few days ago. Only a few days ago? It seemed like another lifetime.

Shaking his head, as much in sadness as in anger, he did what he knew had to be done. As he had with Tighe's, he put a match to the picture, moving it slowly back and forth to fan the flames, then, as it burned down, dumped the charred remains in his ashtray.

"Like the rest of them," he muttered to himself, "like all the rest of them. Unless . . ."

Tighe would have to be disposed of even more quickly than he had originally planned, the preppie bastard. That phone call. And if Meg should persist in *her* cruel notion of leaving . . . then Meg.

Chapter Sixteen

I'm not sure, but if I remember correctly, twenty-five years ago women didn't use to go crazy in bed like they do today. The whole thing was pretty damned civilized. People used to love each other without feeling they had to tear down the bed to prove it.

I'm not really surprised at him—he looks like a degenerate to me anyway. But Meg—well, watching Meg hurt. There was love written all over the way they went at it. God damn, it makes me envious.

If it weren't for that phone call, I'd feel even sadder about Meg than I do. But that phone call just proves how much they're in love. And now I'm aware that he'll be taking her away any day now.

No, he won't, damn it. No one's going anywhere. In fact, just the opposite. First, Tighe out of the way. And if Meg doesn't play ball, then her.

Psychiatric & Personal Observations, The Home, Alan Sommers, M.D., Director.

Earlier, when the infuriating phone call had come, Dr. Sommers was staring out his window, cursing Tighe Devlin, Meg, the capriciousness of love, and the fickle temperament of existence. With a cursory grunt, he had walked over to his desk and picked up the receiver to answer its strident ringing, spoiling for a fight with someone—anyone.

An unfamiliar, deep-voiced woman had rasped at him over the line. "Dr. Sommers?" it had asked. "Esther Groundly here. Real estate. . . ."

"The island is not for sale," Sommers had snapped at her.

Miss Groundly wanted to laugh. No one in the world would want to buy that falling-down heap of wood; anybody in their right minds would know that.

"I'm not calling about the island, Doctor. What I wanted to know is whether you're familiar with a girl named Meg Kendricks. She has another name, too, but just now I can't remember what it is. Anyway, this girl came and saw me last week sometime. I was wondering if she were a patient or what. See, she said she was just visiting The Home to be near her mother, but she was so incredibly vague and mixed up about what she wanted in the way of a house, I wondered if maybe she wasn't a patient rather than a visitor."

"No, she's only visiting." Sommers's answer was so automatically honest, the doctor wondered why he'd given it. In his mind he didn't think of Meg as a visitor but as one of his family. The doctor cleared his throat, about to expand his answer, but the deep-voiced Miss Groundly was already rattling her basso at him again.

"What confuses me, Doctor, is that just a little while ago I got a phone call from a young man named Tighe Devlin. Said he was Miss Kendricks's husband and that they wanted to see some houses—quite large houses— down toward Key West, but not in it. Big enough for the two of them, the girl's mother, and a housekeeper/ practical nurse they are going to hire. I gather they're in a great hurry."

There was a pause as Miss Groundly took a deep breath. "Oh, yes, the girl's pregnant. At least, she said that's what the doctor had told her. So the house would have to be even bigger than she'd originally asked and would have an additional room that could be used as a nursery. Now, as you know, Doctor, Key West is a good way from here—I don't want to waste time chasing phantom sales—but they're apparently moving that far because it seems the girl's mother is ill and needs some sort of special, expert treatment they can only get for her in Key West. Never did explain what she was sick with. In any case I wondered if Mr. Devlin was just visiting, too, or is *he* a patient?"

For some moments there was no answer from Sommers. It took so long, in fact, that a baffled Miss Groundly had to repeat "Dr. Sommers? Dr. Sommers?" several times, not sure at first whether he was still there.

If she could have seen Sommers's face, she would have known he was very much still there, a livid crimson flushing his features. He was so angry he had come very close to hanging up on her without another word, but although trembling with rage, he had struggled and finally brought himself under control. A sharp crack made him look down at his hands; the pen he had been holding—like the pipe he had destroyed the other day— had been brutally broken in two. Sommers heard himself swear, muttering some highly impolite things, and heard Miss Groundly gasp at the language. Again, he struggled to gain control.

With a good deal of effort Sommers was finally able to produce the semblance of a friendly laugh; it was, Sommers decided, distinctly forced-sounding, but passable. "You'll have to forgive me, Miss Groundly, but I just broke my new pen—paid quite a lot for it, too—and the damned thing fell apart in my hands, just like that. Probably Japanese. All you have to do is take a good look at something the Japanese make and it comes apart in your hands. Getting back at us, I guess." The forced laugh again.

"Oh, yes," Sommers said good-naturedly, trying to sound very casual about it, "we were talking about the Devlins. No, Tighe Devlin is just a visitor to The Home, too. Came down to help his new wife—that's Miss Kendricks, or *was* Miss Kendricks—find a house for themselves and her mother."

Sommers could feel the sweat gathering beneath his arms threatening to run down his body. It was impossible. Meg, her mother, and, now—a baby. Tighe's hot semen had been hurled up inside her and was conspiring to produce a baby. Unfair, foul, disgusting. Already planning to run out on him. Unfair, unfair. . . .

But it mustn't be allowed to show, damn it. Tightening his jaw, Sommers was finally even able to add: "I hope you can find a nice home for them. They're a delightful young couple, and Mrs. Kendricks—the girl's mother—is one of my special favorites here. I'll be sorry to see both she and her daughter go. . . ." Somewhere in the middle of this new lie, Sommers's voice had cracked, and he had had to cough to cover his emotions.

He and Miss Groundly chatted for another couple of minutes with Dr. Sommers almost having to become rude to get her off the line. He signed off after a vacuous comment of some sort which, seconds later, he couldn't even remember himself.

The moment he'd hung up, Sommers's fist began beating the desk in fury again, his eyes staring angrily into space. A few seconds later Sommers buried his head in his hands, the fist still pummeling the desk top in a tattoo of naked rage. All his worst fears were beginning to take shape. Not only Meg, but her mother were planning to leave him flat. Desert him. Abandon him. The way everybody—even his pets—always did.

He turned toward the bookcases and opened the front, hoping to draw solace, as he so often had, from its hallowed contents. That's when the objects in the shadow box began taunting him, and Sommers burned the Polaroid he'd taken of Meg. Then the picture of Meg in its ornate, oval frame stared out at him, her warm wonderful smile looking at something beyond his shoulder that he would never see. One hand stretched forward and snatched it off the wall; it deserved to be destroyed, as Tighe's and her other, earlier picture had been. Something stopped his hand. He was too fond of Meg—she was his surrogate daughter, after all—to destroy both of her pictures. Hanging it back in its place on the velvet rear wall, he looked at it again, already regretting having burned the other one.

He sat down behind his desk heavily, cursing the unfairness of the world. Out his window he saw Tighe appear, looking around him like a thief, slipping down the flight of stone stairs, pressed tight against the building. Little bastard. For a second Sommers was confused, unable to figure out where the degenerate prick could be sneaking out to. Thinking no one could see him, at that. *Stupid* little bastard.

The echoing, gravely basso of Miss Groundly suddenly trumpeted in his memory, coming back unannounced and unwanted. The thin, hot wire probed the inside of his brain again. Tighe was slipping off to meet Miss Groundly, trying to sneak away unseen to get crazy Miss Groundly to show him houses to buy. Later, he would take his too-long eyelashes and lithe young body and drag Meg away with him.

Resentment swept over him in waves of anger. The doctor stared at Meg's picture again. Damn it, he *should* burn it; the shadow box was right. But he couldn't bring himself to. Squirming, he stood in front of the shadow box, loathing himself for the weakness that stopped him from destroying Meg's picture.

It was difficult to believe that earlier in his life Sommers had been a topflight psychiatrist in one of the most sophisticated psychiatric clinics in the country. The objectivity had dissolved; he could see very little of the ambivalence he felt toward Meg. Part of him was desperate to love her and protect her and keep her here with him forever; part of him wanted to destroy her for having married Tighe and—Jesus God—getting pregnant. Sommers beat his fist against the wall as he had earlier beaten the desk top. He hoped Tighe would give her the clap or genital herpes or something dreadful like that. In spite of his fury, the thought of Tighe with open, running sores made him smile. Abruptly, the smile vanished.

Mad at himself again, Sommers slammed the doors to the shadow box shut. The part of him that loved Meg had triumphed—for the moment. Tighe he could destroy without qualm; all of his trouble with Meg began and ended with Tighe—Tighe of the rich family in Philly and the warm, phony smile and the festering, running sores.

If Meg was still insistent on taking her mother and leaving The Home after Tighe had been sliced into ten thousand bloody pieces, Meg, too, he knew, would have to be destroyed. Oh Jesus, he prayed it didn't come down to that.

Sommers was surprised to find that he was crying.

Chapter Seventeen

Pregnancy. Usually a time of incandescent happiness for everybody. In books you read of "the glow of expectant motherhood"; friends hold baby showers; strangers look at the prescient bulge and smile with nostalgic warmth.

In the case of Meg's pregnancy, however, I think of it more as an infection. Her body violated by foreign germs, thrust inside her by a malevolent agent—Tighe Devlin. An injection of Tighe-sperm already invading her cellular structure and producing a malignant growth: the baby.

I have noticed no expectant glow; only a slight pallor. Inside her, the malignant growth is expanding in geometric leaps and bounds. Arms and feet being formed; the first vestiges of a brain taking shape; the fish-gills discarded in favor of embryonic lungs. Soon the growth will be expelled into a world where no one will really want it.

There will be no baby showers, no warm smiles from strangers. Only the bitter cries of an infant born with no father.

And if Meg doesn't play ball, no mother, either— not for long.

> *Psychiatric & Personal Observations,*
> *The Home, Alan Sommers, M.D., Director.*

"I'm almost finished. Christ, but it's hard. This crazy little pump isn't worth a damn."

Meg giggled. "I've always liked your little pump. It's sweet."

Tighe raised his head to stare at her, beginning to laugh himself. "Beats me how a place like Little Goat could turn out such a foul-minded woman. Sometimes I think—Hey!" Tighe suddenly shouted. "Damn it, Meg, you're not pressing hard enough on the valve; we're losing more air than we're getting."

Meg and Tighe were on the far side of the island, well away from The Home and Sommers. "I don't think the good doctor would like us having our own way of getting around—to the mainland, for instance," Meg had explained, insisting that Tighe hide the boat far enough away from The Home so that it would not be easily found.

Tighe was manning the pump that was slowly inflating the small rubber boat—a bright blue plastic one trimmed in red—while Meg held the air nozzle to the intake valve on the boat itself. Inflating it was nowhere near as easy as the salesman in Marathon had promised it would be. Tighe cursed and ranted, only making Meg giggle all the harder.

Finally, it was done, and Tighe stood back to look at the little rubber boat, as proud of it as if it were the *Rittenhouse*. "You know," he said, patting the bow affectionately, "it's not bad at all." He grunted and began fastening the small outboard onto the boat's stern, and again stood back to study his boat with pride. Grinning shyly, he turned to Meg. "Can't wait to try her out. Maybe . . . maybe"—the grin broadened in delight—"maybe I'll get a chance to try her out this afternoon when I get back from looking at houses with that weird Groundly woman. Even a little bit of snorkling, too. I should be back soon enough if I can keep the lady's sales spiel from getting out of hand." Tighe's face glowed with anticipation. "God damn. Awesome."

Meg couldn't help but laugh. Tighe was like a little boy dying to try out a new toy. She felt a shudder of love seize and shake her. "Time to hide the *Titanic*," said Tighe, suddenly serious, his brow furrowed, a conspiratorial gleam in his eyes. Together, they pulled the *Titantic* back into the shrubbery, covering it with small branches.

Abruptly, Tighe spun toward Meg. "Christ, I hope I get back in time to give it a whirl this afternoon."

Without warning, Meg suddenly grabbed him and threw her arms around him. There was something irresistibly winning about a normally sophisticated man transmogrified into an excited child by something as inconsequential as a rubber boat.

On their way back to The Home a sharp twinge of sadness shot through Meg as Tighe chattered on about how easily he would handle Miss Groundly today. Originally, Meg had planned to go with him on the house hunt and had looked forward to the excitement of picking their first home together. But then she had suddenly remembered this afternoon was when the doctor in Marathon had said he'd call her with the results of the tests; both Meg and the doctor were pretty certain the tests would confirm what they themselves were already sure of: that Meg was pregnant. This was a call Meg wouldn't miss for the world. At first Tighe had been a little difficult about her not going; so far, Meg hadn't told Tighe anything at all about the baby. First she wanted to be absolutely sure.

"I wish I could go with you, Tighe," Meg again told him. "But if we both start ducking out of here at the same time, Mother will guess something is up. And I can't tell her yet about the house. I don't dare to; she might blurt it out to Dr. Sommers."

Tighe stopped walking and looked at Meg curiously, always baffled by her odd reaction to the doctor. Starting to walk forward again, Tighe shook his head in bewilderment. Both Meg and her mother were always so confusing about Sommers. As if he were an evil madman of some sort. Sommers was a little strange, Tighe would admit, but he'd never seen a trace of madness or evil in the man. Shrugging, he put the whole thing out of his mind.

A little later—about eleven—Tighe was ready to go. In honor of Miss Groundly he was wearing a tie and jacket. "I should be back here by two thirty or three," he assured Meg. "I don't care how many houses old Groundly has on her list; more time than that in one session and I'll be ready to flip out."

Meg walked across their bedroom and folded him into an embrace. God, she loved him—and told him so. "If you don't stop that, Meg," he pointed out, "I'll throw you into the sack and never get to see Miss Groundly at all."

Down on the landing dock Meg kissed Tighe again and watched him climb into the rickety tramcar. "I still wish you were coming with me," he called to her, and then closed the door, reached forward, and pushed the button that sent the tramcar creaking and groaning toward the mainland and Miss Groundly. Meg watched him until he was so far from the island she could barely see him through the ever-present fog. She hated to have Tighe leave her—even for a brief separation like this one—but took comfort in the realization that with every hour Tighe spent looking at what Miss Groundly had to offer the long-dreamed-of house for her mother came a little closer to becoming fact. Along with her own and Tighe's release from this dreadful place. With a final wave at the eyeless fog, Meg turned and slowly walked up the uneven stone steps toward The Home.

*   *   *

Not very successfully, Meg was trying to kill time. Until the doctor called. Until Tighe got back. She and her mother were sitting on the terrace behind The Home, her mother stretched out on one of the chaises, Meg sitting on the foot of the one beside it, too keyed up to lie down. Chattering away, she heard herself bring up a subject with her mother she hadn't planned to.

"You know, Mom, I'm a little worried about Mrs. Belagio. She was a nice lady, and, I guess, your best friend here. . . ."

"My *only* friend here," her mother corrected. "The rest are sick in the head."

Meg wanted to laugh. Nice lady or not, Mrs. Belagio—and her hundreds of thousands of dollars of costume jewelry—was as sick in the head as any of them.

"Anyway," Meg continued, "there's something wrong about how Dr. Sommers explains her leaving." Meg studied her mother; she wasn't reacting at all.

"Mmmfph," was the most her mother could manage, sounding very sleepy and distant.

"You know, she asked me—she said she'd asked you the same thing—to come looking for her if she should disappear suddenly. First, down in the cells, she said. Then, if I still couldn't find her, to go get the police."

Another "mmmfph" was her mother's only reaction. Meg found herself unable to stop, driven to keep a conversation she'd never intended to start going. The logical part of her brain demanded an answer; it verged on compulsion.

"I'd do it myself, Mom, but I don't know the setup down there at all. See, the only time I was ever in that area was the day Dr. Sommers took me on his damned tour. I saw the cells, and I saw his outer workroom, but I never saw what was behind the door to the preparation room. He got very upset when I asked and warned me never to go in there. If Mrs. Belagio isn't in one of the cells, she may be in that room. After all, we have only Sommers's word that it's his preparation room."

Yet another "mmmfph." Meg was stymied; the total lack of response was bewildering.

Suddenly, from her mother: "I know that crazy place down there," she volunteered. Meg turned to look at her in surprise but couldn't get a single word more out of her. In defeat Meg threw up her hands, lay back in her chaise, and studied the cloudless sky.

Her mother, eyes still closed, face steeped in impassivity, had ample reason not to tell Meg anything further. She *did* know the whole area—quite well, actually—and now that Meg had fortified her own fears about Mrs. Belagio, she had decided that this afternoon she'd do a little searching on her own. Mrs. Belagio had been her only real friend at The Home.

She didn't know why, but at the moment she was deep into one of her spells of not trusting Dr. Sommers at all. It was hard to believe he would hurt Bea—Mrs. Belagio—but you could never tell what a man you didn't trust might take it into his head to do.

She ought to take Meg with her, she knew, but for reasons she couldn't understand, she felt this was something she had to do completely on her own.

Carefully, she began planning her search for this afternoon. The idea frightened her, but she owed Bea that much. Old ladies, she told herself, had to stick together.

By the time the rest of the patients were at lunch, one of them was already missing from her usual place. No one seemed to notice. Mrs. Tibald's cell in the basement stood empty, its barred door swinging wide, the interior of her stark cell glaring malevolently into the bare main room outside the other cells. For once, the wild-eyed Mrs. Tibald was neither screaming nor cursing. She couldn't; the gag Sommers had crammed into her mouth and tied behind her head reduced her to a violent moaning and muttering. Wildly, she thrashed and struggled against the restraints of the straitjacket in which the doctor had tied her. The effort did her little good. By a combination of dragging and shoving, Sommers led her out through the back door and down the twisting rear path that ran toward the landing dock for the tramway. Sommers had chosen this circuitous route because, with the exception of the last few feet of open ground, it was not visible to prying eyes peering out of some window in The Home.

Twisting suddenly away from Sommers, Mrs. Tibald yanked herself free of his hold and threw herself flat on the earth. Abruptly, she began trying to rub the gag out of her mouth by pulling her face across the dirt. Fascinated, Sommers stood and watched. Finally, the gag was torn free, and Mrs. Tibald was able to scream. Only she didn't. With a sudden snarling sound, she began eating the loose dirt beneath her face, making strange satisfied moans. Sommers shook his head, reached down, and flipped her over on her back.

"You're a real nut-case fruitcake," he said to her, sitting on her chest and stuffing the gag back inside her mouth. "And fruitcakes call for full fruitcake treatment." He laughed his dry, menacing laugh and pulled a length of leather thong from his pocket, wrapping it around and around her face where the gag was and tying it tightly. "There," Sommers said with a satisfied smile. "This time the damned thing will stay put."

Roughly, he yanked Mrs. Tibald to her feet and started her down the path again, holding her back when they reached the edge of the clearing. Even on tiptoe he could see no one at any of the windows, and he suddenly dragged Mrs. Tibald across the short, open distance to the tramcar. Inside the car he slammed the door behind him and shoved Mrs. Tibald to the middle. Her eyes, always rolling wildly, were more insane-looking than usual; she stared at him with a mixture of loathing and viciousness. Dr. Sommers suddenly hit her behind the legs, causing her to fall to her knees—as if praying to the God of Madness. As she began struggling, trying to get back on her feet, Sommers gave the back of her head a vicious blow with his hand, forcing her face down hard against the seat of the wooden bench that ran across the rear of the tramcar. Quickly, still holding her head down against the seat, Sommers attached a strange wire device to the leather straps which held the straitjacket around her body. Leaning out the tramway door, he hooked the wire onto a loop that hung down from the cable supporting the tramcar when in motion. With a sharp, brutal yank, Dr. Sommers pulled her face off the bench, then doubled her up slightly and shoved her under the deep, wide seat of the bench. The same wire device that he had fastened to the leather straps was now attached to a sort of cagelike door he put in place across the open front side below the bench. Trussed up by the straitjacket and unable to shift even her legs because of the gate, Mrs. Tibald was incapable of moving any part of herself. Before he shut the cage on her, Sommers brandished a razor-sharp meat cleaver in front of her raging, raving eyes, smiling encouragingly as he did. Calmly, he shoved the cleaver beneath Mrs. Tibald's motionless body.

"Old girl," he said with a satisfied laugh, "you're always screaming at me about how all men are out to rape you. Fat chance." Briefly, Sommers pulled the cleaver out from under Mrs. Tibald again, moving its razor-sharp edge back and forth so that the sun glinted off its gleaming chromium blade. Mrs. Tibald's eyes widened; her breathing grew labored from the excitement coursing through her.

"Well," Sommers continued calmly, "you're about to meet a man who really plans to. He told me so. 'I'm going to rape nutty old Mrs. Tibald,' he said. He'll be climbing into this car in—well, maybe half an hour or so. Name of Tighe. The wire I hooked onto your straitjacket will let you loose from the jacket and let the gate across the bottom of the seat fall open when you're riding across in the tramcar with him.

"That's your chance, Mrs. T. . . . your revenge . . . your opportunity to settle up scores with all the filthy men in this world who want to defile your body. Tighe may not make a pass at you right away—he's a devious bastard—but with you loose and with that meat cleaver in your hand, well, you know how to prevent it from happening to *you*. *Whack! Whack!* and you'll have rid the world of one admitted rapist."

Sommers knew from the fevered expression on Mrs. Tibald's face that his planting of the problem and his suggestion of how she could be the solution had struck home. Quickly, he shoved the cleaver back beneath her and put the gate in position beneath the set, forming a cage that would not open until the wire was pulled—by him. "Just lie where you are quietly, Mrs. T.; the less noise you make, the better." Sommers grinned at her through the grillwork of the cage door. "And don't ever say I never did anything for you."

For a moment or two Sommers listened to the groans of rage coming from Mrs. Tibald. He patted the front of the cage affectionately, speaking soothingly to Mrs. T. as he did. She was, after all, his agent in what was coming. Eventually, Tighe would return from his house-hunting with Miss Groundly. When he was riding in the swaying tramcar, far out over the water where there was no escape and no way back, he would discover he had an interesting traveling companion. The small, thin wire would be pulled. The leather straps which fastened the straightjacket around Mrs. Tibald would fall away, the door across the bottom of the seat fly open. A crazed Mrs. Tibald would suddenly emerge, meat cleaver in hand, ready to take terminal action against a man who admittedly planned to rape her, a man who deserved extinction in the name of women everywhere.

Calmly, Dr. Alan Sommers stepped out of the tramcar, locking its door securely with the large chromium handle on the car's outside. Whistling softly, Sommers sauntered back to his office, face wreathed in a satisfied smile. Perfect planning, he confessed to himself as he sank into the chair behind his desk.

Suddenly, he stood up again and opened the doors of the bookcase to study the objects in the shadow box. "Soon," he promised them in a whisper, "soon, it will be all right again." The objects stared back at him in whispering agreement; his father's ear rose to the top of its colorless liquid, then slowly sank back down, nodding its approval. Only Meg's picture appeared to disagree, frowning at him darkly from its frame.

"Please don't," the picture pled in a soft whisper. "*Please.* . . ."

Sommers ignored it, compulsively glancing at his watch. "See?" he pointed out to the objects in the shadow box, holding the watch close to them. "Do you see?

"Maybe in an hour, maybe even less.

"End of Tighe.

"Sad thing for Meg, happy thing for me. Saddest of *all* things for Tighe, I suppose."

But, he added to himself, it couldn't happen to a more deserving guy.

Chapter Eighteen

Long ago, when I was in residency, I learned quite a lot about my childhood from my analysis. (All analysts, you know, are required to undergo analysis themselves.)

A lot of things about childhood I remembered before the analysis; the whole sorry story of my sister didn't come back to me, though, until the doctor went to work on me.

When I was about eight, my sister was my best friend. Even though she was sixteen, we did everything together. And I didn't really think it too strange when she began playing around with my thing, manipulating it and getting me all excited every night when I was having my bath.

Little by little she moved the activity out of the tub and into her bedroom. I could respond but at that age couldn't do anything much more.

It got pretty wild over that year, and pretty soon she wasn't just my best friend, she was really also my lover. I guess she was a pretty sick girl to be doing that kind of stuff with an eight-year-old. Me? Hell, I was only a little boy.

When my father caught us one night—both of us naked, me with an erection and she having an or-

gasm she was producing with one of my hands—he just about blew the house down. She was sent somewhere—a sanitarium of some kind—and I was experiencing my first case of someone's walking out on me. At least, that was the way I looked at it. A year later she died of pneumonia, and I really felt abandoned.

I've never counted on anybody since. And I've been right.

> Psychiatric & Personal Observations,
> The Home, Alan Sommers, M.D., Director.

A little after lunch Meg finally received the call she had been waiting for all day. "The test is positive, Mrs. Devlin," the doctor said. "Congratulations."

Meg gave a whoop of joy. "How long?" she asked, doing her best to control the surge of ecstasy that was rippling through her whole body and made rational speech difficult.

"Oh, I'd say you're a little over two months into the pregnancy. That would make it in a little less than seven months—provided everything goes according to schedule. You're an extremely healthy young woman, so I can see no reason it shouldn't."

"Seven months. . . ." Meg repeated with wonder, still unable to quite accept what was happening. Suddenly, all of the facts broke over her in a great wave, and Meg shrieked with sheer delight. She could hear the doctor laughing on the other end of the phone. "I'm sorry," Meg apologized, "but, well . . ."

"Nothing to be sorry about. A first pregnancy is always one of a woman's most exciting moments. A whole new world. . . ."

A few minutes later, when Meg hung up after a handful of instructions from the doctor, she was sur-

prised—although not really startled—to discover she
was trembling with excitement. It took four tries just to
get the receiver back on its hook. She couldn't wait to
tell Tighe; the idea of a son—she was sure it was going
to be a boy—would leave him happily dumbstruck.
She hadn't told him anything yet, or her mother either.
But now the compulsion to tell someone was burning
hot inside her.

Walking down the hall toward her room, she decided
to tell her mother, but discovered she wasn't in her
room. A cursory look downstairs failed to uncover her
either. Out in the sun somewhere, she supposed. Why
was no one ever around when you had something wonderful to tell them, and always right there when you had
nothing but bad news to report?

Maybe she was out on the terrace. Meg looked, but
her mother wasn't there either. Damn. Slowly, Meg
climbed the stairs to tell the news to the four walls of
her room.

If Meg had known where her mother actually was, her
happiness would have abruptly dissolved. Mrs. Kendricks
wasn't too happy herself; the basement rooms always
gave her the willies. But she, like Meg, had promised
Mrs. Belagio to check out the cells, and if she still
couldn't find her, to go get the police. Mrs. Kendricks,
walking softly around the bare brick and concrete halls
of the cellar rooms, wondered if it might not have been
better had she reversed the process: gotten the police,
then checked out the cells.

Noiselessly, she opened the door to the room where
the cells were. For some reason it always smelled in
there, probably, she suspected, because the poor catatonic was incontinent. He, she could see, was in his
cell, fixed by someone with his legs wide apart, his
hands similarly reaching out over his head, like the

anatomical portrait of Man by Michelangelo. Poor, poor man, Mrs. Kendricks whispered to herself; why didn't someone come and put him in a more comfortable position?

Her eyes moved two cells to the left, from which Mrs. Tibald usually glowered at the world through the bars of her cage. The cell was empty, its barred door yawning wide out into the bare, cement-floored outer room. Possibly, Dr. Sommers had her upstairs, giving her electroshock or something. Mrs. Kendricks shuddered thinking about it. The things which doctors had to do in the name of medicine were sometimes too terrifying even to think about.

Well, one thing was ruled out: Mrs. Belagio—Bea—was not in any of the cells, which her friend had been so fearful of. Mrs. Kendricks didn't believe Dr. Sommers would do anything to Bea, but she'd made Bea a promise to search for her if she suddenly disappeared, and to Mrs. Kendricks a promise was a sacred oath.

Outside the room with the cells, Mrs. Kendricks stood, wondering where to look next. Down the hall she could see the door to Dr. Sommers's workrooms. An improbable place for Bea to be kept—although the thought of Bea's being kept anywhere against her will was improbable in itself. But her promise to Bea bound her to search those rooms, too, she decided. The idea unnerved her. She had been in the room before at Dr. Sommers's invitation, and the clinical aspects of the place—parts of stuffed animals on the table, the shelves around the walls of the room jammed with other, completed stuffed animals—always upset her. Cautiously—she shouldn't be in this part of The Home and knew it—Mrs. Kendricks tried the door, secretly hoping it would turn out to be locked. No luck. The handle turned, and she was able to walk in.

The only light in the room came from two small windows set high in the cement of the wall to her left, which admitted only enough light to make the room more forbidding. There had to be a light switch somewhere, but she couldn't find it. The stuffed animals glowered at her from the shelves, their glass eyes burning into her as if resenting this intrusion into their privacy, staring at her with dark malevolence. Mrs. Kendricks shuddered again; if Bea hadn't been such a close friend of hers . . .

No sign of Bea Belagio in the room, anywhere. The promise she'd made to Bea came back to haunt her, stopping her from the headlong flight out of the room she longed to make. Her eyes fell on the inner door to the preparation room. The doctor—as he had also told Meg—had told Mrs. Kendricks that it was a door she was never under any circumstances to open. To keep her promise to Bea, Mrs. Kendricks decided it was her duty to look in that room, too—regardless of Sommers's warning. Damn the promise to Bea, she told herself, and started to leave the outer room for the relative safety of the hall outside. Mrs. Belagio's voice came to her as if from a great distance, reminding her of what she had promised her, and Mrs. Kendricks stopped in her tracks, halted by the familiar voice echoing through her head. A promise was a promise, and she owed it to Bea to keep her end of the bargain. Oh Christ, oh Christ. . . .

For almost half an hour now Meg had been sitting on the end of the landing dock shading her eyes against the sun with her hand while she tried to make out Tighe's familiar stride as he headed for the tramcar, which was waiting at the mainland landing dock. Every now and then a shudder of happiness would pass through her as she thought of how Tighe was going to react to her news: pregnant, a boy—a miniature clone of Tighe—being built inside her. Would Tighe want it named Tighe Dexter Devlin IV? Meg hoped so; there was something so wonderfully permanent-sounding in a name like that. She squirmed on the hard planking of the landing dock, unable to sit still very long because of her excitement.

Finally, Meg saw him walking along the edge of the water, his long, purposeful strides bringing him ever closer to the tramcar and his return to Meg. Meg jumped to her feet and began waving as hard as she could, jumping up and down, hoping he would see her and know she was waiting for him. The intensity of her thoughts must have reached across the water in a surge of telepathy; he suddenly turned in her direction and began waving back excitedly.

Tighe had his own good news to tell Meg. On their very first day Miss Groundly had shown him a house in Saddlebunch Key, right on the water, and only a little over ten miles from Key West. The house was modern, a tremendous expanse of glass bringing the whole breathtaking view into the house. Even better, there was a semidetached wing where Mrs. Kendricks and the housekeeper/practical nurse could live almost as a separate unit. Perfect.

His father's training kept Tighe from displaying too much enthusiasm. ("Stay cool," his father had once said. "Show interest, and up goes the price.") In spite of himself Tighe was haunted by the fear all people about to buy a house suffer: inevitably, the agent tells them they'll have to make up their minds quickly because, you see, there's this other couple who've already been to see it twice, and . . . Potential buyers always bit; Tighe was no exception.

With a final grinning wave to Meg, Tighe threw back the heavy chromium handle locking the tramcar from the outside and climbed in. It struck him as strange that anyone would bother to lock the car that way, but maybe it was something that happened automatically when the car began to move. Whistling, impatient to give Meg his good news and unaware that she had her own news to tell *him,* Tighe pressed the button in the front of the car and felt the sudden lurch as the battered tramcar began its trip across the water to The Home—and Meg. God, he was happy.

Dr. Sommers was happy, too. He stood beside The Home, not hiding exactly, but partially concealed from prying eyes by the bulk of the building. In his hand he held the thin, taut wire that was attached to the tramcar—and Mrs. Tibald. Sommers quivered in anticipation.

There would shortly be no reason for Meg to ever leave The Home.

Chapter Nineteen

It was a real hoot watching old Mrs. Tibald roll around on the ground eating dirt. In the last few years the old bat's slipped over the edge completely. I should tell myself how much that depresses me, but I'm afraid it amuses more than saddens me.

Originally, her problems were pretty simple: the fear of being raped. That happened because she got married when she was too young and too innocent.

Her first sexual experiences were with her husband, and even intercourse with him she regarded as rape. (Her bridegroom didn't help; apparently, he was a brutal and insensitive man, whose head-on approach to sex was so rough the loss of her virginity was an agonizingly painful experience.)

As time moved on, Mrs. Tibald lapsed deeper into madness; Mrs. Tibald convinced herself that all men were trying to rape her. Like her husband had.

From there, Mrs. Tibald sank further into generalized paranoia. Which is where she is today.

*Her reaction to Tighe the rapist should be an inter-
esting thing to watch. That shiny chromium meat
cleaver has fascinating possibilities as a weapon.*

*Poor batty Mrs. Tibald. As nuts as Evelyn Kendricks
is sane.*

*Psychiatric & Personal Observations,
The Home, Alan Sommers, M.D., Director.*

Nervous, trembling a little, upset to be flying directly in the face of Dr. Sommers's specific dictates,
Meg's mother slipped uncomfortably into the room forbidden her. The place smelled terrible, a sweet, sickening smell that made Mrs. Kendricks almost gag; Dr.
Sommers had warned her of this when telling her she
must never come in here. "It's the damned solution in
the curing vat. Stinks like hell," he'd explained. "Little
half-rotten flesh lying around, too. That's the room
where I cut up the animals before I cure them, you see.
There are a lot of other reasons, too, which I can't go
into now. Just don't ever set foot in there, understand?"

Mrs. Kendricks understood the command, but the
reasons behind it escaped her. Looking around now,
she kept hearing Sommers's petulant warning voice as
she studied objects in different parts of the room. In
one corner she saw a large, waist-high leaden tank. The
light was meager, but as her eyes grew accustomed to
the semidarkness, she could see down through a partly
opaque, foul-smelling solution of some kind. The curing
vat. Animal parts swam into view, tied some distance
below the surface on what looked like shish kebab
spears. Bits of hair and fur and shredded strips of flesh
skewered on spears seemed to be struggling to get to
the surface; occasionally, a bubble of air would burst
from one of the animals and escape upwards, making an
almost live-sounding *baloop* when it exploded through

the liquid at the top. Meg's mother felt her stomach turn and hurried away from the vat to see what was in the other parts of the room.

Looking further, she saw the dim shapes of completed stuffed animals peering down at her from the shelving on one side of the room, their expressions bristling and unfriendly, their plastic eyes picking up little glints of light from the high, barred windows which, as in the antechamber, provided the only light. The trembling inside Mrs. Kendricks grew; the room was steeped in hostility.

Shuddering, Mrs. Kendricks walked over to the far wall, as stark and bare as the concrete it was made of. Just above her hung three large stuffed heads mounted on wooden plaques. For some reason, one of these was completely shrouded beneath heavy cloth. Below each head was a card hand-lettered by Dr. Sommers describing genus and species. Slowly, she moved down the line of heads.

The first was a large deer head, mouth open, head and neck thrown back in pain, as if the deer had just been pierced by a hollow-nosed bullet. Next to this, its card describing it as a dune wolf and providing the Latinized species category, was the head of an unfamiliar but ferocious-looking animal, posed with jaws open and lips pulled back, its teeth bared, as if the wolf were about to leap off the wall and tear her to pieces. The excellence of the taxidermy and the realism of the pose made Meg's mother shudder violently.

Moving down to the last head—the one concealed by the shroud—Mrs. Kendricks read the card beneath it. "Ultimate Stuffed Specimen." There was no other identification of the animal on the card; Meg's mother found both the shroud and the card mysterious. Glancing behind herself, feeling guilty for what she was going to do, Mrs. Kendricks pulled at the shroud. For a moment the shroud would not move; then, suddenly, it responded to her tugging and fell to the floor.

Her breath left her; she could hear her heart exploding against her breastbone; her breathing was suddenly a gasping wheeze of horror and disbelief. Mounted on a wooden plaque identical to the others was the head of a woman, her mouth open, her face twisted out of shape by some unseen agony.

It was Mrs. Belagio.

Meg's mother felt the room spinning around her and grabbed the wall to steady herself. In her head there was a sudden, piercingly sharp pain. Her eyes went out of focus, and she felt the floor begin to shift beneath her feet. Desperately, she wanted to scream, but found that, for some reason, her mouth would no longer work; she could produce no sound of any kind. Before she realized what was happening, Mrs. Kendricks fainted, crumpling to the floor, unconscious.

She had kept her promise; Mrs. Kendricks had searched until she found Bea Belagio.

With one final, cheerful wave to Meg, waiting at the landing dock on the island, Tighe Dexter Devlin III stepped happily into the tramcar still sitting on the mainland dock. There was a wide, happy smile on his face. With reason, he told himself. Wait till Meg heard that he'd found the absolutely perfect house—and one right on the water.

Still smiling, Tighe pulled the door of the tramcar shut behind him. There was a sudden *thunk;* the automatic lock on the car's outside had fallen into place. Damn, he thought, what a crazy setup; with the lock closed from the outside, he was now imprisoned inside. Thank God Meg was waiting for him on the other end; otherwise, he could wind up having to spend the night in the tramcar. Damned uncomfortable. The thought made him smile.

With a shrug he leaned forward and pressed the start button; immediately, he felt the car lurch forward and up, in response. Remaining at the front of the tramcar, Tighe shaded his eyes with both hands and tried to see if Meg was still waiting for him on the island's landing dock.

There was the usual fog that always seemed to swirl over the water between the mainland and the island, but nonetheless, he could still see her—barely—sitting on the dock, waiting for him. He waved, but what with the fog and the dirty window between them, he doubted if she could see him.

Unlike Meg, Tighe genuinely enjoyed these aerial trips across Matecumbe Gut. Today, though, he kept hearing strange moans and thumps as the car moved along the cable swinging from side to side. The wind hadn't appeared to be that strong on the mainland, but it had to be blowing like hell to make so much noise in the tramcar. Dimly, Tighe saw Meg stand up as someone else—the filthy windows made it impossible for him to recognize who—walked out on the dock to join her. Sommers? Ernie? One of the patients? Tighe couldn't tell.

About halfway across, a sudden noise spun Tighe around. A strange, thin wire he had not noticed until now, running along the ceiling and down to the deep wooden seat behind him, had suddenly gone taut, then snapped with a sharp crack like a whip's. Mystified, Tighe saw the grating below the seat fall open like an out-of-control drawbridge across a castle moat. From under the seat Tighe was stunned to see a wild-eyed woman, her hair falling down over her face, her upper body wearing some sort of white canvas jacket which was beginning to fall off her, suddenly crawl out and stagger unsteadily to her feet. She ripped a gag out of her mouth, threw back her head, and began screaming wildly at the ceiling. It had to be one of the patients, he told himself, nervously edging as far away from her as he could get. The tramcar struck him as a very odd place for one of the patients to be.

Then Tighe saw it. Clutched tightly in her hand was a wicked-looking meat cleaver of some sort, the late-afternoon sun glinting ominously off its chromium blade. For an instant the screaming stopped. The woman's rolling eyes fastened on him with a venomous look. "Rapist," she hissed at him, a thin line of spit running from one corner of her mouth and falling lazily to the floor. "Flesh-eater," the woman added, her eyes burning into him.

"Look," Tighe began. "You've got me mixed up with somebody else. I've never seen you before. I've never raped anybody. I don't understand what—"

"The doctor *told* me you were a devious bastard," the woman said in her ugly, whispering voice, each sibilance accompanied by the running of more saliva from the corner of her mouth.

"Look," Tighe began again. He never got to finish. Before he could even brace himself, the wild-eyed woman gave an unearthly shriek and threw herself at him, the meat cleaver spinning viciously above her head.

Helplessly, Tighe threw both arms up in front of his face. He was young; the lady was not. He was strong; she looked emaciated. If he could just knock the cleaver out of her hands. . . . But the wild-eyed woman had the advantage of surprise and the savage potency of that damned weapon. He felt the cleaver sink into one of his upraised arms and screamed in pain. Tighe clutched the arm in his hand, startled at the amount of blood that was spurting from the wound. The cleaver was an intimidating weapon; Tighe knew he had to get it away from her if he was to survive.

Watching the woman warily, Tighe sidestepped her next lunge. With all his strength, he seized her wrist and twisted it until the woman gave a high-pitched anguished squeal and dropped the cleaver to the floor. Tighe felt her fingernails ripping his face and trying to get at his eyes. She screamed, she shrieked, she tore at him savagely. Tighe countered as best he could, but the arm she had damaged with the cleaver was no longer working, hanging limp to one side.

They swayed back and forth, making the tramcar lurch from one side to the other, the cables that supported it groaning in warning. Desperate, Tighe clutched her in a bear hug, forcing her arms to her side. "Rape! Rape!" the woman screamed. Suddenly, the hug was broken. Tighe yelled again in pain. The woman had leaned forward and bitten him on his face in two different places. More blood spurted from him. The wild-eyed woman gave an unearthly laugh and dove to the floor to retrieve the cleaver. Tighe dove, too, and they rolled on the floor, each one trying to get their hands on the savage weapon. She'd seen how much pain her bites caused Tighe; now the woman continued to tear at his face with her teeth. From one side to the other, the two of them rolled and grappled, each one with one hand reaching out for the cleaver.

It was a furious battle. Sometimes it was fought rolling on the floor, hands stretched out to seize the elusive cleaver. Sometimes it was staged wrestling upright, crashing into the sides of the tramcar, bouncing from side to side. The tramcar swayed, lurched, pitched, and yawed. The cables screamed. Yelling and screaming, each tried to seize the cleaver before the other did. Their outstretched hands tore at each other to grab it first, because in the cleaver lay the answer to who would emerge from the car alive. Tighe's breath was coming in short, painful gasps; the loss of blood was beginning to tell, while the woman's strength seemed to grow with her escalating rage. Both had their hands on the cleaver, rolling back and forth, struggling to possess it, battling to survive.

On the island landing dock, completely unaware of what was happening out over Matecumbe Gut, Meg still sat and watched the tramcar slowly move toward her. On her face a puzzled look began to take shape. She knew the tramcar always swayed and rocked, but today it appeared to be swinging from side to side with unusual violence. Funny, there wasn't that much wind. . . . For a moment Meg felt a passing premonition of something dreadful about to happen but erased the thought by remembering what Tighe's reaction would be when he learned he was going to be a father. It was a delicious picture, and one Meg never tired of imagining.

A slight sound from behind her made her look around. It was Dr. Sommers walking out onto the dock to stand alongside her. Meg scrambled to her feet. "Oh, hello, Dr. Sommers. I didn't hear you coming."

"I'm sorry if I startled you."

"I wasn't startled. I just didn't hear you coming up behind me, and I guess it threw me a little. Nothing to worry about."

Nothing to worry about, Sommers parroted silently in his head.

Meg looked at Sommers. His face was wearing an expression of resigned sadness, as if he knew of an automobile accident about to happen that he couldn't prevent. Meg heard him sigh softly and look at the tramcar moving ever closer to them. "Well," he said casually, "I guess the crazy old thing has decided to come back. I feel like I've been waiting for hours."

In confusion Meg looked at him questioningly. Sommers kept staring at the tramcar, but his comment made no sense. Crazy old thing? Crazy old thing *who*? "I'm sorry, Doctor. I don't get you."

Dr. Sommers spread his hands and gave a little laugh. "Mrs. Tibald. Poor creature. She managed to get out of her cell somehow, swiped a meat cleaver from the kitchen, and disappeared. A little later I saw her climbing into the tramcar. If she ever got loose on the mainland, there'd be hell to pay. She'd be swinging that meat cleaver all over town. It's a big damn cleaver, too. Terrible. At the last minute, fortunately, I managed to lock the door on the tramcar from the outside, so at least she couldn't get out. I was afraid for a while some idiot on the mainland would open the door and get inside, but I guess I got lucky. . . . Now she's on her way home. Damn bitch."

Slowly, throughout her whole body Meg could feel the cold dread of realization seeping into her every fiber. She seized Sommers, unable to speak, a strange gurgling sound coming out of her mouth instead of words. Sommers stared at her, a look of bafflement on his face. "Meg—" he began.

The realization exploded into a screamed torrent of words. "Tighe—Tighe—he just got into that car before it left—Tighe, my God, Tighe—"

"Meg," Sommers said again, trying to calm her. He blinked at her, feigning confusion.

"Tighe's in that car with that crazy woman," Meg screamed, shaking Sommers as hard as she could with her hands. "That vicious crazy woman. Tighe. For God's sake," she screamed at Sommers, shaking him even harder than before. "Do something, for Christ's sake, do something. Tighe. She could hurt Tighe," Meg shrieked. "Oh my God, she could even kill him.

Do something, do something, Oh, my God, my God—
Tighe—"

Sommers swore loudly, pretending horrified surprise.
"Meg," he said, his voice rising even as he tried to calm
her, "Meg, get ahold of yourself. It doesn't help to—"

"Do something," Meg screamed, beating him on the
chest with her fists. "Jesus Christ—Tighe, Tighe, Tighe!"

Sommers seized both her hands and forced them
tightly together. "Look, Meg. There's nothing I *can* do
until the car gets to this side. I have absolutely no
control of it when it's in motion," Sommers lied. "What
we have to do is—"

Meg was no longer listening. "Do something," she
shrieked again, and began running up and down the
landing dock from where she had been standing to the
end of the dock and back. Suddenly she stopped in
front of Sommers, crying and sobbing and racked with
convulsions. "Oh my God, Jesus Christ, please, please,
please, Doctor, *do* something," she pled, the tears pouring down her face. "There must be some way. . . .
There's got to be something. . . . Oh my God, Tighe . . ."

Meg was reacting so wildly Sommers finally did the
medically correct thing. He slapped Meg hard across
the face. The crying stopped, and she stared at him
blankly, one hand to her face where he had struck her.
"I'm sorry, Meg. But you were becoming hysterical.
Look. Don't worry; Tighe is strong; he can take care of
himself. Get a grip on yourself, Meg. Everything will
be all right. . . ."

Hypnotized, Meg watched the car's slow progress
toward the island. She felt that somehow the hand of
God had reached down and was holding it back, pulling
on the cables so the car couldn't move any faster. Every
now and then she could see the shadows of Mrs. Tibald
and Tighe against the car's windows, apparently locked
in a furious battle. Then the shadows would disappear,

as if the fight had moved to the floor. Then the shadows would appear in the windows again. The car inched forward toward them, swinging wildly from side to side with the force of their struggle. Several times it looked as if the car must tear itself loose from its supporting cable under this sudden new set of forces.

The tears began again. "Oh, please, Dr. Sommers. There must be something you can do," she sobbed, aware for the first time of her own total helplessness.

Sommers abruptly turned away from her, swearing heavily. "I have to go for a minute, Meg. I have to get help for when the car reaches here." He squeezed her arm and trotted off toward The Home; even some distance away, Meg could hear what sounded like him swearing as he ran. It was just as well she couldn't hear him very clearly; the sound Meg heard was Dr. Sommers laughing to himself in satisfaction.

Meg heard herself begin to pray, pleading with God, trying to make a deal with God, promising God she would do anything, be forever His, if He would only spare Tighe. The words sounded childish and she stopped, threw her head back, and screamed incoherently at the cloudless sky, damning God for the unfairness of what He threatened Tighe with. The heavens did not answer.

A babble of voices made her turn around. Down the dock toward her came Midge Cummins, Ernie, and the two young practical nurses, led by a harried Dr. Sommers. All of them were watching the car as it inched its way the final yards to the landing dock.

Beside her Meg saw Sommers move away from the others to join her, putting one restraining hand on her arm. As the car moved closer, Meg thought it suddenly seemed strangely quiet; the car no longer lurched and swayed from the struggle. The awful dread grew inside Meg; she bit her lip to keep control of herself.

Finally, with a sickening thud the car touched down

on the dock, dragged itself forward a foot or two, and came to a full halt. There was no one visible in the windows. Meg tore herself free from Dr. Sommers and raced toward the tramcar door. She felt herself suddenly seized from behind; it was Dr. Sommers again. "Let me, Meg, let me. . . ." he said urgently. Meg shook her head and began to move forward again. Sommers nodded to someone behind him, and Ernie stepped forward, taking hold of both of Meg's arms and keeping her from getting to the door. "Let me go, let me go," she screamed. "I want to see, I've got to see."

Grimly, Dr. Sommers walked up to the car, threw back the lock, and yanked open the door. Meg kicked Ernie as hard as she could, knocked him off-balance, and darted forward.

Shoving Sommers out of the way, she stuck her head inside the car. Meg shrieked. It was an unearthly sound, piercing, shattering, pulverizing.

A moment later she crumpled to the landing dock's wooden deck, the sudden silence as loud as her shriek had been.

Chapter Twenty

Women are all a little bit nuts. Even Meg. Hell, by now she's obviously figured out that her mother is as sane as they come, yet she's never mentioned a damn thing about it to me.

I also can't believe she doesn't know I'm keeping her here without any medical reason at all. She never mentioned that either.

I wonder. She saw the mess in the tramcar. Is she going to ignore that, too?

She was planning to take her mother and go someplace else. No longer. With Tighe out of the way, she and her mother will stay right here with me until the place falls down around their ears.

Well, it's one way to keep your family together.

Psychiatric & Personal Observations, The Home, Alan Sommers, M.D., Director.

The ringing in her ears was so loud she tried to put her hands up over them to shut out the sound. Mysteriously, her arms wouldn't cooperate, and she lay on the cement floor trying to figure out why. For several moments she couldn't understand where she was; the ceiling gave no clues, and her head, like her arms, refused to move when she told it to. Her vision was fuzzy, and what she could see was out of focus.

Slowly, movement came back to her, and she was able to turn her head enough to see something of the room besides the ceiling. As full consciousness slowly returned to her, it hit her all in one piece: she was lying on the floor of Dr. Sommers's forbidden room. Had she fainted or what? She wasn't sure. Meg's mother still had considerable difficulty moving anything, something that puzzled her at the same time it frightened her. It didn't make sense. What was happening to her? Punishment maybe for being in a room where she'd been told not to be. That didn't make sense either.

With great effort Mrs. Kendricks managed to turn her head in the opposite direction. Staring down at her from the wall, her face tortured and wearing an agonized expression, the stuffed head of Mrs. Belagio still hung where she'd first seen it. A terrible sinking feeling swept over Meg's mother. That sight was what had made her faint—or whatever. Good God, Bea Belagio had been her one real friend at The Home, and now she had been stuffed and mounted and hung on the wall like one of Dr. Sommers's animals. Mrs. Kendricks suddenly felt sick, and there was a strange pounding on the left side of her head she'd never felt before.

The thought of Dr. Sommers and his stuffed animals began tearing at her. The connection between them and Bea Belagio was too obvious to ignore. She had to get out of here; she had to find Meg. They—all of them—had to get away from this awful place as fast as they could. She should have seen it a long time ago, but Sommers's charm and kindness when she had been all alone here had blinded her. Dr. Sommers was completely, absolutely insane. A dangerous lunatic who would kill them all if they didn't put The Home behind them quickly. To the police. To the mainland. Anywhere but here.

Meg's mother knew she didn't have the luxury of feeling sorry for herself, or even for poor Bea. The doctor might come in any minute, and God alone knew what Sommers might do if he came across her in his forbidden room, particularly now that he would know she'd seen Bea. Find Meg, find Meg. Run, run. Mrs. Kendricks tested her body again; there seemed to be more feeling in her arms and legs, although the thumping of her heart and the dreadful throbbing in her head made movement of any sort painful. She had to, she *had* to.

Slowly, unsteadily, Mrs. Kendricks struggled to her feet, which made the shooting pain in her head hurt worse. She was still very dizzy and had a terrible suspicion she was going to throw up. Testing again, Meg's mother discovered she had mobility once more, but that it was very limited. Her feet didn't answer her commands as quickly as they usually did. Her eyes—Mrs. Kendricks tried to avoid looking in its direction, but found herself unable *not* to—swept past poor Bea's head. She wanted to talk to her, but was unable to think of what to say. What *could* you say to the stuffed head of your best friend, anyway?

Fighting off her unsteadiness, holding onto walls and woodwork and doors, Meg's mother slowly, painfully inched her way up the stairs to her bedroom. Meg, she had to find Meg. She wasn't in her room; to check, she'd pushed open Meg's door on the way to her own. Empty, with a forlorn, deserted look. The waves of nausea swept over her again, and Mrs. Kendricks staggered to the bathroom to be sick. Instead, she fainted again. The unconsciousness seemed briefer this time, although she had no way of knowing how long she had been out either time. Coming to, she rose unsteadily and sat on the edge of her bathtub. She couldn't understand what was wrong with her; neither could she understand where Meg was. She'd seen her outside just before she herself had gone down into the damned basement. She had to be somewhere, and she fought to remember if Meg had said anything about going out earlier. She needed Meg, my God, but she needed her. Where *was* she?

At that moment Meg was on the landing dock in hysterics. Just before Sommers had opened the tramcar door, she had broken away from Ernie and raced to Sommers's side. "Damn it," the doctor had exploded when he saw her. "Ernie! Take her away from here. *Ernie!*"

Ernie tried to respond, but he had not reached Meg before she'd stuck her head into the car and *seen*. The entire interior of the tramcar was a swamp of dark, glistening blood. In one place a thick patch of it still moved heavily down the wall in a thick line; the seat in the car's rear had a pool of blood stagnating in its center; wide streaks of blood were smeared across every window. Tighe lay sprawled in the middle of the slatted floor, the meat cleaver still sticking out of his forehead looking like a child's drawing of a settler after an Indian massacre, a tommyhawk left in place for artistic clarity.

Mrs. Tibald watched as Sommers's and Meg's heads appeared in the doorway. Suddenly, she threw back her head and gave a terrible laugh which turned into a scream as it poured out of her. Sommers had summoned Ernie and Miss Cummins; the three of them gingerly made their way into the tramcar, while Mrs. Tibald, her dress black with Tighe's blood, stood up on the seat, pressing herself against the wall behind the seat in an effort to keep their hands off her.

Her eyes rolled savagely, the laughter pouring from

her as she watched them advancing toward her. Meg tried not to look at Tighe's body—no doctor was needed to know that he was dead—numbed and paralyzed by all that had happened. In spite of herself she couldn't keep her eyes away from what was left of him; she stared vacantly at his torn body as if passionate wishing could somehow bring him to life again.

From the rear of the tramcar came the sudden sound of a new battle. Numbly, Meg turned her eyes to see what was happening. Sommers, Ernie, and Nurse Cummins were trying to move forward in a body, but their maneuvering was limited by the cramped interior of the car. Before they could reach Mrs. Tibald, the woman had hurled herself on top of all three of them, bringing them down to the floor with a splintering crash. She snarled, she bit, she clawed; more blood was added to the carnage. Quickly, though, Ernie's strength and Sommers's expertise began to overwhelm her. Sommers and Ernie struggled and grunted and cursed; Mrs. Tibald screamed and ripped and tore.

It didn't take long. Held down, punched, and sat on, she was quickly subdued enough to let Cummins force her arms into the long sleeves of the straitjacket and tie the restraining straps behind her. The two practical nurses and The Home's cook—he had shown up unexpectedly, curious to find out what was happening down on the dock—were able to drag the still-screaming and struggling Mrs. Tibald off to her cell downstairs.

Going back into the car, Dr. Sommers examined Tighe. It had been his plan, and he had executed it, but the violence of Mrs. Tibald's attack on Tighe left even Dr. Sommers shaken. Tighe's whole forehead and skull had been split down the middle by what must have been a tremendous blow of Mrs. Tibald's cleaver; his hands had been badly sliced trying to fend if off. How Mrs. Tibald could have gotten into position for such a clear shot was hard to imagine; Sommers shrugged. No one would ever know. Besides, to Sommers it didn't make one hell of a lot of difference; Tighe had been eliminated.

Stepping out of the car, Sommers looked at Meg. She was sitting on the ground, her head lowered, no longer even able to cry. "Meg," the doctor said. "Meg."

There was no answer, only a slow, agonized movement of Meg's head from one side to the other. He couldn't get her to utter a sound. With a sigh Sommers stood up and walked over to Midge Cummins. "You'd better take her to her room; stay with her, try to get her to talk. I'm afraid she's going into shock."

"Sedation?" Miss Cummins asked.

A little annoyed that his head nurse had beaten him to the obvious, Sommers studied the air as if weighing her suggestion. "It's not always a good idea in situations like this," he explained. "We'll see later. I'll be along in a minute, but there's some things here I have to take care of first."

Midge Cummins took Meg gently by the arm and pulled her to her feet. Meg gave no resistance; Nurse Cummins felt as if she were handling a lump of children's modeling clay—soft, rubbery, totally pliable, cold. On their way up the steps back to The Home, the cold clay suddenly turned to fire. Before Cummins knew what was happening, Meg had bolted away from her and raced up the stairs into the mansion. By the time Cummins reached The Home herself, Meg was nowhere to be found. Methodically, Midge Cummins began searching the building room by room, pausing only once—to stop off at the nurses' office and gulp a shot of vodka.

Upstairs, Meg raced down the hall, her breathing reduced to gasps, the sobs and the tears finally beginning to come. Her mother. She had to tell her mother what had happened. They had to get off this crazy island. Tighe had been wrong in pressuring her into staying here when she'd wanted to move them all into a motel. Very wrong. Then suddenly, the memory of Tighe's kidding her about her fear of The Home and his childish delight in his new rubber boat came back to Meg. A piercing stab of pain shot through her. Oh God, Tighe. He was so damned wonderful, so damned lovable, and now, so damned dead. . . .

The tears flowing, the sobs out of control, Meg looked around her mother's room. Nowhere. With something between a wail and a scream, Meg threw herself down on her mother's bed, sobbing, the tears running down her face and dripping onto the bedspread, her whole world crumbling around her.

An unexpected noise raised Meg's head. Out of the bathroom stepped her mother, walking shakily, her footsteps awkward and unsteady. She saw Meg lying on her bed. Tears ran down her face, too; Meg half sat up to tell her what had happened. But her mother was trying to tell her something herself. They both began talking at the same time, their speech interrupted by sobs and tears.

"Mrs. Belagio . . ." her mother wailed. "Bea Belagio . . . Dr. Sommers, he—"

"Tighe . . . Tighe . . . Tighe . . ." Meg sobbed. "They killed Tighe. Oh, Mother. . . ."

For a moment Meg's mother just stood where she was, staring at Meg, stunned by what her daughter had said, unable to accept it, listening to her own heart pound. "Too much . . . too much . . ."

Her words had a muffled, indistinct sound, as if her mouth wasn't shaping them properly. Suddenly, she gave a piercing cry of pain, her face contorted in agony, and she grabbed both sides of her head with her hands. Strange animal noises came from somewhere deep inside her; she swayed back and forth, teetering, the noises transformed into a succession of soul-shattering groans. Her head wobbling on her shoulders, her mother's eyes fixed Meg with a pleading look. A second later her mother crashed heavily to the floor.

Meg screamed. She called her mother's name several times but got no response. Meg watched in horror as her mother's body began thrashing against the floor, the strange noises still pouring out of her. She put both hands beneath her mother's head so that she wouldn't hurt herself by her violent movements. Looking closer, Meg was afraid she was going to be sick.

Her mother's eyes had bulged wide, and her whole face was twisting and writhing, one side drawn sharply upward, the other side pulled violently down. Suddenly her mother gave one final groan and became limp. "Mother?" Meg asked urgently. "*Mother?*"

There was no answer, but Meg could hear her breath, a curious rasping quality to it, being drawn in and let out; even without a stethoscope, Meg could hear her heart pounding. At least, she told herself, her mother wasn't dead—yet.

Tearing herself away, Meg stumbled across the room, yanked open the door, and began screaming for help. A few moments later Dr. Sommers and Midge Cummins were on their knees clustered around her mother on the floor. A lot of medical double-talk passed between them, and Dr. Sommers called for a shot of something to be given her mother—*stat*. When Cummins came back, the shot was administered, and between them— they kept telling Meg to stand back, please—Mrs. Kendricks was lifted onto her bed. Without removing her clothes, they pulled the covers up over her.

By the time Sommers made his pronouncement, Meg had already guessed what he was going to say. "It's a severe stroke, I'm afraid, Meg."

"*How* bad?" Meg asked, one eye still glued on her mother.

After pondering a moment, Dr. Sommers gently led Meg away from her mother over near the room's door. "That's a hard question to answer," Sommers whispered, as if Meg's mother might hear. Meg asked herself, *Could* her mother hear? Did the victims of severe stroke hear what was being said to them, even if unable to respond? Meg didn't know; she *did* know it was no time to ask.

"There must be an answer of some sort," Meg suggested.

"Not really." Sommers looked at the floor as if depressed by his own lack of ability to provide a better response. "For the moment," he added grimly, "your mother is completely paralyzed, unable to speak, unable to move, unable to do anything but lie where she is. Whether she will ever regain her faculties"—the doctor put one hand on Meg, looking her in the eye sadly—"and this is just one of those things you have to face, Meg—whether she'll regain her faculties wholly or in part—or even survive—there's no way yet of knowing. In matters like this, time is the great healer. Or the great killer."

"Shouldn't she be in a hospital, Dr. Sommers? Shouldn't we at least have a specialist look at her?"

"We're quite capable of caring for her here," he said. "All analysts, as you know, have to be fully qualified M.D.'s or they wouldn't be allowed to call themselves analysts. Hospitals, outside help—well, they're frequently more trouble than they're worth. A trip in an ambulance to the hospital in Key West at this stage could easily do her more harm than good."

Meg wasn't sure she really agreed with this at all. She wanted to argue but suddenly felt enormously tired. The feeling left her too weak to fight. The day's events had suddenly closed in around her like a black shroud. Trembling, she stared at Dr. Sommers. "Oh my God, Doctor. Just one day. Tighe—wonderful wonderful Tighe—and now this. It's too much, too damned much." She swayed so badly the doctor held out one hand to steady her. The tears were streaming down Meg's face again; the confusion and worry brought on by her mother's stroke had erased from her mind for a brief few minutes that Tighe was dead, that she was a widow, that there was a baby growing inside her who would be born fatherless, and that, with her mother probably dying, she was now completely alone in the world. The one person she'd always loved, the one person on the face of the earth who loved her back, her sustenance, her life, the beginning and end of each day, was gone, hacked apart by a madwoman who had been carelessly allowed to escape her cell.

Convulsed by sobs, she leaned against the doorway, crying bitterly that it was unfair that God should forsake her so completely.

"Miss Cummins," barked Sommers. Between them they helped Meg to her room. Gently pushing her down on the bed, Miss Cummins quickly undressed her. Even though Sommers was standing right in front of her, staring, Meg did not protest; she was unable to find the strength.

"I'm sorry, Meg; I really am," Sommers said gently. "Sorry for everything." Abruptly, he turned on his heel and walked out of the room. Midge Cummins produced a hypodermic syringe and advanced toward Meg, lying on the bed, now too exhausted even to cry.

"You can't," Meg sobbed softly. "Mother. I have to stay awake in case Mother needs me."

"Don't worry yourself, dear. There's nothing you can do. Really. Dr. Sommers and I will keep a very close eye on her and do anything that has to be done. . . ."

When Cummins picked up Meg's arm, lying limply on top of the bed, Meg snatched it away. "No, no, no. Mother . . ."

Cummins retrieved the arm. This time Meg didn't pull it away; the effort was too great. "It'll make you sleep, dear. After all you've been through today, sleep is what you need. There." The needle went in painlessly. Meg looked at Cummins curiously. The words she'd just spoken were the first gentle words Meg had ever heard come out of her mouth. Nurse Cummins looked at Meg for a moment. "Try and relax, dear. Don't fight the sedative. Just give in to it. I'd stay, but I think Doctor probably needs me. Sleep, sleep. . . ." Hazily, Meg watched Head Nurse Midge Cummins go out through the door, leaving one small light burning softly in the semidarkness.

Almost immediately Meg could feel the shot beginning to take effect. Through the fuzzy cloud in front of her eyes, Meg watched a cavalcade of pictures pass by. Waiting on the dock to tell Tighe the wonderful news about the baby. The tramcar swaying violently; the shadows against the windows—Tighe and Mrs. Tibald locked in an unfair battle which Tighe would lose; the blood-filled interior of the car, the hatchet still sticking straight out from Tighe's forehead.

Her mother, saying something about Mrs. Belagio, something she never got to finish. The dreadful stricken look; the sudden hands to her head; horrible noises, like the demons of hell; crashing to the floor and the writhing and thrashing. Her mother's eyes bulging, the face, half twisted up, half down; the sudden silence, a silence as final as death itself.

The shot of Thorazine continued to wrap Meg more deeply in its embrace. She was floating, a free body falling through space. As if from a great distance, she could hear her own voice hissing thickly at Sommers.

"You killed him, you stupid bastard. You didn't guard that woman carefully enough. Or maybe you let her out on purpose. . . . You killed him. . . ."

Darkness closed around her.

Chapter Twenty-one

---

*In my books, yesterday was the Day of Screams.
Mrs. Tibald, doubtless, screaming when she was carving up Tighe. Meg screaming when she saw his body.
The staff and a lot of the patients screaming at the
whole thing.*

*Meg screaming for help when she saw the stroke
hit her mother. Her mother probably screaming when
she saw the stuffed head of Mrs. Belagio. Great
buddies, those two.*

*For a while there it seemed to me every damned
person at The Home was screaming for one reason or
another.*

*Except Roger—that kid's always laughing. Well,
maybe he has the right idea. Laughing is a lot more
fun than crying or screaming; we should all do more
of it.*

*I'm afraid there's one person who won't ever have
much reason to laugh again, though—that bastard,
Tighe.*

> *Psychiatric & Personal Observations,
> The Home, Alan Sommers, M.D., Director.*

Tentatively, she opened one eye, baffled by the sun. Because Meg's windows pointed west, sunlight only fell across her bed in late afternoon. Yet, it was sun that had just awakened her, sun that streamed across her eyes now. It should have been morning, yet the sun was acting like late afternoon.

Slowly, Meg sat up and glanced at her watch. Five o'clock. No sun at five in the morning, that was for sure. That made it late afternoon. My God, could she possibly have slept that long?

The effects of the drug had been prolonged and brain-numbing. At first, Meg woke up with no recollection of yesterday at all, only confusion that she could have overslept so badly. Feeling somehow guilty, she threw her feet over the edge of the bed and was about to head for the shower.

Then, everything that had happened hit her with thunderous impact. Unsteadily, she sank back down on the bed, incredulous, as bits and pieces of yesterday took shape in her head. Tighe. Tighe, butchered by a wild-eyed, insane woman from a cell downstairs. How could that possibly be? Slowly she remembered everything from yesterday, her eyes swimming, unable to accept the finality of Tighe's death.

Tighe dead, Tighe murdered. A child inside herself. A sudden, tangential thought that sprang into Meg's consciousness caused her to burst into tears again. She had never gotten to tell Tighe that he was going to be a father. My God, it would have made him ecstatic, the glorious anticipation of having a son that he could shape and mould after himself. Now, though, Tighe would go to his grave without ever knowing. It was sad, so terribly sad. Increasingly, tears and sobs racked Meg's body; a river of salt filled her mouth and nearly made her gag; the bed beneath her shook from her crying, making strange little *poingg* noises as the springs shifted from her writhing.

A moment later the searing reality of Tighe's grue-some fate was underscored by the sudden awareness of her mother's stroke. "Mrs. Belagio . . . Mrs. Belagio . . . Dr. Sommers, he—" her mother had just finished saying seconds before the stroke.

What *about* Bea Belagio? Meg wondered dully. Would she ever know what her mother had been trying to say about her? Would her mother ever be able to speak again and explain what she meant? "Dr. Sommers, he—" Somehow, whatever it was was connected with Sommers. Everything in this damned place always turned out to be.

The thought of her mother dying made new waves of tears engulf Meg. With Tighe gone, with her mother more than probably gone, she had no one left in the entire world. Her stepfather? She shuddered through her crying. Never.

She fell back on her pillow, staring listlessly at the ceiling. The image of Tighe, tall, blond, godlike, that first day she had seen and fallen in love with him, suddenly became all mixed up in her head with what he'd looked like when they hauled him out of the tramcar. The tears began again, but were more muted—and possibly more eviscerating—than before.

Cried-out, Meg lay there, trying to pull herself together. She knew she should eat; she knew she should go see her mother. Oddly, she found herself hungry, although unable to face the thought of the dining room. In her drugged sleep she must have sweated a good deal; her entire body felt sticky. She needed no mirror to know that her face must look as terrible as her body felt.

She would take a shower. That was it. She would have a shower; she would see if someone could bring dinner to her room; she would find out what she could about her mother.

Meg let the water stream across her body at full force, running the water as hot as she could stand it. For some time she stayed there, feeling some of the tautness slip away under the water's therapeutic caress. She kept feeling that somehow the steaming rush of hot water was washing not only the tension out of her own body, but the blood off Tighe's. Suddenly, Meg wondered where they were keeping Tighe. Somewhere in the basement, she supposed. Rigid, cold, silent—and terribly alone. Part of Meg wanted desperately to go see him; another part screamed in protest even at the thought of it.

Coming out of the bathroom into her room, Meg decided she felt a little better, but then realized it was hard to tell; Tighe's death had left her completely numb. She stood in front of the mirror over her dressing table, drying herself vigorously. Blinking at the reflection, Meg saw she looked as if her face had been held under water for a week—puffy, bloated, eyes red-rimmed, her skin grotesquely creased. Shrugging resignedly, Meg went back to toweling herself, rubbing as hard as she could stand it.

Suddenly, something made her stop abruptly; a sinister shudder she couldn't explain was running through her. It made no sense, but Meg had a curious feeling that eyes somewhere were fastened on her, hungrily drinking in the sight of her body. Shaking her head at the silliness of such a notion, Meg shrugged and returned to her toweling.

Not as silly as Meg thought. Outside her bedroom Dr. Sommers was looking in through his peephole. Meg had a glorious body; in spite of himself, her nakedness excited him. Staring at Meg, her body golden in the last rays of the sun, a flash of errant recall raced across Sommers's brain; his older sister, the inevitable bathrub, himself, the wild, erotic games. With his sister it had always been connected with the bathrub, as it was now, with Meg. Strange.

Abruptly, Sommers shook the meandering thoughts from his head. Tonight, he wasn't here to think about his sister or even spy on Meg. Rather, he was aware that it was only a matter of time before Meg would demand to go to the mainland on one pretext or another, and that was something that had to be prevented at all costs. Her mother's stroke would, of course, keep her at The Home for the moment, but in town Meg might find a doctor and question him as to whether it was really advisable to have her mother treated here at The Home instead of at a hospital. Sommers could guess what the man's answer would be. Meg had to be rendered *unable* to go to the mainland.

Deliberately, he took the flat of his hand and made a loud, sharp sound against the outer side of Meg's bedroom wall. Virtually at the same time he took his flashlight and flashed it briefly once or twice through the peephole and into her bedroom. He put his eye back to the eyepiece of the peephole, slapping the outer wall again. It was happening just as he had planned.

The slapping noise had made Meg look around the room for its source; the light had drawn her eyes directly to the peephole. For an instant Meg appeared confused. Then, wrapping the towel indignantly around her, she raced across the room and put her own eye to the peephole to see which of the patients was spying on her. All she saw was a giant eye staring in, greedy, unidentifiable.

The eye widened as if surprised, then abruptly disappeared. Sommers had swung himself around flat against the wall so there was nothing to see but empty hall. For a couple of minutes, Meg stood, staring out, waiting for the eye to reappear. It didn't.

Outside her room Meg heard what sounded like someone running down the hall and starting down the stairs. It wasn't. (Sommers had made the noises she heard, then ducked soundlessly around a corner of the hall to wait.) So far, everything was going precisely as Sommers had schemed it to go.

The rest did not go the way Sommers had planned it at all. He was sure an outraged Meg would come running out of her room to find out which patient had the gall to peer into her room—particularly since she had been naked that moment—and follow the sound of the footsteps down the stairs.

There, he was ready for her. At the top of the stairs Sommers had earlier put a trip wire and an open noose. The trip wire was designed to make Meg lose her balance, while the noose would encircle her foot and tighten. With the noose around one foot as she started to hurtle down the stairs, she would at least break a leg as her body fell forward, the foot held stationary by the noose. The cast he would put on her leg would leave Meg unable to go to the mainland—or anywhere else—for a long time. Perfect.

The scheme quickly fell apart. Meg started toward the door as Sommers had planned and was about to follow the sound of the mysterious running footsteps, but as she came out into the hall, the door a little down the way sprang open, and the lady who thought every new face was a new doctor, popped out.

"Doctor," she screamed, almost pinning Meg against the wall with a jabbing finger. "You never kept your appointment, damn it." The woman advanced on Meg, her hands and fingers outstretched as if to claw Meg's eyes out. "You're just like all the others, Doctor. Damned bitch. Trying to stay away from me because you know

I'm sane and don't belong here. . . ." She kept coming, her fingers ripping through the air to get at Meg's eyes.

Meg mumbled something and retreated back into her room. Anything to escape that carzy woman. As for the peephole, the hell with who was staring into her room. Too much had happened yesterday for her to care. With a resigned sigh, she put a Band-Aid over the peephole and let it go at that. The Band-Aid would keep whichever patient it was from seeing in anymore, and that was all she cared about right now.

All of the patients were crazy anyway, and under the strain of Tighe's death and her mother's stroke, she was beginning to think she was going a little nuts herself.

Grumbling, Dr. Sommers finally had to accept that Meg was not coming out of her room to conveniently fall into his trap. He looked in through the peephole and discovered he could no longer see. Damn it, he muttered to himself, and went downstairs to his office, sulking.

Meg, now dressed, lay on her bed and stared at the ceiling. The ability to cry had left her; too much had happened. A sudden noise from her stomach made her realize how hungry she was. She supposed that was a good sign, a start on the path to getting over the wave of shocks that had hit her yesterday, but while her stomach was hungry, the actual idea of food was nauseating to Meg.

Feeling faint and miserable—the image of Tighe's body never completely left her mind—Meg finally came out of her room. Any thought of the dining room was impossible. But maybe if she went into the kitchen they would give her a little something she could take back to her room. Listlessly, she headed for the stairs.

As she did, Sommers's original plan unwittingly met with partial success. Sommers, when he had gone back to his office, had been so frustrated and angry he'd forgotten to take away the trip wire. As she started downstairs, Meg tripped on it, falling partway down the stairs. Because Sommers was not there to sneak up behind her and give her the sudden shove he had originally planned, her foot did not become anchored in the noose as Sommers had planned. Instead, Meg only took a sudden, precipitious dive down the stairs, screaming when she landed halfway down, her leg crumpled beneath her and hurting like hell.

Her screams produced Midge Cummins and a startled Dr. Sommers. "What happened, what happened, Meg?" Sommers asked as he reached her lying on the stairs.

"Something tripped me," Meg answered angrily. "Or maybe I just forgot to watch where I was going. Christ, but it hurts."

"It could be broken," Sommers noted, reaching down and feeling her ankle; in his mind his original scheme had somehow been carried to its planned conclusion: to break Meg's leg so she would be immobilized by the heavy cast he would use on the break. Midge Cummins, running her fingers expertly over Meg's ankle and lower leg, promptly threw cold water on Dr. Sommers's hopeful statement.

"Nothing feels broken anywhere, Doctor. It may be nothing more than a bad sprain—not that those don't really hurt."

Sommers looked at Nurse Cummins with irritation. Damn it, the leg was supposed to be broken, not sprained. "We'd better get her into the examining room in any case. A simple sprain would certainly be wonderfully good luck." Dr. Sommers winced as he said the words, smiling at Meg, hoping his utter hypocrisy wasn't too transparent.

Between himself and Midge Cummins, with Meg

hopping on her good leg, they came down the stairs and into the examining room near Sommers's office. With each hop Meg would give a little yelp of pain; sprain or break, the damned thing hurt like hell.

Carefully, they helped Meg up onto the examining table and had her lie down. By now Sommers was livid with frustration. The heavy cast with which he had planned to immobilize Meg—in a sense, holding her prisoner on the island—was no longer viable. He might be able to get away with it with Meg, but Nurse Cummins would be well aware that you don't put a huge, cumbersome cast on even the most severe sprain.

Instead of the kind of cast he'd had in mind, Sommers knew he would have to satisfy himself with a small cast to keep Meg's ankle rigid and a lot of bandages wrapped around and up her leg. It would slow her down, but not completely immobilize her. He sighed. Some other plan would have to be resorted to.

On the table Meg tried to think of anything but what was happening to her. She knew in advance whatever Sommers and Midge Cummins did it was going to be extremely painful; anything to do with broken bones or torn, sprained muscles always was.

Her thoughts were prophetic. Suddenly, Meg—she had been lying back, still trying to keep her mind on anything but her leg—sat bolt upright with a terrible scream of pain. Sommers looked at her. He had been rotating her ankle and had somehow moved it into a position that produced searing pain through Meg's whole body. "Sorry," he said to her. Oddly, he meant it. No one likes to hurt their child, even when it's only a surrogate daughter.

Lowered gently back into a prone position by Midge Cummins, Meg found herself cursing under her breath. She knew that the manipulations of her foot and ankle would get to be even more painful before Sommers and

Midge Cummins got through. Inside herself she kept wondering why Sommers hadn't called the G.P. in Marathon to deal with the painful work on her ankle instead of trying to do it himself. Tighe would have insisted on it. But Tighe was dead. My God, Tighe was dead. It all caught up with her again.

Sommers looked at her oddly. He couldn't understand why Meg should be crying before he'd even gotten to the really painful part.

Chapter Twenty-two

Some people are brave, some aren't. Meg, it seems, is not one of the brave ones. Whether the pain she's exposed to is physical or mental, she reacts violently—a low threshold of pain, I guess. She did a lot of screaming when I was working on her ankle; she screamed just as much when she saw Tighe hacked up.

I should be able to empathize. Hell, when I was a kid, I used to yell my head off at the slightest scratch or the littlest frustration. They called me a big baby—and I have to admit they were probably right. I was a baby, and Meg's a child.

I hope some of the terribly unpleasant things I'm going to have to do to Meg if she doesn't toe the mark won't harden her; I want my little girl to stay as fragile as when she was a child and as vulnerable as I suspect she still is today.

Psychiatric & Personal Observations,
The Home, Alan Sommers, M.D., Director.

When they really got down to it, the repair work that Dr. Sommers and Midge Cummins did for Meg's sprained ankle hurt more than Meg would ever have believed. "You hold her by the calf; I'll do the stretching,"

Sommers directed Cummins. He leaned up toward Meg.
"This is going to be a little painful, I'm afraid. But we
have to stretch the muscles into the proper configura-
tion before we put on the ankle cast, Meg. I'm sorry."

"I have it, Doctor." Midge Cummins's face was grim,
knowing precisely how terrible what Dr. Sommers described as "a little painful" was actually going to be.

Sommers looked up at Meg. "Okay, Meg, here we
go."

"Ready." Midge Cummins turned her eyes away.

"Now!" Sommers said. Midge Cummins held Meg's
leg firmly in place; simultaneously, Dr. Sommers turned
her ankle and pulled as hard as he could. The shriek
that came from Meg was unearthly. By the time Sommers finally said, "There. That ought to do it," Meg
found she was unable to breathe. The pain in her ankle
felt ten times worse than it had before Sommers had
started; rivulets of sweat were running down the inside
of her dress; her whole body was trembling and shuddering from the pain.

"Oh Jesus Christ God." It was all that Meg could say;
she slumped back onto the table, swallowing hard, gasping for air.

A lot of the pain was actually unnecessary. But Dr.
Sommers hadn't been deliberately trying to hurt Meg;
like most analysts, he had practiced very little actual
medicine. The unnecessary pain rose not from deliberate cruelty but from simple incompetence. Yet, inside
himself, Sommers couldn't escape a fleeting sense of
pleasure when Meg screamed; he hated himself for it.

This duality of feelings had been growing in him ever
since Tighe's arrival—Tighe had been like the trigger to
a powerful explosion. Miss Groundly's innocent telephone call about Meg's wanting to find a house for her
mother had fed the explosion; watching Meg and Tighe
in their thrashing, writhing ecstasy through his peep-

hole had produced the final, convulsive detonation. Inexorably, it had slowly transformed his original feeling for her into alternating spasms of hatred and love. For Sommers this was not an unusual phenomenon.

In Meg's mind she had expected putting the cast on would be relatively painless. It wasn't. At one point Meg fainted. At another she suddenly cried out in agony as Sommers turned her ankle again.

"Doctor," Midge Cummins began, "you know, if we gave Meg just a small shot of Thorazine, it would reduce the pain a little. This is brutal." Cummins said it with the expression of a child who already knows he is going to be beaten for suggesting something her parents will not like.

Sommers spun on her angrily. "No. It's inadvisable."

"But, Doctor—" Midge Cummins continued, seemingly possessed by a death wish.

Sommers smiled at her grimly. "You've been a nurse long enough, Cummins, to know better than to question the doctor," he snapped, obviously enjoying himself. "But you won't be a nurse much longer if I write the County Nursing Authority and tell them about your habit of being half-bombed on duty. . . ."

Midge Cummins paled, her jaw set, and she said nothing further, carefully avoiding Meg's eyes, ashamed to be so powerless.

"There. All finished, Meg," Sommers said with a satisfied sigh. "Sorry if it hurt, but medicine is an inexact science when it comes to things like sprains and breaks." Between Sommers and Ernie they carried Meg upstairs to her room; Midge Cummins remained downstairs, about to head for the nurses' sitting room and her own private relief.

In Meg's room, after the doctor and Ernie had laid her gently down on the bed, Sommers was determinedly cheerful. "I'll bet you're glad *that's* over." He laughed to Meg. "Now, doctor's orders: Keep off your feet; do nothing that will put any weight on it at all. Your meals will be brought to you up here, and Ernie will get you a pair of crutches so you don't have to stand on that ankle even to go to the bathroom. All of this is very important: It takes time and rest for something like your ankle to heal, and any weight you put on it will slow down the healing process. If you need anything, we'll bring you a big bell that someone will answer. Whatever you do, don't—repeat *Don't*—put any weight on your ankle until I tell you you can."

"But my mother. I should be seeing her; she's going to think she's been deserted."

"Absolutely not. Too much strain on your foot."

Meg started to argue, but Sommers was halfway out the door. There, he paused only long enough to give her a cheerful wave, then disappeared. Downstairs, he ran into Midge Cummins on her way into the nurses' sitting room. Sommers treated her to another of his grim smiles. "Oh, go get yourself a belt *now*, Cummins. You're shaking like a leaf."

On the way down the hall to his office, Sommers reflected on recent events. Yesterday had been a good day for him. So had today. Meg wouldn't be going anywhere for a while. And if he played his cards right, Meg wouldn't be going anywhere—*ever*.

Stay off your feet, the doctor had said. Take time to rest and heal, the doctor had gone on. A time for complete peace of mind, he had added. A crock, nothing but a goddamned farce, she told herself. A sudden sound in her doorway made her look up. It was Midge Cummins.

"Here are a couple of pills, dear, that ought to help a little. If you're still in pain, they should reduce that. In any case they'll relax you a bit; after everything you've been through the last couple of days, you need something to relax you. I don't know why that damned doctor—"

Midge Cummins stopped in midsentence as if she were afraid the room was bugged. Or perhaps it was her years of medical indoctrination. Shaking her head to dismiss her own intransigence, she handed Meg two large, multicolored capsules and a glass of water. "They're quite powerful, dear. Doctor would skin me alive if he knew I'd given them to you, but the hell with it. I suspect you didn't get too much sleep last night."

Meg thanked her and watched as Cummins unsteadily made her way to the door; it was vodka that had given her her bravery. At the door Midge Cummins stopped and turned toward Meg. "Good night, Meg. Try and get some sleep." A moment later she was gone.

The head nurse had been entirely right on one point: the pills were more than a little powerful. Ten minutes after Meg had taken them, she felt herself drifting into a twilight haze, a world without boundaries, a fuzzy, distorted void. From nowhere she heard a music box playing "London Bridge is Falling Down." She remembered that music box well. Her real father had given it to her when she was a very little girl. It was brightly painted with characters from nursery rhymes, *Alice's Adventures in Wonderland*, and *Grimms' Fairy Tales*. The music box kept tinkling happily, and the pills Midge Cummins had given her stopped Meg from asking herself why she should be hearing and remembering the little toy this many years later.

The room was spinning; the bed was whirling; Meg was flying into the blackness of space.

Three minutes later, her brain as numbed as her body, she fell back flat on the bed, dead asleep.

Chapter Twenty-three

Okay. I was the guy who put the trip wire across the stairs in the first place. It was necessary. But most of the time I feel lousy about having to do it. On top of the injury, straightening out that damned ankle hurt my little Meg more than I expected. I don't like to even think about the moments I sort of enjoyed it. Sick.

Meg keeps asking if we shouldn't take her mother to a hospital, and of course, we probably should. But fond as I am of Evelyn Kendricks—that's an understatement—if she went to a hospital, Meg would be right behind her. Can't have that.

Mrs. Kendricks is the anchor that holds Meg here. That and the sprain. The sprain itself will keep Meg from doing anything for a while, but I'll have to think of other precautions as well. I have several in mind—none of them, unfortunately, very pleasant.

That's the price you pay for having a bright daughter like Meg—sometimes they're too damned smart for their own good.

Psychiatric & Personal Observations,
The Home, Alan Sommers, M.D., Director.

"You look a little better each day, Meg," Dr. Sommers said, standing halfway across her room. In his hand he held a clipboard with the nurses' notes and charts on it. "Eating better, staying off your feet and—well, the only thing I don't like is the number of sleeping pills you keep asking for. I mean, I'll give them to you of course, but it's not a good idea to become dependent on them." Sommers smiled at her. "Can't have you turning into a junkie, can we?" The doctor gave the awful dry little laugh he used when he was trying to seem jolly. More and more, Meg kept asking herself how she could ever have considered the man charming. He wasn't. He was a self-conscious, sometimes unpleasant, always thoroughly unsympathetic, man. Only his pleasant appearance, which he wrapped around himself like a saintly shroud, had any real kindness to it.

"I don't like the pills at all," Meg argued. "But—well, with everything that happened . . ." She left the sentence unfinished, afraid if she said more she would burst into tears. These days a continual compulsion to cry hid just below the surface. Dr. Sommers fixed her with his cold gray eyes. "Your mother, oh, yes. I'm terribly fond of her myself. . . ." It struck Meg as odd Sommers made no mention of Tighe at all, merely shrugging when he'd finished talking about her mother.

Sommers stared at Meg, a sad, troubled look crossing his face, his head swinging slowly from one side to another. Meg assumed it was a gesture of sympathy. "Would you like to talk this over with me, Meg?" he asked. "I'm a shrink, don't forget. And with all these things going on . . . well . . . maybe it would help if you talked about it with me. . . . In my business, you get to be a damned good listener. . . ."

Meg shook her head violently, repelled by Sommers's

offer. Christ, of all people to talk about her troubles to. . . .

Looking at his watch, Dr. Sommers suddenly seemed to remember a forgotten appointment somewhere. "Anyway, Meg, keep eating, stay off that foot, and don't worry about anything. I'm always here." A perfect example, Meg thought, of how little Dr. Sommers understood her.

Meg watched him go through her door with a cheerful wave and disappear down the hall. Shit. For several days Meg *had* followed Dr. Sommers's orders and stayed completely off her feet. The only time she was standing upright would be when she hobbled unsteadily across the room on her crutches, making a painfully slow crossing from bed to bathroom. Lying in bed was becoming increasingly impossible for her; to cheer her up, Sommers had had one of the television sets brought up and put at the end of her bed. It was better than staring at the ceiling, she supposed, but not much.

Suddenly, Meg sat up. She could stand it no more; lying in bed gave her too much time to think about everything that had happened to her.

She threw back the covers with finality and dangled her bare feet over the edge of the bed. The hell with Sommers. She couldn't shake the feeling that somehow he was responsible for Tighe's death.

Meg pondered a moment. Sommers had told her not to do any walking. Screw the doctor. He was nowhere around. Down in his office, he'd told her. Slowly and painfully, Meg hobbled down the hall and went into her mother's room, opening the door only a crack at first to be sure there was none of the staff inside. Inexplicably, Meg found her heart pounding against her ribs.

Dreading what she was going to see, Meg slowly

pushed open her mother's door and walked into the room. The sight was a painful one. Her mother lay motionless in her bed, open eyes staring ahead unmoving. She made no sound whatever. All Meg could hear was the funereal *drip-drip* of the catheter into its bottle, the hollow tattoo of slow death. Intravenous tubes surrounded her head like birds of prey. Uncomfortably, Meg squirmed on her crutches, staring miserably at the silent, shrunken shadow of the woman who had raised her, cared for her, and loved her above everything else. From her suddenly came a rasping, breathy groan, as if her mother were desperately trying to talk to her. Only her chest had moved; the rest of her stayed as motionless as a tortured rock. The sound stopped as suddenly as it had begun.

In spite of what Dr. Sommers had once said about not speaking to her, Meg limped painfully over to the bed and struggled to talk with her mother, reassuring her of her recovery, telling her that soon they would all be together in the dream house they'd been talking about for years. All together? Hardly. Tighe would not be with them. Meg felt herself crumbling as the words passed through her head. She studied her mother but could see no reaction whatever; if she *could* hear, she had no way of signaling the fact to Meg. Not knowing if her mother even heard a word of what she said was an unsettling experience for Meg. She shuddered, bent down on her crutches as far as she dared, and tried to kiss her. Even that attempt was a failure; with the crutches she couldn't lean down far enough to reach her and had to settle for kissing her own fingers and then touching them to her mother's lips. Unsettling, miserable, painful.

Slowly, she walked back toward the door and softly opened it partway. Turning, she again stared at the silent, motionless body on the bed, and wondered. Certainly, by now, they should have taken her to the hospital in Key West, shouldn't they? Why was Sommers insisting on treating her here? The answer was to torture Meg for hours after she'd left her mother's room.

A sudden voice from behind her almost made Meg lose her grip on the crutches and topple to the floor. "What the hell are you doing in here?" Sommers demanded.

"I was just wondering—"

Sommers was furious. "As far as medical things go, let me do the wondering. I'm the doctor, damn it. I made it quite clear you were to stay in bed, not go roaming around on your crutches. I was also very explicit about your not coming to see your mother. Apparently, you think you know better," he added sarcastically. "Go back to your room this instant, do you hear me? I'll think of a fitting punishment for you later." Abruptly, Sommers turned his back on Meg and walked over to her mother's bed. Her heart still pounding from the way Sommers had suddenly materialized behind her, Meg backed out of the room, feeling guilty. Stupid, she supposed, but his scolding had sounded like an angry parent yelling at his child, and she was reacting accordingly. Even more stupid.

Meg began to grow angry. She wasn't his daughter; she wasn't a little girl. Sommers was acting more and more crazy; to Meg everything he did now seemed tinged with madness. Added to the already overpowering sense of fear attached to The Home, the idea of the place under command of a lunatic took Meg's breath away.

She tried to hurry to her room—anyplace where Sommers would not be—but the crutches slowed her down so much she might as well have been going backwards.

There had always been fear implicit in her appraisal of The Home: the terror now was beginning to close in around her. As she crept back toward her room, emotionally drained, the hollow, echoing sound of her crutches on the bare wooden floor added an ominous counterpoint.

Christ, she told herself, in this hellhole, even a bare floor would have sinister overtones.

If Meg could have been downstairs in Sommers's office at that particular moment, she would have realized how sinister things at The Home were actually getting.

Sommers stood in front of his open shadow box looking at a new addition to the strange collection of stuff inside. It was a picture, but a picture that made no sense. Framed and hung below the photograph of Meg was a new rectangular frame. In it were two illustrations cut out of a medical journal. One was a four-color photograph of an embryo, the other a black and white photo of an infant in its crib.

Sommers disconnected the frame from its velvet wall and stared at it, at first almost fondly, then as he studied it further, with hate. A surging maelstrom of curses poured out of him. The frame was opened and the picture of the baby taken out.

For a few moments Sommers was busy with his scissors and his pen. Then, he carefully returned the picture to the frame and the frame to the rear wall. A satisfied smile wreathed his face. Hanging along with the other photos and objects, the new picture presented a strange sight: the baby's head had been cut off at the neck. A deep red torrent of blood—product of

Sommers's dark scarlet Magic Marker—poured from the baby's torso where the head should have been. The stuffed animal, his daughter's china doll, his father's ear, all of the things in the shadow box began applauding, then began cheering.

The effect pleased him. This baby's father had been killed by a madwoman who had bathed the tramcar in his father's blood. When his baby was born, he himself would take care of the infant. Perhaps the tiny head should be stuffed and hung alongside Mrs. Belagio's. Or maybe he should stuff the whole damned baby; that would be something new.

For a moment Sommers stared at the picture, then grimly turned and strode out of the room. There was so much to do, so much.

The next morning Meg set her jaw and decided she couldn't take lying in her room anymore. There was too much upsetting her, too many things that kept intruding into her brain, reminding her of Tighe. This room was too filled with objects, thoughts, remembered conversations, forgotten laughter.

In defiance of Sommers, she slowly and painfully made her way downstairs into the Main Room. The patients appeared to ignore her. None of them seemed interested enough to voice sympathies about Tighe's death—something she decided she was thankful for— or her mother's stroke, or even to ask what had happened to her leg. It was as if she'd never been away, had never had a husband, and had always used a crutch.

Meg saw Midge Cummins across the room advancing toward her. The woman's face appeared set in a scowl, but with Cummins, it was always hard to tell. "How are you, Meg?" she asked. "I didn't really expect you'd be able to stand it up there alone for very long. Just watch that you don't bump into things with your leg and you'll do all right. And one thing to be really careful of is . . ."

Midge Cummins had to stop; one of the practical nurses was tugging on her sleeve and whispering into her ear. Cummins never got a chance to return to her instructions; she left hastily with the practical nurse, giving Meg a desultory little wave as she hurried to some other part of The Home.

As Meg hobbled across the room—she intended to go on through the French doors and out onto the terrace for some sun—a sudden violent fight broke out between Roger and Kenny. Or perhaps it would be more apt to describe it as a continuation of the same old fight, only this time intensified in violence. The subject was unchanged.

"She is not, I tell you, she's not," screamed Kenny, grabbing Roger's shirt.

Roger laughed. "She sure as hell is, Kenny-baby," Roger hissed meanly. "Like the hamster you had when you were a kid, or the pet fish of yours that turned up one morning floating upside down in their bowl, or the family dog that ran out into the street and got run over. Five years ago. Dead. Dead and buried." Roger paused a second, then giggled. "I mean, I *suppose* they buried her, Kenny. Kind of smelly if they didn't. . . ."

A second later, Kenny, screaming, and Roger, laughing, were thrashing on the floor. Roger's laughter disappeared as he realized he had a real fight to handle. Furniture fell over; furniture was smashed; furniture flew through the air as they heaved it at each other. A small crowd gathered, some cheering one, some cheering the other. It was the inevitable Ernie who finally broke it up, the watching patients grumbling because the show was over.

Without even realizing it at first, the madness of

what she'd just seen—the screaming, the violent, senseless fight, the other patients cheering them on, loving the brutal excitement—had pushed Meg into a decision. Somehow, she had to get off this insane island and find a doctor who would arrange to have her mother taken to a hospital. She had to go to the police and demand that they look into Tighe's death. She had to get away from here and from Dr. Sommers once and for all.

There was only one path open to her. The damned tramcar. She hated the idea—the place where Tighe had been killed—but she had no other choice. Outside, she dragged herself slowly and painfully down from The Home toward the landing dock and the tramway car.

Wobbling, the crutches suddenly disobedient, Meg advanced toward the tramcar. As she dragged herself close, something looked strange about the car. At first she couldn't figure what it was; then, Meg saw a large, hand-lettered cardboard sign hanging across the door. Shaking her head, Meg hobbled the rest of the way to the tramcar. Written in tall Magic Marker letters— Sommers's writing, she was pretty sure—were the words: Out of Order Until Further Notice.

Meg felt the dock crumbling beneath her. She wanted to scream. Now she was a prisoner on this damned island. A captive just as surely as if she were chained to the walls of The Home's basement dungeon. Christ, could Sommers read her mind?

Taking a deep breath, Meg turned and made her way back up the steps to The Home, the crutches biting into her underarms, each step an agony. It was all too neat. Finally she had decided to do what she knew she should have done a long time ago—leave the island— and conveniently, the tramcar was suddenly out of order. Very, very much too neat. Meg was gasping for air and moaning softly by the time she reached the level of The Home. Having started her escape and then been stopped, Meg's resolve had grown even stronger, nourished on frustration.

She had to get off this island if it was the last thing she ever did.

The finality of her own words left Meg more frightened than ever.

Chapter Twenty-four

I wasn't very popular as a kid. Too smart-ass, the other boys said. Oh, I got fabulous grades—always better than anyone else's—but that only seemed to make the guys dislike me even more. I really tried to be one of the guys—it's tough not having any friends— but the other boys ran when they saw me coming.

After putting up with that crap for years, I decided to change direction completely. Hell, if you can't be liked, you can always be respected. So I doubled the time I spent studying and got even higher marks. That didn't work either: instead of respect, I got loathing.

I did have one friend—Corky Lummet—but then, he was pretty strange himself. So strange, matter of fact, his family finally put him in a sanitarium someplace, sort of like The Home, I guess. I wrote a lot of letters to Corky there, but he never answered one of them. I finally realized the bastard didn't really give a damn about me, and all those close times we had were just because he didn't have any friends either. That hurt. Being deserted always does.

I bet Meg got good marks at school, but I bet no one ever hated her for it. No one called her a *smart-ass or ran when they saw her coming down the hall.*

I must have been doing something wrong.

> *Psychiatric & Personal Observations,*
> *The Home, Alan Sommers, M.D., Director.*

Meg had to be scared. Scared into realizing that only in himself lay safety. Scared into seeing that he was the only person in the world she had to turn to. Scared into realizing that only he, Sommers, could protect her, guard her, save her. Then, any notion she might have of leaving The Home would slowly wither into nothingness.

Downstairs that morning, Sommers set in motion what he would admit was the most dangerous maneuver he'd tried yet. He stood outside Mrs. Tibald's cell door, looking at her wild, raging eyes and listening to her labored breathing. "You killed her husband, you know. And she told me just how she plans to get back at you."

Her eyes fastened on the cell door in which Dr. Sommers had ostentatiously left his key ring. Mrs. Tibald snarled and stared at him without apparent comprehension. Suddenly: "He tried to rape me; the bastard tried to rape me!" she shrieked. Sommers ignored her statement.

"Well, Meg Kendricks *has* a way to get back at you, a pretty good way, I think, Mrs. Tibald. This." Sommers suddenly opened something he had been holding behind his back and held it up in front of her, waving it slightly. Mrs. Tibald shrank back at the sight of it. It was the one thing at The Home she feared. "Right, Mrs. Tibald, it's a straitjacket. Meg Kendricks is insisting you be kept in one all the time; otherwise she'll go to the police about her husband—the man you killed. I don't know; maybe she's right, Mrs. Tibald."

The poor creature didn't understand a lot of things, but the sight of the straitjacket was one thing she did. She began cursing Meg and swearing that she'd get her—then all her threats about the straitjacket or going to the police would become meaningless. She'd get her, damn it to hell Jesus Christ goddamn Mother of God she would.

Dr. Sommers shrugged, turned around, and walked out of the room, his footsteps echoing eerily on the bare cement floor of the antechamber. Behind him in the lock of Mrs. Tibald's cell, the key ring hung pendulous. It glistened in the sun briefly as Mrs. Tibald—she'd never taken her eyes off it for an instant—quickly snaked one hand through the bars and unlocked her cell door.

Halfway around the corner, Sommers waited expectantly. He would have to follow Mrs. Tibald everywhere she went. Meg was to be scared, not killed. How would Mrs. Tibald try to do it? he wondered. Another meat cleaver? A kitchen knife? Strangling? He didn't know. But there was beautiful poetic justice, Sommers decided, in Mrs. Tibald having killed Tighe in *one* of his plans, while in another, Meg would suddenly believe she was going to die by the same hands. If only Mrs. Tibald didn't find some way to get around him, Meg was safe. But the woman was devious—almost as devious as he himself was. Sommers had a gnawing worry inside him telling him that there was an awful lot that could go wrong.

Watching, he saw Mrs. Tibald come sneaking out of the cell room and start up the stairs, muttering and cursing under her breath. Softly, Sommers followed her.

No damn woman was going to put her into a straitjacket for the rest of her life, Mrs. Tibald hissed to herself.

She'd killed the rapist.

Now she would kill his wife.

After breakfast, Meg climbed painfully back upstairs. Halfway up, she reached the same conclusion she'd come to once before: the hell with Dr. Sommers's orders. She would go into her mother's room and try talking with her again. It was terrible to let her lie there endlessly, alone, staring at the ceiling. Even if her mother couldn't move, who really knew whether she could *hear* or not?

Sitting beside her bed, holding one of her mother's hands in hers, Meg talked quietly. She kept up an endless monologue about the new home she was sure they would soon find, of how happy they would be living there, and of minor, funny incidents that had happened at The Home in the past few days.

Her mother's eyes never even flickered; her expression never changed, even a little. The only movement of any kind that Meg could detect was that her chin had drooped infinitesimally lower, making her mouth sag even more grotesquely than it had before. The catheter dripped, the breath rasped, the cardiac monitor on the table beside her mother's bed beeped softly as glowing dots of light moved sideways across the monitor like errant blips on a radar screen.

Meg sighed. The lack of reaction from her mother, the lulling effect of the stillness in the room, made her eyes droop. A second later they flew wide open, terrified.

Mrs. Tibald exploded from the closet, shrieking as if all the devils in hell were beside her, urging her on. In her hand she held a long kitchen carving knife high in the air as she dove toward Meg. Meg couldn't believe what was happening. The woman who had butchered Tighe was back now to butcher her; the weapons were different, but the end result would be the same. Meg screamed, trying to keep a chair between herself and the wild-eyed Mrs. Tibald, who was snarling like a jungle predator. From one corner of her mouth, saliva ran loosely. Moving around the room to keep as far away from the woman as she could, Meg heard, as if from a distance, her screaming something about the straitjacket they were going to put on her for the rest of her life and how Meg was responsible for the whole thing. It made no sense, but more things that made less sense were happening at The Home every day.

Her heart shriveling inside her, Meg suddenly discovered Mrs. Tibald had her trapped in one corner of the room. Desperately, she searched the room for a way to avoid Mrs. Tibald and her brutal knife. Wild-eyed, Mrs. Tibald kept moving the knife-slashes ever closer, playing with Meg, prolonging her pleasure by making the process of killing Meg a slow and terrifying one. Her voice rose in an insane laugh as it struck her how long she could make this game last; maybe she could get Meg to plead for her life before she plunged the blade into her neck or body. "You bitch woman," she screamed. "Trying to get them to put me in a straitjacket forever. Just because I killed the pretty-boy rapist." A peal of laughter shook her whole body. "He deserved every slice I took out of him. Boy, did he scream! Just like you're going to when I stop playing with you and get down to business."

In Mrs. Tibald's eyes Meg saw the sudden change of attitude. The fun had gone out of the game for her; now was the time to finish it. Meg cajoled and pleaded, but Mrs. Tibald only laughed grimly. The slices through the air suddenly came much closer to Meg than they had; the maniacal look on the woman's face deepened as she got down to the serious business of killing. "Now, you dyke-whore," screamed Mrs. Tibald. "Now you get it!"

"Put that thing down," roared Dr. Sommers from the doorway. He had been waiting outside the room and from the sounds Mrs. Tibald was making knew he had to move in before it was too late. "Ernie! Cummins! Anybody. Quick, come quick!" he yelled out the door.

It was as if they had all been outside waiting for his summons. From the hall Ernie and Midge Cummins ran in; a moment later they were followed in by the two young practical nurses. Mrs. Tibald had turned away from Meg, apparently quickly forgetting she was even there. With the knife swinging wildly in front of her, she turned on Sommers. Ernie was moving in from one side, Midge Cummins from the other, but the knife in Mrs. Tibald's hand seemed reserved for the doctor. Without even thinking, Meg, still standing behind her but forgotten, reached over the woman's shoulder and grabbed her by the wrist, twisting it so hard that the knife clattered uselessly to the floor.

In one movement Sommers, Midge Cummins, and Ernie threw themselves on top of Mrs. Tibald, knocking her to the floor. One of the practical nurses produced the straitjacket. Mrs. Tibald shrieked in fury at the sight of it, kicking, clawing, biting the four people who were trying to hold her down. By grinding her face into the floor and sitting on her head, the four of them were able to inflict enough pain so Mrs. Tibald's struggle weakened, and they could finally jam her arms into the hated straitjacket.

Quickly, the arms of the jacket were crossed in front of her and the sleeves fastened behind her with the leather straps. As they dragged her out of the room, Mrs. Tibald suddenly saw Meg, looking at her as if she hadn't been there the whole time. By planting both feet in front of her, she was momentarily able to keep them from dragging her any farther. "You finally got me into the straitjacket, you whore-bitch. The doctor told me that—"

Midge Cummins stopped Mrs. Tibald from saying anything more; she hit her hard behind both knees with a night stick she had grabbed from the supply room. Mrs. Tibald's legs buckled. Between Cummins, Ernie, and the two practical nurses, they were able to drag the woman out of the room. From the doorway came her voice shrieking at Meg: "I'll kill you. I killed your pansy husband; now it's your turn. I'll—" Meg could not see what they had done to Mrs. Tibald in the hall as they dragged her back to her cell, but she heard a scream of pain—and then silence.

Shaking, her whole body trembling, Meg turned around to look at her mother's bed. The woman had not stirred. All the noise, the screaming, the wrestling, and the shouting apparently had not reached her.

From downstairs, Meg heard Mrs. Tibald scream and the sound of something breaking; she must have torn herself away from her jailors long enough to run into something with glass in it. She heard other voices shouting at one another. You could hear the scuffling and banging clearly, even here, one floor up. Suddenly, a final scream from Mrs. Tibald; then her voice grew muffled as she was dragged down the stairs to her cell.

All the shouting and confusion mixed in with Mrs. Tibald's screams reminded Meg of the dreadful day Tighe had arrived back at The Home after being attacked by Mrs. Tibald. Meg shuddered, remembering the sickening sight inside the tramcar.

Shaken, Meg went over to her mother's bed and took her hand, speaking reassuringly to her; if she was able to hear at all, the bizarre sounds of the battle—it had taken place no more than ten feet from her bed—must have been terrifying. A sudden noise from behind her made Meg turn around. It was Sommers, his face flushed and angry. "I told you to stay out of this room, damn it, Meg. You could have been killed. Now you see what can happen when you don't follow my orders."

Meg looked at him in amazement. His statement

made so little sense she simply ignored him and left the room.

Once again lying on a chaise, trying to calm her taut nerves after her encounter with Mrs. Tibald, Meg drank in the rays and waited for some sort of calmness to come back to her. It didn't. Wave after wave of inescapable fact crowded into her brain. Suddenly, the most inescapable of all hit her. Somehow, someway, however dangerous and difficult, she had to get off this damned island. While she still could.

She had no idea of how—the tramcar was still out of order—but her life was in jeopardy. So was her mother's. It was already too late for poor Tighe.

Thinking about Tighe always brought Meg to the edge of tears; tonight, the sensation was compounded by the sight of a small boat bobbing along on the twilight waters of Matecumbe Gut. She couldn't help but remember Tighe's boyish pride in the rubber *Titanic*—the smile on his face as he put together the boat he never got a chance to sail.

Meg sat bolt upright on the chaise, ignoring the pain that shot through her ankle when she did. The crazy, damned rubber boat. Dr. Sommers might have fixed the tramway so it no longer ran, effectively holding her prisoner on the island, but the man didn't even know the rubber boat existed. Beginning to quiver with excitement as she suddenly saw escape materialize before her eyes, Meg mentally ran over where the boat was. She could remember exactly. She could remember the path they took; she could remember the clearing where they had inflated the damned thing, laughing wildly; she could remember how they had had to struggle hiding it—some distance from the water and under a light covering of tree boughs. It would be easy to find it again. Even if she couldn't start the outboard, there was a pair of oars inside.

Meg began to fidget. Her excitement made her want to start this minute. Escape. She looked up at the sky, and her enthusiasm suddenly sagged with disappointment. The sun, a hazy red globe, was about to slip under the horizon; soon it would be dark. Damn. She would have enough trouble in broad daylight getting to the other side of the island, dragging herself on wobbly crutches, but the dark would make it damned near impossible.

With a sigh, Meg stood up. Tomorrow, then. First thing tomorrow. Off this insane island and to the safety of the mainland. The police. Safety from Dr. Alan Sommers. Killing Tighe had not been enough; now he was trying to kill her. Slowly, she limped back inside, her ankle throbbing with every movement.

Meg went directly up to her room, stopping off only to pick up a sandwich from the kitchen. She didn't go to sleep at all that night, but sat in the chair by her window, watching the sky, waiting for the first pale rays of sun to tell her morning had come.

At the moment, sunrise was about the only thing in Meg's life of which she was really certain.

Chapter Twenty-five

Sometimes, I'm not as cruel and callous as I think I am. See, there's this crazy streak of softness that keeps getting in the way. It bugs the hell out of me.

For instance, when I was watching Mrs. Tibald moving in to carve Meg up, well, that was something I should have gotten one hell of a boot out of.

And part of me did. The look of unadulterated terror on Meg's face as Mrs. Tibald advanced on her, the carving knife slicing the air in front of her, gave me a charge that was almost sexual.

But then, suddenly, from deep inside me, came an unexpected surge of sympathy for her. Concern for her. Empathy with her terror. A sudden urge to fold her in my arms and tell her everything was going to be all right.

Damn it, what's wrong with me?

Psychiatric & Personal Observations,
The Home, Alan Sommers, M.D., Director.

The morning finally came. But with it, no sunrise. A thick, misting rain made it as wet and dreary as it had been a few days before. Still sitting in her chair, Meg woke with a start, annoyed to realize she had dozed off, and angry when she looked at her watch and saw how late it was: 7:05 A.M. Damn. She had planned to be already out of the house and halfway across the island by now. How could she have been so careless? Early morning would have suited her purposes far better: no one else would have been up, there would have been no one—not even Sommers—to see her downstairs, or later, to notice she'd slipped out of the house. Cursing herself, Meg knew she had already blown this part of her plan; the staff would be up, along with some of the patients. It was her own stupid fault.

Downstairs in his office Sommers had his own reasons to feel stupid. Because he'd had trouble locating the office key, he'd had to go back upstairs to get the copy. By the time he got back downstairs, the staff was already moving around The Home. Quickly, he took refuge in his office.

When he opened his shadow box, Sommers saw that, just as he had expected, his father's ear was again floating near the top of the peanut butter jar; the pressure gauge on his barometer gave such a low reading he was surprised the ear hadn't risen right out of the jar. Looking at the barometer again, Sommers wondered how much this extraordinarily low reading would affect his mind. Before the day was over, he suspected, he would do something unusually bad—even for him. Probably to Meg.

The inhabitants of the box were unusually vocal today. "Stop staring at me, boy," his father's ear said gruffly. "Stop staring and get on with it."

His daughter's china doll rolled her eyes and screamed at him. "Remember how you loved her laugh? She was laughing at *you*, you creep, every minute, every day. Making fun of you, you old fart. If you've got an ounce of guts, you'll take care of her today. *Today*, understand?"

"You've burned the picture of her, now burn *her*,"

the stuffed animal screamed. "Oh my, oh my, oh my!"
He laughed, holding his sides from the pain of it.
Turning around, the stuffed animal led the unholy gath-
ering in song. "Good night, Lady. . . . Good night,
Lady. . . . Good night, Lady. . . . It's time for you to
go. . . ."

Sommers laughed. They were being so funny today.

He shook his head. No matter how often he ran into
it, he could never get used to the duality of his feelings
toward Meg; one minute he'd want to love her and
keep her with him always. The next, he'd want to kill
her and get it over with. Stupid, stupid, stupid, he told
himself, shutting the bookcase to hide the shadow box
when he heard his bell chime and knew a patient was
waiting for his appointment.

Carefully, Meg was pulling her things together for
her trip across the island—to freedom. No, she wouldn't
take her raincoat; she was afraid Sommers might see
her in it and know she was going out.

God alone knew what one or the other of the crazier
patients might do if they caught her alone outside the
relative safety of The Home. There would be no one to
hear her scream, no one to see her thrash as she was
thrown to the ground and strangled. Knifed? Sliced into
strips with a cleaver like poor Tighe? As always, the
thought of Tighe—oh God, he was so great and now
was so dead—cast a pall over Meg; she had to shake
herself and force her hands to stuff the things she was
taking with her into her sleeves and pockets. A couple
of small snapshots of Tighe crammed into one pocket.
Something with her name and address on it, in case the
fragile rubber boat swamped and she was drowned. A
short note to her unborn son. Meg didn't know why she
wrote it; if she died during the escape attempt, so
would the baby inside her. A second note—this one to

the police—telling them to go get her mother from The Home and for God's sake to investigate Tighe's murder. A postscript putting the finger squarely on Sommers in case the police were too dense to get the picture for themselves.

There. For better or for worse, all ready. The words "for better or for worse" immediately conjured up the rest of the service. The damned trapped pigeon screaming its warning at her. The pigeon had been right, so terribly right. Death had them parted, certainly far earlier than the man who wrote the prayer had ever envisioned. Only the pigeon had known.

Furtively, she made her way out the side door near the kitchen into the rain; you very rarely ran into anyone in that virtually abandoned part of The Home. The rain was not heavy but the thick misting kind that drifts down steadily, shrouding trees and bushes in what appeared to be a fog-wrapped harbinger of misery.

For a brief moment she stood where she was, swaying slightly on her crutches, taking what she hoped would be her last look at The Home. With the exception of a handful of good memories about Tighe there, there were nothing but terrifying associations connected with this dreadful place. At the moment her only regret about leaving like this was that she had not been able to get into her mother's room and whisper a few words of encouragement in her mother's probably unhearing ear. Meg had longed to explain that, no, she was not deserting her, only going to the mainland to get help.

Meg began painfully pulling and dragging herself across the narrow width of the island. Her heart was pounding with excitement—and fear. Fear that something would go wrong. Fear that Dr. Sommers somehow knew what she was up to and would suddenly pop out of the bushes somewhere along her route and drag her back to The Home, fear of the upcoming trip across the raging waters of the Matecumbe Gut. The prospect of battling the powerful, angry current in a tippy rubber boat was frightening—so risky she wasn't sure even an expert sailor like Tighe would have tried it.

As the terrain along the path grew more overgrown and hilly, each step became an agony. Small branches from the tangle of bushes on either side of the path tore at the crutches. A malevolent web of vines reached out and tried to fasten their tentacles to her feet; it was as if they were the clutching fingers of some purposeful demon determined to bring her crashing to the ground.

To Meg the journey seemed to take forever; yet glancing at her watch, she saw that the trip so far had consumed only a half-hour. Suddenly, dead ahead, an angry patch of ominous gray water sprang into view: the far side of the island. Ten minutes later, thrown to the ground twice by the spiteful tangle of vines, she stood on the narrow, stone-strewn strip of beach along the shore. Meg was so exhausted she found it difficult to breathe and sat down for a few moments on a rock to get her breath back. Farther down the shore she could see the large fallen tree that stretched from the undergrowth halfway to the water; it was the landmark Tighe had chosen to make finding the rubber boat easier.

Getting painfully back to her feet, Meg started along the shore; the drizzle continued to fall; her hair was plastered across her eyes; she was soaked through, and she began to shiver from the drenching chill. Moving seemed twice as hard now, partly from exhaustion, partly because the crutches kept sinking into the sand.

Following the fallen tree a few yards back into the underbrush, Meg finally saw it; a surge of new hope flowed through her as a tiny flash of bright blue revealed itself under the branches. It was the *Titanic*, exactly where she remembered it, still mostly hidden beneath the camouflage of branches with which she and Tighe had covered it. She was going to make it.

Fingers trembling, Meg pulled off the small branches and greenery they'd used to hide the boat; its blue and red plastic seemed startlingly bright when the boat was stripped of its concealing cover, a splash of Day-Glo brilliance in the misty dullness of the day.

Quickly, she dragged the fragile little boat to the water's edge. It should have been easy. It wasn't; trying to pull something, however light, while having to use crutches, was a nightmare. Carefully, she attached the outboard to the stern, and, wincing, hauled the *Titanic* into the shallows.

Meg had seen Tighe start the outboard several times, and began with confidence. It was the kind with a self-starter and should have been easy, but there was some button or lever on the motor she didn't know about, and the outboard stayed as silent and dead as poor Tighe. Standing up on her crutches, Meg leaned over the stern to take a look at the outside rear of the motor to see if there was something there she could push, turn, or engage, but could find nothing.

Meg sat in the stern, trying to recover her breath. The motor was beyond her; she would have to use the paddlelike oars lying in the bottom of the boat. There were no oarlocks, and with no one to row but herself, she would have to use one of them more as a paddle than an oar. Not good, but she had no other choice.

A moment later she was maneuvering the craft as close to the shore as she could manage. By using all of her strength and trying to ignore the pain each stroke of the paddle sent shooting through her ankle, Meg was able to get the boat as far as the far end of the island.

Then it happened. As she came around the island's end and out of the protection it had been giving her, Meg felt the tide surging through the gut seize the craft and spin it wildly. It was totally out of control, completely at the mercy of wherever the gut wanted to take it. Meg stroked as hard as she could, but the small wooden paddle was virtually useless against the surging tide of the gut. Meg's immediate fear was that the roaring current of the gut would drag her tiny ship out to sea, spinning and turning as she watched the shore move farther and farther away, helpless to even slow down her voyage into nowhere; Meg's second fear was that the roaring current's high, choppy waves would swamp the low-sided, fragile boat. The wind moaned; the current raged; the boat spun helplessly.

A few moments later, she heard a terrible scraping sound, the rubber boat's paper-thin bottom striking against something. Grabbing the rubber sides, Meg braced herself for the worst. At first nothing seemed to happen, then came a long, whining hiss like a punctured bicycle tire. The raging current had driven her onto a barnacle-covered rock not far from shore; there was a fevered bubbling sound as the air raced out of the rubber boat. Meg's heart sank almost as quickly as the boat did.

As the water rose around her, Meg grabbed her crutches and gingerly lowered herself over what was left of the gunwales. At first, she closed her eyes, trying to keep the bitter salt water from blinding her; the thought of swimming to shore, somehow hanging onto the crutches without which she wouldn't be able to stand once she made it back to land, her ankle throbbing and aching as she struggled toward the shore, was a dreadful one. To her surprise she found she could touch bottom; the water here was far shallower than she had expected. The natural buoyancy of the water made the crutches unnecessary; she floated them ahead of herself so that she would have them when she got ashore. For some reason—one she never understood—

she towed the punctured rubber boat behind her; it was useless, but maybe it would come in handy for something in her next escape attempt.

Once ashore, hobbling across the sand on the crutches, Meg suddenly found herself exhausted—physically and mentally. Her escape—which seemed so possible a little earlier—had been a miserable failure. Exhausted, she sank onto a boulder down the beach. For the first time, she had a chance to realize the effects of the steady, misting rain on herself; Meg was soaked through; her shoes sloshed each time she took a painful step in them. Christ, she could never remember being this wet or miserable. She should get back to The Home, she supposed, and dry off; maybe she'd even be able to cadge a little something to drink out of Midge Cummins. Meg sighed, forcing herself to get going, shivering, drenched, and defeated. Just as she stood up, a new idea struck her.

The tramway's breakdown had obviously been no accident; it had been deliberately put out of operation by Sommers to keep her from going ashore. If he could make it *stop* running, obviously he could make it *start* running—whenever he chose to. Meg searched her mind, trying to remember what he'd shown her about the motor's operation the day he'd taken her on his tour. Looking back, it seemed pretty simple. She dreaded the thought of riding in the crazy little car, but getting to the mainland could save her life and her mother's. *And* the baby's.

Almost crawling, the pain growing worse as she put weight on the ankle, Meg slowly crossed the island again—this time to the rickety-looking shed where the motor that sent the battered tramcar back and forth was. At least the place was relatively dry inside; she found some smudged and slightly oily rags in one corner of the shed and, dirty as they were, used them to dry off a little. Especially the sopping tangle of her hair.

Discovering what Sommers had done to keep the tramway from running was not hard, even for someone as unmechanical as Meg. He'd unscrewed all the fuses from their sockets. They had to be here somewhere, Meg told herself, but could find them nowhere. Meg sat down on the pile of rags, her heart withering with discouragement. The bastard must have taken the fuses with him; no matter how hard she looked, she couldn't find them.

Suddenly, she remembered a trick from her childhood. The boys in Little Goat used to talk about it frequently, proud of their own ingenuity. If you didn't have a fuse, you used a penny. With trembling fingers, Meg opened the small wallet she'd stuffed into the pocket of her dress. At first she could see only bills and silver; abruptly, some pennies surfaced. One . . . two . . . three—she needed four, and the damned supply of pennies stopped at three. Not expecting much, Meg fished frantically around in the other pocket of her dress. *Bingo! Four!* At first Meg had trouble believing it. God, who had been treating her so badly for the last couple of weeks, had suddenly smiled down on her.

Gingerly—hoping the small boys in Little Goat had known what they were talking about—Meg pushed the pennies into their sockets. She set the motor's switch at a trial setting of On. Nothing happened. Then, a second later, the motor suddenly began turning over, whirring, whining, stuttering, but definitely running. Quickly, Meg pulled the switch back to the Off position. She wasn't ready yet and didn't want any movement of the car to give her away.

Meg was brimming with excitement. She walked over to the battered door of the shed and looked out. Still raining, but with considerably less intensity, she decided. Meg was torn. It wouldn't be safe to try her escape in the tramcar until dark, yet she was too cold and uncomfortable to stay much longer in her soaking clothes. Hard as the thought was to accept, Meg knew she had no choice but to stay here until night fell—wet, soaked through, shivering. With a sigh of resignation she sat down on the pile of rags in the corner to wait, burrowing down into the filthy mess a little for what little warmth it could provide.

It was a melancholy place; on the tin roof above her the rain beat steadily—an ominous tattoo. The shed smelled, and Meg kept thinking she heard the scurrying feet of mice running across the low beams at the ceiling line. All she had to do, she kept telling herself, was wait until dark, climb into the tramcar, and make her escape. Meg wished she felt as sure as her words sounded.

At about three, Meg heard the rain stop. Sticking her head out the door again, she could see the sky had suddenly become quite light. By three-thirty the sun was shining brightly, hazily. Meg grew bolder as the weather grew better. Cautiously, she stepped outside and pressed herself against the wall of the shed, letting the sun warm her and at least partially begin to dry out her clothes. By about four forty-five, Meg decided her hair and her clothes were dry enough to chance The Home. If any of the staff happened to run into her, they might think she looked unusually unkempt and messy, but their curiosity would go no further. She was aware it would be far smarter to stay right where she was until darkness finally came, but a wave of guilt had been tearing at Meg.

This morning she had not gotten to say good-bye to her mother. Now, she could. It would be dangerous—Sommers had a way of popping into her mother's room at odd moments—but it would give Meg a chance to reassure her mother she wasn't abandoning her, merely

going to get help. If her mother *could* hear, the visit
would eliminate any possibility of her mother's thinking
she had been deserted by her daughter—left alone to
lie as she was forever.

Going up the side stairs, Meg, trying without too
much success to make no noise, finally reached the
landing and hobbled down the hall toward her mother's
room. There was, thank God, no sign of Sommers.

Her mother lay in her bed, soundless, motionless,
her eyes staring blankly at the ceiling. Meg leaned over
to whisper to her, but something made her heart freeze.
It was, she realized, the complete absence of sound: no
dripping catheter, no muffled electronic bleeps from
the heart monitor. Trembling, Meg touched her mother's
face; it was as cold as stone.

The scream that had been buried inside Meg for days
wanted to find voice. To rise and fall in shrieking tatters
of sound, splitting the air around it, tearing at the walls
of the room as if it were some malevolent demon. With
all the effort she could summon up, she managed to
stifle it and stood motionless and silent, staring in disbelief.

Her mother was dead.

Chapter Twenty-six

I feel awful about Evelyn Kendricks. First the stroke, then—well, you know.

And I feel pretty awful about Meg, too. I can remember when my own father and mother were killed in the car accident. At least, though, their deaths were in an honest-to-God accident. Nothing very accidental about poor Evelyn's.

Which makes me feel even worse. I loved that woman—God, but I loved her. When she first got here, right off she made me feel like I had a family again. She was the replacement for that crazy damned wife who walked out on me, only, unlike her, I knew Evelyn would never run out like that.

Then, Meg showed up, and my family was complete. She was the replacement for my daughter. Willingly or unwillingly, she deserted me, just like her mother. The two of them—Meg and my daughter—were so alike it was eerie: the same smile, the same laugh, the same sweet disposition. And Meg would never have tried to leave me either, if it hadn't been for that bastard Tighe.

Well, you saw what happened to Tighe. And sad as it made me, to Evelyn Kendricks, too. Now, I guess it's going to have to happen to Meg. God, I love her so much I don't know if I can bring myself to that. But I'm getting surer and surer she's going to make a break for it; and at that point, I won't have any choice.

So long, little Meg.

Psychiatric & Personal Observations, The Home, Alan Sommers, M.D., Director.

Even though her whole body was still shaking from shock, Meg was in control of herself enough to realize that the chances of a second stroke had been high right from the beginning. She seemed to have read somewhere it was what doctors feared the most. One of the reasons, she told herself, her mother should have been in a hospital instead of being given makeshift treatment here at The Home. Damn Sommers.

Meg wasn't sure what to do next. Obviously she was the first person to know about her mother, and the fact made her uneasy. Looking at her, Meg remembered all the wonderful things her mother had done for her as a little girl—her kindness, her warmth, her love. With effort Meg pushed from her mind all recollections of how strange she'd become as she grew older—the memory lapses, the inability to cope, the sudden fits of depression. They were what had brought her here to The Home and terrible Dr. Sommers. In an odd, removed way, they were what had killed Tighe—Sommers had engineered that, she was now sure—they were what might kill her herself unless she could find a way to escape from this island. It wasn't just a selfish thing: she had Tighe's baby inside her, and she owed the embryonic boy survival.

Wincing, Meg reached over and closed her mother's

eyes. As she did, she began to notice things that upset her. The eyes had been motionless and staring ever since the stroke; now, though, they seemed to be bulging. The effects of the second stroke, Meg supposed.

But as she continued to look, other things she had not noticed at first began to surface. One of her mother's arms had moved—it must have been the first time her muscles had worked since the first stroke—and was halfway up to her face. Meg's first thought that it, too, was the effect of the second stroke didn't make sense. The arm was raised as if fending off someone or something unknown. No, Meg told herself: people in the throes of a stroke probably don't have spasms of involuntary movement that put their arms and legs in strange positions. The long string of strange events at The Home was getting to her, Meg decided.

Meg sat in the chair looking at her mother. Slowly she began realizing how many strange things the new stroke had done to her mother's appearance. The face was frozen in terror. It looked as if there were purple marks of some kind around her neck, but Meg wrote that off to some medical aberration connected with sudden death. The pillow, tossed to one side, was ripped in a couple of places; either it was an old one, or her mother's death throes had torn it.

Ordinarily, Meg, with what she knew about Dr. Sommers, would have been suspicious that her mother's death also had something to do with Sommers. But that was ridiculous. A stroke is not something you can bring on; it just happens. She herself had been the first person to know her mother was dead, and as much as she loathed and was frightened of Sommers, her mother's was one death she couldn't blame on him.

Meg was wrong on virtually every point of logic she used about Sommers and her mother's death. It was a curious kind of leaning over backward so as not to have to face reality. She was so terrified of what Sommers could do to her unless she escaped to the mainland, she descended into massive rationalization.

Quite simply, she had not been the first person to know of her mother's death at all; Sommers was. He had gone into her room that morning and while examining her had been startled to see her begin to move. This, he knew, was not an unusual medical phenomenon in cases of stroke. The victim suddenly enjoys a partial remission of symptoms, sometimes permanent, frequently only temporary. So when Evelyn Kendricks's arm had abruptly moved, pushing him away from her blindly, Sommers knew precisely what was happening.

Her eyes were following his movements now, and although it was obvious she could not see clearly, the fact that they could follow shapes at all indicated the remission was a profound one. "How are you, Evelyn?" he asked rhetorically, knowing it was impossible for her to answer. A small knot of fear was beginning to grow in his stomach; if she had a full remission for any length of time, she might even start talking. "My," he added, "but you gave us a scare. . . ."

Sommers could see her mouth struggling to form words, but failing. It was as he had expected: nothing— although her damned mouth kept trying. Suddenly: "You . . . you bastard . . . stuffed . . . poor Bea . . . poor Bea Belagio. Wait . . . you murderer . . . wait until . . . until I . . ."

Dr. Sommers did not hold off to discover what he should wait for. The last thing in the world he had expected was for Evelyn Kendricks to regain her speech. He had no choice. If she could talk—even if only temporarily—she could tell about Mrs. Belagio and say where her stuffed head was. Even if she told no one but Meg, it was something he could not afford to have happen. The thought hurt him; he genuinely loved Mrs. Kendricks.

Quickly, Sommers yanked the pillow out from beneath Evelyn's head. "I'm sorry, Evelyn, I really am," Sommers said sadly. Then he pushed the pillow down on her face as hard as he could. To his surprise, she battled him, scratching him with her untrimmed fingernails, making a desperate moaning sound as her body thrashed to avoid the suffocating pressure of the pillow. Sommers began to sweat as Evelyn Kendricks continued to fight, twice pushing the pillow far enough off her face to manage a weak scream.

Sommers found he was shaking with a combination of anger and frustration—along with a dread of having to smother this woman he genuinely loved. One more time the pillow was pushed away from her face, its case ripping in the process. The strangled cry rose again. Stronger measures had to be taken.

Hating himself as he did it, Sommers flung the pillow to one side and fastened his fingers around her neck, choking off Evelyn Kendricks's supply of air completely. Her eyes bulged, staring at him with hatred. A moment later the look of hatred was replaced by a consummate look of panic. It was hard for her to believe, but Dr. Sommers was really going to strangle her, his iron grip pressing hard into her neck, his breath coming in gasps as he followed through on what he knew had to be done.

For some minutes Evelyn Kendricks continued to struggle against him. Her fingernails drove deep gashes into his arms, tearing his watch from his wrist; her body rose and fell on the bed as she struggled to survive. A mottled look came into her skin; the thrashing and heaving grew more rapid; her lungs swelled in search of air they could not find. There was a sudden rapid movement of her feet as if she were trying to tap-dance her way to safety, then a sudden stillness.

Slowly, Sommers relaxed his grip. For several moments occasional spasms of thrashing ran through her as her autonomic nervous system reacted to death. Then, she grew as motionless as she had been during the depth of her stroke, the eyes staring into space, but an expression of terminal agony frozen into her features.

Briefly, he stood rooted to the spot where he was. So much to do. The evidence of what had happened had to be cleaned up. There was nothing he could do about the bruises on Mrs. Kendricks's neck, although possibly later he could apply Covermark or some other kind of makeup. Quickly, he began straightening the covers on the bed and putting Evelyn back into a more normal position. Just as he reached over to pick up the torn pillow, Midge Cummins came into the room and told him that Mrs. Tibald needed sedation immediately; she had gone after one of the practical nurses again and was now in a state of screaming violence.

Sommers shrugged and followed her downstairs; the rest of the tidying up of Evelyn's room would have to wait until later. "Same as before," Sommers muttered to Cummins when she asked if Mrs. Kendricks was making any progress. "It's quite possible she will never regain consciousness," he added. "These damned stroke patients are tricky."

It was something of an understatement.

Slowly, Meg was adjusting to the shock of discovering her mother dead. As her mind cleared, some of the odd features of the death began to bother Meg again. She sighed. Sommers terrified her so much she supposed she wasn't thinking straight. Slowly, she straightened out her mother's body—one of her legs was in a strange, pulled-up position—and patted the covers smooth. They seemed terribly messed up. The pillow on the floor still baffled Meg, and when she picked it up, she was further troubled to discover there were several patches of blood on the ripped case—Meg had no way of knowing that it was Sommers's blood, smeared on the pillow when her struggling mother's nails had slashed his forearm.

It was while she was adjusting her mother's head on the pillow that the truth of the whole thing struck Meg with shattering force. Partly concealed by her mother's long, tangled hair, Meg found Sommers's wristwatch—it was a highly distinctive Girard Perregaux, gold, with a stylish jet-black face—so distinctive it was impossible not to recognize as the doctor's.

Staring at it, Meg saw that the gold watchband had been torn almost in two and the crystal broken, with a large piece of it missing. Like the pillow slip, the stylish black face of the watch was similarly smeared with blood.

The bruises on Evelyn Kendricks's neck suddenly made sense—as did the torn pillowcase and the disordered bedcovers. Her mother had not died from a second stroke at all; she had been strangled with Sommers's bare hands.

The horror of it—and the threat it represented to herself—abruptly hit Meg with stunning power. Sommers was a killer—first of Tighe, now of her mother. Meg knew she should stay quiet and go ahead with her escape plan without raising a fuss. But the shock was too much for her.

Meg raced out into the hall, shrieking with all the strength she could summon. Virtually the same moment as she gave in to her emotions and ran screaming from the room, Meg realized how stupid she was being. Now that it had grown dark, she could get to the tramcar and make her escape; doing anything that would alert Sommers or draw attention of any kind to herself was to invite disaster.

From downstairs, as if confirming the appraisal of her own stupidity, she began hearing sudden voices. An excited babble. Above it rose Dr. Sommers's strident, commanding voice, issuing unheard orders to people unknown. Meg listened, trying to hear what he was saying, but loud as he was yelling, the words were lost in the confusion; the only thing Meg was sure of was that he yelled her name several times, following each mention with stern, abrasive-sounding orders.

Dear Christ . . . Sommers . . . now he was after *her*. Standing in the hall a few feet from the door of her bedroom, Meg's mind suddenly went blank. It was as if the terrifying chain of shocks had pulled a switch in her brain somewhere, making the world around her unreal and distant. She could remember she had felt a little the same way at her wedding when the pigeon in St. Bardolph's had swooped down on her, screaming its raucous warnings.

Dimly, Meg became aware she was swaying back and forth, almost fainting but fighting it with all her strength. The realization was redoubled that—if only for her baby's sake—somehow, she had to get away from The Home. Away from Sommers. In one piece.

The calling back and forth downstairs penetrated her hazy consciousness, along with the sound of people's feet beginning to pound their way up the stairs. Meg tried to ignore the waves of fear running through her; Sommers would be here any moment, and Meg was aware that by now the doctor must have realized she knew he had killed her mother. Probably he had intended to come back and find his watch, then clean up both her mother and the room before Meg could see them. The waves of fear turned into breakers, crashing along the shore of Matecumbe Gut. Sommers had only one sure way to silence her effectively; she would join Tighe and her mother in the safety of everlasting silence. Along with the baby. Oh, God, the baby—Tighe's baby—somehow it had to be saved.

As she leaned against the wall, trembling and terrified, desperation summoned up the memory of the side stairs. Steep and hard for her to maneuver on crutches, they were a possible way out. The thought of trying to negotiate the steep, narrow treads appalled her, but the alternative appalled her even more. Dragging the foot with the cast painfully behind her, Meg began down them.

Each step had to be taken one foot at a time; then she would bring the other foot down alongside it and pull herself together for the next. The pain was so fierce she wanted to cry out. Behind her, upstairs in the hall, she heard the same babble of voices she had before. By now she was almost to where the stairs took a sharp right; if she could get around that, no one upstairs would any longer be able to see her. The babble grew louder as Meg raced to get herself around the stair corner and out of sight. She felt a scream almost tear itself free of her as the crutches slipped out from beneath her when her effort at speed pushed prudence too far; for a second she teetered back and forth, fighting to regain her balance, praying to God she would not fall and give away where she was. Finally, Meg gained control of her balance again, thanking God for having spared her and her baby. The fall would have been murderous enough; the sound of it would have brought Sommers racing to her side, intent on—on what?—well, Meg wasn't precisely sure except that it would be something terminal.

The sounds of shouting upstairs, followed by a hollow series of thuds as someone started down the side staircase, pushed Meg through the side door and out into the rainy darkness. Gritting her teeth, Meg hobbled painfully down the incline from The Home, the huge house looking ghostly and sinister in the occasional flashes of lightning that still rolled in off the waters of Matecumbe Gut.

With the exception of these brief, episodic bursts of lightning, Meg knew that by now it was dark enough so she could go directly down the steps to the landing dock without fear of being seen. She grimaced; soon Sommers would discover she was nowhere inside The Home and come looking for her outside. The landing dock was a logical place to begin, though Sommers would be confident that since he had taken the fuses she couldn't go anywhere in the tramcar.

Out of the darkness the tramcar suddenly loomed into view, silhouetted against the fitful flashes of lightning. Meg's whole insides were churning as she climbed into the car, closed the door, and fumbled in the dark for the button that would start the tramcar on its way to freedom for herself and her baby.

With a mechanical grunt the car lurched forward and up, moving quickly out over the raging waters of Matecumbe Gut. Looking down, Meg could see, by the eerie light of a stuttering lightning flash, the tide racing through the gut, angry, gray plumes of water hurled into the darkness where the surging current of the narrow channel crashed into the calm of the ocean beyond.

As Meg knew it would, the tramcar swayed back and forth wildly when the full force of the wind began clutching at it; the cables that supported it groaned and shrieked from the strain on them. Today, while the old fear still clutched at her, Meg didn't mind. She had made it, goddamn, she'd made it. She and her baby would finally be safe. Her mother was dead, her wonderful, fabulous Tighe was dead, but she and the

baby were going to make it. There was nothing now that
Sommers could do to stop her; he himself had told her,
when she was pleading with him to do something about
Tighe's deadly trip across from the mainland with Mrs.
Tibald, that he had no control at all over the tramcar
once it was set in motion. And she doubted if Sommers
knew where she was even yet. Her whole being was
suffused with a great sense of relief; to escape, to be
free, to raise her child—these were now things within
her reach.

Swaying and lurching, creaking and groaning, the car
moved slowly toward the mainland. Oh God, but Meg
wished Tighe were here with her to see how she managed the escape and saved his baby. He would have
been so damned proud.

But Tighe was *not* with her and never would be
again. He and his humor had been reduced to dust
and scattered on the winds. Suddenly, through the
tramcar's rear window, Meg saw, back on the island,
all of The Home's outside lights go on. Sommers—
someone—had seen the tramcar on its careening trip
across the creaking cables and alerted the staff.

For an instant it scared Meg, but she reassured herself with Sommers's own words that still lodged in her
brain: once the tramcar was in motion, he had no
control over it at all.

The lights were brilliant, casting the long shadows of
many people running back and forth. There seemed to
be a great deal of activity on the landing dock and near
the motor shed. In spite of Sommers's statement, Meg
felt a small tug of fear pull at her heart. But no, Sommers had said what he had said: no control once the
tramcar was in motion. She was safely on her way to the
mainland, and there wasn't a damn thing that crazy
doctor could do about it. Escaped! Free! Safe!

Suddenly, panic seized and shook her to the very

soul. She was only about halfway across, but the car
ground to a jolting halt. Twisting around, Meg saw
more people gathering on the island's landing dock, and
the distant shape of what she supposed was Sommers
staring up at the tramcar from the doorway of the motor
shed. But Sommers had said . . .

Meg swore loudly. She should have known better
than to believe anything Sommers said. As the car hung
motionless over the gut, Meg again looked back toward
the brightly lit area outside The Home. The memory of
seeing Dr. Sommers leaning out the door of the motor
shed swam back into her mind. Maybe he couldn't
actually control the tramcar, but he *could* stop it or
start it. Maybe he'd found the pennies in the fuse box,
pried them loose, and stopped the motor. Or maybe
there was a main switch inside The Home which con-
trolled the electrical feed to the motor.

My God, Meg told herself. Sommers couldn't get at
her, but he was entirely capable of keeping her suspended like this indefinitely, swinging and lurching in
the wind but unable to get to the mainland. Would he
let her starve?

The answer came quickly. There was a succession of
sudden lurches, and the car jerked roughly forwards
and backwards, beginning to move. For an instant Meg
again thought she was going to make it to the mainland.
Then, it hit her. There was now no question that the
car was once again moving—only *back* toward the Home.

Meg could feel cold panic seize her; in her mind
there was little doubt that Sommers would kill her the
moment the car landed. He almost had to, to silence
what she knew about her mother's death.

Frantically, Meg looked down at the surging waters
of Matecumbe Gut, more menacing than ever, lit only
by the eerie streaks of lightning that were cascading
across the sky. She shuddered as she began to wonder

if it might not be better if she opened the door, jumped, and tried to swim through the treacherous water to the mainland. She already knew the answer before she asked herself the question: even in the best of circumstances, the current alone would probably be fatal. But hers were not the best of circumstances. With her severely disabled right foot, the feat would probably not only be fatal, but probably very nearly impossible.

For a moment or two, Meg stood staring out the window at The Home, realizing how little chance of success her swim for it really had. It was a project that virtually screamed to be abandoned. Then, in the brilliant, stark light outside The Home, Meg again saw what she was pretty sure was Dr. Sommers, standing now at the end of the dock, doing what almost looked like a little jig of success. The project that cried to be abandoned suddenly came to life again. Anything was better than letting that bastard Sommers get his hands on her. The hell with the risk. She would jump for it.

"Oh God, God, Tighe," Meg whispered to herself, aware it sounded like part of a prayer. "If only you were here to help, Tighe . . . to tell me if I'm doing what's right, Tighe. . . . The baby's yours, too. . . . Tell me, tell me, Tighe, tell me, what I'm doing's right. . . ."

There was no answer. Except the creaking and groaning of the cable as the tramcar slowly moved back toward the island; except for the screaming of the wind as it rattled the tramcar, making it groan in protest; except the moaning sound of the elements as they seized the car with malevolent fingers and tried to hold it captive.

Meg swallowed hard and reached for the door handle. It wouldn't move. Below the handle—the way you see the *Occupé/Libre* signs on European railroad cars—was a small sign in a window reading Locked.

That bastard Sommers. Creepy, murdering bastard.

She should have guessed he'd do something diabolical like lock the damned door. Somehow, he must have known all along exactly what she was up to, letting her go ahead and try for it for the sadistic kick he'd gotten out of her attempt's futility. Son of a bitch, cocksucking bastard.

All of the pieces fitted. When she was climbing into the tramcar, congratulating herself on her own cleverness, he'd slipped up to the car in the darkness and thrown the outer lock of the tramcar's door. This would have been just before Meg started across. Dimly, Meg could remember the soft whisper of the lock being thrown——a meaningless sound to her at the time——just before she had pressed the start button that made the car start moving. Meg's fury flared, and she hit the hard, metal side of the car with her fist. She could imagine Sommers smiling to himself as his victim began a journey she expected to end in freedom. Sommers already knew better.

Desperate, willing to tackle anything to avoid falling into Sommers's hands again, Meg searched for alternatives to the door. She beat on the car's windows as hard as she could; if she could break one of them, she could crawl out, hang onto the tramcar's sides, and drop to the water below.

She kept hammering on the windows as hard as she could, but they must have been made of Plexiglas; nothing happened. In the corner she saw a bucket of sand marked Fire and tried to break a window with that, but it didn't work. She felt the car slowing down and heard it clank over the cables where they passed by the landing towers, and her heart sank.

Slower and slower it went. As the car began nearing the landing platform in front of The Home, Meg started screaming——senselessly, uselessly, almost hysterically. Below, in the glare of the lights on the landing dock,

Meg could see a reception committee waiting—Dr.
Sommers, Midge Cummins, the giant Ernie, and the
two young practical nurses. Behind them, gathered in a
whispering little mob, were some of the patients, drawn
by the lights and curious to find out what was happening.

The moment the door was unlocked and opened, Dr.
Sommers walked over to it. "Good evening, Meg," he
said benignly, the shadow of a smile playing across lips
washed thin by light. Still smiling secretly to himself,
Sommers executed a courtly little bow. "Welcome to
The Home."

Chapter Twenty-seven

I suspected Meg would try it, I was afraid Meg would try, and damn it, Meg went right ahead and tried it. Not successfully, of course, but what counts is that she tried.

Sad. She wanted to walk out on me, just the way my wife did. My daughter, too.

I said I was afraid Meg would try the same thing, but I've got to admit I never really believed she'd do it. She doesn't realize, I'm sure, how much that hurt.

Now, I'll have to hurt her, something the nice part of me doesn't want to do at all. If I can't shape her up, she'll have to be disposed of, something the nice part of me wants to do even less. I need her.

The fact is I don't have any choice. If she ever got away from The Home to the mainland, she'd have every damned cop in Florida breathing down my neck by morning.

Hell, why couldn't Meg just be content staying here with me? I've always tried to be nice to her.

Like a lot of people, I guess, Meg plain doesn't realize how nice a guy I really am.

> *Psychiatric & Personal Observations,*
> *The Home, Alan Sommers, M.D., Director.*

Meg was still screaming when Ernie and the two
practical nurses—Midge Cummins standing slightly behind them and supervising the trio—dragged her from
the tramcar and threw her roughly on the ground. Meg
couldn't believe it. In the hard, brilliant light of the
floods burning outside The Home, Ernie and the two
nurses moved like long shadows, their faces pale in the
harsh incandescence, their movements exaggerated—
blue-white demons dancing in an eerie floodlit circle
that pierced the blackness of night.

Not looking at her but beyond her, Dr. Sommers
appeared out of the darkness and handed Cummins a
straitjacket. Midge Cummins looked at him questioningly for a second, then stooped down to the other
three with it. Fiercely, Meg thrashed and screamed
and fought, trying to keep them from putting the jacket
on her. With all her strength, she struggled to keep
them from forcing her hands and arms through the
long, white-canvas sleeves, but there were too many of
them to resist for long. The sleeves were fastened,
criss-crossed, over her chest, and then tied tightly behind her by heavy leather straps.

"Get something in her mouth," commanded Midge
Cummins. "With all that screaming of hers she could
swallow her tongue." One of the practical nurses took a
gauze-wrapped tongue depressor and stuffed it into Meg's
mouth, tying it there with long strips of bandage.

"Good," Cummins said, testing the device. "That'll
keep her quiet, too."

Wild-eyed, gagged, and trussed up like a turkey,
Meg was surprised that Midge Cummins and the two
practical nurses should be party to Sommers's madness
and treat her this way—like a violent, dangerously insane patient. Like Mrs. Tibald, Meg suddenly realized.

Why, in spite of her screaming and pleading and
welter of rational explanations, would they all go along

with Sommers in something as blatantly illegal as this?

The answer was simple. None of them thought for a moment they were doing anything in the least bit illegal. Earlier, while Sommers was waiting on the landing dock for the tramcar to return, he had addressed the others quietly but urgently. "This," he told them solemnly, "is something I hoped would never come up. The doctor-patient relationship made my mentioning it earlier impossible. It's a very sad, regrettable story—I mention it now only because I have to—but about a year ago Mrs. Devlin became for a time hooked on LSD."

Sommers turned away for an instant, as if too moved to continue. "One of the more frightening aspects of LSD, as you probably all know, is that even years later, when a former user is under any kind of unusual stress, the original dosage of LSD can reactivate itself and produce the same weird hallucinations the original dose did. Terrible," Sommers added, his voice breaking slightly.

"You're aware of the pressures Mrs. Devlin has recently been under. The shock of her husband's death, followed almost immediately by her mother's stroke and subsequent demise, were simply too much for her. She was already on the verge of a breakdown, I believe," Sommers noted. "Some of you know that Head Nurse Cummins discovered poor Mrs. Devlin—a truly wonderful person we had all come to appreciate—had discovered Meg sitting in her room talking to people who weren't there. Bad enough, but under all this strain, you see, the residual LSD in Meg's—Mrs. Devlin's—system suddenly became active again. With the hallucinations and everything else. Tragic. Worse, we have no way of knowing how long it will take Meg to recover. If ever. Even more tragic."

Looking down, Sommers studied his hands as if deeply

buried in thought, although a careful observer might have noted he kept a sharp eye on the tramcar to see how soon it would arrive at the landing dock. Sommers sighed. "In any case I must remind the staff that, until further notice, Meg will have to be treated as a psychotic, probably self-destructive patient. Maximum confinement, minimal freedom of movement. No access to belts, straps, or even stray pieces of cloth she might use to hang herself." Sommers sighed again. "I realize this will be an unpleasant assignment for all of us. Because we know Meg as well as we do, the temptation to relax our vigilance will be tremendous. On the other hand, I don't think any of us could face ourselves if under the guise of mistaken kindness any of us found ourselves responsible for her suicide. I know I can count on the staff to perform its duty with its accustomed efficiency and expertise."

Since Meg had not been privy to Sommers's address to the staff, she was still confounded by what she considered their grossly illegal performance. She struggled and thrashed, trying to wrench her body free from the straitjacket. She got nowhere. Ernie was holding her motionless, sometimes sitting on her chest to control her. Fighting hard, Meg struggled so wildly the gauze-wrapped tongue depressor broke in her mouth, and she was able to talk in short, gasping pants. Shrieking, she pled with them for God's sake to help her, that Sommers was nuts, that Sommers had killed Tighe, that Sommers had killed her mother. Couldn't they see he was a murderous psycho?

With a pitying look, Midge Cummins jammed another gauze-wrapped tongue depressor into Meg's mouth, this time tying it with triple widths of bandage. As Meg's words and shrieks were reduced to a muttered groaning and thrashing, Cummins shook her head sadly. Ordinarily she rarely admitted this, but what Dr. Sommers had said was absolutely accurate. Meg's bizarre hallucinations—Sommers's killing Tighe Devlin, Sommers's killing her mother—were the hallmark of a totally unbalanced person. It was somehow strange to think of Meg this way; Cummins had always rather enjoyed her.

"Now?" Cummins asked.

"Now."

Grimly, Cummins nodded at Ernie and the two practical nurses. Between them they carried Meg back into The Home. At first Meg couldn't figure out where they were taking her; then, it hit her. Struggling with every bit of strength she had, heaving and thrashing in the straitjacket, Meg kicked and heaved and fought against them. The gauze-wrapped tongue depressor again broke, and Meg began shrieking in protest—screams that had no beginning or end, no top or bottom, sounds that tore at the air around her and brought most of the patients out of the Main Room into the front hall to see what was happening. There was a lot of whispering and muttering among them, but no one said anything out loud except the crazy, frightening old lady who lived down the hall from Meg and kept seizing her and demanding the new doctor give her an appointment.

"My God," she hissed at a perplexed Kenny, who stood beside her watching Meg struggle inside the straitjacket and shriek at anyone who would listen. "My God," the old lady whispered, "look at what they're doing. They've taken the new doctor prisoner. Oh, terrible, terrible, terrible. . . ."

Kenny didn't say anything. Something was bothering him. For Meg to be hooked on LSD—even briefly—didn't make sense. She wasn't the type. It was all out of character. She wouldn't—not in a million years. So why was Sommers accusing her of it?

Something else was bothering Kenny. He'd never

been overly fond of Meg—she'd never been mean to him about his mother like some of the other patients, but there was often a strange look on her face which made him wonder about her—but a conversation he'd heard between Cummins and the two practical nurses had begun to change his feelings about her.

"I heard about that," one of the practicals had said, shaking her head.

"Sad," Cummins had noted. "I mean, she's at the perfect age and all that, but with everything that's happened to her—her husband, her mother, her leg and everything—well, it's one hell of a time for a girl to be pregnant. . . ."

Now, watching poor Meg struggle, Kenny suddenly felt infinitely sad. All this, with Meg pregnant. To Kenny a child and his mother were of almost sacred significance, and it made him shudder to think of the mother—Meg—being strapped tightly in a straitjacket and locked in a cell—possibly forever. The child, what would happen to the child? For no reason he could think of, Kenny suddenly wanted to cry.

Shrugging, Kenny told himself it was none of his business. He had plenty of problems of his own. With a small, sad sigh he turned away and watched to find out what they would do with Meg next.

Halfway across the hall Ernie and the two nurses steered Meg's struggling body down the staircase, Midge Cummins bringing up the rear, issuing a series of commands.

At the bottom of the stairs, while Ernie stood guard at the door to keep the patients from following any farther, they carried Meg across the cement-floored antechamber and into one of the cells.

Farther down the row of cells, wild-eyed Mrs. Tibald saw Meg and laughed and laughed and laughed, alternating the laughter with little screams of delight. Seeing

Meg in a straitjacket—Meg, after all, had tried to have her put in one for life—struck her as a hilarious joke; justice, for once, was being done.

In the cell no effort was made to release Meg from the straitjacket. "It's too soon, dear," Cummins told Meg. "You'll have to quiet down first." Cummins reached over and took off the remnants of the device that had held the tongue depressor in place; broken this way it was too dangerous.

"Listen, listen," screamed Meg at her. "You've got to listen. What I'm telling you is true. Sommers *did* kill Tighe, he *did* kill Mother. You've got to listen, Miss Cummins," Meg shrieked. The sound was so loud Midge Cummins winced, patting Meg on the shoulder to try and soothe her, slowly pushing her back onto the steel cot in one corner of the cell. Meg kept screaming and stood up again. As gently as she could, Midge Cummins forced her back down on the bed, shaking her head, looking at Meg with pity.

Meg fought against the restraining straps of the straitjacket, yelling at Cummins and cursing, but realized she was completely helpless, so trussed up even a gentle push from Cummins couldn't be resisted.

"When you calm down a little, dear," Cummins said soothingly between Meg's screams, "I'll come back and take that jacket off. I know it's very uncomfortable. Just try to be calm, dear, just try to be calm. . . ."

For an instant Meg stared at Cummins with disbelief. None of this could be happening to her, yet it was. She watched, helpless, as Midge Cummins turned away, still shaking her head sadly, and slammed the cell door shut behind her.

With a long key Cummins slid a bolt across the bars; the lock in the door snapped shut with a terrible finality. Moving from her cot to the cell door, Meg listened as Cummins's footsteps echoed hollowly across the concrete floor outside and receded up the stairs, each footstep eerie proof that her freedom was vanishing into the infinity of hopelessness.

The silence that followed seemed to Meg the stillness of death. Somewhere inside her the baby moved. Down the corridor in her cell, Mrs. Tibald suddenly screamed with laughter once again.

Upstairs in his office Alan Sommers, M.D., was smiling himself. The shadow box was open, and Sommers stared at his father's ear in wonder. The crazy Keys weather, he supposed. A half-hour earlier the weather had been furiously stormy, but this was the Keys and the weather could change in a matter of minutes. The ear was making no sense today. It floated near the top of the peanut butter jar, ignoring the immutable laws that dictated on a clear, brilliant night such as this one—a night so clear the orange moon seemed close enough to reach out and touch—the ear should have sunk to the bottom under the influence of the high pressure ridge sweeping across Matecumbe Gut. Sommers was baffled; the ear had never behaved like this before. It was trying to tell him something. For once, the other objects were mute.

Sommers studied it for a few moments more, then shrugged and followed the ear's unspoken instructions. The last remaining vestige of feeling for Meg had vanished with her attempt to leave him and go to the mainland. All that remained was a chilling compulsion to punish her for her faithlessness.

From the drawer beneath the shadow box, Sommers grimly pulled the remaining picture of Meg. As he had Tighe's, he held a lit match to one corner of the picture, letting it burn until he could dump the smouldering cadaver of Meg's photograph into the ashtray.

Watching the last of the flames gutter out, Sommers snickered. Goddamn, but he was clever. Brilliant. That scene he'd played for the staff—the LSD, the reactivation of the drug's hallucinations, the terrible tragedy of it all, even the slight quaver in his voice when he'd talked of his fondness for Meg—well, he might have pushed credibility to the limit, but, goddamn, he'd gotten away with it. A magnificent performance. Worthy of Burton. Clever, clever, clever.

Like Mrs. Tibald, Sommers suddenly exploded into insane laughter.

Chapter Twenty-eight

Women are all alike. In spite of everything, Meg isn't one damned bit different from the rest. Looking back, I have trouble imagining I was ever so fond of her. Or of her mother.

Bitches, both of them, just waiting for me to turn my back so they could run off.

I suppose I ought to be sorry for what Meg must be feeling—her mother's past feeling anything—but, somehow, I just can't bring myself to. Sometimes, in my mind, I try blaming it on that little prick Tighe, but hell, he wasn't forcing Meg to go anywhere; she must have made that decision all by herself. Particularly since by the time she tried to take the ultimate powder, he'd been chopped up like salami. Hell, sliced, circumcised sausage.

As for the baby Meg is going to have, well, I don't feel a damned thing about it either; how could I? Its father was sure no prize. The only thing in its favor is that this time I'll be able to bring up a kid right, not the whining, run-off kind my own daughter was.

Jesus, the island's suddenly gotten very lonely.

Some days I'm afraid I'm going as bats as my patients.

They're still here, at least.

> *Psychiatric & Personal Observations,*
> *The Home, Alan Sommers, M.D., Director.*

The days had a terrible sameness to them. At seven the lights would go on. Almost immediately, Mrs. Tibald would begin shrieking and cursing the world. At seven thirty, the identical gloppy breakfast would be served—invariably half-cold and heavy on the stomach. There is nothing, Meg had long ago decided, worse-tasting than cold oatmeal. Because she was pregnant, she was given a glass of orange juice every morning, something that invariably made Mrs. Tibald—Sommers had had her moved into the next cell four days ago, purely out of meanness—shriek with fury.

"You only get that," she would scream, "because you shacked up with crazy old Sommers. You think anybody believes Tighe what's-his-name was the father of your kid? Don't make me laugh." Mrs. Tibald threw back her head and loosed a cascading, insane cackle. "Sommers was the father, and you damned well know it. He raped you and knocked you up. Just like the bastard wants to rape *me.* All that crap he feeds me about wanting to take my pulse or blood pressure. Hands all over me. A trick to give him a cheap thrill. I know what he wants, and one of these days I'm going to kill him for it. Your precious husband was a rapist, too—just like Sommers— only at least he was a young rapist. Well, you saw how I took care of him; now watch how I take care of fat, old, half-bald Sommers. They both wanted me. They both deserve to be knocked off. Pity I only got to your husband; Sommers is next."

Granted Mrs. Tibald's rape-fixation was naked madness, what she said made Meg furious. Meg walked
over to the heavy bars separating their cells and threw
the glassful of orange juice all over Mrs. Tibald, leaving the woman's dress soaked in an orange-colored mess,
pieces of pulp and seed clinging all over her. "There,"
Meg spat at her. "Your own glass of O.J. Now *you* start
shacking up with Sommers, and maybe he won't *have*
to rape you, you fucking bitch."

Muttering and cursing, Mrs. Tibald retreated to a
corner of her cell, her burning eyes glowering with
hate. Jesus, Meg thought to herself, she was getting as
crazy as the rest of the patients at The Home. To pick
on someone as patently nuts as Mrs. Tibald showed
how badly her mind had deteriorated since she'd been
locked up down here.

Disgusted with herself, Meg sat gloomily in her cell,
staring at the blank rear wall as if there were words of
great importance written on it. There was nothing, only
irregular cracks running up the cement of the wall,
once white, now a peeling, mottled gray.

On the lower corner of one of the walls, Meg could
see the scratched lines she made to keep track of the
days. Christ, there were a lot of them. By her count
six months and two days. Sommers had to let her out
of here soon; she was now in her eighth month, she
figured—and as a doctor, Sommers must know she
needed sun and fresh air and exercise and an end to
the eternal dampness of the cellblock.

Sourly, Meg crossed to the corner of the wall with
the makeshift calendar and added another line for another day. Then, she went back to staring at the wall.
God, they didn't even let her have an old magazine to
thumb through.

Half an hour later, at 9:30 sharp, Meg heard the door

to the cellblock open and the sound of crisp footsteps on the cement floor. Meg didn't bother to look up; she already knew it was Sommers on his daily morning visit. Just outside the closed cellblock door—she was also aware—Midge Cummins stood waiting, in case Sommers needed her for something. Meg sighed. The same dreadful sameness to this visit, as with everything else. She couldn't remember Dr. Sommers's ever being more than five minutes late to show up. As if triggered by some invisible switch, he would stride in exactly at 9:30.

"Good morning, Meg," Sommers would say, coming over close to her cell. "How are you today?"

"Bored as hell. Today, like every day."

"Contemplation is good for the soul," Sommers would answer. "If you had thought more and acted less, Meg, you wouldn't be here, you know."

"I was wondering, Doctor," Meg said, smiling a little at him to make him feel less hostile, "when you planned to let me out of this cell. It's not good for the baby. I should be getting sun, fresh air, and a little exercise, don't you think? I mean, as a doctor, you of all people must know that."

Sommers shook his head sadly. "Yes, you probably should be getting all those things, Meg." Sommers's face grew sadder, and again he shook his head. "But I can't trust you. You'd just try to run away again."

As Meg began to protest that of course she wouldn't, Sommers held up his hand toward her. "Don't add lying to your other crimes," he snapped. A little startled, Meg sat down on her bed. "I wouldn't," Meg pled. "I really wouldn't. The baby . . . I wouldn't do anything that might hurt the baby. . . ."

"I'm sure," Sommers snickered. "You must think I'm a fool."

"No, Doctor, I didn't mean—"

Once again the upraised hand from Sommers, shutting Meg up. His shoulders slumped as he stood staring at Meg in her misery, seeming almost moved, but more moved by things and events foreign to her. Only the words were familiar. "I can never understand it," he explained mournfully. "People are always trying to leave me, to run out on me, to desert me. They seem to think I won't mind being left all by myself. Alone. I don't know why." Unconsciously, Sommers began pacing the area outside Meg's cell, reciting the words with which Meg was so familiar her lips sometimes moved along with Sommers's as he spoke, like one actor silently mouthing another actor's words in a too-familiar play.

"Think of them," Sommers noted, ticking them off on the fingers of his left hand. "Think of them all: my father and my mother—one day, just gone. They can't have cared much. Oh, people said there'd been an accident, but they probably just told me that to make me feel better. My father and my mother, my wife and my daughter. You and your sweet mother had sort of replaced them, you know."

The softness suddenly left Sommers's voice, and when he turned back toward Meg, the words had a bitter, acrid tone of accusation to them. "But then I found out both of *you* were trying to leave me, too. Sneaking out. Slipping off into the night. Deserting me. Trying to run away. Bitches, damn it."

This was one part of Sommers's speech where Meg always avoided saying anything. The insane glitter that always came into Sommers's eyes when he reached the part about trying to leave him had a savage intensity to it; Meg was never sure he wouldn't suddenly come into her cell and strangle her—along with her unborn baby.

The glitter receded, and Sommers went back to sounding more sad than angry. "It's all very disappointing. My patients did the same kind of thing to me—always. They wanted to get out; they wanted to leave me; they wanted to run away and leave me behind. Never could get them to understand they belonged to *me*."

When Sommers turned his head to look at her again, Meg could see that his eyes were filled with incipient tears. A sudden thought made him smile weakly through his misery. "But *you*, my dear little Meg, well, *you'll* never be leaving me. Not ever. You're here for good."

In the past Sommers had occasionally made veiled references to this article of faith; today was the first time he'd ever come right out and said it. But then, today was a day when Sommers appeared to be changing the rules. As the full impact of Sommers's statement hit her, Meg exploded. She ran to the door of her cell and began yelling at him. "Keep me here forever!" she gasped. "You can't do that. Make me a prisoner for life? Lock me up for the rest of my days? You're crazy to even think of something like that. You can't do it, I tell you, you can't do it."

Condescendingly, Sommers smiled again, spreading his hands to show he had no intention of changing his mind; it was obvious he was enjoying himself. "Out here," he said smugly, "out here on the island—at The Home—out here, I can do anything I choose to. And, for a variety of reasons I won't go into, I choose to keep you locked up. Forever. After all, it *is* better than being executed," Sommers added with another smile, adding, "which if I chose to, I could also do."

By now, Meg was screaming incoherently. Behind what Sommers said lay such a tenor of reasonableness it made the horrible position she'd suddenly found herself in even more untenable. "You can't, you can't," Meg screamed, "Jesus Christ, even murderers are given a trial. I tell you, you can't."

For a moment Sommers appeared to ponder her remark. "A trial," he said, more to himself than to Meg. "You have a point," he conceded. "A trial is part and parcel of American justice. That can be arranged. A trial . . ."

"What?" Meg stared at him in wonder. What was Sommers talking about now?

Turning, Sommers walked across the room to where some heavy black cloth—it was sometimes used to cover the windows during certain kinds of treatment—lay folded up on a table in one corner of the antechamber. "Every accused is, if I remember my Constitution, entitled to a speedy trial," Sommers noted. "So your trial will be held today. In fact, right now." Unlocking Meg's cell door, Sommers marched in and seated himself behind the stark little table that stood in the center of Meg's cell. Carefully, he adjusted the black cloth around his shoulders in an effort to appear to be wearing a judicial robe. His eyes rose to meet Meg's. "Sorry this is a little makeshift; I don't usually have to deal with capital cases."

Sommers rapped on the table with his pipe. "Court will come to order in the matter of one Margaret Kendricks Devlin versus the People. Accused may sit over there," he added, indicating Meg's cot with his head.

"Very well. Court is in session. How does the accused plead?"

"Not guilty."

"Of course you'd say that. However, the accusations against the defendant speak for themselves; the accused's crimes were such that there is no basis for a not guilty plea. Guilty," he declared, knocking his pipe on the table again. "Guilty as charged." Sommers made a note on a piece of paper sitting on the table in front of him.

Meg stood up openmouthed. "You're absolutely crazy, Sommers. That wasn't a trial. It was a farce. A fiasco. Worse, I don't think you even realize it. Bats, bonkers, crazy as a loon . . ."

"Silence!" barked Sommers, and he made Meg stand up and face him. "We come now to the sentencing." He fixed her with a stern expression, referring to his notes on the table. There appeared to be nothing written on the paper except for one word. "Guilty." Feeling herself beginning to sway—she supposed it was the shock, the realization of Sommers's degree of insanity affecting her system—Meg sat down on the bed again. Sommers looked displeased but didn't try to make her stand up. He was too lost in his own fantasy.

"Margaret Kendricks, alias Margaret Devlin, once your baby is born and weaned, I sentence you to be executed, cured, and stuffed, as your mother was before you. I shall allow you to be mounted alongside her; the court always believes in keeping families together, even in death."

Meg groaned softly and began trembling when she heard what had happened to her mother, but made no effort to answer; she knew anything she said would be wasted on this lunatic—a madman who had her completely in his control. Briefly, he appeared to consider something before speaking, clasping and unclasping his hands in front of him. "The infant—well, the child will be raised by *me*. I shall try to forget who his father was. And since, as the child grows up, he will be told I am his natural father, he is not apt to ever abandon or desert me."

Meg shot to her feet and raced over in front of Sommers, one trembling finger pointed directly at his face. She could feel herself shaking as she swayed unsteadily back and forth. "You can't," she shrieked. "Not you—not my baby! Do what you want with me, but not my baby. . . . No, my God, no! . . ."

Drawing himself to his full height, Sommers stood up and rapped loudly on the table with his pipe again. "This court stands adjourned," he declared, turning on his heel, unlocking the cell door, and walking out of her cell, through the cellblock antechamber, and up the stairs.

Meg sank back onto the bed, her head in her hands. Mrs. Tibald sneered at her through the separating bars, shrieking with laughter that was as insane as Sommers himself was. The sound of Sommers's voice pronouncing his bizarre sentence echoed through Meg's head and made her shudder. Her baby . . . the baby . . . Sommers was planning to bring him up as his *own?*

Long ago Meg had resigned herself to what Sommers would probably wind up doing with her, but the thought of her about-to-be-born son—last remnant of an almost holy love between Tighe and herself—being brought up by someone as completely crazy as Sommers turned her blood frigid. And Sommers was so totally insane he doubtless meant to carry his sentence out.

Oh Jesus, Tighe, why couldn't you be here when I need you the most? No, that wasn't fair; poor, wonderful Tighe had had nothing to say about what had happened to him. Any more than her son had anything to say about the horrible fate that awaited him once he was born. Worse, with Sommers's lying, the child would grow up never knowing that that wasn't the way things had been at all.

For the first time since she had been locked away in

this dreadful cell, Meg lay down on the bed and cried until the walls seemed to move, shaking and sobbing and weeping for Tighe, for her mother, and for her poor, unborn son.

Chapter Twenty-nine

The more I've thought about it, the more the idea of raising Meg's kid has grown on me. My own son. Son? Well, about a month ago, before I'd told Meg she was here to stay, she told me she was sure the baby was going to be a boy, and I've always trusted a mother's instincts in things like that.

My son. He'd be raised believing I was his father. I don't know why, but that makes me kind of feel good. He'd never desert me, that much I'm sure of; boys are much more reliable than girls in things like that. Alan Sommers, Jr.? I don't know yet.

The staff will have to be shaken out so that no one here knows who his father really was. Midge Cummins will be the only tough one to replace, but I think it's about time she left for someplace else anyway.

Alan Sommers, Jr.—definitely. It has a real nice sound to it, doesn't it?

Psychiatric & Personal Observations,
The Home, Alan Sommers, M.D., Director.

Meg spent every waking moment furiously trying to get someone to believe her story. By now, she knew, it was too late to do anything for herself, but that didn't really matter. Her son's whole future hung on getting someone—anyone—to realize that she wasn't hallucinating, she wasn't crazy, and that every word she'd said about Sommers was true.

What progress she made was painfully slow and seemingly insignificant. To Midge Cummins, to Ernie, to the two practical nurses (they brought her her food and sometimes stayed to chat with her), Meg kept repeating her story over and over again every chance she got. Listen, for Christ's sake, *listen:* Sommers killed Tighe, killed her mother, and now, once the baby was born and weaned, was planning to do the same to her.

None of the people she talked to ever contradicted her outright—in fact, Midge Cummins appeared to make considerable effort to pretend she accepted every word of what Meg said as gospel—but just behind their serious, sympathetic faces Meg couldn't miss what they were really thinking. Hallucinations brought on by a breakdown—on top of a pattern of past drug usage. Terrible stuff, that LSD. It had left Meg as looney as any of the patients at The Home. Worse than many, in fact. The straitjacket was kept folded in the antechamber, just in case. Stronger restraints were in a cellblock closet farther down the anteroom.

Every now and then Meg would think she'd seen a glimmer of belief in one or the other of those she repeated her story to, but then Meg would see the story eclipsed by a sympathetic smile. It was infuriating not to be able to get a single person to believe what was so terribly true.

Understandably, Sommers had forbidden any of the patients to visit Meg. With their curious, disordered minds they would probably have accepted every word Meg said as the truth—that it was was beside the point— and he couldn't afford to have any of them believing it.

One patient consistently ignored Sommers's rule:

Kenny. He was fascinated by the approaching birth and spent as much time with Meg as he could manage. It was not hard for him; he had the staff's schedule down to the last minute. Watching and talking to him, Meg discovered Kenny was the patient who snuck into the cell early every morning and placed the catatonic—the man in what Sommers had called a "state of waxy immobility"—into his new, awkward position. "He doesn't feel a damned thing," Kenny assured her. The bizarre positions—they looked impossibly uncomfortable—bothered Meg nonetheless, and by talking to Kenny enough, she was able to get him to abandon his crazy game. It surprised Meg that Kenny was that easy for her to influence. It surprised her, too, that of all the people she had told her story about Dr. Sommers to, Kenny was the one who seemed to accept it completely. There was a way, if she could just find it, Meg decided, to turn this facet of Kenny's pliability to her own advantage in getting at least the baby safely out of The Home, but she couldn't quite fasten her fingers around a method for pulling it off.

A few days later Meg suddenly felt it. The baby was coming. The waves of pain were almost unbearable, but she couldn't face calling Dr. Sommers. Finally, Midge Cummins, down in the cellblock for some reason or other, saw her and her twisted face. "Have you timed them?" Cummins asked. Meg shook her head, unable to speak. "Should I get Dr. Sommers?" Cummins continued.

Meg shook her head, but as she did, another wave of labor pains swept brutally across her. "Get Dr. Sommers," Meg contradicted herself, hating herself for being so weak. Meg began shrieking with pain and was only dimly aware that Sommers was standing beside her in her cell.

Three hours later Meg, groaning, screaming, and pushing on command, suddenly felt something strange happening to her. It was followed by a sharp slapping noise and the sound of a baby crying.

"A boy. A baby boy," Sommers announced. "Just as you predicted." Sommers wrapped the baby in a small blanket and gave it to Meg to hold. "Ordinarily, I would offer my congratulations. However, you will enjoy the delights of motherhood for so short a time, congratulations would seem both cruel and grotesque."

For hours Meg studied the infant—Meg quickly named him Tighe Dexter Devlin IV—filled with wonder at the miracle of it, noticing all the things about the boy that reminded her of poor Tighe. He had Tighe's eyes, Tighe's hair, Tighe's lopsided little smile.

Every day, when Sommers would arrive in her cell for his daily visit, he would devote an unusual amount of time to little Tighe. Invariably, this would make Meg both angry and nervous; she could not forget that part of Sommers's sentence included his raising Tighe as his own child. Maybe, Meg comforted herself that Sommers had forgotten all about that part of it and would leave the baby with Meg to bring up. Even being brought up in a barred cell was better than being raised by Sommers. Or maybe he would send the baby to someone on the mainland. An orphan, true, but it was better than having his entire life shaped by a psychopath with several murders already on his record.

Although Meg might try to push this part of her plight out of her consciousness, Sommers quickly made it clear he had neither forgotten the entire sentence nor had any plans other than to raise little Tighe himself. On only the second visit he paid her—two days after the baby's birth—he looked at Meg with what she thought was perhaps just an ounce of sympathy. "What's his name, Meg?" he asked.

"Tighe Dexter Devlin IV," Meg answered, her pride swelling at the marvelous sound of it.

"Terrible name," Sommers snapped. "After that pretty-boy bum." He suddenly laughed. "Well, we'll change that quickly enough. Once the kid's been weaned."

Meg started to protest, but Sommers quickly cut her off. "Don't get into a tizzy about his name, Meg," Sommers said with a faint smile. "You won't be around long enough to know if I've named him after Yasser Arafat." With another grim smile and a small wave, Sommers stalked out of the cell, slamming Meg's steel-barred door shut with a particularly final-sounding *thud*.

For hours after that confrontation Meg went back to working on various plans for saving little Tighe. The idea only came into place when Kenny was standing outside of her cell making one of the many visits he made to her each day. Meg was too busy thinking about plans to get Tighe off the island to pay much attention to what Kenny was talking about—ever since the birth of the baby he had managed to spend hours with her downstairs—but something he said suddenly put the whole plan together for her. Wild, dangerous, but given the circumstances, absolutely necessary.

"I hope you don't mind my spending so much time down here with you," Kenny said suddenly. "See, it's just that I love to see a mother and child together the way they should be—the way Mother and I should be." The pieces suddenly all came together, and Meg lied, assuring Kenny she loved his visits.

Quickly, Meg seized the opportunity that Kenny's crazy mother-fixation offered her. "I know, I know, Kenny," she said softly. "But this poor baby will never really get to know his mother. Once he's weaned, crazy old Sommers plans to kill me—just like he did the others—and bring him up himself. He'll be as mother-less as Dr. Sommers has made *you*. Terrible . . ."

Kenny became indignant. "That bastard. That son of a bitch. He shouldn't do something like that. At least I know that eventually Mother will come get me; that poor little baby won't ever have anyone to come get *him*."

"Unless," began Meg, and deliberately stopped without explaining any further. The time wasn't right yet. But from the gleam of fascination she could see in Kenny's eyes, she was sure she had him halfway to buying her scheme already.

Every day, Kenny managed to spend a bit more time with her. The combination of Meg's reckless go-for-broke gamble and Kenny's insane delusion about his mother slowly fused together. Carefully, little by little, she worked out the plan with Kenny. There was no question any longer that he was completely dedicated to the scheme. It was a dangerous one.

The first thing Meg did was to tell Kenny of the punctured rubber boat and where it was. When Kenny wasn't with her, he was on the other side of the island, secretly patching up the rubber boat where it had been torn on the barnacles, inflating it, and then hiding it again.

"We'll need a key," Meg pointed out. "Something so I can unlock the cell and get Tighe out of here. Maybe you could steal one or something."

Kenny smiled widely, proud of himself as he was proud of everything he could do to keep this child and mother together. From his pocket he produced a small, metal object. "Already have one," he explained. "It's how I used to get into the catatonic's cell to put him in a new position every day. So, no problem about the key; all these cells have the same key, so if mine will work in his, it'll work in yours." Kenny tried the key in Meg's cell door; he was right. The key worked. His smile of pride widened.

One morning, perhaps three days later, Kenny told Meg that he had finally tried the boat in the water and that it stayed afloat easily. "Not a drop inside, even after half an hour," he announced proudly. "You and little Tighe can make it to the mainland in it easy."

"It's all right for me—I'll try to get away in it—but it's too dangerous for Tighe. The damned thing already sank on me once. Look, could you—I mean, I know it's asking a lot—could you get Tighe ashore in the tramcar? Under your jacket or something? I hear it's running again."

Kenny first looked startled, then nervous. "If I got caught," he began, "well, Sommers might send me someplace else so my mom would never find me." Shifting his feet uncomfortably, Kenny studied his shoes. Then: "But hell, he might do something like that out of pure spite one day, anyhow. Son of a bitch. Sure, damn it. They're used to seeing me go to the mainland. I'll go when no one else is even near the tramcar. Hiding Tighe under my jacket will be a cinch." He studied his feet again. "I got to grow up and be a man *some* day. This is as good a place to start as any."

"Oh, Kenny," Meg said excitedly, and leaned toward the bars to peck him on the cheek. Kenny blushed deeply, trying to hide how pleased the kiss had made him. Suddenly, a strange look came over his face.

"I don't know quite how to put this. But suppose—I mean, I'm sure it won't happen, of course—but suppose, well, hell, you said the boat sank on you once. It won't do it again, naturally, but, just in case . . . you . . . well . . . hell, I mean . . . you know . . ."

Meg *did* know; the same worry had been plaguing her for some time now. "What do you do with Tighe? I have it all figured out," she told him. Meg explained that if something should happen to her—she couldn't explain why, but she had a gnawing fear that that was exactly what was going to happen—he should call Miss Groundly and deliver the baby to her. Granted, Miss Groundly was no prize, but she'd told Meg she had been desperate for years to have a child of her own. That would keep her from just taking Tighe back to Dr. Sommers.

At the same time Meg planned to pin a note inside Tighe's baby basket asking Miss Groundly to notify the baby's grandparents—the Devlins—in Philadelphia. This, Meg was aware, was something Miss Groundly might or might not do, but at least the pride of her life—her son—would be safe. Miss Groundly was a long way from being her favorite person, but Meg could think of no one else nearby to call on.

Little by little, the final details of the plan were carefully stitched together. Meg, lying sleepless in the night, had difficulty believing she might actually pull it off. Some inner voice kept whispering it was an awful lot to ask of God.

The morning of the actual escape, Meg felt her nerves drawn taut as bowstrings. All of the things and people that could go wrong crowded her brain; the idea of Miss Groundly became an increasing source of doubt; the whole operation seemed suddenly flimsy, childish, and improbable. Kenny stood outside her cell, trying to hurry her along. Meg clung to Tighe—so tightly he began to whimper—holding him, kissing him, fondling him, praying to God they soon would be reunited and she could smother him in kisses of *hello* instead of *good-bye*.

"It's time," Kenny said, looking increasingly nervous. Just outside the side door of The Home, she and Kenny parted from one another, Kenny with Tighe to go toward the tramcar, herself to head toward the far side of the island where the rubber boat was hidden. Watching them as they left, Meg's eyes filled with tears, blurring her vision, and making it hard to even see Kenny and her baby any distance away. Her own progress was slow and painful; although the ankle bandage had long ago been removed, her whole leg was still weak and unreliable; the tangle of vines on either side tore at her feet and the pockmarked, uneven ground kept putting pressure on odd parts of her leg, frequently twisting it beneath her and hurting like hell.

Once Meg was out of sight, Kenny dramatically changed Meg's carefully worked-out plan. He had earlier called Miss Groundly and prepared her to receive the baby on the mainland loading dock as he and Meg had agreed, but everything else was different. Miss Groundly had sounded ecstatic, as Meg had said she would, but Kenny had absolutely no intention of delivering Tighe himself.

The bravery he had shown when they were first discussing the plan had quickly dissolved. Every time he thought about it, the idea of trying to smuggle little Tighe to the mainland himself became more frightening. Finally, Kenny abandoned it entirely, telling himself he had no choice. By sheer chance he might stumble across someone on the tramcar, or after Tighe had disappeared from The Home, questions might be asked him. He knew precisely what Dr. Sommers, the bastard, would do by way of punishment: ship him to some other asylum. His mother would finally come to pick him up, but she wouldn't be able to find him. Sommers wouldn't tell her either. He would spend the rest of his life in some terrible place waiting for his mother, while she went futilely from asylum to asylum searching for him.

His own plan for getting Tighe ashore was ingenious enough, but terrifyingly hazardous. In the lee of The Home, where no one could see him, Kenny hooked the small basket that held Tighe to one of the cables which carried the tramcar across to the mainland. Working quickly, Kenny then hooked a thin, strong wire to a series of pulleys he'd attached between the cable and the basket holding Tighe. When this wire was pulled, Tighe and his basket would move slowly across from the island to the mainland landing dock. Reeling the line in hand over hand, Kenny carefully started little Tighe on his way across Matecumbe Gut, the angry water racing fiercely below the baby's basket. On the mainland Miss Groundly watched spellbound, having trouble accepting that soon she would have the baby she'd wanted for so long, but deathly afraid that Kenny's curious, makeshift device might dump the child into the water before he reached her.

On the far side of the island, paddling furiously, Meg had almost reached the tip of the island. Kenny had done a good patching job; so far the only water inside the *Titanic* came from the splashing of the waves. Confidently, Meg turned the corner and came around the island's end, suddenly nervous because this was the spot where she had come to grief on her last try for the mainland.

Automatically, she looked toward the tramcar, expecting to see it slowly making its way across. Instead, she saw the small, fragile basket inching its way across the raging waters of the gut. The sight terrified her, seizing her and squeezing her insides with panicky fear. Tighe, little Tighe, hanging up there, alone, unprotected, dangling over a watery nothingness. What in God's name had Kenny been thinking of? Why the hell had he chickened out on her, damn it?

Transfixed, Meg stared at the basket and its precious cargo. Because the basket was light, it swung dangerously back and forth in the high, fickle winds over the gut, several times almost tipping completely over. She wasn't sure, for once or twice Meg thought she could hear the sound of a baby shrieking in the distance. Calling to her, Meg told herself, desperately calling for help she couldn't give him.

Meg wanted to scream, to shout, to yell—to do *something* that might make little Tighe's perilous journey a little safer. Instead, she did the only thing she could do. Putting her head down and setting her jaw, Meg paddled the damned rubber boat with every ounce of strength she had, trying desperately to force it through the choppy waters beyond the headland fast—faster—to get to the mainland shore. The paddling suddenly became harder; the exposed water of the gut tore at the sides of the rubber boat, the current ripping at it, and twice, almost swamping it completely.

There was a new hazard which Meg only realized as she neared the shore. Apparently Sommers, too, had suddenly seen Tighe's fragile basket slowly nearing the shore of the mainland. He and Ernie were using axes, frantically trying to break into the motor shed where the engine that drove the tramcar back and forth were. Kenny, though, had not only padlocked the shed, but reinforced the shed's only door with heavy planking. You could hear the thump of the axes against the wood and the scream of the planks, as, one by one, they shattered under the brutal battering.

Sommers, Meg knew, was well aware that once they got inside and started the tramcar back toward the island, it would dump the baby into the tumultuous waters of Matecumbe Gut, but had decided, apparently, that if *he* couldn't have the baby, no one could.

Finally, enough of the planks had been caved in so that Sommers could squeeze into the shed to throw the switches that would start the tramcar back toward the island.

His hands were trembling so much he had difficulty

making the preparatory adjustments. Finally, he grabbed the main switch and gave a cry of triumph. The motor wheezed, refusing to start, and gave a grunt of electrical disobedience. Sommers swore. Some days the motor was like that. You just had to keep trying.

Meg's race to get her boat to the mainland before Sommers started the tramcar abruptly collapsed around her. She was only about fifty yards from shore when her reckless paddling and the fierce chop of the water swamped the boat; Meg floundered. She tried to swim— once she had been a strong swimmer—but her mouth repeatedly filled with water as the waves dashed against her face. Lack of exercise had left Meg badly out of shape; she gasped and choked and flailed, but her forward progress was agonizingly slow.

Miss Groundly stood on the mainland dock; the basket was almost to the shore. Then, something went wrong. The tramcar sitting on the dock began to move, heading straight for the basket; a triumphant Sommers had finally gotten the motor to cooperate. Her hand automatically moved to her face in horror. For a second, she stood frozen, then she moved quickly. The basket was now close enough to the dock that she was able to swing out on the small jetty beneath it and grab the basket before the tramcar moved far enough out to upset the basket. Panting, Groundly stepped back off the jetty onto the landing dock and gazed down into the basket with love. The child was still screaming, but when Miss Groundly reached down and brushed her hand lovingly across his cheek, the baby suddenly smiled and made a contented gurgling sound.

Quickly she read the note; the happy smile disappeared from her face. Like hell she would notify those people in Philadelphia. Like hell she would let them know the baby even existed. Grandparents, the note said. Well, she had as much right to the baby as any old grandparent did. More, in fact. She had saved the child's life, hadn't she? The baby was hers. Patting his face again and watching, fascinated, as the baby once more smiled up at her, she crumpled the note and threw it away, taking the basket by the handle and starting toward her car with it, face wreathed in a fulfilled smile.

A voice from behind her froze Miss Groundly. Slowly, she turned around. It was Meg, dripping wet, panting with exhaustion from her desperate swim the last fifty yards between the boat and the mainland shore. With a grateful smile, she held out her hands for the basket holding her son. "Oh thank you, thank God for you," Meg gasped. "You saved my baby. You saved his life. God damn, God damn it, Miss Groundly, you saved poor little Tighe's life."

Miss Groundly stared at her for an instant, then held the basket with Tighe in it as far away as she could get it from Meg. "It's not your baby anymore. You're too late. Too late, I tell you. It's my baby now. . . ."

Meg didn't argue with her. Without even thinking, she lunged forward, grabbed Tighe in her arms, and raced down the street clutching him tightly to her sopping wet body. She never even looked back.

Tighe Dexter Devlin IV, product of the passionate love between Margaret Sayre Kendricks and Tighe Dexter Devlin III was, at last, safe. . . .

L'Envoi

To anyone who stands in the crumbling, sun-bleached town of Matecumbe Gut today and looks out to the island where The Home was, the place appears very much as it always had—a huge building, forlorn, falling down, near collapse.

There is only one major difference; no one any longer lives there. Meg had had a difficult time getting the State Police in Marathon to believe her story; their initial reaction was that she must be as crazy as most of The Home's occupants. They tried to call Sommers, but got no answer. Finally, grumbling and reluctant, they investigated. What they found stunned them.

Knowing it was only a matter of time before the police showed up, Dr. Sommers had long ago disappeared. Most of The Home's staff, Midge Cummins, the two young practical nurses, the people who worked in the kitchen—and everyone else except Ernie—had followed Sommers into benign obscurity.

Ernie had done his best. But the police found the patients half-starved, dirt-encrusted, and totally out of control. One by one, the police had located their families—The Home's records were still in their files beside the nurses' station—and had the patients picked up, or sent on to other sanitariums. All but one. One patient had completely disappeared, and the police were still searching for him up and down the Keys.

Kenny. Once the other patients and the police had left, Kenny had slipped back and was still living on the island, afraid to leave, because surely it was only a matter of time before his mother came to The Home and took him away with her. If he left before she got here, how would she ever find him? Although they had searched the building carefully, The Home was the one place the police never thought of rechecking.

In the lonely, rattling emptiness, Kenny moved from room to room, listening to the ghosts of voices long departed, hearing the shutters bang emptily against the windows, wandering through the deserted skeleton of The Home, listening intently for the sudden sound of his mother's voice.

Far, far from Matecumbe Gut, Meg and Tighe lived in Paoli, a pleasant, expensive suburb just outside Philadelphia. Although the elder Devlins supported her handsomely, they were neither kind nor unkind to her, treating her, rather, with regal indifference. On the other hand they adored their only grandson; it was obvious to Meg they tolerated her, if somewhat distantly, only because of him. Meg could understand their feelings. Tighe Dexter Devlin IV, after all, was the sole living embodiment of their own son, and from the first, she had been a not overly welcome outsider.

They worshipped the little boy, bought him lavish toys and clothes, showered him with their love, but kept up a steady flow of oblique conversations with Meg suggesting it might be better if he were moved to Philadelphia and was raised by them. She could come there and see him any time she wanted to, of course. . . . Meg simply ignored it whenever this painful subject was brought up, although always grateful for the other bounty they showered upon him.

Far away, in the foothills of Big Sur, a heavily bearded but youngish-looking man sat in his office and talked earnestly to the woman sitting across his desk. "I think," said Dr. Stanton, "that you're making genuine progress, Mrs. Lambert. You've improved enormously, I'd say, and my professional assessment is that your problems only need a little more time and some fine-tuning to complete your treatment."

The doctor swiveled in his chair, puffing on his pipe and appearing to ponder something. Still lost in thought, he spun his chair to face her. "I have a suggestion that may appeal to you for that period." Once again the doctor turned his back on Mrs. Lambert, staring at a section of the bookcase behind him. In it was a new shadow box, filled with the same curious collection of objects he had had at The Home; these items were the only things he had brought with him the night of his abrupt departure from The Home.

More slowly this time, the chair once again swiveled, and he looked intently into Mrs. Lambert's eyes. "A couple of months ago I bought a small island off the Baja, and when the rebuilding is completed, I shall open it as a very superior sort of rehabilitation sanitarium. It has a beautiful, rambling old house on it, and a highly competent staff already lined up. When the refurbishing is finished, it occurs to me that it would make an ideal place for someone such as yourself to spend a few months while moving toward complete psychological recovery. There are so few really pleasant places where persons like you can get both the psychological help and a feeling of real security. Not so much an institution, as a home. . . ."

The doctor smiled at her, giving the bookcase with

the shadow box a sideways glance as he did. "I don't want to pressure you in any way, of course; the decision, Mrs. Lambert, must be entirely your own. But I sincerely hope that when it's ready, you'll decide to be one of my first patients there." The doctor smiled at her, calmly lighting his pipe, and watching her reaction. It was as he expected.

A shudder of happiness ran through Mrs. Lambert. Smiling back at Dr. Stanton, she nodded gratefully.

The doctor was *such* a nice man.

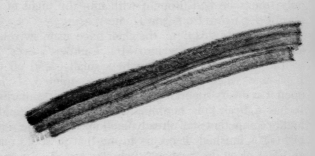

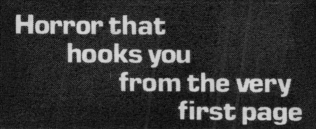

If you enjoy squirming
through scary books,
you'll shiver through the stories of

MARY HIGGINS CLARK

☐ THE CRADLE WILL FALL	11545-0-18	$3.95
☐ A CRY IN THE NIGHT	11065-3-26	3.95
☐ A STRANGER IS WATCHING	18127-5-43	3.95
☐ WHERE ARE THE CHILDREN	19593-4-38	3.50

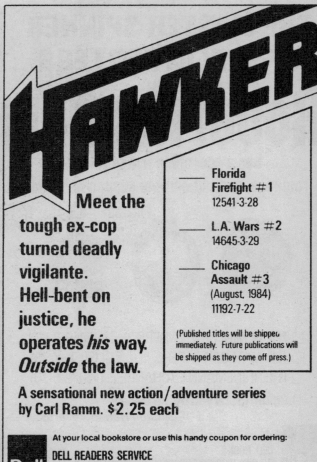